DIVISIBLE MAN™
THE SEVENTH STAR

by

Howard Seaborne

ALSO BY HOWARD SEABORNE

PRAISE FOR HOWARD SEABORNE

"This book is a strong start to a series…Well-written and engaging, with memorable characters and an intriguing hero."
—*Kirkus Reviews*
DIVISIBLE MAN [DM1]

"Seaborne's crisp prose, playful dialogue, and mastery of technical details of flight distinguish the story…this is a striking and original start to a series, buoyed by fresh and vivid depictions of extra-human powers and a clutch of memorably drawn characters…"
—*BookLife*
DIVISIBLE MAN [DM1]

"Even more than flight, (Will's relationship with Andy)—and that crack prose—powers this thriller to a satisfying climax that sets up more to come."
—*BookLife*
DIVISIBLE MAN [DM1]

"Seaborne, a former flight instructor and charter pilot, once again gives readers a crisply written thriller. Self-powered flight is a potent fantasy, and Seaborne explores its joys and difficulties engagingly. Will's narrative voice is amusing, intelligent and humane; he draws readers in with his wit, appreciation for his wife, and his flight-drunk joy…Even more entertaining than its predecessor—a great read."
—*Kirkus Reviews*
DIVISIBLE MAN: THE SIXTH PAWN [DM2]

"Seaborne, a former flight instructor and pilot, delivers a solid, well-written tale that taps into the near-universal dream of personal flight. Will's narrative voice is engaging and crisp, clearly explaining technical matters while never losing sight of humane, emotional concerns. The environments he describes...feel absolutely real. Another intelligent and exciting superpowered thriller."

—*Kirkus Reviews*
DIVISIBLE MAN: THE SECOND GHOST [DM3]

"As in this series' three previous books, Seaborne...proves he's a natural born storyteller, serving up an exciting, well-written thriller. He makes even minor moments in the story memorable with his sharp, evocative prose...Will's smart, humane and humorous narrative voice is appealing, as is his sincere appreciation for Andy—not just for her considerable beauty, but also for her dedication and intelligence...Seaborne does a fine job making side characters and locales believable. It's deeply gratifying to see Will deliver righteous justice to some very bad people. An intensely satisfying thriller—another winner from Seaborne."

—*Kirkus Reviews*
DIVISIBLE MAN: THE SECOND GHOST [DM4]

"Seaborne...continues his winning streak in this series, offering another page-turner. By having Will's knowledge of and control over his powers continue to expand while the questions over how he should best deploy his abilities grow, Seaborne keeps the concept fresh and readers guessing...Will's enemies are becoming aware of him and perhaps developing techniques to detect him, which makes the question of how he can protect himself while doing the most good a thorny one. The conspiracy is highly dramatic yet not implausible given today's political events, and the action sequences are excitingly cinematic...Another compelling and hugely fun adventure that delivers a thrill ride."

—*Kirkus Reviews*
DIVISIBLE MAN: TEN MAN CREW [DM5]

"Seaborne shows himself to be a reliably splendid storyteller in this latest outing. The plot is intricate and could have been confusing in lesser hands, but the author manages it well, keeping readers oriented amid unexpected developments...His crisp writing about complex scenes and concepts is another strong suit...The fantasy of self-powered flight remains absolutely compelling...As a former charter pilot, Seaborne conveys Will's delight not only in 'the other thing,' but also in airplanes and the world of flight—an engaging subculture that he ably brings to life for the reader. Will is heroic and daring, as one would expect, but he's also funny, compassionate, and affectionate... A gripping, timely, and twisty thriller."

—*Kirkus Reviews*
DIVISIBLE MAN: THE THIRD LIE [DM6]

"Seaborne is never less than a spellbinding storyteller, keeping his complicated but clearly explicated plot moving smoothly from one nail-biting scenario to another. As the tale goes along, seemingly disparate plot lines begin to satisfyingly connect in ways that will keep readers guessing until the explosive (in more ways than one) action-movie denouement. The author's grasp of global politics gives depth to the book's thriller elements, which are nicely balanced by thoughtful characterizations. Even minor characters come across in three dimensions, and Will himself is an endearing narrator. He's lovestruck by his gorgeous, intelligent, and strong-willed wife; has his heart and social conscience in the right place; and is boyishly thrilled by the other thing. A solid series entry that is, as usual, exciting, intricately plotted, and thoroughly entertaining."

—*Kirkus Reviews*
DIVISIBLE MAN: THREE NINES FINE [DM7]

Any reader of this series knows that they're in good hands with Seaborne, who's a natural storyteller. His descriptions and dialogue are crisp, and his characters deftly sketched...The book keeps readers tied into its complex and exciting thriller plot with lucid and graceful exposition, laying out clues with cleverness and subtlety...Also, although Will's abilities are powerful, they have reasonable limitations, and the protagonist is always a relatable character with plenty of humanity and humor...Another riveting, taut, and timely adventure with engaging characters and a great premise."

— *Kirkus Reviews*
DIVISIBLE MAN: EIGHT BALL [DM8]

THE SERIES

While each DIVISIBLE MAN ^{TM} novel tells its own tale, many elements carry forward and the novels are best enjoyed in sequence. The short story "Angel Flight" is a bridge between the third and fourth novels and is included with the third novel, DIVISIBLE MAN - THE SECOND GHOST.

DIVISIBLE MAN ^{TM} is available in print, digital and audio.

For a Cast of Characters, visit **HowardSeaborne.com**

For advance notice of new releases and exclusive material available only to Email Members, join the DIVISIBLE MAN ^{TM} Email List at

HowardSeaborne.com.

Sign up today and get a FREE DOWNLOAD.

ACKNOWLEDGMENTS

This is the Divisible Man's fourth mission. The flight crew continues unchanged, poor devils. Stephen Parolini continues to navigate the mission through his editing expertise. My test pilots, Rich "Maddog" Sorensen, Judethe "English Ace" Johnson and Robin "Polly Pureheart" Schlei, deserve special thanks for the initial airworthiness inspection. The ground crew at Trans World Data—David, Carol, Claire, April and Rebecca keep the machine running and Kristie and Steve continue the reconnaissance so I can concentrate on flying. Roberta Schlei's thorough copyediting spots the bandits lurking in every paragraph.

And thank you, Robin, for keeping me in the air.

For Tom.
Everyone should be lucky enough
to have a brother like you.

Author's Note

This story begins where the Divisible Man short story "Angel Flight"
ends. If you haven't read "Angel Flight," now might be a good time.

The song playing in the Black Box Theater is "Adore" by Amy Shark.
A beautiful, heartfelt song.
You should download it when you read that chapter.

"ANGEL FLIGHT"

We crossed a parking lot. Evenly-spaced lamps all around us cast down cones of lighted mist—creating a magical forest of transparent Christmas trees. I felt the girl moving now. I felt her small arms around me and a weak but steady embrace. Her head lifted from my shoulder. I felt her looking around. I wondered if being in the vanished state gave her strength.

I aimed for the Emergency entrance.

I eased us onto the concrete outside broad glass doors. With a last pulse of the FLOP, we stabilized and stopped. Somewhere in the distance I heard the airplane high in the fog. Engine song faded into the silent night.

Fwooomp! I let gravity reacquire us. I settled onto my feet.

I looked down at the bundle in my arms. A set of wide, bright eyes stared up at me from an expression so serene, so at peace, it took my breath away.

"Are you an angel?" she asked.

"No, honey." I smiled down at her. "That's all you."

PART I

1

W *ell, this Christmas sucks.*
        My hypothesis solidified when the so-called heater in my motel room issued a scream just before two a.m. The scream perfectly accented a nightmare knifing into my sleep cycle.

In the dark dream, my wife Andy fell backward. Not in cinematic slow motion. She was ripped away. Violently. Down a stairway that morphed into a shattered open window on the thirty-eighth floor of a Chicago high-rise office building. She reached for me. I lunged for her. Our fingertips touched.

Then we both fell.

And I woke up sweating.

After a moment, I remembered where I was. I realized the scream wasn't my wife plunging to the pavement, but the mechanical workings of the in-room heater performing an operatic death scene.

The heater howled long enough to bounce me out of the bed looking for a baseball bat or an ax or something of equal menace with which to kill the demon. Management didn't stock the room with baseball bats or axes. Before I could locate an equivalent weapon, the device gave out a fatal *Clunk!* and fell silent.

I stood breathless in my underwear and sweat as the nightmare released its grip on my jangled nerves, only to reveal hip-hop bass beats throbbing through thin motel room walls.

Marshfield, Wisconsin has the usual array of fine hotels, inns and suites. The Pineview Motel is not one of them. I had called every listing on my phone. Except the Pineview. The Pineview displayed one pathetic star and carried an encyclopedia of negative reviews.

One by one, the more reputable options reported being booked. It did not amuse me that I arrived in Marshfield on Christmas Eve bearing a child and there was no room at the inn.

Accepting the inevitable, I called the loser on the list. I should have read the warning sign when no one answered. Ever the optimist, I made myself vanish and set off on a short flight across town using the remaining battery power in my hand-held FLOP (Flight Launching Operational Propulsion) unit.

After I zigzagged above all-but-empty streets, avoiding wires and stoplights, the Pineview Motel materialized out of dense fog. It crouched on cracked asphalt and dirty snow between a car wash and an auto parts store. Judging the book by its cover, I nearly turned around and went back to the Marshfield Clinic to sack out in one of the nicely appointed waiting rooms. The flaw in that plan was that I had no good answer should anyone ask why I was there. I didn't know the name of the little girl I dropped off at the emergency entrance. And I didn't want to answer any questions about the fact that I *had* dropped off a little girl.

I eased to a landing at the front entrance of the Pineview, cleared the area to be sure no one was watching, then reappeared and stepped inside.

The kid manning the motel's front desk had an understandable excuse for not answering the phone. He sailed higher than the cruising altitude Pidge and I had maintained on the flight to Marshfield. The visibility inside the motel approached instrument flight conditions and carried the rich aroma of burnt cannabis.

Not my problem. Or passion. I just wanted a room.

"I'm not sure, man, but I think somebody just left," the kid told me after I flagged down his loosely tethered attention.

"Maybe you could check and see?"

On the count of five the notion took hold. He looked down at the desk and found a plastic key card laying on an open *Sports Illustrated* photo spread that had nothing to do with sports. He picked it up and handed it to me with a big smile.

"Yeah, they did. Here." I took the key card. He didn't ask me to register. He didn't request a credit card imprint. He didn't inquire as to whether I might be staying the night or moving in permanently.

"Does this key card have a room number to go with it?"

"Oh, they all do," he assured me.

I waited a moment and might still be waiting if I had been determined to make him figure it out for himself. Instead, I asked, "Could you look it up for me?" I handed the card back.

"Good idea!" He swiped the card through the desktop reader and handed it back to me. "Twenty-two."

"Right."

Everyone I ever tell this story to in the future will be able to guess what happened next. Room twenty-two throbbed with music that attempted to drown out the voices of the room's partying occupants. On top of that, the card didn't open the door.

I hiked back to the front desk.

"Sorry, man! I meant room Two. I saw the two, and then I saw it again, and I put two and two together." This struck the kid as funny. After some helpless giggling he said, "But that key is totally for room Two."

"You're certain?"

"Oh, yeah. We only have one room Two," he solemnly held up his right hand.

The card opened room Two.

Where I stood in my boxers at one-fifty-four *ante meridiem*, peeling away the clinging threads of a nightmare and presiding over the dramatic death of an in-room heater.

Christmas morning.

ANDY and I spoke earlier in the evening. I called her immediately after delivering the tiny Angel Flight girl to the Marshfield Clinic Pediatric Hospital. I placed the child in the arms of the first nurse I found, gave the nurse just enough information to send her rushing away, then discretely made for the exit.

Standing outside the hospital entrance on a holy night made silent by thick fog, I fished my phone out of my pocket and touched the contact line for my wife.

"Hey," I said. "The delivery has been made. They were ready for her and took her straight in for treatment."

Andy relayed the news. I heard a shriek and clamor.

"I told the girl's mother to stay here at the airport," Andy explained. "I convinced her to wait for word." I heard a bit of a commotion and chatter. Andy relayed a question to me.

"Honestly, she was looking pretty good," I answered. "She was awake, talking. She seemed to enjoy the flight."

Andy relayed. More excited, relieved chatter.

"I don't know," I answered the next question. "Probably best if her mom calls the clinic. They'll have information. After you tell her that, could you find someplace quiet? So we can talk?"

Andy repeated my suggestion and then excused herself from the escalating joy. A minute later she closed the door to Earl's office. I closed my eyes and pictured her standing in her patrol sergeant's uniform beside his old government-issue metal desk surrounded by a forest of piled maintenance manuals.

"The ambulance crew waiting at the airport called about fifteen minutes ago. They said the plane flew over but couldn't land," Andy said. "I told Rosemary II not to tell the mother. I knew you would try again. You obviously got in on the third try."

"Yeah...no. We didn't land. That ambulance crew might still be waiting at the airport."

Andy gave me silence. I didn't take it as judgment or confusion. Just the silence she needed as she computed the variables.

"Oh—my—God."

"Andy, the kid was in bad shape. We had nowhere to go. Pidge busted minimums and we still couldn't see anything. It was zero-zero."

"You—didn't."

"Yeah, I did." I gave her an abbreviated version of the Angel Flight.

"What about the nurse?" Andy immediately grasped the consequences of me disappearing and reappearing in front of a witness—not to mention jumping out of the airplane with the nurse's patient. "What about the ambulance crew? And the people at the hospital?"

"I'm counting on a little chaos, I guess. She got there. The people treating her might wonder, but they've got bigger problems."

"And the nurse? Will, you're not thinking this through!"

"I explained to her that it was the only way. She knew we were out of options, and she swore she wouldn't tell." I realized how weak that sounded. "Don't mention this part to the mother, but it looked bad for the girl. I think when the nurse finds out the kid made it, she'll keep her word."

"Oh—my—God."

"I'll send Pidge a text. Tell her to emphasize the need for secrecy. Call it the price of a Christmas miracle. She'll probably be landing somewhere in the Dakotas tonight."

"Where are you now? What are you going to do?"

I told her not to worry. That I would check into a hotel and I would call her in the morning to work out a way home.

Does two o'clock qualify as morning?

Technically, yes.

But Andy might not agree.

I PUT on some pants and my boots, picked up my key card and slipped into the hall where the visibility continued to rival this night's flight in the fog. I wandered the length of the hall, making a note of which rooms were still registering music and voices on the Richter Scale.

On the way back, I stopped at each one.

"POLICE! OPEN UP!" I turned my back to each door and kicked three times with the flat bottom of my boot heel. "ESSEX COUNTY NARCOTICS SQUAD! OPEN THE DOOR!"

At each door the result was the same. Sudden silence replaced the thumping music. A patio door slammed open. Feet pounded.

Following my final stop, I heard vehicle engines start in the parking lot beside the building. I heard tires squeak followed by one very satisfying fender-bender.

"Dumbasses," I muttered. "This is *Wood* County."

By the time I got back to the one and only room Two, the fabulous Pineview Motel had fallen silent. It may have been my imagination, but the air in the hallway seemed clearer.

I stood in the empty room, fairly certain sleep wasn't in the cards.

2

—————

"So?"

"I don't want to talk about it." Andy tried to sound light-hearted, but I wasn't buying it. "We can talk about it when you get home. I wish you'd let me drive up and get you."

I sipped the Kwik Trip coffee and surveyed the vacant gas pumps beneath the canopy. Christmas morning lay under the same blanket of fog that complicated my Christmas Eve arrival in Marshfield. The fog amplified the eerie absence of traffic. My already low mood deepened.

"The bus is safer. I have a ticket." Only partly true. I needed to get to the CVS pharmacy on Ocean Street to buy the ticket and then figure out what to do for a couple hours.

Despite the wait, the bus remained the better option. Andy driving in low visibility worries me. On top of that, I didn't need a full briefing to know that her sister's attempted Christmas Eve family reunion had not gone well.

The Trailways bus from Marshfield to Milwaukee makes a stop at the Park 'n Ride on Highway 34 at the western fringe of Essex County. Despite the fog, the company predicted the bus would run on time. I expected to be in my loving, emotionally-charged wife's embrace by four o'clock.

Not a minute too soon.

Three weeks had passed since someone tried to kill Andy's sister, thinking she was Andy. I spent those three weeks with a knot in my chest, one that tightened whenever Andy was out of my sight.

"That's fine," I said, "we can talk later. Maybe open a bottle of wine."

I felt relieved that Andy didn't want to discuss The Shitstorm, our pet name for her rocky relationship with her parents, specifically her father. She would want to vent, and that's a delicate procedure best performed in a controlled environment.

"Lydia of course played the big sister card," Andy launched into it. "She always thinks she knows best. I was afraid she would do that. I mean, fine, she already apologized for how she was toward me, but—I don't know—the minute Mom and Dad walked through the door it's like this programmed response kicks in. I get it. She's had it pounded into her. To be fair, she has overcome *a lot* of that. And I know she's dealing with serious issues of her own. But it was still there, you know? Just these little —*oooh!*"

I decided if Andy wasn't going to talk about it, I better sound interested.

"How did it go with your dad?"

"Oh, boy. No. We'll talk about that later. Not on the phone."

So, not well.

"Right off the bat, he gets into it about you. 'So sorry your husband decided to miss this family time.' Like you had a choice. Like you went looking for something else to do. I told him about the Angel Flight and how important it was, but then Ellis made some comment about you still flying puddle jumpers, and why couldn't they transport the patient in something bigger? Like there's 747 service to Marshfield! I mean—my brother can be such an elitist. And just like that, it became a doubles match with Dad and Ellis pairing off against me and Lydia. Liddy called Dad on his tone and reminded him that he agreed to a truce. But this is his idea of a truce? I'm supposed to give him kudos for not jumping all over me for my career choices while he puts on his robes and sits in judgment of you? For God's sake—you were out there trying to save a little girl's life!"

I switched the phone to my other hand and opened the pack of C cell batteries I bought to replenish my dead FLOP unit.

"And Mom, oh—my—GOD! She actually asked why someone else

9

couldn't have taken the flight. Why it had to be you. Do you believe that?"

Andy went on for a while about her mother, bringing Lydia back up for a few choice observations on how it would have been nice if her sister had been stronger in pointing out their mother's insensitivity. I added an occasional "uh-huh" and "oh" and threw in a few keen questions to prove I was listening. Mostly, I sipped my coffee, replaced the batteries, watched the unattended gas pumps and counted my lucky stars that Andy didn't want to talk about all this over the phone.

"And then here it comes, right in the middle of dinner," she said. "Lydia doing the big sister thing again—thinking she's helping. She brought up Lane's case and then she brought up Cinnamon Hills, and my promotion, and that gaudy business with the governor at the capital. Yeah, okay, fine, she meant well. But I mean, I don't need her validation. I don't need her going to bat for me with Dad! And the whole time I'm waiting for the inevitable hammer to drop about me being a cop, like it always does. And you know it's right up there, hanging from the chandelier along with the mistletoe. And sure enough! Dad, of course, says, 'This kind of life experience is powerful resume material.'"

Silence.

Crap. She wanted me to respond.

"I...um ...."

"Do you believe that?! Resume material! Will, he didn't say it, but I *know* he's just waiting to lay all that same old shit on me about getting me into law school! He didn't come right out with it, thank God! Because I swear, I would have walked out. I would have lost it! And not just me. I think Liddy would have butter knifed him right there, right in front of her kids, all over the tuxedo cake. He still hasn't given up! You just wait. He's going to slip it in somehow. He'll say, 'I've got contacts at Harvard.' All that old-boy BS. I should ask him if he thinks admissions will offer extra credits when I put down on my application that I blew off the top of a raging pedophile's head!"

"You had tuxedo cake?"

"And God forbid he should find out about Rahn!" I didn't need to be reminded of the threat to her life. The knot tightened. "God!" she cried out. "So *fucking* not cool!"

Andy rarely curses. This was getting serious.

"And on top of that, it's Christmas! And I—*I miss you!*"

The sentiment and its sudden tenderness signaled an end to the rant.

"Miss you, too," I said, wanting with all my heart to believe we were done *not* talking about her Christmas Eve at Lydia's lake house.

I listened to her breathing for a moment.

"I'll be home soon. Meet me at the bus."

"Fine."

"I think I have to go. My phone battery is about dead. I asked at the motel about a charger. They offered to sell me one for thirty bucks."

"That's crazy."

"Well, I think they lost some money at the Pineview Motel last night. Some of their regulars checked out suddenly without paying. Plus, they never charged me for the room. Hey," I said, seeking a more intimate tone. "Maybe we could do a nice quiet dinner tonight, just you and me. Have Christmas together."

Andy's Christmas present lay unopened under our small artificial tree.

"Everyone is still at Lydia's until Friday. They want us to come for leftovers tonight, so they can meet the man I've been married to for three and a half years."

Shit.

3

———

Andy met me as I stepped off the bus, her arms out, looking like the dream girl in a movie where the hometown sweetheart meets her serviceman beau at the station. She missed me, I missed her, and we missed spending Christmas together. We were all over each other for a moment in that Park 'n Ride lot. The people remaining on the bus gawked at us.

We broke it up after the bus driver wished us a Merry Christmas and told us to get a room.

"I talked to Pidge about twenty minutes ago," Andy reported as I slipped into the police cruiser she drove. She'd been using one of the Essex PD squad cars ever since her car sank in Leander Lake. This one, unit twenty-three, perpetually smelled like french fries.

Andy threw the car in gear.

"Where did she end up?" I asked.

"Bimmidy?"

"Bemidji?"

"Yes! Bemidji, Minnesota. She said she found a hole in the fog. Otherwise she would have been visiting South Dakota just like you said."

"I'm surprised she got in at Bemidji. Is she back now?" I don't know why I asked. The fog still hadn't lifted.

"No, and she may not be back tomorrow either—and not just because of the weather," Andy said, cracking a smile. "She and that nurse went out and got wasted. Epic Christmas-Eve-in-Bemidji wasted, according to Pidge. When I talked to her, she said the nurse was still passed out and it sounded like Pidge was still drinking. The City of Bemidji has asked them not to come back."

"Might be a good strategy. Convince the nurse that she doesn't clearly remember what happened."

"Oh, no. Pidge said you were the subject of many a toast last night. I think you're right, however. I talked to someone at the hospital. The girl seems to be doing better than anyone expected. It's a Christmas miracle and that might do the trick."

"How's the mom? Is she on her way up there?"

"She took off last night, right after you called. I didn't want her to drive but couldn't really stop her. Tom came out and drove her over to Al Raymond's car lot and they set her up with a rental. Well, a loaner. Tom persuaded Al to cough up a little Christmas spirit." Al Raymond is a stingy old bastard, but Tom Ceeves, the Chief of the City of Essex Police Department, goes six-six and two-seventy. Persuasion follows him into a room. "The poor woman couldn't wait another minute. I made her promise to text me when she got there, but I haven't heard anything. I'm sure she had other things on her mind."

"I have no doubt she made it."

Andy nodded.

"So, what's the plan?"

"Well," Andy said. "You and I are going home to get cleaned up and presentable, and then I'm going to take my new boyfriend to meet the parents. And if they like him, I might let him ask me to marry him."

"What if they don't?"

She tipped me a light shrug.

"Guess I start shopping around again."

4

Andy dressed in a knee-length plaid skirt of Christmas green and red and topped it with a cream-colored angora sweater that made me want to touch more than usual. I asked her if I should suit up, but she told me a nice shirt with dress pants would be fine. I knew better. I brushed off my one-and-only suit, a crisp white shirt and a cranberry-red tie I keep around for holidays.

My wife gave me a pleasing once-over when I descended the stairs. "Giving it the full-court press, I see."

"I better, if I'm going to ask the old man for his daughter's hand. Do you come with a dowry?"

"How do you feel about goats?"

Breaking with routine, I drove us to Lydia's house in my car. With the arrival of evening, the relentless fog intensified. I didn't want to show up at this event with my heart in my throat thanks to Andy's driving. I also allowed a machismo instinct take hold and decided I would not appear at this first parental meeting with their daughter at the wheel. Plus, I thought showing up in a squad car might needlessly press the point about Andy's career choice.

The route to Lydia's lake house took us through the curve where Lydia went off the road into Leander Lake. By the time we rolled past the spot, a combination of pitch black and fog obscured the lake, less than fifty feet from the road. Still, Andy reached for my hand.

Electric tension settled into my neck and shoulders.

"Thank you," she said quietly.

I felt grateful for the darkness and the fog. I've seen the spot numerous times since pulling Lydia from the black water. It gives me a chill.

Still, I checked the rearview mirror to make certain nothing rushed up behind us.

LYDIA'S LAKE house belies the term. Done in multi-layered slabs that descend a slope to a vast patio overlooking the water, the wood and glass architectural award-winner bears little resemblance to 'casual' or 'cottage.' I marvel that it's available for rent. Lydia has hinted at buying the place. Given its location and price, I decided Lydia wasn't kidding when she told me she planned to financially castrate her philandering soon-to-be-ex-husband.

She met us at the door beaming. Andy wrapped a hug around her sister, mindful of the baby bump between them. I stepped into the warmly lit modern interior and immediately dropped to one knee. I knew what was coming.

"Uncle Will!"

"Unca-woo!"

Harriet, the five-year-old, and Elise, the two-and-a-half-year-old, collided with me. Arms entangled around my neck, I scooped them off their feet and stood, squeezing and gently jiggling them, giving their help-less giggles a nice *vibrato*.

"Ladies! Oh, it is *soooooo* good to see you! It's been forever! Days and days! Plus, even some hours! How have you been? Have you been desperately lonely without me?"

"We have!" Harriet cried. "Come and see what we got for Christmas!"

"Come and see!" Elise bobbed her head and pigtails like a pair of antennae wiggled.

Since Lydia moved to Essex County, and especially during her short hospital stay, I have become acquainted with my nieces. As I looked at their faces, at their alert, beautiful eyes, healthy skin and strong little bodies, I thought of the bundle I carried into the pediatric hospital at the Marshfield Clinic. I thought of the way her eyes had been bright, and her face serene and glowing in defiance of the disease killing her.

Dammit. Lydia must have been cutting onions in the kitchen.

I pressed a kiss into Harriet's hair, and another into Elise's forehead. And blinked the sting out of my eyes.

"In a minute, ladies. I have important people I must meet first, but then there better be some pretty fantastic toys for me to play with!"

"Harriet got a Frozen Castle!" Elise announced as I lowered her to the floor.

"Ellie! Stop!" Harriet cried out. "Mom, she's telling everything!"

I pulled Harriet close and whispered in her ear, "I didn't hear a thing. And you can show me first."

The reassurance earned me a smile.

"Girls, go and play by the tree until dinner," their mother commanded.

A young woman appeared. Taller than Pidge, but sporting the same short blonde hair and pixie looks, she reached out to corral the children. There was no way to miss the baby bump she, too, carried. Not for the first time, I directed a thought at Lydia's dirtbag husband. *Jesus, Davis, did you climb off your wife and onto the nanny?*

"Hello Mrs. Stewart—Mr. Stewart," the girl said with a hint of an east European accent.

"Hi, Melanie."

"Please excuse me while I see to the girls," she said. Her eyes dropped, and she turned away. I caught her pulling at her open sweater. Extending it. Hiding the bump.

Lydia gave us raised eyebrows as the nineteen-year-old nanny shepherded my nieces away. She waited until the trio disappeared down a set of steps into another room.

"I can't get her to stop feeling ashamed. I'm seriously considering counseling. Seriously."

"Or maybe swearing out a warrant," I muttered to Andy. She jabbed me with her elbow.

Lydia took our overcoats but not before I patted mine to ensure that two ready propulsion units remained tucked in a pocket. I noted the location of the closet where Lydia found hangers and hung the coats. Andy pushed her purse onto the top shelf of the closet. The move told me she carried her Glock 26. We both came prepared.

"Where are Mom and Dad?" Andy asked.

"Getting ready."

Andy rolled her eyes. "Really? They couldn't meet us at the door?"

"It's all about the grand entrance, Katie," Lydia said, letting Andy's childhood name slip. "Will, regardless of the raging temperance in this house, we are well-stocked. Can I get you something?"

"The stronger the better," I said.

"He'll have a Corona Light with lime. I will, too," Andy said, firing a warning shot at me about getting shitfaced, which I will admit I had considered.

Lydia ushered us into a vast room with night-black windows that, in daylight, offered an expensive view of the south end of Leander Lake. I knew from previous daytime visits that a stand of trees to the left obscured the place where Andy's car had been pulled out of the deep end of the lake.

The room was tastefully furnished. Contemporary but comfortable-looking sofas and chairs attended the broad span of windows. Recessed lighting warmed wood-paneled walls. I wondered about anyone who could own such a beautiful property and not seek every opportunity to enjoy it, instead renting it to a stranger.

A bar occupied one corner of the room, just inside the entrance, opposite the windows. Lydia stepped into the role of bartender and produced two bottles of Corona. She deftly wedged lime slices into the necks, handed them off and picked up a tumbler filled with ice and what looked like cranberry juice.

"Okay, maybe not perfect, but one of the best Christmases I've had in a while," Lydia raised a glass with a special glance at Andy. We touched our drinks to hers.

Pregnant. Marriage falling apart. Nearly killed. I had to give it to Andy's sister. She mined the silver lining.

We drank.

"Lydia, you're toasting without us?"

I knew Andy's mother was attractive. She was her daughter's mother, and I'd seen photos. But it was instantly apparent that the woman entering the room lacked her daughter's accessibility and warmth. A couple extra decades gave Eleanor Taylor a sharp edge I hoped Andy would never acquire. She wore her hair shorter than either of her daughters, yet more expensively styled. She wore makeup carefully applied to suggest she wore none. She entered the room like someone who knew where the best light fell.

She traded a brisk hug with Andy, then turned to be presented to me.

"Mom, this is Will." I caught my wife's eyes flaring at me and the beer in my hand.

I dropped the cold beer bottle on the bar and quickly wiped my hand on my pants before extending it.

"A handshake? For your mother-in-law? Nonsense!" she pulled me into a hug, the temperature of which I could not determine.

"I'm very pleased to meet you, Mrs. Taylor."

"Finally!" She left the word hanging, perhaps so that blame could be randomly assigned.

"Dad, this is Will," Andy said, pulling me away from her mother.

I turned around and met my wife's father. He posed at the entrance to the expansive room. He looked younger than the photos I'd seen, fit and dressed to perfection in an expensive suit and tie. He had a businessman's look and a businessman's silver-touched haircut. I flashed on the notion that if you slit him open, he would bleed spreadsheets.

I had just enough time to feel glad I dressed up, sorry I didn't own a better suit, and foolishly confident that this might go well.

Then he spoke.

"You want to explain to me how you almost got my daughter and her unborn child killed?"

The doorbell chimed.

5

————

The left engine gave out a loud bang and a piston blew through the side of the cowling. The oil pressure dropped to nothing. Ice broke from the props and slammed into the fuselage. The fuel tank feeding the right engine read empty and the valve for switching tanks stuck. The flight controls heaved as the electric trim ran away.

In my head, it was that kind of moment.

"Hello!" A voice called from the front door.

"I'm leaving," Andy announced. She planted her barely-sipped beer on the bar.

"Dad!" Lydia scolded her father. "Andy please! Don't!"

Andy marched past her father on a line for the front hall, which was now crowded with two new people who appeared cheerfully unaware of what was happening.

"Girls! Come back here!" the nanny cried as the two little girls thundered toward the sound of the doorbell.

"Mom! Do something!" Lydia snapped at her mother.

I stared at Andy's father, who tried to fry me with an expression likely used to good effect in board rooms, or for welding. Andy charged back into the room from the front hall, trailing her brother and his wife who were quick to conclude that something pungent had hit the fan.

Andy whirled and confronted her father.

"Overlooking how monumentally wrong you are, I have to ask, Dad, how could you be so insufferably rude?!"

"And I have to ask both of you girls why you thought I didn't deserve to know?"

Lydia and Andy traded glances and gasps—then both spoke at once—a rapid-fire response mixing disclaimers and dismissals with angry assertions that the car-in-the-lake incident was none of their father's business.

"None of my business? One of my children almost loses her life thanks to *his* irresponsible action and it's none of my business? I expect that from you, Andrea Katherine, because you've decided nothing in your life is my business, but from you Lydia? I expected better—although your judgment at present is seriously open to question." Louis Taylor marched to the bar and poured a drink from a decanter of something glittering and golden.

"Oh—my—God!" Andy exclaimed. "You waited for this moment, just so you could blow everything up! You are UNBELIEVABLE!"

"My judgment? My judgment?" Lydia demanded.

"Look at you," her father said, swinging his tumbler in the direction of his daughter's belly. "Do you really feel this is the time to break up your marriage?"

"Are you kidding me?!"

"I think Dad just means—"

"SHUT UP ELLIS!" the sisters snapped at their brother who edged into the war room with a dark-haired woman wearing a friendly face.

"He—fucked—the teenaged—nanny!" Lydia enunciated every word to perfection. "Probably because none of his regular sidepieces were available that night!"

I shot a glance toward the front hall. Thankfully, Melanie had already shepherded the girls to another room. I hoped it had a door. A solid one.

"Lydia! There's no need to talk that way!" Eleanor Taylor scolded.

Lydia slapped her forehead, gaping at her mother for apparently thinking foul language was the greater sin.

I picked up my Corona and took a long slug.

Kill the engine and feather the prop before it freezes up. Pull the circuit breaker for the electric trim or else kill the master switch until you can. Grab a pliers from the flight bag and crank the fuel selector over. Hit the de-icing boots.

I got this.

I flexed my fingers. I thought about vanishing. A hearty pull from the beer substituted.

"Wait a minute! How did you find out what happened to Lydia?" Andy demanded.

"So, you admit to hiding it from me."

"Dad, you may think you're the center of the universe, but people do have the capacity to deal with things without your sage counsel!"

"Oh, that's more than evident and you've certainly paid the price."

I wondered if *paying the price* meant marrying me.

Another slug of Corona went down. The floating lime tap-danced on the bottom of the bottle. I began mapping a path to the back side of the bar for reinforcements.

Andy's light caramel complexion, a genetic gift from her mother, took on a deeper shade.

"Answer—my—question. How did you find out what happened to Lydia?"

"Your chief of police told me."

He dropped the statement like a stone.

"You went to my work?"

"I did. I wanted to find out if anyone there had the sense to help you see that there are better paths for your future. Imagine my surprise when a stranger told me what a blessing it was that my *other* daughter was not killed. And then having to hear the whole terrifying story. Not something you expect. No thanks to *him*."

Andy's father gave me a sneer. An actual sneer.

"Of course, your father and I felt the complete fools for not knowing a word of it," Eleanor Taylor contributed smartly.

"Clearly, Mother, your embarrassment is the real headline here," Lydia said.

Lydia's phone woke up, broadcasting a pop tune ringtone. I recognized the song (something snappy about a lying cheating bastard) and assumed the call came from her husband, Davis. She extracted the phone from a pocket and jabbed a finger at the screen, killing the music and the incoming call.

"If that's Davis, shouldn't you let the man speak to his children?" Lydia's mother suggested. "It is Christmas, after all."

"He was probably calling to chitchat with Melanie!" Lydia fired back. "See if she wanted to—I don't know—go roller skating or go to the prom!"

"Don't be absurd. You shouldn't keep him from his children."

"Which *children*, Mother?"

Andy moved to face her father as he stood at the bar.

"The whole story?"

"Yes, the whole story," her father said. "How your pregnant sister found herself stranded in a storm and *he* didn't have the sense or courtesy to drive her home. How *he* sent her out in a strange car—an *old unreliable* car with no four-wheel-drive—on unfamiliar and dangerous roads that are obviously not well maintained in this part of the state. How she slid into this God-forsaken lake and nearly died!"

Somehow, I couldn't picture Chief Tom Ceeves telling the story like that.

A shade of red, not far from the color tinting my wife's cheeks, climbed the sides of her father's neck.

"Whoa, Liddy? You drove into the lake? This lake?" Ellis asked.

"Oh, my God!" his wife exclaimed. "Are you okay? Is the baby okay?"

She seemed nice. I put out my hand.

"I'm Will."

"Mary," she smiled warmly and with her eyes. "Oh, and this is Ellis."

We shook, but he guarded his half of the transaction. The Buffalo Springfield lyric about battle lines played in my head.

Lydia's phone beeped. She ignored it.

"I'm fine," Lydia said tersely.

"Are you sure?" Her mother put her hand on Lydia's belly. "Have you seen a doctor? Is there even a doctor *around here* you can see? You should come home with us."

"God, Mom! This isn't The Oregon Trail!"

My wife stood silently facing her father. He glowered at her. At any second, I expected her to switch back to 'We're leaving' and take me by the hand. Instead, she tipped her head to one side. A dimple appeared at one corner of her mouth. Given the moment, I didn't initially recognize the sign, but then the dimple's twin joined.

She giggled.

This brought stunned silence to the room.

She giggled and she turned to face me. Her gold-flecked green eyes, alight, met mine. A smile blossomed.

"I'm not sure what you think is so funny," her father said.

I had no idea what was so funny either, but it was infectious. I felt a confused smile break out on my face.

Andy blew out a deep breath. She put one hand over her mouth, but the giggle slipped between her fingers.

"Whatever she's drinking, pour one for me," Ellis said.

Lydia, still fuming, gaped at her sister.

Andy reached out and touched my arm, just for a moment, just to connect. Our eyes locked as she gathered herself. Then she turned and pulled her father into a hug. He stiffened. His drink spilled a few expensive swallows onto the hardwood floor.

"Oh, Daddy!" she said. "I love you."

She pushed back from him and looked at his stunned expression.

"That's right. I love you. And I just realized I don't care if you remember it or not. I remember it. I love you and that's all that matters to me. You can get onboard or get off. You can chase my lost future for the rest of your life. I don't care. It only matters to me that I love you."

She planted a kiss on his cheek.

"And whether or not you ever say it—you love me. Because all this—all this awful behavior—it's because you found out today that you almost lost a child, isn't it! A child you love."

"You're being simplistic."

"God, please help me to see simple truths! You love your children. And like it or not, that means you love me. I never saw it before, but I see it now. You always act your worst because you love me."

"Well, dammit, of course I do! What's that got to do with anything?"

She smiled sweetly at her father. "I'm sure you will figure it out."

She left him frowning and took me by the arm.

"Everyone," she announced. "This is William Stanley Stewart. He is the love of my life. I know this to be true, because my father just treated him like crap. I know this to be true because the first time I saw him, I vomited. He is a pilot and he loves airplanes and flying more than he loves me—" I started to protest, but Andy suppressed it with her hand on my arm "—but I am blessed to hold second place, because I love him more than you could ever imagine. Daddy, he came here tonight to ask for your blessing and my hand, and I hope you give it—but as you may one day realize, *my* blessing is all he ever needed and all that ever mattered."

Louis Taylor wasn't buying any of that.

"Oh, and Daddy, this isn't the man who caused Lydia's accident—this is the man who saved your daughter's life, and the life of your unborn granddaughter. You might want to thank him."

The magenta color under his skin turned blotchy. He had no words.

"You vomited?" Ellis asked.

"Several times," I said, slipping my arm around Andy's waist.

"*That* is a story I need to hear."

"You have my blessing, Will Stewart." Lydia came close and gave me a kiss on the cheek. "Anyone who can make snow angels when no one else is watching has the right heart for my sister."

Her phone beeped again. Mildly exasperated by the interruption, she plucked it from her pocket. I thought she might turn it off once and for all.

"Davis again," she muttered. "Dammit."

She poked the screen then froze. I was close enough to catch the phone when it slipped from her fingers. Andy caught Lydia by the arm when her whole body quivered.

I looked at the screen. A text message displayed one word.

Bitch.

The image above it displayed a selfie taken from arm's length. The man in the photo wore a terrified expression, thanks to the heavy orange outdoor extension cord wrapped tightly around his neck, knotted and extending upward to a point beyond the frame of the picture.

6

———

"**I** am the fabulous Prince Moose and I have come to rescue the princess!"

"That's not a moose, Uncle Will, that's a reindeer!" Harriet set me straight.

"Come!" I hopped the stuffed animal to the castle wall. "Jump down on my back and I will ride us into the sunset!"

Ellie plucked her favorite princess, a doll with hair the color of a firetruck, from the balcony and dropped it on my moose-reindeer. I held the two dolls together and hopped them toward the Christmas tree, which we had designated the Green Forest of Dancing Fairy Lights.

Andy hurried down a half-set of stairs into the informal sitting room that also overlooked the lake. This room nestled half a level below the space containing the bar and the adults. I missed the bar. I didn't miss the adults.

She crouched where I lay on the floor and whispered in my ear.

"D.C. Metro police are there."

I looked up. She shook her head, then looked at two small girls who just lost their father and didn't know it.

I stroked Ellie's hair, thinking, S*fhe eventually won't remember him.* Looking at Harriet, who was busily arranging tiny furniture in the castle, I knew this would scar. In her world, the cowardly lying sack of shit was

'Daddy' and only the ideal lived in her heart. Only the ideal ever tucked her in at night.

"I'll stay here," I said. "We will be having a princess tea party soon."

"Lydia is sending Melanie down to get the girls and give them dinner."

The news had shaken Melanie. I volunteered for princess-rescue duty while the nanny collected herself.

"We're fine here. I got this."

Truth be told, I preferred it.

Andy gave me a kiss and a squeeze on the arm.

"I love you."

She hurried back up the half-stairway.

"Auntie Andrea looks like a princess," Harriet observed.

"Which is most wonderful," I pointed out, "because that makes me a prince!"

And God knows, you're going to need one.

7

The remainder of the night passed like an old truck, shuddering and rattling down a dirt lane, cylinders missing and ignition stammering. A relic on the verge of quitting at any moment. Something that should never be taken out of the barn again.

Andy divided her attention between her sister and her phone, stepping away to speak in low tones to the police in Washington, D.C. Mary took over in the kitchen and produced the delayed meal, leftovers from the Christmas Eve dinner I missed. Instead of attempting an organized sit-down dinner, Mary put the food out in a haphazard kitchen-countertop buffet. We grazed our way through an unenthusiastic meal. Melanie saw to the children. They made one last appearance in colorful nightdresses, doling out hugs and kisses to aunts and uncles, and Mama and Papa, as they called Lydia's parents.

Everyone put on brave and cheerful faces for the children.

Midway through the goodnight process, Lydia hurried away to the kitchen to prevent her children from seeing tears. Andy and Mary followed, leaving me at the table with Ellis and Louis while Melanie hustled the little girls off to bed.

"I'll be there in a minute!" Lydia called after them.

Anchoring the head of the table, Louis nursed his third Scotch, turning the tumbler slowly clockwise on the white tablecloth. Andy cut me off after my third Corona. She left her first unfinished. I sipped an ice water in the uncomfortable silence.

"How are the pelvic bones these days?" Ellis asked.

"Hurts when I play rugby," I tossed off. Then, thinking better of dismissing his attempt at small talk, I added, "They're doing well, thank you."

"Must have been terribly painful. I hear that's not something you can set or have in a cast."

"It is not. But on the upside, I don't have to go running with your sister every morning."

"This is a bad business. With Davis."

"I never knew the man."

Louis said distantly, "He ruined a good thing with Lydia."

Then you might try hating that *sonofabitch instead of me,* I thought.

We slipped back into silence. After a few minutes, Louis broke it.

"Will."

I looked at Andy's father. He sat back in his chair. He let his eyes rest on the tumbler of scotch as he turned it around and around.

"Sir?"

"Thank you."

His eyes came up briefly, narrowed to slits in a granite expression. I nodded acknowledgement.

"Anybody else need a drink?" he stood up suddenly, finished off the last gems of amber in his glass and stalked toward the bar for his fourth.

"Wow." Ellis watched him go. "That must have hurt."

8

S hortly after ten, Andy concluded a final call with the on-scene detective in Washington, D.C.

"They're done for the night. He gave me a number to call in the morning," she said. She turned to me. "I offered to stay, but Lydia said no. We should go home."

I went for the coats while Andy engaged in a lengthy goodnight discussion with her sister.

At the door, Louis and Eleanor doled out a cordial but stiff "it's good to finally meet you." In the car, Andy called that a win. I considered her assessment generous. I was more pleased that Andy seemed to have found some release from the expectations her father had held over her. I thought of her outburst of giggles; it made me smile.

On the ride home, Andy sidestepped details about Davis's suicide. Instead, she talked about the logistics of helping her sister. Of dealing with the D.C. police and medical examiner. Of dealing with Davis's family and the looming issue of a funeral. Would it be in Washington? Or would it be in Michigan, where his family originated? What role would Lydia play? What about the children?

"I'm worried that Lydia will blame herself," Andy said.

"That's ridiculous."

"She did love him once, you know."

"And his unworthiness of that love grows bigger every day," I argued, with apologies to the nanny's belly.

"You're right. And that's completely not the point."

I wasn't sure how that worked but having identified a new minefield I marked it on the map and moved gingerly around it.

The house was cold and dark. Andy slipped out of her coat and made a quick examination of the first floor doors and windows. She double-checked the front- and back-door deadbolt locks and turned on yard lights, then secured the weapon she had been carrying in her purse.

Security checks and lighting up the yard at night had become the new routine. Like the squad car in the driveway.

I hovered a bit, waiting for a sign, which came at last when Andy closed her arms around me in a loving and distinctly unsuggestive embrace.

"Can we do presents tomorrow evening? I'm beat. I hardly slept last night. And you've got to be dead on your feet. Did you get any sleep?"

"Plenty," I tried to lie. The look on her face told me I failed.

"There's so much to do tomorrow. I need to call the Chief and see if I can switch shifts with somebody. Lydia will need me."

She stood against me for a moment, resting her head on my shoulder, absorbing something she needed. I slipped my hand under her sweater and lightly ran my fingernails over the skin between her bra strap and the waistband of her skirt. I didn't touch the bra.

Just as a part of me woke up to argue that nobility wasn't all it was advertised to be, she said, "If Lydia goes to D.C., I'm going with her. Let's get some sleep."

This Christmas sucked.

9

"Dammit." Andy muttered, standing over the dining room table in the gray dawn light.

She snapped the laptop shut and shoved her fingers deep into her thick auburn hair. A lock of it fell angrily over one eye.

"It's been three weeks!" she complained.

This was about Bob Thanning. He had been spread out on our dining room table since the day of his murder, the day Lydia nearly drowned. Andy scooped up the photos, printouts, documents and maps that erupted like a paper volcano each time she sat down to study the case. She tamped everything into a tight sheaf and shoved it all back into the case file. The file traveled with her to the station every morning and returned to our dining room table every evening.

I resumed scrambling eggs. Andy doesn't appreciate the clichés. *It takes time. Look at it from a different angle. Don't worry, something will pop up.* The last time I said *Maybe if you step away from it—* she threw a pen at me.

I knew what she was up to when she crawled out of our warm bed at four-thirty in the morning and padded downstairs on bare feet. Even with Lydia and Davis on her mind, she remained driven by Bob's murder and the attempt to murder her/Lydia. More than a few early mornings, after showering and dressing, I found her at the table, chasing information on her laptop, reviewing emails from the investigators in Montana, sending new emails to law enforcement agencies around the country or rearranging the photos and documents.

Someone who doesn't know Andy might have suggested she was driven because Lydia had nearly died. Or because she, not Lydia, had been the intended victim. That wasn't the full story. Sister or not, a crime had been committed in her jurisdiction. A murder.

Though that's not what the official record said.

THE ESSEX COUNTY CORONER ruled Bob Thanning's death an accident.

Ten years ago, at a machinery auction held at the Edwin Orth farm, Bob purchased a snowblower. Not your typical pull-start, walk-behind snowblower. Constructed by the Heath Machinery Company of Hibbing, Minnesota in 1947, this monster made of heavy steel, blades and chains, ran the width of a car and had been built to be mounted on a tractor. The machine used an auger to pull snow into a channel at the center, then used a fan-type blower to launch the snow into the next county.

Bob nurtured the bright idea that the beast could be mounted on the front of a pickup truck and would make his winter snowplowing avocation the star of Essex. Unfortunately, the Heath Machinery Company built the snowblower like a battleship. With the added weight of an engine he mounted to power the rig, Bob had yet to come up with a method of attaching the machine to the front of his Dodge Ram diesel pickup without tipping the rear wheels in the air or crushing the front suspension. The engineering question regularly sparked debate on fall Saturday mornings at the Silver Spoon Diner. Marching into another snowplowing season, Bob found himself forced to serve his clients the old-fashioned way.

According to the coroner, Bob had been tinkering with the beast when he reached into the running unit to retrieve a screwdriver that was later found mangled in the auger. The machine snatched his arm and pulled it into the auger and fan, which painted the roof and wall of his garage workshop with skin, bone and blood. Bob managed to avoid being pulled bodily into the machine only because the auger chewed his right arm off at the shoulder.

Linda Thanning found Bob lying prone in front of the bloodied machine, which stopped running after the engine ran out of gas. Later, the coroner would say that if the shock of the violent amputation hadn't killed him, carbon monoxide from running the engine in the closed garage would have.

An accident.

A lie.

Andy proposed letting the lie stand. Chief Tom Ceeves approved. They cemented their conspiracy two days after Bob died—on the day Andy and I drove Lydia home from the hospital.

Tom met us at the lake house.

"Are you finally going to tell me what's going on?" Lydia asked Andy when she saw the Chief. Andy said yes.

Lydia moved slowly. She had bruises on her legs and one knee was swollen, causing a limp. At the hospital they pronounced the injury a mild sprain, probably caused by twisting the leg when she was pulled from her submerged car. Her throat hurt, she said. Her voice had a rasp to it.

We took seats in her large sitting room overlooking the frozen, snow-covered lake. A severe-clear blue sky hung over the fresh blanket of white on the early-season ice.

"The Chief and I have already been over most of this, but we need to brief the two of you," Andy said. I tried to look curious. Andy had already shared her plans with me under the terms of our Usual Disclaimer.

Andy opened her laptop and turned the screen to face Lydia. "His name is Mannis Rahn."

"Is that him? Is he the bastard that pushed me?" Lydia pointed.

"We think so," Andy said. "Rosemary II thinks he's the one who pretended to be an insurance adjuster. The one who was interested in my car. He also struck up a conversation with Bob Thanning when Bob stopped at the airport to set up driveway markers on Thursday morning."

"Bob is a—was a talker," Tom explained. "Ask him the time of day and half an hour later you still wouldn't know what time it was."

"Rahn probably pumped him for information," Andy said. "I think that's how Rahn found out that Bob plowed for us and where we live. Rosemary II said she heard them talking about the big storm coming."

"It's not hard to imagine Bob telling someone all that," I said.

"So, who is he? Why did he come after me?"

"This has to do with the Cinnamon Hills Robbery case, Liddy. I don't know how much you followed the story—"

"Every word of it," Lydia said, "that I could find. Not just because it was my kid sister leading the charge, but because it had Davis and some of his colleagues awfully upset. A lot of lobbyists worked for those private prison companies."

"Montana is prosecuting the case against Parks, but they're keeping me in the loop on their investigation. I asked for a copy of the Evergreen population database and a list of inmates classified as Discharged by Death in Custody. It's a long list. It happens more than you would think. On that list, I found four who fit the profile. Two of them we knew about. One actually *was* a death in custody. Another was Garrett Foyle—"

"The Nazi?"

"Everything but the little Hitler moustache," I interjected.

"Two more are ranked as highly probable. Evergreen says they died and were cremated. We think one may have been seen going into Mexico. We thought the other had equal chances of being dead and alive. Now we know." Andy gestured at the screen. "Rahn."

"Time out!" Lydia held up her hands. "If these men were part of a scheme by this Pearce Parks character—what on earth would that have to do with me?"

"Liddy, he wasn't trying to kill you."

"Oh, beg to differ! That sonofabitch came up behind me and rammed me. And the moment he hit me I heard him rev his engine. He—he—!" Lydia choked on the words. She put her hands to her lips. "I'm sorry! I will never—*never*—be able to forget that moment!"

I wondered if that was a blessing or curse.

My accident—the one that cracked my pelvis and put me in the hospital six months ago—existed only in the form of what I could imagine and its aftermath. I normally nurtured a little self-pity over my memory loss. Looking at Lydia, I wasn't so sure that I didn't have the better deal.

"I will never forget going into the water," Lydia whispered. "Thinking for a crazy moment that the ice would hold me—and then it didn't. Breaking through, and the front of the car going straight down. I opened the door, but the car just filled up. Not like in the movies. Not this slow rise of water. It was a flood! A tidal wave! And it was black, and I didn't know up from down! And—oh, Katie!—all I could think of was the girls! What would they do without me?"

Tom and I exchanged a glance across an uncomfortable silence while Andy reached for and held her sister. Lydia shuddered.

I stood and walked to the nearest bathroom. I returned with a box of tissues. Andy took them and plucked one for her sister.

"Dammit!" Lydia swore, taking the tissue. "Ever since I met your husband, all I do is cry in front of him!"

"I've noticed that," I said. "It's giving me a complex."

Lydia let a laugh break through.

"I'm so sorry, Liddy," Andy said. "It never should have happened. I wasn't saying he wasn't trying to kill you. I mean, he wasn't trying to kill *you*. He was after me. He thought you were me."

"Well, that doesn't make it better! Why is this *asshole* after you? Why would he do Parks' bidding? I presume this Rahn had a life sentence like the Nazi, right?"

"Multiple life sentences," Andy confirmed.

"But he's free. He's out. And the devil he made a deal with is in jail now. So, if he answers to no one, why would he come after you? Why isn't he on a beach somewhere?"

Tom spoke up. "Andy thinks that Parks still has some sort of hold over Rahn. The world thinks Rahn is dead. Maybe Parks threatened to expose him. Maybe he's using that threat to get one more job out of him."

"Why?" Lydia asked.

"To eliminate me as a witness for the prosecution," Andy said. "Parks' legal team has been rolling out claims he never knew about any of it. Cal Richardson, the Montana Attorney General, thinks they're going to try and deflect everything onto a lackey named Leeson. He was a captain in the ranks at the prison in Sioux Valley—and in Tulsa before that. I met him. He disappeared when everything went bad for Parks."

"That's a body that will never be found," Tom muttered.

"I'm not their entire case," Andy said. "But Parks has a lot of money and a lot of legal firepower at his disposal. He'll chip away at the prosecution's case, move the venue, file motions to create delays—*eliminate witnesses*—and eventually muddy the waters so much it's hard to bring a conviction."

"But he tried to kill your friend Sandy! He killed her father!"

"Foyle killed her father. As for Sandy, Parks is laying all that on Jameson. He claims he had no knowledge of Todd's intentions," Andy said. "He's claiming that when Will and I rescued Sandy, we invaded his home and injured one of his employees, who plans to sue. He probably will sue, at Parks' bidding, just to throw the kitchen sink at me."

"That's insane!"

"No, that's civil law," Andy said. "Although the two are often one and the same."

"Don't get us started," I added, thinking of a recent encounter with another stellar member of the legal profession.

Lydia gestured at the laptop and looked at the Chief. "This Rahn. You think he killed your friend? Mr. Thanning?"

"Yes," Tom said.

Andy explained. "We think Rahn killed Bob, then took Bob's truck and came looking for me. He thought you were me and followed you. The snowstorm, the lake, the slippery roads—he improvised. He put you in the lake with no witnesses and returned Bob's truck to his machine shop and left it."

"Wait!" Lydia interrupted. She turned to Andy. "You think we look alike? I don't see it."

"Me either," Andy shook her head, puzzled.

I looked at the two of them like they were nuts.

"It was all supposed to look like an accident," Tom said, pulling everyone back on track. "Bob fiddling with that damned snow blower. You, sliding into the lake. It might have, too, if Will hadn't pulled your car back on the road and followed you."

I made a point of not trading glances with my wife. Andy had engineered a sanitized version of Lydia's rescue in which I managed to get Lydia's car off our mailbox, chased after Lydia, happened on the scene moments after she went into the lake, pulled her out, and raced her to the hospital in her Mercedes. Not the best lie ever told. Certainly not one that will stand up to close examination.

"Taking Bob's truck in a snowstorm made the perfect camouflage. No one would think twice about him coming or going. If not for you surviving, we might never have looked at the truck," Tom said.

"You found it? The truck that pushed me?" Lydia asked.

"It was never lost," Andy said. "It was right where Bob always parks it, at his machine shop."

"But how?" Lydia asked. "How could he put the truck back? You told me you were called to his shop when his wife found—you know…"

"Bob was found in the garage behind his home. Rahn returned the truck to the machine shop Bob owns in town. We were all at his garage, which is about half a mile out of town."

"The truck didn't have as much snow on it as it should have, if it had been sitting the whole time. It's the sort of thing you only notice if you're looking for it," Tom added. "We're having the blade tested. We expect to find paint transfer from Andy's car. But again, we never would have looked at it, if not for you surviving."

Lydia studied the three of us.

"Why does this feel like an intervention?"

Andy deferred to the Chief.

"Ma'am," he began.

"Ugh! Don't call me that. Tom, is it? I'm going to call you Tom. You're going to call me Lydia."

"Lydia," Tom began again. "I've got a citizen dead and—accounting for mistaken identity—an attempt on the life of one of my officers. Four of us, in this room, know neither was accidental. Four of us know that a convicted murderer who is supposed to be dead, or at least locked up for life, is responsible. We know what and who we're dealing with here, but we don't want him—or Parks—to know how much we know. And we don't want to give him—or them—reason to come after you again."

"You want me to keep quiet about being pushed into the lake."

Andy tapped her nose.

"So basically, I'm supposed to tell people I just drove off the road into a lake?"

"Better that you say you have no memory of the accident," Andy said. "This is why I told you not to discuss it with anyone in the hospital."

"I can coach you on the memory thing," I offered.

"We're putting added patrols on both you and Sandy Stone," Tom said. "You, because we just want to be sure. Sandy because, if they're really trying to eliminate witnesses, she's a prime target."

"And Andy! I want you to protect my sister! I don't care how tough she thinks she is!"

"Yes, Liddy. Me, too. I'll have a squad car in our driveway every night," Andy said. "Until we get this sorted out. It's also best if you don't mention any of it—the accident—any of it, to Davis."

"We're not exactly speaking."

"It's best you don't. If there's any kind of custody battle coming…"

"Oh fuck that! Davis is not getting anywhere near my children! And he fucking well knows it!" Lydia declared.

"Absolutely, but lawyers can twist things into pretzels if they want. There's no point in giving them material to work with," Andy said. She quickly changed the subject. "We're putting a lot of resources into finding Rahn. Not just local—I doubt he's anywhere near Essex right now—but state and federal, too."

Lydia gazed out at the frozen lake.

"I won't be able to identify him. If you catch him. I never actually saw him."

"Sweetie," Andy patted her sister's hand, "the man is supposed to be dead. And before that, he's supposed to be serving a triple life sentence. I don't think your testimony will be needed."

10

Bob Thanning was memorialized at the Grace Lutheran Church in Essex. Family and friends filled the church. The casket lay open. The right arm in his Sunday suit was stuffed with sawdust. Following the service his remains were interred at the Lutheran Cemetery behind the church. Due to the fresh snow, the graveside proceedings were limited to immediate family and the crew from Ron Anderson's funeral home.

Despite being planted under the snow and frozen earth, Bob regularly appeared on my dining room table as Andy threw herself into the investigation, pouring through the files and photographs. She stayed at the station well into the evening the initial week after the murder. I worried about her leaving the building alone and driving home late. I demanded that she agree to an escort.

"I'm fine," she said. "I'm in a unit, and Mr. Glock travels with me wherever I go."

"It's your theory. About Parks eliminating witnesses. Either you believe it, or you don't."

"Fine."

After that, Tom Ceeves put her on days and gave permission for her to take the file home with her.

I contributed to the security detail in my own way. Each evening after she returned home I slipped into the back-porch mudroom in the dark and—

Fwooomp!

I vanished.

"I'm doing a patrol," I called out to Andy. I thought it sounded official.

"Mmm-hmm," came from the dining room table where she sat shuffling papers and checking national crime databases on her laptop.

Wrapped in the cool sensation and shifting to weightlessness, I slipped out the back door. I pushed upward, letting myself rise in silence to a height of two or three hundred feet. At that height, I pulled a battery powered propeller-driven propulsion unit from a pocket in the old fishing vest I wore. I eased the power on the propulsion unit to a low growl. The quiet low power setting pulled me in a spiral above the house, ever widening, checking the landscape for signs of an intruder.

Our farmhouse offers its own security. We're the only house on the road. Harvested cornfields extended in all directions around us. Anyone approaching would have crossed half a mile of snow-covered field leaving telltale tracks. Except for deer trails, the snow in all directions remained virginal.

I put some genuine effort into those patrols. Flights lasted up to half an hour. I cruised across fields, up and down our road, in and out of the trees on a winter landscape glowing with moonlight.

Weaving and flying, chasing shadows, breathing in crisp air.

Skimming the tops of winter-black trees.

The flying helped loosen the knot in my chest.

On the fourth night, just to be a paragon of thoroughness, I ranged as far as the edge of Essex, then flew back across the airport, catching sight of Pidge as she taxied the Piper Mojave to the hangar after a charter flight. The fifth night I followed the winding road to Leander Lake, checking the property around Lydia's house. I noted an Essex PD car parked two hundred yards down the road.

That patrol took nearly forty-five minutes and used up two power units.

"Did you have fun?" Andy asked without looking up when I slipped back in the house and pronounced us safe again.

She doesn't miss a thing.

11

The morning after Christmas Andy dropped the Rahn file into her shoulder bag with an air of frustrated finality.

"Honestly, I am getting nowhere," she slid onto a chair facing the breakfast I laid out. "The man is a ghost. I've emailed his photo to every hotel within a hundred miles. No hotel, motel, B and B records. No rental car plates popping up on Vantage. Nothing! I can't figure out how he got to Bob. I can't figure out how he got Bob's arm in that contraption. I can't make sense of his transportation."

"What do you mean?"

"He needed a means to get to Bob's garage, right? From there, he took Bob's truck. So, did he leave a car out near Bob's home? He left the truck half a mile away at the machine shop. And by the time he was done with the truck, we had the full fire drill going on at Bob's garage. We would have seen something," she said.

"Eat."

"I checked traffic cameras. I checked security cameras. It was a snowstorm, for heaven's sake! People don't take long walks in a snowstorm. I spoke to every employee of every business on that side of town to see if someone saw something while they were driving home that day. Somebody walking. Nothing."

"Eat."

"Rahn is a loner. His record indicates he's a thinker. Making murder look accidental is his thing. They convicted him for three deaths, but his file lists nine other possibles. Accidents related to him. Going back to his parents when he was fourteen."

"Eat!"

"What?"

"Eat your breakfast," I said.

She put a fork to the eggs I had scrambled.

"I need to put it aside anyway," she sighed. "We have this thing with Davis. Lydia wants me to go with her."

"Wait—what?"

"She sent me a text—time stamped something like three a.m. She booked two tickets for D.C. for tonight."

"Tonight? What about the kids?"

"Mom and Dad will stay with the girls."

"I don't understand. Why is she going at all? The guy was a shit. She left him. Isn't this a job for his family?"

"Probably, but this changes everything. She's not a divorcee in the making, she's a widow. She needs to settle his affairs—no pun intended. They have a house there. *She* has a house there."

"A house that he hanged himself in."

"I doubt she plans to move back in," Andy said. "But there will be things to attend to. It's only for a couple days, Will. Besides, it might do me some good. I'm nowhere with this Rahn thing. Maybe if I get away for a couple days—step away from it—get a fresh angle on it..."

She looked at me. I gaped at her with a fork full of scrambled eggs hanging in front of my face.

"What?"

42

12

To make an evening flight out of Milwaukee, Andy and Lydia departed Essex early in the afternoon. I kissed my wife goodbye after extracting a vague promise that she would be back in a couple days, at most. She set off at the wheel of Lydia's Mercedes, leaving Unit 23 on guard duty in the driveway.

I felt marginally better about her driving. The fog lifted. Fresh cold air from the arctic pushed the stagnant air east. New snow frosted the landscape, and more was expected by the weekend. I wasn't happy about her being away but reasoned that travel to another city would be hard for Rahn to follow.

Andy screwed up. It happens so rarely, I considered marking it on the calendar. Her screwup became apparent just after dark.

"Hi, Mr. Stewart!" Lane Franklin stood at my back door flashing a bright smile.

"Lane!" I greeted the girl. "Who're you gonna fly for?"

"Norwegian Air Shuttle. 787 Dreamliners!"

Rosemary II had her car in reverse on the driveway. She waved. Lane waved back at her mother and stepped into our mudroom.

"You're here to see Andy."

Lane read the expression on my face. "She's not here is she?"

"I'm so sorry, kiddo. We've had an emergency. It's been a bit chaotic."

Lane quickly checked the driveway, but her mother was already on the road, taillights headed west.

"Andy will feel terrible. I know she would have called…"

"Oh, no, no! She probably just forgot. I'm so sorry to bother you!" Lane dug into her coat pocket and pulled out her phone. "Let me call Mom and turn her around!"

"Hang on!" I stopped her.

I considered the situation.

Not counting my neurologist, Lane, Andy and Pidge are the only people who know what I can do (I don't count the nurse who saw me jump out of the Angel Flight airplane on Christmas Eve). From time to time, Lane visits, and I treat her to a flight in the barn. To be proper, and in part because Andy claims Lane carries a crush for me, I make a point of having Andy present. Andy watches from the sidelines, unable to suppress her own laughter when she hears Lane giggling and laughing from the high corners and rafters, unseen.

Ordinarily, obeying a rule of caution around a fourteen-year-old girl, I would have insisted Lane call her mother back to take her home. But Rosemary II trusts Andy and me with the very life of her daughter.

I decided to bank on that trust.

"Hold up," I said. "I'll take you home. There's something I want to show you."

The fourteen-year-old bubbled to the surface of her sometimes-too-serious face. She grinned. "Is it about *the other thing?*"

"We really do have to come up with another name for it. Yes. There's been a bit of progress at Area 51," I said, referring to the barn and my experiments with flight. "You and I haven't been flying for a while."

"I know!"

Lane bounced on the balls of her feet in anticipation. I reached into a cabinet and pulled out my old fishing vest and two pairs of ski goggles. I handed one set of goggles to Lane.

"Here. Put these on."

"Oh! This is new!"

"AREN'T you going to wear a coat?" Lane asked as we stepped out the back door onto the concrete stoop.

I slipped on my goggles and gave her a secretive smile. "Don't need one. Ready Orville?"

"Ready Wilbur!"

I pulled her into as paternal a hug as I could manage and pushed an imaginary set of levers in my head to their imaginary firewall.

Fwooomp! Lane and I vanished. The dual sensations of coolness and weightlessness enveloped us. I relaxed my embrace and flexed my ankles to give the concrete a gentle push. We launched upward.

"You're doing this outside!" Lane exclaimed. Until now I restricted our flights to the interior of the barn, where walls, rafters and the roof offered grips and pivots for maneuvering—and protection against drifting away untethered. "Are you sure about this?"

"Stand by," I said. We continued our climb, slowly approaching rooftop level. Lane tightened her grip. "Okay, now I'm going to hook my arm in your arm. Don't worry. Andy and I have done this. You don't need to keep a death grip on me." I rearranged us until we were arm-in-arm. "See? You can ease up, Lane. I've got you."

She relaxed, and I pulled a propulsion unit from one of the pockets in my fishing vest.

"Okay, I know you can't see it—but, behold! The FLOP!"

I pressed the unseen flashlight tube and propeller combination against her hand. I felt her take the device. For a moment I wondered if it might reappear. Objects, when I let go of them, reappear, regain the influence of gravity, and fall.

In Lane's hand, the FLOP unit remained unseen.

"Flop?"

"Flight Launching Operational Propulsion unit. Awesome name, right?"

"It is!" she exclaimed. "Is that a propeller? Ohmigod! Does this do what I think it does?"

"Hold it in your hand like a flashlight," I said. I found her hand and helped her find the right position. "There's a slide control on the side. Do you feel it? Put your thumb on it, but don't move it yet."

"This is what you were doing with those model airplanes last summer!"

"Sharp eye, kiddo," I said. "Like all great inventions, there's been an evolution." I didn't tell her that the first version nearly killed me. "Okay, hold it out, away from us. Point it."

"On the axis of the propeller shaft?"

"Yeah. You get it. Now ease the slide switch forward. Just a hair. Just to get the prop turning. And be careful. That's a carbon fiber prop and it's sharp as hell. It will take a finger off if you put it in the blades."

The FLOP growled. I felt the wind generated by the propeller. We immediately moved forward, away from the house.

"That's it. You point. We fly."

Lane released a sparkling laugh.

"OH—MY—GOD!"

We eased forward over the long shadows cast in the snow by the yard lights. The garage roof slid toward us.

"Oh-my-God-oh-my-God-oh-my-God-oh-my-God!"

"That's it. Give it just a hair more power," I said. "Not too much. This baby has a lot more thrust than you might imagine."

"Of course, it does! Thrust without having to overcome inertia!"

We floated forward over the roof of the garage. The open fields beyond the low structure spread before us. The afternoon's lingering cloud cover had broken up, revealing moon and starlight that painted the snow-covered landscape. Light pollution from the City of Essex gave the few remaining clouds a soft glow. Our eyes adjusted as we moved away from the blazing yard lights.

"This is amazing!" she cried.

Snow-covered corn stubble flowed beneath us. Lane accepted the side-by-side posture but squeezed her arm tightly against mine. I reached over and closed a grip on her forearm to offer reassurance.

"You're doing great. Add power."

She complied, and we picked up speed. The FLOP unit hummed.

"Hey! I'm not cold!"

"Right. I can do this with no jacket on. All I feel is—"

"That coolness! That's amazing! I can feel the wind, but *the other thing*—it's thermal insulating! Amazing! What am I saying? This whole thing is AMAZING!"

"It gets even better. Use your wrist to turn."

She did. We changed course.

"Work your hand back and forth."

We curved right, then left.

She laughed. The sound danced across the snow-covered landscape.

"See the woods coming up?"

"Uh-huh!"

"Okay, change your power vector upward," I said. "This is three-dimensional flying."

She moved. We began to climb. In a moment, we were above the plateau of treetops.

"See how it works?"

"UNBELIEVABLE!"

"There's a thrust reverser, too. Try it. Slide the switch back until you feel the neutral detent."

I heard the power change its tone until it stopped. We continued to glide above the black tops of the trees.

"Now ease it back. You have the same thrust in reverse as you have going forward."

She did as she was told, and we stopped. Then we began to back up.

She laughed again.

"Okay, Captain. Your aircraft. You have the controls. Let's go!"

Lane stopped the unit again, then gave it forward thrust. We reverted to forward flight.

"Don't be afraid. Give it some power. See what it can do."

Slowly, ever the cautious child, she tested the power, adding to it, gaining speed. As the relative wind sweeping around us grew and tugged at our clothing, she laughed and cried out.

LANE GAINED confidence quickly and took us on a winding path across the Essex county farm country. I monitored her movements like I would any flight student, checking the route ahead, watching for obstacles, protecting the margin for error. With my free hand, I slipped another power unit out of my pocket and held it in reserve. If Lane encountered trouble, I planned to tell her to cut the power on the unit she held. Then I would take over with mine. Reaching for a spinning propeller that I couldn't see wouldn't be in the best interests of my fingertips.

We flew.

We skimmed over dark wooded expanses and broad open fields. Over frozen marshes and snowplowed back roads. The world lay still and white beneath us, with accents of black trees and brush. Fresh winter scent filled our nostrils. Crossing roads, I instructed Lane to avoid the wires by flying over the poles. Twice, we followed cars moving through the night below us. In an open field, we found a small herd of deer. Their ears shot up and they stood still at the sound of the buzzing propulsion unit. They listened but did not hightail it away. Lane eased off and performed a wide circle around them with a degree of finesse that I complimented.

She turned toward the herd and slid the power to neutral. We coasted in silence just yards above their alert heads. I wondered if they sensed us. As if in answer, their tails twitched and went up, and they bolted away across the field.

Lane did not resume powered flight. She let us glide in silence until the deer disappeared in a thicket of brush on the edge of the field. We floated thirty feet above the snow. I was about to ask if the power unit had died when she spoke up.

"Can I talk to you about something?" she asked.

"Anything you like."

She let a long pause hang in the air with us.

"There's a boy in my class."

Oh, no... I tensed.

"Lane...is this what you wanted to talk to Andy about?"

"Uh-huh."

"Because she'll be back in a day or two. Plus, you know you can always call her."

"You're turning red right now, Mr. Stewart! And NO, this is not *that* kind of boy thing. Oh, my God!"

"I am not turning red. See?"

"Funny," she said flatly. "No, this is something else. I thought I should talk to Andy about it because she is a police officer. But now I'm not sure that's the best idea. I think maybe I should talk to you first."

"Uh...okay." I couldn't imagine how that was a better idea.

"Okay," she said, and I could feel her posture change, seeking resolve. "This boy in my class. I don't think he's a bad kid. I mean, I talked to Sarah and some of my friends about him, because they knew him from grade school, before I came here. And they said he was always nice. But his mom died a few years ago. And he's had a hard time of that, and it's just him and his dad now, and...um, his dad is kind of a big old racist. I've seen him. He has stickers on the back of his truck that totally spell out his feelings about anybody who isn't white. The Confederate flag is there, too. And some other stuff. And I get it. I get there are people like that. But now, well, now this boy is...I don't know...changing."

We continued drifting. I noted a string of power lines bordering the field, half a mile away. No need to adjust yet.

"I think he's becoming like his dad."

"Racists aren't born, honey. They're made."

"I know that. I don't blame him. I know it's coming from his dad. And his dad is all he has. Like me and Mom. I know how that feels. But now he's—I don't know how to put this. I think he's using me like a test subject. Like a way to test out his new, um, way of thinking."

My protective instinct kicked in.

"Has he done something to you?"

"No! No, nothing. Well..."

"What?"

She hesitated.

"He gives me looks."

"What kind?"

More hesitation.

"Just...I don't know. Sometimes when I walk past him in the hall. He looks at me like I'm some kind of bug."

"Has he threatened you?"

"Nothing like that." Lane fell silent again. I waited. After a moment, she said, "He, um, he doodles stuff. In class. He's a really good artist. I think he likes graphic novels. Sarah said he was always good in art class."

"What kind of doodles."

"Stuff. He does it sometimes with his paper angled so only I can see them."

"What kind of stuff?"

"Lots of stuff."

We approached the road. I gave her time. But in minutes we would have to divert or rise above the power lines.

"Swastikas." She said it in a small voice. "And that SS symbol—the lightning bolts. And..."

She let the vast silence of the winter night press in on us.

49

When she finally spoke, the words slipped free just above a whisper.

"Last week he drew a cross and I think it was supposed to be burning."

"Hang on," I said. I pulsed the power unit in my hand and we stopped drifting. "A burning cross? Did you report him?"

"No."

"Lane this is serious shit! Stuff. This is serious stuff!"

"It's serious shit, Mr. Stewart. But no, I didn't report him."

"Why not?"

She hesitated.

"I don't know. I guess because I don't want to let him push me into becoming what he's trying to see me as. I mean—he wants me to be his enemy so what better way for me to become his enemy than by ratting him out?"

"Well, okay," I said. "That's a ridiculously mature chain of thought, but he's only going to become bolder. You need to report this to someone. There could be more to this. Does he ever talk about guns?"

"He doesn't talk to me at all. I just think I'm his guinea pig. There aren't all that many kids who look like me in Essex, in case you haven't noticed."

"Beautiful? Smart?"

"Brown. Mr. Stewart, I'm not going to become one of those people whose whole identity centers around the color of their skin. I'm just not. I mean, that's almost as bad as what he's doing."

"It's nothing like what he's doing!"

"I don't know what to do. I don't want to escalate this!"

"Okay. Okay. Let me think." We drifted. An owl made an early territorial call. After a minute, I said, "Okay. First off, maybe it's good you told me before Andy. I mean, you know you can talk to Andy, but she might have gone all Essex PD on this. Let me give it some thought. And let me tell Andy. Is that okay?"

"Sure."

"You don't see this kid during winter break, do you?"

"He comes into the store with his dad sometimes, but otherwise, no."

"You're working again? At Farm and Fleet?"

"Uh-huh. God, it took me four months to get Mama to let me go back!"

Last summer, Lane persuaded Leo Willis to let her work at Farm and Fleet, stocking shelves. Her abduction happened after work one Saturday night. I knew that the idea of Lane returning to the part time job terrified her mother. I was a little surprised that Rosemary II relented.

"Are you working during break?"

"A couple days during the week. And Saturday. But only days, and only until five. Mama drops me off and picks me up."

"What's his name?"

"Corey Braddock."

Shit. Of course.

"Don't let it worry you. I'll talk to Andy about it."

"I guess… it's just…please don't let her get too upset and do something—I don't know, harsh?"

"Lane, I can't guarantee anything. It's a different world now. Too much has happened in schools that might have been prevented if people spoke up sooner."

"I know, but…"

"Andy will be cool. I'll chat with her about it and make sure she understands the way you feel. If she needs to take steps, I'm sure she'll do it in a way that doesn't implicate you. Maybe there's a way to head this off. But you *definitely* should not do anything on your own. And promise me, swear to me that if anything, and I mean *anything* escalates, you will tell me. Does this kid have friends? Kids with the same attitude?"

"He hangs with some other boys, but I've never seen them show the same—I guess—symptoms."

Maybe not, I thought, but boys tend to spin each other up.

"If you get a whiff of anything, you take it seriously and tell me—and if you can't reach me, tell your Mom and find Andy."

"Oh, God, Mom will freak!"

"Freaking isn't the worst thing sometimes. Promise?"

"I promise."

"Good. Okay." We drifted toward a country lane. Beyond the road, a farm spread out in the dusky gray night. Squares of bright yellow light lay on the ground outside the windows of a milking parlor. The vacuum system compressor sounded lonely in the winter night.

"Let's get you home," I said. "Fire it up and set course for Essex. Mind the power lines!"

"Seriously!?"

"Why not? Let's get you home in style!" I declared.

I LET Lane do the flying, the same way I would have given a student pilot the controls in an airplane. I gave her a hint here and there, but she managed the power unit and determined the flight path. We skimmed over the farm country, then angled higher as city street lights sprouted in front of us. She expressed electric wonder at the way the landscape flowed below us, and her laughter broke over the steady sound of the power unit. I liked the sound. It suggested that by telling me about Braddock, she had unburdened herself.

We flew across town to where the streets became orderly and cookie-cutter houses stood in rows that sprouted when young soldiers returning from the Second World War fulfilled a need to create life. I told Lane to cut the power. With my FLOP unit I showed off by flying a sweeping arc around her small house and landing us on the front sidewalk.

I performed a quick search to ensure there were no eyes on us, and—

Fwooomp! We reappeared. Gravity re-established its relentless grip and we settled onto the concrete.

Lane threw a healthy hug around me.

"That is so awesome!" she bubbled. "We *have* to do that again! Soon! Promise?"

"Promise. Listen, Lane," I stopped her. "I need you to do something for me. Something online." I explained what I was after, knowing she could run rings around me with a mouse and keyboard. She accepted the assignment enthusiastically. I proposed a deadline. "Tomorrow okay?"

"No problem, Mr. Stewart! I can have my mom bring me over again."

I recognized the play. She wanted to fly again. And I wanted to take her flying again, but I preferred it be with Andy around.

"Just call me. We'll talk on the phone," I said. "Tell your Mom I said Hi!"

"I will! Thank you! This was absolutely awesome!"

She handed me her goggles and the FLOP unit and skipped toward her front door.

Fwooomp!

I kicked the pavement away.

13

Andy and I traded late night text messages. Hers arrived after midnight to let me know she and Lydia landed two hours late in D.C. after a delay in Atlanta. She didn't sound happy. I kept my response short. A simple wish for her to have a good night and a request that she find time to call me in the morning.

We didn't speak until almost noon on Thursday.

"How's it going?"

"Troubling."

I took the call in the pilot's office at Essex County Air Services. She spoke softly, suggesting that other people hovered within earshot.

"I'm at the house. I'm here with the D.C. Metro detectives. They have a forensic unit here."

"Seems a bit much for a suicide."

"Mmmm-hmmm. That's where this gets troubling. Everybody here thinks Davis died by accident."

"What?"

"They found Davis with that extension cord wrapped around his neck —the one in the photo. It looks like he climbed up on a chair in the foyer. There's a stair that goes up to a landing on the second floor. It's got one of those wrought iron railings. Not a wooden one. You know? This one is heavy and ornate. I don't know what it's called. But it's got lots of curls and swirls."

"Got it."

"Wait. Let me back up." She gathered a breath. "They checked Davis's credit cards. He went to a bar on Christmas Day, spent most of the afternoon there. The staff remembers him pounding drinks with a woman. One of the bartenders said she was 'pretty hot.' Davis settled his tab at seven-twenty, Eastern Time. The bartender remembers him leaving a stingy tip but doesn't remember if he left with the woman or alone."

"And we got the text and photo at—what?—around seven Central Time? Maybe seven-fifteen?"

"Seven-oh-nine. Forty-nine minutes after he signed for the tab, allowing for the time zone difference. The bar is twelve minutes from the house."

"Okay. Drinking all afternoon. Morose. It's Christmas Day. Lydia won't let him near the kids and is about to kick him in the bank account. Why the house? Was he living at home?"

"No, Liddy booted him out weeks ago. He's been living at a hotel."

"So, he went there to make a point. This still sounds like suicide to me."

"It would seem. Remember he tried to call Lydia? That call came into her phone at six-fifty-six, our time. So that means he had about twenty minutes from the time he got home to when he called, right?"

"About that."

"Then thirteen minutes between the time he called and when he sent the text."

"He went there with a purpose and he got right to it. No hesitation. Suicide."

"No. Accident."

Andy let it hang for a moment.

"I don't see how you come up with 'Accident' when you have a selfie of the guy with an extension cord wrapped around his neck."

"I'm getting to that. The team here thinks his purpose was to send a message. And when you send a message, you expect a response. Suicides *leave* messages," Andy explained. "This is how the detectives here see it: Davis drank all afternoon. Spent time with one of the girlfriends. Some-thing got him wound up. Lydia's ignoring his calls. He decides to show her. He came to the house. More than a little drunk, by the way. The medical examiner established he had a blood alcohol level of point one six."

"Was he drinking at the house?"

"There's no liquor here. Lydia got rid of it all."

I wondered if there was more to that.

"Anyway, he tries to call Lydia. She still doesn't pick up. He decides to show the bitch—literally, by texting 'Bitch' and sending her a photo of himself pretending to kill himself."

"How do you come up with 'Pretending?'"

Someone in the background spoke to Andy. "Be there in a minute!" she told them. "Because it was all for show. He wrapped the cord around his neck a couple times, then tied it with a pretty good knot, climbed up on the chair and then sent the selfie to scare the crap out of his wife."

"How did you come up with him doing it all for show?"

"Because he didn't tie off the other end of the extension cord."

Andy waited for me to get the picture.

"Not tied off?"

"No," she said. "He simply took the other end and tossed it up over the railing. To make it look like he meant it. He made it look like the cord was secured above him and took the selfie. Then hit send."

"You could have led with that. Are you telling me the other end wasn't tied to anything?"

"That's exactly what they found when they got here."

"Then how did he...?"

"You're not going to believe this. When he threw the cord up over the railing, the plug at the end got caught in the wrought iron. Like a grappling hook."

"You have got to be kidding me!"

"I wish I was," Andy said. "The cord caught. I guess he wasn't aware it had caught. He took his selfie, sent his text, and now he's up on the chair with the cord knotted around his neck and he can't get the other end to come down. It's tight enough that he can't get any slack to undo the knot or release the plug. Drunk. He panics. Loses his footing. Tips over the chair."

"Son of a bitch!"

"Will, they showed me scene photos. The plug was stuck—just barely

—like a quarter of an inch from being free. If he could have given it the tiniest bit of slack, it would have fallen out. If you tried a hundred times, you probably couldn't have gotten that plug caught. But he did. And he clawed at that knot. There's no doubt in the medical examiner's mind that he tried to abort. He tore the skin on his own neck. But with his weight on it, there was no way to create slack."

I couldn't help but think of a few times in my own life when I'd done something stupid and managed to narrowly escape paying the consequences.

Nothing like this. This was stupid for the record books.

"They're going over the scene thoroughly, to be sure, but all indications are that this is going to be ruled an accident. A dumb, tragic, drunken accident."

I had already been wondering how Lydia would explain to her daughters that their father was dead. Given this, I couldn't imagine.

"Jesus Christ," I said. "No disrespect to the dead...but what a fucking idiot! Are you onboard with all this?"

"These guys are good. They've looked at the scene from every angle. Nobody here is trying to fasttrack this or minimize it. Lydia and I spent most of the morning being interviewed. They dug deep. The separation. Davis sleeping around. All of it. We're talking to people in his office this afternoon. This isn't some slapdash conclusion."

"And you agree with it?"

She hesitated. "I can't argue with it. The police work on this is impeccable. They're doing a serious dive into forensics, which they could have skimped on. They're trying to identify the woman he was with."

"Do they think she was there?"

"No. The neighbor has security cameras showing him arriving home alone."

"How's Lydia taking it? This accident theory?"

"At the moment, she doesn't know. The lead detective gave me a professional courtesy pass to tag along but made her stay at the hotel. I'll fill her in when I get back."

The picture in my mind sharpened. Davis up on the chair, posing for the selfie. Davis convinced he would scare the pants off his wife. Then trying to climb down and feeling the noose tighten. Then panic. Panic that killed him. He had a phone in hand. If he had remained calm—even if he couldn't free the knot—he could have called for help.

"Stupid."

"Yeah. Listen, I gotta go. They're looking for me. Gotta go! Love you!"

"Love you!"

"Be careful, okay?"

"You, too."

I sat staring at the phone.

After a moment I remembered that I wanted to talk to her about Lane.

14

Thursday afternoon, on deadline, Lane called my cell phone while I was airborne. Earl booked me out as right-seat pilot on a charter in the King Air. It was unofficial, of course. Just to keep me sharp, he said. I listed myself on the manifest as "flight attendant." Dave Peterson flew as pilot-in-command and gave me good-natured shit about my title until I took the controls and made him serve the soft drinks in the back. The run took us to Louisville. I saw the missed call and dialed Lane from the pilot lounge while Dave and I waited for the charter clients to return to the airport. We talked for twenty minutes. She gave me more than I originally asked for. Typical Lane.

DAVE and I landed back at Essex County Airport just after eight. Andy called a little after ten as I arrived home and dropped my keys in the dish by the door.

"Hi," she sounded more relaxed, less rushed.

"Hey."

"Sorry I had to cut you off this morning."

"Where are you now?"

"Back at the hotel. We're at the Mayflower."

"I can understand not wanting to bunk at the house," I said. "I don't mean to be petty, but please tell me Lydia is picking up the tab."

"She insisted. And no, Lydia won't go to the house. Will, I can't get her to tell me for certain, but I'm starting to think Davis was more than just philandering."

"As in?"

"I think…" Andy hesitated. "I think his drinking might have been a serious problem, and he might have been putting his hands on Lydia."

"As in…abusive?"

"As in."

"Just Lydia?" I didn't want to consider other possibilities.

"I don't know. I don't know. It's just a feeling right now. But it explains her taking the liquor out of the house and wanting to get far away from him."

"How did the afternoon go? Did you go to his office?"

"Brogan Wayne. Davis's lobbying firm. Yes, we went. The D.C. detective and me. We got *a lot* of stock answers. Great guy. Lovely couple. Perfect entertainers. Charming wife. The more nice things people said about Davis, the less I believe any of it. I think he had Liddy boxed in. Trophy wife. A nice body and big smile for the clients. She used to be blonde, you know. He always wanted her blonde. And I looked in her closet. At the clothes she left behind. Very expensive things I doubt I would wear except alone with you. I get why she left the lot behind."

"An asset." I said. "She was a business asset."

"I'm not pushing her to reveal. Yet. Anyway, at Brogan Wayne it was like they're all reading from the same script. Also, there were a couple women— I'm pretty sure they were sleeping with him."

"How could you tell?"

"They saw me and looked guilty. Involuntary response. I guess I do resemble Lydia a little."

"She resembles you. There's a difference."

"You're sweet."

"I'm sorry, but it sounds like this couldn't have happened to a nicer guy. Tell me Lydia—and I mean you—isn't getting sucked into handling his funeral. Giving him a glorious and hypocritical send-off."

"Yeah, well, that's where it's getting a little cloudy. Turns out Davis's family knew nothing about the separation. As far as they're concerned, it's still one big happy."

"Do they know now?"

"Well…no. I talked to his father. Briefly. Kind of avoided the topic. They've been blowing up Lydia's phone ever since they were notified. I've been gatekeeping her calls. I don't know about the funeral. Nothing is clear yet. Lydia has the girls to think about. They're going to need—I don't know—something."

"*Please please please please* don't get pulled in."

"Trust me, it's the last thing I want, but I have to help. You know that, right?"

"I know. Just...come home as soon as you can."

"Lydia wants to sell the house. I told her I would help her meet with a realtor, and I want to make sure the cops here have everything they need, but then I plan to book it for home. God! I've missed so many work days in the last two months! Oh, and on that note, I got an email from Richardson in Montana. They're scheduling interviews right after New Year's."

"Really? Montana in January? Do you know how cold it gets there?"

"I don't control the schedule."

"Tom has to let that be on the clock, Dee. That's Cinnamon Hills."

"I know, I know."

She heaved a sigh.

"Did Richardson have anything new on Rahn?"

"Nothing."

We talked for close to forty minutes. Lydia had the two of them booked in something called a Congressional suite, and had gone to bed in her own room, leaving Andy alone on a sofa in the living area. Andy said it had a fireplace. I told her I wished I was there.

We revisited the bizarre nature of Davis's death, talked about the kids, and drifted on to a few housekeeping topics. I told her that Al Raymond had heard about her car and has been leaving messages about "absolutely cherry" vehicles he has on his lot. She said she would sooner arrest him than buy a car from him. I asked if she had any hope of being home before Sunday. She hedged her answer. I didn't push.

I told her about the charter flight to Louisville with Dave. She worked up excitement in her voice for me and the fact I was flying, albeit unofficially. Something about her chipper tone made me feel the opposite. I didn't like the feeling and moved on to other topics. I made her laugh a few times. Then, before long we were both yawning.

After exchanging sleep-well wishes, we ended the call. I sat for a moment, looking at my phone and letting her soft *I love you* echo in my head and mingle with memories of her touch.

"Oh, and there's something I need to talk to you about. It's about Lane," I said to the silent phone.

Definitely stalling.

15

"Okay, I get a call from dispatch," Tom Ceeves shoved a sausage back and forth through a lake of maple syrup on his breakfast plate. "Motorist calling it in. The woman is following an SUV up on County D. Says the guy is dragging a pair of wheels all over the road behind his truck. He's not going fast, but she's afraid to pass because the thing is on a chain, swinging all over hell and back."

"Christ almighty," Earl Jackson commented. The Silver Spoon Diner equivalent of giving a story start a thumbs-up.

I sipped my coffee and glanced at the door. The place was busy for a Friday morning. Most of the Saturday regulars were in a day early, thanks to the holidays. I had two reasons for attending. The first was Andy's absence, which gave me a chance to avoid cooking breakfast and hang with the boys.

I sat beside Earl, kitty-corner to Tom, and shared the rest of the table with Joe Boetcher, the fire chief, James Rankin, my farmer landlord, and two other large-acreage farmers, Jack Hindman and John Manke. Milton Cain, the retired former owner of a Harley-Davidson franchise rounded out the group.

"I was only a few minutes away, down on Stone Hill Road, so I cranked up the noisemaker and went west, over to Landry, then up to D. Figured I could intercept the doodler. Sure as shit, here he comes over that hill by Chester Neuman's old place—the one with the gravel pit—and from half a mile away I can see he's got all kinda commotion going on behind him. Whatever he's got on that chain is flying back and forth and it's hitting the snow banks and throwing up snow like a geyser."

Tom stopped marinating his sausage in syrup and took a sip of coffee to let us all admire the image.

"What wazzit?" Cain asked.

"Well…" Tom said.

I've known the chief since I've known Andy, and he's not a talker, except when it comes to storytelling. He enjoys a bit of theater with his tales. He let the question hang in the bacon-scented air for a moment, using the time to lower his coffee mug to the crowded tabletop. The mug looked like a child's tea set cup in his massive hands. He had to pinch the handle with his thumb and forefinger, and his pinky extended regally.

"I come roaring up from the west to intercept. This guy sees me coming, 'mergency vehicle and all, and does his civic duty and pulls over. So I swing over to his lane to block him. Well, he must'a thought I was trying to ram him because he slammed on the brakes and locks 'em all up. No ABS. Next thing I see is glass flying every which way from the back of his truck. It was one of those older Broncos. Jumpin' Jesus, I thought maybe the woman who called it in rammed him or something."

Tom went for his mug again.

"Them old Broncos were good trucks," Jack Hindman opined. "Had a seventy-eight. Er, might'a been seventy-nine, now I think about it. After they switched to the F-series chassis."

"Oh, ferchrissakes, Tom, you drag out a story like my wife. Takes her twenty minutes to tell me my lunch is packed," Milton Cain grumbled. Tom acknowledged the compliment with another long draw from his mug.

I checked the restaurant door again.

"I dismounted and approached the vehicle, and just about passed out from the alcohol fumes. It was Ed Hale. That horse-farmer lawyer. Drunk as an Irishman at a wake. Smelled like he took a bath in bourbon."

"That old horse fucker hasn't been sober since Bush Forty-One," Earl said.

"Sonofabitch will live forever 'cuz he's pickled," Manke said.

"I told Hale to shut her down and hand over the keys, and he did. I made sure he didn't have a cigarette or open flame about because, whooo!

63

the vapors would'a lit him up. I told him to stay put and went back to see what rear-ended him."

"And?" Earl prompted Tom. The look on Earl's face suggested impatience layered over malice, but that was just his breakfast face. At the Silver Spoon, prompting is considered good form.

"I get behind that Bronco and here's a full solid axle rear end with two wheels attached, and about fifty feet of logging chain, mashed up in the back window. He's lucky he wasn't going any faster or that whole rig would'a gone through the back of his head. Course, he didn't have a clue."

"Drunks never do," Milton Cain said. "I seen a drunk take out twelve highway marker posts—those black and white ones? Twelve of them. Four of them went through the windshield and landed in the back seat. Couldn't have missed the dummy's head by more than a red hair. He never knew a thing. Sat there hung up on a culvert revving the engine, makin' the wheels spin, thinking all the while he was driving home to his old lady."

"Hale was towing a rear axle? With a chain?" I asked.

"Not exactly," Tom said. "I stopped back at his window and asked ol' Hale just what he thought he was doing, and he said he was helping his buddy get his car outta the ditch. Mind you, Hale can barely string a sentence together, and he's having trouble getting both eyes pointed in the same direction. But he explains to me that his buddy got his car stuck in a ditch and called him up to pull him out. That's what he was doing. Pulling him out. I said, 'Ed, you only got part of the car attached back there,' and he says, 'Well, thassa part that was stuck!'"

Tom took another sip and let a laugh circulate the table.

"I think it was a seventy-nine," Hindman said, although he still looked perplexed.

"Well, just about the time I'm picturing how one drunk got another drunk to yank a car out of the ditch by wrapping a chain around the rear axle, I hear this God-awful commotion comin' down the road."

"You gotta be shittin' me!" Earl exclaimed.

"As God is my witness, I am not," Tom said. "At first, I couldn't make out what was going on because all I can see is a pair of headlights aimed up at Saturn—and behind that what looks like the Fourth of July. Fireworks and sparks flying all over the road! Looked like a damned UFO coming down County D. Sure as shit, this other drunken idiot pulls up and stops alongside Hale. It's Ray Nelson in that damned Chevy 'Cadavalier' rust bucket he usta drive, and being front-wheel drive, he's piloting that wreck down the road with just the front wheels, draggin' a rear end that's got no wheels, 'cuz they're up in the back of Hale's Bronco."

A round of comments circled the table, sprinkled with laughter and some genuine admiration for an enterprise so skillfully misguided.

"I get around to Ray's door and snatch up his keys," Tom said, "and he compliments me for stopping his buddy Ed because it looks like there's something stuck in the back of his friend's Bronco."

"Surprised he noticed," Earl said.

I shifted my attention. My second reason for breakfast at the Silver Spoon stepped through the door.

Ben Braddock stomped snow off his boots on the rubber door mat. He wove his way through the diner and dropped the keys to his GMC pickup on the Formica counter before taking a stool. Braddock could have tipped a hello to any of half a dozen of his Essex neighbors. Except for a word muttered to one of the high school girls taking orders and serving coffee, he said nothing. In a moment, his breakfast would arrive, and he would eat it in silence, largely unnoticed.

The last time I watched this man eat, he sat in a bar booth hunched over a plate of meatloaf. Then, like now, he dined alone. On that occasion, I stole his cell phone. Andy was investigating the Cinnamon Hills robbery and Braddock's cell phone provided Andy with a vital lead. As for the cell phone, she neither reported it, nor returned it.

Andy later told me she tried to solidify Braddock's connection to the nest of Nazis responsible for the robbery at Sandy Stone's wedding but could not conclusively say he'd been involved. All we knew for certain was that he seemed to sympathize with the sons of Hitler, and tried to call a woman who lived, and then died, with the thieves.

I gave him the corner of my eye as I finished my coffee.

"...don't know how many times I've had that drunk son of a bitch locked up," Tom Ceeves shook his head. "He hasn't had a license for the last ten years. That sure as hell doesn't stop him."

"You ever get an earful of his conspiracy bullshit?" John Manke asked cautiously.

"I did," Milton Cain replied. "Holy Jesus, I ran into him at the fireman's picnic and he about chewed my ear off all about the Democrats and their international child sex slave ring." Cain shook his head. "And don't get him going on the wetbacks!"

"Three rules," Earl announced firmly.

"What rules?" Cain asked.

"Three rules for dealing with people like that," Earl said, taking center stage from Tom who went back to work on his syrup-swimming sausages. "You can't fix stupid. You can't talk to crazy. And you never negotiate with terrorists."

"Drunk, stupid and crazy amount to pretty much the same thing for ol' Hale. But how do you get terrorist?" Joe Boetcher asked.

"He terrorized the shit out of the back of that old Bronco, wouldn't you say?"

I pushed my chair back and stood up.

"Gentlemen," I said, "I would love to stay and see who can top that one, but my wife is out of town, and you know what that means."

"Honey-do list," Earl said.

"Reads like an encyclopedia," I said.

I peeled a ten from my wallet to cover breakfast, the coffee I'd been served and a generous tip for the girl doing the serving.

"How's that sister of hers doing?" James Rankin asked.

"Well."

"That was a nasty thing, going into the lake like that."

"Heard you went for a swim, too, Will," John Manke commented. I gave him points for understatement. "How did that go?"

The incident with Lydia was three weeks old. I hadn't been in the Silver Spoon since. I had hoped it would be old news.

"Cold," I said, hoping to let it go at that. "You fellas have a good day!"

As Joe Boetcher began explaining the intricacies of extracting a sedan from Leander Lake, I made for the exit. The clock was ticking.

16

The Braddock father and son duo occupied a square two-story house on Paradise Road three and a half miles north of Essex. Most of the land in that part of the county belongs to farmers, but a few lots fronting the road had been sold off for individual homes. Country living. Or sub-suburban living. Homes on these isolated lots ranged from ranch style to clapboard to Cape Cod in all states of repair. Some lots displayed attentive landscaping. Others ran thick with buckthorn scrub and unkept lawns. A few sustained classic rural collections of rusting junk that blossomed into view in winter when the shielding vegetation went bare.

The Braddock homestead numbered among the latter.

I arrived overhead after leaving my car in a remote corner of the Piggly Wiggly parking lot. I figured I had about half an hour while Ben Braddock huddled over his breakfast hash at the Silver Spoon counter.

I eased into the yard without a plan except a vague hope that Brad-dock's only child, Corey, would not be at home. From there I had a full range of felonies at my disposal, starting with breaking and entering.

A freestanding four-car garage dominated the backyard. Judging by the tire tracks in the snow, only one of the bays served a vehicle. I maneu-vered closer, eased up to a dusty window and looked in. The interior lay dark, yet familiar shapes and glints of metal told me the garage had a workbench, tools, gas cannisters for welding, and racks of collected machine parts. I smelled grease and oil. The bay aligned with the tire tracks stood empty. Another bay held a vehicle under a dirty tarp.

I turned to the house and pulsed my power unit. Allowing for a cross-wind, I eased up to a set of windows on one side of the back door. The windows revealed a kitchen, dark and cluttered. Dishes occupied the sink. The table wore a green checkered plastic tablecloth under piles of papers, mail and what looked like a toaster undergoing surgery. Clutter mounded the countertops. Potted plants sat on the window sill sporting dry, cracked earth and the skeletal remains of whatever the plants had been.

I moved on. At the next window I surveyed a sitting room. An upright piano nudged one wall, topped with family photos in a variety of frames. Some showed a man, woman and small boy. A few showed just the man and the woman. One, prominent in the center, showed the woman alone. She had a warm smile and hair that might have been styled for the portrait. She looked happy. Other photos showed the boy. These were framed copies of school photos. The boy looked happy, too. Before cancer came to this house.

The rest of the room seemed ordinary enough, except for subtle hints that the woman's touch had left the building. A pile of magazines sat beside a recliner, leaning precariously. A cluster of empty long-neck beer bottles stood without coasters on a coffee table.

I backed away and pushed off the window sill to rise.

Looking through the windows into the second floor, I found two bedrooms with unmade beds. I found piles of laundry at the baseboards. I found bathroom countertops randomly strewn with men's products. Deodorant. Shaving supplies.

No makeup. No women's hair care products or lotions.

I tried several windows, but they were either locked or painted shut.

In the bedroom that belonged to the boy, the dresser top was cluttered with die-cast toys. Cars. Trucks. A helicopter. Posters lined the walls, featuring comic book characters, rock bands and NASCAR heroes. I looked for something suggesting a neo-Nazi bent but saw nothing overt.

An upstairs window at the back of the house got my attention. The shades were drawn, and the room was dark. Through a narrow space where the edge of the yellowed old shade curled, I spotted a desktop. A laptop computer occupied the center. Boxes of ammunition, a bottle of gun oil, and what looked like gun cleaning supplies shared the desktop surface with the laptop.

I tried the window, which had no screen. It refused to move.

I made a note of the location of the room.

I dropped back down and angled toward the back door. Three concrete steps climbed to a concrete stoop. I settled onto the stoop and had just reached for the levers in my head that would make me reappear when I froze.

A black plastic eye stared down at me from under the eaves.

Camera.

For a freakish instant, I thought I had blown it. I thought it could see me. A jolt of panic toured my veins.

Close. Damned close.

I settled myself and tapped my toes on the concrete to rise. Pulsing the power unit, I moved laterally along the back side of the house. The camera hung below the eaves near the corner of the house, transmitting a view of the backyard.

A second camera viewed the side yard.

A third camera surveyed the front.

A fourth, the opposite side yard, completing the coverage.

Two more cameras guarded the garage. I kicked myself for missing them.

This changed the situation.

I bugged out.

"What's with all the cameras, Braddock?" I asked aloud after snapping my seatbelt back at the Piggly Wiggly lot.

17

"It's awkward," Andy told my left ear via cell phone speaker. "Lydia still hasn't given me the okay to tell Davis's family about the separation."

I pulled a Corona from the fridge and performed a deft one-handed cap removal with the opener we keep magnetically attached to the door.

I sat down, switched the call to speaker, and laid the phone on the table beside my chair.

"Dee, please tell me that Lydia plans to come clean with them."

"I could, but it might be the precise opposite of true."

"Might be?"

"Let me think out loud for a minute, okay? There could be an upside to not telling them. Never telling them. They can stay connected to their grandchildren without an elephant in the room. Their son's memory isn't tarnished. Time passes. Davis fades into family history. Someone lost, rather than someone booted out. Will, you have to see what a blessing it is that Lydia and the girls won't have to go through years of court battles and custody skirmishes and being shuttled back and forth between parents."

"Say that around those D.C. Metro detectives and they'll start rethinking that this was a freak accident."

"Lydia has an alibi. Seriously, as bad as it is, what Davis did changes everything for his children and his parents."

"It's a cover-up and I can't believe you're suggesting it."

She sighed.

"Fine. Let's agree that Lydia has to tell the girls the truth. When they're old enough. But by then, what today is a marriage implosion, ten years from now can be described as 'we were having problems.'"

"Andy, do you hear what you're saying? Put yourself down that road, ten years from now. You have a couple of rebellious teenaged girls who, by then, will have glorified the memory of their lost father. Now their mother tells them he was a shit and the marriage hit the rocks and Mom kicked his ass out—and he committed suicide—or whatever it was! Who do you think they will blame for that?"

Andy said nothing.

"I'm not saying that all the dirty laundry gets dumped on the lawn. But a frank conversation with his parents is the only way."

Andy said nothing.

"I don't mean to pile on here, but there's one more thing. Melanie. Her child is Harriet and Elise's half-sister, and a grandchild to Davis's parents. They shouldn't find out about that ten years from now."

"I get it." Andy gave it a beat, then said, "You are an amazing, brilliant man, Will Stewart."

"That's what they say," I said, lifting my beer and toasting myself. I should have known better.

"Which is why you can help me with all that after you arrive here. Tomorrow."

"Tomorrow?!"

"With my parents. And the girls."

18

Plan A. I vanish and make the flight to D.C. coiled near the overhead in the crew galley.

Plan B. I flash my pilot's license and persuade the Southwest Airlines flight crew to let me drive their Boeing 737.

Plan C. An over-the-horizon distant third. I endure awkward semi-silence with Andy's parents driving from Essex to Milwaukee, where we board a Southwest flight to Washington National. I ride seated in the same row as the Great Stone Face himself, who barely has five words for me.

Plan C it was.

Two things made the trip tolerable. First, the flight was nonstop. Second, I took a middle seat between the two girls after they each demanded to sit by Uncle Will; at least that put an aisle between me and Andy's parents. Like the flight, the energy from Harriet and Elise was nonstop. They must have swapped seats six times. I brought along one of the Essex Air Service iPads and tried to use the Foreflight application to show them our route, speed and altitude, and cities passing beneath us along the way. Harriet showed an interest, especially when I pointed out that we were flying higher than the tallest mountain on Earth. Elise wanted to use the device to play a game in which flying toads eat candy.

Andy and I have talked about having children. I'm fond of my nieces, but that flight may have put procreation on the back burner for a couple years.

Upon reaching the baggage claim at Washington National, the girls found and all but tackled their mother. Andy strolled up alongside her sister and gave me an extra-appreciative squeeze.

"You okay?" she asked softly, in my ear.

"Nothing alcohol can't cure."

"I may have something better. Later."

I liked that idea, but then Andy did something that nearly topped it. She turned to her parents.

"Mom, Dad," she announced, "Lydia will go with you to the hotel. I have to meet with the police. Will is coming with me."

"What happened?"

I slid into the back seat of the blessedly quiet car with Andy. The Uber driver eased away from the curb, negotiating the land-based airport departure traffic. He seemed competent enough. Andy endorsed him by paying no attention to his navigation.

"Someone broke into the house last night," she said. "I got the call just before we left for the airport. We're meeting one of the detectives there."

She pulled out her phone and thumbed a short text message.

"I'm just letting him know we're on our way." She hit Send then secured her phone in her purse.

"This suggests...what?"

Andy shrugged.

"We'll see. Just part of the rich tapestry that seems to be my brother-in-law's departure. His parents and one brother are arriving this afternoon. They'll be at the Mayflower with all of us."

"Well, that should be uncomfortable."

"We'll deal with it. Davis's body is being released today, too. Lydia made arrangements with a funeral home to fast-track a viewing tomorrow. She's telling the girls tonight and thought a viewing was important."

Maybe so, but I still couldn't imagine explaining all this to a child just out of diapers. Coward that I am, I hoped Andy and I could keep our distance from that part of the planned events.

"It will be private. Just us and his family," Andy went on. "But there's a memorial this evening."

"That was quick."

"Brogan Wayne approached Lydia and insisted. They're putting it all together."

"Seems like a nice gesture, if a little rushed."

"Rushed because of the holidays. And nice...maybe. They're a lobbying firm. They have event planners on staff."

I looked at her. "Okay...that sounded a little judgmental."

She made a half-apologetic shrug. "I guess. I don't know. It was just the vibe I got from them. Yes, it's nice they're helping Liddy. I wonder, though, how much of that is guilt. He was more married to them than to her. Top management avoided me like the plague."

"Maybe they're thinking of all the women who need to pay their respects."

"Stop it."

"And speaking of women, did the police identify who he was with on Christmas Day?"

"Not yet."

"So many from which to choose."

Andy turned and gave me a slap on the arm, but it was delivered with dimples peeking from the corners of her mouth.

"You better get that out of your system, Pilot," she warned me, suppressing a grin.

"It might be hard," I said. I gave her an innocent look. "But the mortician can probably deal with that."

"Oh! You're terrible!" she laughed, but for appearance's sake, she slapped my arm again.

I'M A BETTER than average navigator. In the air and on the ground. But by the time the Uber driver pulled up to the Bates house, my sense of direction and location lay in a shredded heap. A leaden overcast obscured the sun, stealing my compass orientation. The District of Columbia streets made no sense to me. Avoiding heavy arterial traffic, the Uber driver followed a navigation display through residential backstreets, zigzagging his way through expensive real estate. I had hoped to spot some familiar monuments or buildings along the way, but none of the tourist attractions peeked between old-money homes. By the time the driver double-parked I gave up.

The driver gave us a friendly send-off and we hopped out.

An unmarked cop car sat in the narrow driveway of a two-story red brick house, squeezed between a brick wall that delineated the neighboring property and a brick terraced garden that fronted the house. To my eye, the entire neighborhood had been constructed of the same red bricks, with the same walls, gardens and steps. Young trees, leafless now, lined the sidewalk. I pictured this street in a romantic comedy, with the lovely lead actress jogging to the coffee shop I noted at the corner of the block.

Andy would look good running on these sidewalks.

The cop car driver's door opened and a detective in a gray suit stepped out. He looked about my age and height, with a close-cropped military-style haircut that could have been light brown or red. It seemed to depend on the light. His face had wider than average dimensions, still within the boundaries of handsome. He cultivated a rugged look with a perfectly cropped growth of beard meant to suggest he just hiked home from a rafting adventure in Utah.

He held a tall coffee in each hand. One was obviously meant for the smokin' hot visiting detective standing at my side. His eyes warily jumped from Andy to me. I watched his plans to hit on my wife flash and burn like a magician's paper. I gave him a friendly smile.

"Detective Fanko," Andy greeted him.

"Detective Stewart," he said. He rounded the trunk of his car and stepped to the sidewalk, extended the coffee for Andy. "Thought you might like a cup."

"Oh, thank you, but I had too much with my sister at lunch. My husband is probably dying for one, however." She passed the tall, warm cup to me. "Will, this is Detective Mike Fanko. He's been exceptionally gracious through all this."

I bet.

I switched hands for the coffee and extended a hand to the D.C. Metro detective, who did the same. We shook. He went for car crusher. I countered with tectonic plate collision.

"Good to meet you, Will," he lied.

"Same here."

Andy cast an appraising eye toward the house. Yellow police tape crisscrossed the front door.

"What happened?"

"'Fraid we might have put a sign on the place with the tape," he said. "It's not the first time. Thieves cruise by. See the tape, but no units. Guarantees there's no one home. They make a quick hit. We're pushing for a policy change, but some pencil neck in the department counsel's office insists we have liability if we don't tape up."

Fanko climbed a flight of concrete steps to a landing at the front door. He pushed the door in with his free hand, then pointed at the jamb where splintered wood marked the previous existence of a deadbolt.

"They're buying battering rams online, just like the ones we use." Fanko pushed aside the yellow plastic tape and held it for Andy and me to enter.

The house was a wreck.

From the front foyer, I could see the damage done to the living room and dining room. A china cabinet stood with the doors open, the shelves stripped, and pieces of smashed china on the hardwood floor. Picture frames lay in puddles of broken glass on the floor. In the living room, a television stand showed a dusty footprint where a flat-screen TV had been. Half a dozen children's DVDs lay strewn across the floor beside a DVD player.

The doors to the front hall closet hung open. Boxes that had occupied an upper shelf lay on the floor, exposing a tablecloth and placemats. A box that had held silver napkin rings in a sculpted velvet tray lay open, empty.

I took a moment to look up. A wide, curved staircase rose to the second-floor landing. A wrought iron railing lined the stairs and the landing. I guessed at the spot where Davis made his dramatic exit. The chair he used came from a set in the dining room. It now stood off to one side in the foyer. One dark wood arm of the chair was broken. I wondered if he had been standing on the arms, rather than the padded seat—or if he had tried to step up onto the arm in his struggle.

I looked up at the wrought iron scroll work and tried to imagine the heavy-duty plug from a thick orange extension cord catching in the iron leaves.

"Stupid," I said.

"Did the alarm trigger?" Andy asked. She pointed at the keypad near the door.

Fanko nodded. "A unit arrived in seven-and-a-half minutes. By then they were long gone."

"Wow," I said. "Seven-and-a-half minutes for all this?"

Fanko said nothing.

"Video?" Andy asked.

"Some. Same source we had showing Bates arrive. The neighbor," Fanko said, gesturing with his thumb at the house next door. "The neighbor already turned it in. Three young men, hoodies, looking the part."

I wondered if 'looking the part' was a racial euphemism. "How come Lydia and Davis don't have video surveillance?"

Andy walked across the foyer. "The house came with a security system. It's older, though. No video. Lydia said they talked about upgrading, but it's a good neighborhood."

I followed her through a back hall into the kitchen. Drawers were pulled out and dumped. Cabinet doors hung open. Dishes lay in shards on the floor. A glass coffee pot had been smashed against the brushed aluminum front of the refrigerator. The freezer door had been left open. Several frozen food items lay on the floor.

Some of the destruction seemed to be the result of plunder. Some of it seemed wanton. Some made no sense whatsoever.

A drawer full of household bills, pens and paper clips had been dumped. Another drawer full of utensils had been pulled but left untouched. Several of the utensils were sterling silver.

From the kitchen I entered a sunroom at the back of the house. A utility hallway exited the sunroom and ran to a bathroom. The hall was lined with storage closets. The storage closets were open and ransacked. Children's coats and accessories littered the floor.

One of the cabinets contained an assortment of lightbulbs, a few tools, and a role of tape. Another contained cleaning supplies. A box of laundry detergent powder had been dumped on the floor.

"...junkies grabbing up anything they can pawn," Fanko's voice carried from the kitchen. "Your sister will have to put together some kind of inventory for insurance, but frankly, it sounds like she has most of her valuables out of the house already."

"She does," Andy said. Her voice sounded closer to me than Fanko's. She poked her head into the sunroom. "Whatever they got, it was probably here because she left it behind for Davis. Did they hit the upstairs bedrooms?"

"All of them."

Fanko led the way. The damage on the second floor resembled the first floor. Andy found the master bedroom and entered. She checked a chest of drawers. Fanko stepped up behind her, a little closer than I liked.

"Looks like almost everything of Davis's is gone," Andy said. "Whole drawers emptied out. The jewelry, watches, that stuff makes sense. But look at this. I think his sock drawer got cleaned out, too."

"Why the sock drawer?" I asked, immediately regretting it.

Fanko replied, "Joe Homeowner likes to keep his pet Glock in the sock drawer. Easy pickings for a break-in."

"I like to keep mine on my wife," I muttered.

"Why take the socks?" Andy asked.

Fanko shrugged. "Homeless junkies. Means they can skip laundry day."

Andy hurried out of the room. That she seemed to be on the hunt for something prompted Fanko and me to follow. She led us to a bedroom the little girls recently shared.

"They hit this, too," she said. "But here again, almost everything was already gone. Still...look at that. They went through drawers. The closet."

She said nothing more. She took the lead again. We returned to the first floor foyer.

"We've got a guy, a crime scene tech. I could see if he can come over and secure the front door. Nail it shut," Fanko offered. "But I don't think he's on today."

"Oh, that's not necessary. My husband is very handy with that sort of thing. If there's a hardware store around here, he'll know what to do."

I gave Fanko a smile. It had nothing to do with being handy.

"Well, I'm so sorry this had to happen on top of everything else. You know how to reach me if I can help in any way. Can I give you a lift somewhere?"

"I appreciate the offer, but we'll manage. I want to call my sister before we leave here."

Fanko took the cue and made for the door. Andy followed him out.

"Call me if you need anything," he said to Andy. He ignored me.

Andy and I watched him pull away.

"Do you see anything wrong with this picture?" Andy asked. She turned and marched past me into the house.

"A five-hundred-dollar cappuccino maker left sitting on the kitchen counter?"

"I was going to say the DVD player laying on the floor," she pointed. "What junkie can't sell a stolen DVD player?"

"You also have a drawer full of personal paperwork ransacked, but a drawer with a set of sterling silver serving spoons untouched. And what are they doing going through the kids' underwear drawers? Perverts?"

She stood in gray light, her hands on her hips, her lower lip expressing intense thought at work.

"Liddy moved a lot of stuff the girls had, but she said they still had some toys here. I looked. There are no dolls upstairs."

"Socks and dolls?"

I looked around. She looked around. She looked at me.

"This is bugging you, isn't it," I said.

She said nothing for a moment, then, "I hate that Lydia has to come back here and deal with this. Was it okay? What I said about the front door? Can you fix it?"

"Hang on a sec," I said. I jogged back through the house, to the back hallway. Andy caught up with me as I poked through the cabinets.

"What are you looking for?"

"Tools."

There were none of any use. A drawer I noticed earlier had a pliers, three scissors and a useless bicycle wrench kit. We left the house and checked the garage. Nothing. Andy locked the garage door behind us and we walked to the curb.

"The answer is Yes. Get me to a hardware store and I'll get something to secure that front door. We can start by taking down the crime scene tape. Your key opens the back, right?"

"Yes," she said. She took three steps down the sidewalk, then stopped because I hadn't moved.

I stared at the front of the house.

"What?"

I looked at the house. Looked at the neighbor's house. Looked at the houses across the street. Then back at Lydia's house.

"Where are the Christmas lights?"

Andy came up beside me.

"The rest of the street...just about everybody has lights up." I pointed. "You've got little kids in the house. They would have done something."

"Lydia told me they hire a service every year. I guess she knew, before Thanksgiving, she would be in Wisconsin in early December. She must have cancelled it."

"A service? Davis didn't do it?"

"According to Lydia, Davis didn't do anything around the house unless it involved a laptop."

"Then why," I asked, "would Davis have a heavy-duty outdoor extension cord?"

19

The coffee shop on the corner didn't serve sandwiches, but a deli half a block away came through. While I devoured a tuna melt, Andy worked her phone. Like clockwork, when I finished, another Uber appeared in front of the deli. He took us to the nearest hardware store and agreed to wait.

Before buying supplies to nail the front door shut, or board it up in some way, I checked with the service desk. Yes, they had a locksmith, and yes, they had emergency service. They could be there in the next two hours, and yes, they had plenty of experience with forced doors. Andy made the arrangements.

On the way back to the front of the store and our ride, we passed the electrical department. Andy stopped.

"What?" I asked. She pointed at a rack of heavy-duty outdoor extension cords.

"It was like this one." She studied the display for a moment. "I need to call Fanko."

"Why?"

"Look." She pointed. "Six. Fifteen. Twenty-five. Fifty. One-hundred foot."

She pulled out her phone and dialed.

· · ·

Fanko didn't answer. Andy called his station. The officer answering said Sunday was his day off. Andy explained she had just seen the detective, but that didn't change the response. Andy asked for any other available detective in his division, spoke to a woman named Appleby, and explained her request. She left her name and number.

After the call, I pointed out to my wife that Fanko made the trip to Lydia's house on his own time.

"I think he had plans. Show you around the crime scene, get a coffee, maybe dinner?"

Andy shrugged it off. "I'm sure he did. It got me access. My gain. His poor choice."

We returned to Lydia's house to wait for the locksmith. Andy entered the foyer and stopped, gazing at the spot where Davis died and the railing above it.

I knew better than to interrupt her thoughts. From the request she made of the D.C. Metro detective named Appleby, I had a pretty good idea what she was thinking. She would share it with me when she was ready. Or not.

"We should clean up," she said, returning to the moment.

"Why?" I asked. "Lydia should just hire movers to come in and box everything up that isn't furniture. Ship it all to Wisconsin. Leave the furniture for real estate showings and offer it to the buyer as a package." It seemed like a perfectly viable excuse not to spend the remainder of the afternoon cleaning.

"Movers are not going to clean up the broken glass and dishes. Come on."

20

—————

"Are we going to talk about it?" I asked Andy. "Because if we are, we better do it now. Once we go in there," I pointed at the entrance to the Mayflower Hotel, "we're likely to get sucked into the vortex and won't get another chance until we get to our room. What time does this memorial thing start?"

"Eight."

Andy hadn't said much at the house, other than to comment on my broom work and finally tell me to use a vacuum cleaner she pulled from the utility closet. She remained absorbed during the Uber ride back to the hotel, communicating in monosyllables.

Standing on the sidewalk in front of the hotel, I stared at her until she emerged from the shroud of her thoughts.

"Let's get a drink," she said, taking my hand. The doorman opened the door. It wasn't quite five. Early evening traffic flowed through the busy lobby. Even on a Saturday, people seemed to move briskly, as if chasing something, or being chased. A few individuals sat in overstuffed chairs, but even they seemed anxious and watchful. The men stole glances at my wife.

We diverted to the bar and found a high-top table at the far end of the room, near windows offering a view of Connecticut Avenue. Andy took the mobster seat, facing the door. I pushed my chair around to be adjacent to her. A waitress dropped coasters and took our order for a pair of Coronas.

Light piano music floated in the air, along with a hint of vanilla. Scented music, I thought randomly. I laid a hand on the table and Andy took it, stroking her fingers across my palm.

"Usual Disclaimer?"

"Really? Are you officially on a case? Your new boyfriend, Fanko, isn't going to like that."

"He's not so bad," she said lightly. "For starters, he doesn't accuse me of having a new boyfriend."

"Point taken. Okay. Usual Disclaimer." She substituted a smile for a patronizing pat on the head.

The waitress arranged our drinks on the table. Instead of arriving in bottles, the Coronas were poured with a lime wedged on the rim of a tall glass. A reminder that we were navigating a little outside our social strata.

We paused and touched glasses.

"Us," I said.

"Us."

We sipped. She squared herself on her seat.

"Davis Bates, my sister's despicable husband, accidently kills himself while pretending to commit suicide."

She stopped. Stared. I let her tour the avenues of her thoughts.

She brushed back a stand of hair and went on.

"Using a heavy-duty outdoor extension cord he had no reason to own—."

"Unless he was just a dumb homeowner who needed an extension cord and bought the first one he saw. Bigger and heavier must be better. Or maybe his idea of a backyard barbecue was to take the cappuccino maker outside."

"—a cord which just happened to be the perfect length to get caught in the upstairs railing like a grappling hook. Too long and it flops over the rail and lays on the floor. And even if it gets caught while he's climbing down, so what? He has plenty of slack. Too short, and it doesn't make it over the railing to create the illusion of suicide."

"May I give you a pilot slash mechanic perspective on that?"

"Please."

"Gravity. If he tossed that plug over the railing just for show, it never would have stayed. The weight of the cord running down to his neck would have pulled it back over on him."

"Unless he went up there and hooked the end in first, then got up on the chair and put the other end around his neck."

I gave a skeptical shake of the head. "That version gives him no slack for tying the knot. He had to have been up on his toes."

"The chair arm was broken. Possibly when he tried to create slack to untie the knot."

"Being drunk, I can't see any way he could tie the knot, behind his head, balancing like that. I bet he tied the knot first, like tying a tie—looking at himself in a mirror."

"Okay. While he's still on the floor, he wraps the cord around his neck, ties an elaborate knot. Then he climbs up on the chair, balances, tosses the remaining length of cord up over his shoulder and over the railing to take the selfie. You're saying it wouldn't stay up there?"

"It only stays if it gets caught the way it did. In which case he's in trouble long before he has time to pull out his phone and smile for the selfie. But—!" I held up a finger. "That might explain the photo. The one he sent. It's bothered me ever since it showed up. How would you describe his face?"

Andy pointed at me. "I thought the same thing."

"Terrified," we both said.

"He was terrified." Andy ran with it. "Not the look of someone posing for a selfie meant to make the ex- sorry she walked out. On the other hand, to explain that, one might say he got to the money shot moment, lifted up his phone, then at that very moment realized the cord was caught and snapped the picture, but—"

"No way. He would have dropped the phone without taking the time to type out the text message and send the picture before dealing with what suddenly became a serious problem."

"Agreed," she said.

She sipped her Corona. I followed suit.

"But someone else could have texted. After. While he was up there."

"You think someone else was there?"

"Maybe up on the landing, holding the end for him?"

"Maybe telling him they'll hold the end for him, then wedging it into the railing?"

"Sending the text…"

"While he's dangling and kicking. Wow. That's cold," I said.

Andy took a sip.

"That is a serious left turn, Dee. But you were already there, weren't you," I said. "That's why you called and talked to that detective. Appleby."

She smiled.

"And today," I said, "there's a break-in. It's a junkie B and E if this was an accident. It's a ransacking meant to look like a break-in if it wasn't an accident."

"Uh-huh."

"Somebody looking for something."

"Uh-huh."

"So? Spell it out for me, Detective. What's going on?"

I leaned back to give Andy her moment.

She looked at me, then shifted her eyes to the window behind me. She leaned to one side to get a better look past me.

"What?"

She stood up and opened her purse, pulled several bills from her wallet and placing them under her unfinished drink. Cocktail hour was evidently over.

"Why don't we ask my new boyfriend that question. Coming?"

I followed her eyes to the hotel lobby where Detective Fanko walked purposefully toward the front desk.

21

"Mrs. Stewart, I need to speak to you and your sister in the matter of Davis Bates' death," Fanko said when we caught up to him at the bank of elevators. His officious tone spoke volumes.

"It's Detective Stewart," Andy countered stiffly.

"Not here, not officially," Fanko said, drawing a line.

"Are you here to speak to us officially?"

He hesitated, then said, "Look, I let you in as a professional courtesy. That was when we thought we were dealing with a dumb act worthy of a Darwin Award. That's changed. This is now a homicide investigation, and you know what that means. You're family. You're involved. So, you're out."

"When did this become a homicide?" Andy asked, showing no hint that she and I had just been discussing the same conclusion.

"When extension cords come in nine-foot seven-and-a-half-inch lengths and I get called in on my day off. But you already knew that."

The elevator arrived. We stepped in. A woman with shopping bags hustled to catch the door. Fanko pulled out his badge and used it to wave her off.

"Ma'am, please take the next one," he said politely. The doors closed before the woman could react. Andy touched the button for Four.

Fanko looked at Andy, then me, then made a face like he'd been caught in the act of something.

"Fine," he said. "It was your idea. You called in the question. The techs measured and took a closer look at the—I guess we can call it 'murder weapon.' It's not a standard length. It's been modified, making it the perfect length for an 'accident.' And you have the fact that Bates was a D.C. suit who probably wouldn't know which end to plug into an outlet. Toss in a picture of the guy looking like he's facing a firing squad, and we all arrive at the same unhappy conclusion."

The car stopped on the fourth floor. Fanko didn't wait. He took the lead. I let Andy keep pace with him.

"But that means you're on the other side of the line now," he said. "Just to be clear."

"Suspect?"

"You know how this works," he said.

I couldn't help myself. "You do realize that Lydia and my wife were a thousand miles away at the time, and literally witnessed the event in real time."

Without looking at me, Fanko said, "Mr. Stewart, your sister-in-law has a lot of money. In fact, she has a lot more money now than she had a few days ago. I've seen what money does in this town. We'll get to who was where when I decide to get there."

Andy shot me a look that said it would be best to stay silent. I held my tongue.

Midway down the hall we stopped. Fanko stepped aside, letting Andy approach the door with her key card.

Before slipping in the key card, Andy turned to Fanko.

"One thing. The break-in. It wasn't just junkies."

Fanko studied the pretty woman he had planned on getting to know better before her husband showed up. I wondered at what point he would start thinking with his big head.

"It's under investigation."

Not soon, apparently.

THE DOOR swung open on the sitting room of the Congressional Suite. Andy stepped aside and let Fanko enter first, which caught him off guard.

He took several steps and stopped. The scene he encountered derailed him.

Lydia sat on the floor with her legs folded under her. Each of her small daughters lay curled beside her, their heads in her lap, crying. Tears streamed down their mother's face, too.

Out of sheer cowardice, I had hoped to miss the moment when Lydia explained to her children that their father was gone. Now, my unease intensified and mixed with anger as I watched Fanko barge in on it. He stood in silence, swallowing whatever he had planned to say.

Andy pushed past the detective and hurried to join the trio. She dropped to her knees. Harriet tumbled into Andy's arms.

"Auntie Andy! My daddy died!"

Andy pulled the child to her bosom and let her own tears fall.

I stepped up beside Fanko.

"Do you want to cuff her now or wait for SWAT?"

22

"He refused to speculate about the break-in," Andy said, emerging from the bathroom wrapped in a plush hotel robe. I sat in a bedside chair with my feet on the mattress. While Andy had been in the bathroom, I slipped into my black suit, a white shirt and my other tie, the blue one. Now I sat idly stroking the wrinkles out of the suit pants.

Caught off guard, Fanko, instead of pressing to interview Lydia, had asked for a word alone with Andy. They conferred in the hall. I took up station on the sofa where Elise crawled in my lap and let me cradle her while she cried. Less than ten minutes later, Andy returned but waved off my questions.

Lydia eventually managed to get the girls to bed by crawling in with them. She told us she had no intention of attending the lobbying firm's memorial. She called it a phony tribute attended by people who were already jockeying for her dead husband's office. She added something about all the people he had been screwing, figuratively and between sheets.

Lydia's parents checked in with Andy and announced they too would not attend the memorial. Thinking we were not required to go either, I envisioned other plans for the evening. Andy had moved out of the suite she shared with Lydia and into a separate room with me. Not a Congressional Suite, but exponentially nicer than the last hotel I visited. I thought we might find someplace close for a nice dinner.

Andy derailed my plans by telling Lydia we would go to the event in her place. Now she busied herself with trips between the bathroom and her suitcase, doing whatever she does to make the transition from beautiful to stunning. I watched from the room's only chair.

"C'mon, he can't have missed the same signs you saw," I said.

"I didn't say that. He did, in fact, note the anomalies. Even caught a few I missed," she replied. "He's a good detective, Will."

Defending him. I decided to dial down my hostility.

"But," she added, "he doesn't want to be blinded by what appears obvious."

"Of course. Don't let the obvious get in the way. I have a question. Why would someone ransack the house with a separate break-in? If someone was there to engineer the fake suicide turned accidental death, why not do it once Davis was dead?"

"Because a person committing suicide doesn't ransack their own house," she replied. "You can't have it both ways."

I caught a glimpse of her tinkering with eye makeup.

"Also, if it really was a homicide, we're dealing with two very different crimes. One is a staged suicide-turned-accident. The other is a rough-around-the-edges B and E. That suggests two different skill sets."

"What does that mean?"

"Okay. Let's assume someone was with Davis and killed him—engineering an elaborate fake accident. That must have taken planning and coercion, or God only knows what to get him to cooperate, right? There were no signs of a struggle, except his ultimate struggle to get at the knot. And let's assume that ransacking the house has a related purpose. They had less than eight minutes. Wouldn't that require its own skill set? And many hands?"

"Six hands, according to the neighbor's video."

"It also required some police tape on the door to make it look like a crime of opportunity."

"So, he let you back in? Fanko?"

"Not full professional courtesy, but a little bit of blue brotherhood, yeah."

"Anybody have a clue what they were looking for? The B and E artists?"

Andy emerged again, long enough to pull a dress from the tiny hotel closet. I recognized it and approved, but she studied it as if she'd never seen it before.

"Not yet. I'd like to chat with Lydia when she's in a better place."

"As would Fanko."

"Yes. I promised him we would meet with him tomorrow. He gets that her children need her tonight."

"He can't seriously consider her a suspect."

"Cheating husband. Lots of money. It's always the wife," Andy tossed off. "Or the husband."

"Always the wife? Should I be worried?" I smiled.

"Should I?" She smiled back.

"If I cheated on you, I'd lose my membership in the Society of Half-way-Smart Men. And then the other two guys wouldn't have a quorum. And God knows there's no money."

She held the dress against her bosom. "Is this okay? It's all I have in black. It says 'funeral' and not 'party?' right?"

"Absolutely."

"Liar." She swept it into the bathroom and closed the door behind her.

23

I tapped the key card in my pocket out of habit as Andy closed the hotel room door behind us. We headed for the elevator and I tried not to stare at her dress, which definitely said 'party.'

"I was thinking about doing *the other thing* and visiting the White House. You know, take a tour of the Rose Garden. Maybe poke my head into the Oval Office. Wanna come along?"

"Don't you dare!" Andy stopped suddenly, looking panicked. I grinned at her. She pursed her lips and rolled her eyes, then resumed her path to the elevator.

"What? I'm serious! I have a couple FLOP units in my suitcase."

"Flop?" She stabbed the call button with a finger. I noticed she painted her nails and wondered when she had time.

"Flight Launching Operational Propulsion."

"No." I got the look. "And no! You are not going to violate the most heavily defended TFR in American airspace!"

"Look at you! Talkin' all piloty! TFR. Nice."

"I'm serious, Will. You can't be sure they don't have motion sensors or heat sensors or some high-tech system that can lock on and shoot you down. We already proved you show up on x-rays. I forbid it!"

We waited for the elevator.

"Okay. I'll make you a deal. I'll skip the White House, but after we do this thing, let's go over to Smithsonian Air and Space."

"We're not here as tourists, dear."

"I won't be long. I just always wanted to sit in the cockpit of the Spirit of St. Louis. It's hanging from the ceiling at the museum."

If looks could kill, I'd be a smoldering heap of bones in that Mayflower Hotel elevator.

24

"This is an art gallery."

We stood on the sidewalk as the Uber pulled away. Andy double-checked the address in her phone. Numbers above the ornate door to a behemoth Victorian house matched the instructions she received from Brogan Wayne. A subtle sign composed of marble and brass lettering proclaimed the building to be The Styles Markham Gallery. Aside from wondering who those people were, I wondered what an art gallery had to do with a memorial service.

Andy pulled her coat tighter around her waist. Her high heels clicked on the concrete sidewalk, which I noticed had been embedded with chips of something that made the surface sparkle. The entire building façade was illuminated, but by means I could not determine. Light seemed to glow from the eaves and window frames. The building had been a house once; an icon of nineteenth century wealth. Oil, maybe. Or railroads. It was huge. Between the lighted gingerbread façade and the warm light streaming from every window, the structure looked like a giant Christmas card, though it had none of the gaudy light strings that mark the season.

I checked my watch. Andy can be a speed demon when dressing for an evening out, but time spent with Lydia and the little girls put us behind schedule. My wristwatch said we were twenty minutes past the eight o'clock start time.

"Looks like they started without us." I worried that we would be conspicuous, slipping into a subdued room full of mournful people and hushed conversation. Or worse, causing a pause in a clergy-led memorial service or interrupting tearful speeches.

Andy pulled open the big front door.

The sound hit us with tactile intensity; a steady, loud symphony of chatter, boisterous conversation, and even laughter. I couldn't make out a single word in the wall of noise.

Andy and I stepped into a warmly lighted space filled with people. On three walls, arches opened to more spaces and more people. Flat panels rose from the polished wood floors at intervals, each bearing samples of the gallery's goods. Some pieces were framed. Some were simply wall-mounted canvases. Some were mysterious three-dimensional constructs. One connected to our purpose for being there.

Facing the door, standing at least nine feet tall and four feet wide, a panel displayed a photo of Lydia's deceased husband Davis. The black and white image caught him in a cluster of suits, all with their backs to the camera or cropped at the edges. Only Davis's face acknowledged the photographer, transmitting a sly look that seemed to say, *Watch me go to work on these rubes.*

Outside of Washington, D.C., I didn't think the photo would have been complimentary.

A single word had been printed in the upper left corner of the image. *Davis.*

Dwarfed around the image, people stood in clusters chatting over cocktails. I spotted wait staff wearing bow ties on white over black, weaving through the crowd with trays of drinks or hors d'oeuvres like nothing I'd ever seen at the Silver Spoon Diner.

I leaned close to Andy. "Yup, they definitely started without us."

Before she could answer, a young woman touched her shoulder.

"May I take your coat?" She offered Andy a numbered plastic chit.

Andy reluctantly slipped out of her coat. The young woman took the garment and disappeared in the crowd. I didn't see anything resembling a closet.

"I don't think you need to worry about what you're wearing," I said. A quick survey told me her little black dress was far from the most provocative gown in the room.

"This isn't what I was expecting."

"Do you suppose there will be some sort of...service?"

"Yes. Cocktail service." She pointed.

On cue, a young man bearing a tray of red and white wine glasses drew a bead on us and approached. Before he could deliver, another young man, this one in a tight-fitting suit of charcoal gray, touched his arm and sent him off in another direction. He approached us with a solicitous smile.

"Mr. and Mrs. Stewart? I'm Trent Dougherty, Ms. Brogan's personal assistant. How do you do?" He delivered crisp handshakes. Andy's was light and delicate. Mine drove in and went for firm, but not competitive. The young man had practice.

"Yes," Andy said. "I saw you at the office yesterday."

"Of course," he said. "I was so sorry I couldn't introduce myself then. Ms. Brogan sends her apologies for not being here to greet you. She's running late as usual." He made a theatrical face that attempted to say, *What's new?* "She will be here soon. Is Mrs. Bates with you?" Dougherty looked over our shoulders at the door.

"She won't be attending," Andy said. "She's with her children."

"We completely understand. And you have our sincere condolences. We have all suffered a great loss, but ours can never compare to losing a husband and father. May I offer you a beverage?"

Before I could accept, Andy declined for both of us, setting the ground rules. In her case, I understood. The slender handbag slung from a thin strap on her shoulder didn't contain cosmetics.

"Please, come with me," Dougherty gestured. "I'd like to introduce you to some of Davis's colleagues."

We trailed the young man through the milling, chattering crowd. Faces swung in our direction. Heads leaned together to exchange comments. Both the men and the women focused on Andy. There are times when I don't need special abilities to vanish alongside my wife.

"What is this place?" Andy asked.

"Styles Markham?" Dougherty laughed. "It's not Gagosian or Zwirner, and D.C. hardly holds a candle to Soho, but in our little political swamp, it is the premier gallery in town. D.C. is a revolving door, and there's always a new Congressman's wife who uses her checkbook to keep pace. This is as good as it gets. And of course, it doubles as a setting for social functions. Mr. Markham, God rest his soul, was a chemical industry lobbyist. But they say his heart was too tender, and his love of art too deep. He chose this as a means of marrying his past with his passion."

Dougherty led us through one of the arches into another room. Four starkly white walls displayed more framed and unframed art at discrete intervals. In the center of the room two full mahogany bars—back-to-back and presumably portable—dominated the space. Men in suits and women in elegant dresses surrounded the bars. Four bartenders performed a nonstop ballet of drink service. Except for tip jars, no cash flowed over the polished mahogany. The only hint that this was a memorial function came from the overwhelming selection of black apparel by both the men and the women.

In this room alone, I estimated attendance at well over a hundred and fifty.

Dougherty tapped into a cluster of three women and two men. All seemed young to me. Mid-twenties at most.

"People, this is Davis's sister-in-law and her husband, Mr. and Mrs. Stewart."

Hands were shaken and waved. First names exchanged. Condolences offered.

"This is the brain trust of the new Brogan Wayne," Dougherty went on. "John and Carla here head up what we call the Green Team. I don't know if you're aware, but since Ms. Brogan took over for her father six years ago, we have become one of the leading social responsibility legislative liaison firms in the country. Certainly in D.C."

John, tall and thin, said, "Yes, it sounds like an oxymoron, but we are a lobbying firm with a social conscience."

"Ms. Brogan took the firm in a new direction," Dougherty picked up the thread. "She realized that small individual groups fighting for clean water or clean air or land preservation didn't have the resources to combat the kind of lobbying firepower that typically writes the laws of this country, so she introduced the concept of a co-operative. We represent, without exaggeration, hundreds of environmental and social justice groups. We often find ways of intersecting diverse interests on a single, focal issue."

I wondered if I might find that speech in a brochure somewhere.

"That sounds like fulfilling work," Andy offered.

"It is an absolute nightmare," Carla replied. She had an academic look and projected a hint that polish wasn't her priority. Instead of an evening gown, she wore a dark sweater over black slacks. "But you're a police officer, Detective Stewart, so you know what it's like doing battle with scum on a daily basis."

"I'm a small-town police officer. Our scum tends to drive on the neighbor's lawn or steal street signs."

"Ours write laws that line billionaire's pockets while allowing legislators to turn around and tell Joe Middle Class they're preserving their values and defending their daughters' virginity from people with different pigmentation," Carla said, looking at Andy through wire-rimmed glasses. "And, by the way, you are too modest, Detective. Nice work putting that rat bastard Parks where he belongs."

"I was under the impression that Davis's firm was not pleased to see one of its private prison clients brought to justice," Andy said smoothly.

Carla laughed. "Oh Lord! Parks? No, he wasn't one of ours. Missed bullet. We turned him down. But you're not far from the mark. In fact, you're only about six feet from the mark."

She pointed at another cluster of people at the bar. These were older men in conservative suits, more what I expected from a lobbying firm.

"That's also part of the Brogan Wayne family, of course. The original gene pool. And while we may be the new Green Team, they're still paying the bills, even if it means selling their souls to the dark side. Do you remember that private prison scandal in Missouri? That was theirs."

"I see."

"Carla," Dougherty warned. "I don't think Mr. and Mrs. Stewart are really interested in our client list."

"Oh, stuff it, Trent," Carla said. She abruptly leaned past us and swapped her empty wine glass for a fresh one from a passing tray. "Don't you have some boots to lick or dick to suck?"

Dougherty's face reddened but he forced a smile. "And now you can see why we value Carla's panzer leader style, which also explains her couture. That kind of enthusiasm on The Hill serves our clients well." He touched his hand to his ear. I noticed a Bluetooth earpiece like the one Andy made me carry. He listened for a moment, then said, "Would you excuse me? Ms. Brogan is arriving." Without another word he slipped away.

"Fucking weenie," Carla said. "Detective Stewart, can I ask you a question?"

"Anything."

"Did you like your brother-in-law?"

"No," Andy replied without missing a beat.

"Well neither did anyone in this room. If not for the free booze and free whatever-the-fuck those little gray things are—and oh, my God, *are they good!*—no one in this room would be here tonight. Look around you. It's not just our people here. Josiah James, the Internet radio hate-monger, he's here stuffing his fat face. That's Congresswoman Chatham over there —champion of her Gold Coast one percenters. There's a whole pack of wolves from Justice on the other side of the bar, drinking side by side with people they should probably prosecute. Davis Bates cultivated a lot of contacts. Half are here tonight to celebrate his departure; the other half are here to hook up with his replacement. And this isn't even the top tier room."

"Top tier?" I asked.

"Buddy, you're slumming in here. You want to rub some gilded elbows, go over to the other side of the building. I think that little Nazi political strategist from The White House is over there trying to feel up some of the interns. I know I saw their chief economic advisor, that dumbass they found on the Internet. And the Russians—well, they're keeping a low profile these days, but they field plenty of surrogates."

"Honestly, Carla," one of the previously silent women said, "I think we may have to cut you off."

"My point, well-lubricated though it may be, is that your brother-in-law was as big a shit as anyone in this room or any other room full of big shits in this town. That's probably what made him good at what he did, but it didn't make what he did good."

"Brutally honest," Andy said.

"Be warned. It might be the only honest thing you hear tonight," Carla said. "And now, before I say something offensive, I think I will find the women's toilet to make room for more wine." She tipped her glass in our direction and slipped away.

The others stood awkwardly in her wake.

"Um, not everybody feels that way," John offered. The two women remaining in the small circle traded uncomfortable glances.

"Then I don't think I would trust them," Andy said with a smile. "Would you excuse us?"

She hooked my elbow before he could answer and pulled me away.

"Bit of a snake pit," I said.

"That's the job. How long do you want to stay?"

"My target departure time was ten minutes ago."

She wove her way through the cocktail crowd toward the main room where we had entered. I nurtured hope that we might be making our escape, but she said, "We can't leave yet. There's something I need to do. Do you see Dougherty anywhere?"

I scanned the crowd. No sign of the executive assistant.

"Hey! You're Will Stewart!" Someone scooped up my right hand and shook it. I stopped and turned.

A man, shorter than me, overweight and squeezed into a suit two sizes too small, pumped my hand vigorously.

"I just gotta say Hi! I read all about you. The crash. Last summer." He grinned up at me from a broad fleshy face mounted beneath receding short black hair.

"I'm sorry..." I said, giving him a have-we-met? turn of the head.

"Oh, you don't know me. But I'm a fan. Big fan."

I glanced at Andy for help. She gave me a bemused look.

"I have a fan," I said.

"I'll let you two talk," she said. She pressed through the crowd, abandoning me.

"I'm Tim Revell." More hand pumping. "I work legislative affairs for the Aviation Counsel. It's a coalition of small secondary manufacturers who supply the aviation industry. Parts for Lockheed-Martin, Boeing, Textron. Anything airplanes, man! That's my thing!"

"Right. Do you fly?"

He struck a pose. "I took some lessons when I was in college. Did pretty well. 'Bout twenty hours. Almost soloed. Always wanted to finish up, but you know. Life. I want to get back into it someday. Just need to find the time. I love Microsoft Flight Simulator! Any chance I get, I'm there! Do you fly a Lear?"

I ignored the question, thinking if you haven't soloed in under fifteen hours, something's not right. "So how do you know my name?"

"Are you kidding? I saw you on the news! I read the accident report.

Well, the preliminary report. Amazing! You're a miracle, man! It must have been crazy, having an aircraft break up like that and living to tell about it! No parachute! Wow!" The admiration oozing from his expression made me want to step back. I didn't want to get any on me. "I want to know all about it. Piper Navajo! I have one programmed on my simulator. Great airplane, right? Great airplane."

A drink tray floated by and I snagged a glass of wine. Red. I didn't care. I took a substantial and inelegant hit.

"So, what happened? What were the warning signs? Was it flutter? I've been waiting for the final NTSB report. Those guys take forever, am I right? I bet it was flutter. Did you have any warning? Was it control failure? I know, I have a million questions. I never thought I'd get to meet—"

"Mr. Stewart, I believe they're ready for you."

Someone touched my arm. I turned toward a woman taller than my new fan. She had a perfectly proportioned face framed in golden blonde hair, the kind that caught light and hoarded it. My immediate impression, however, was of dark eyes and bright red lipstick. My second impression came from the outside of my bicep, which the woman pulled firmly against her chest. She wore a black dress like Andy's, but hers had no neckline. The two halves simply plunged toward a belted waist. It was a mystery to me, how the fabric managed to remain concealing. My arm confirmed what my eyes told me—that she wore nothing beneath the dress.

"Thank you, Tim," she said, and she moved us both forward, leaving Tim open-mouthed and speechless.

She maneuvered me toward the back of the vast room. I saw people watching us. Some shifted and stepped aside, clearing our passage.

"It may be presumptuous of me, but I suspect you have no desire to recount your survival experience with someone who captains Microsoft Flight Simulator," she said.

"Not my favorite topic," I replied. I wanted to extract my arm from her embrace, but she nestled it home.

"Understandable," she said. Her voice carried a silky smoothness yet sounded capable of command without requiring volume. "Even more so if you have no memory of the event in question. Hello, Senator! Thank you for coming."

A man I recognized from news footage tried to say something nice to the woman about Davis Bates, but she continued past him and cut him off with, "Thank you so kindly."

A few steps beyond the Senator, she turned her head so that her red lips aligned with my ear. "The gentleman from the senate has expensive tastes. Davis helped him sustain his lifestyle. Now he's afraid Davis may have left details behind."

"Did he?"

She shrugged, putting most of the movement into her chest.

"It doesn't hurt for a man like that to feel a little uncertainty. The kind we all feel when he and his colleagues touch things that matter in our lives."

She aimed me at an archway. Now, not only her breast pressed against me, but she managed to brush her hips against mine, and fall in step with me. We moved forward like dancers. I was not leading.

We skimmed through the archway into a new gallery space exhibiting sculptures and what I can only guess would be called unframed art. None of the art made any sense to me. I've seen airplane parts thrown in a pile that looked better.

As if a noise-cancelling switch had been thrown, the room pressed a silence upon us that contrasted with the boisterous outer spaces. There was no bar. No servers skittered between clusters of people. Which made sense. There were no clusters of people. A few individuals wandered among the sculptures cradling cocktails. All of them glanced at us as we entered, and in a moment or two, trying not to look conspicuous, they made their way to the exit.

A single padded bench faced the far wall of the room, which had been hung with what looked like pieces of a shredded mattress. She guided me toward the bench. I wasn't certain the seat didn't belong to the exhibit until she released my arm and sat down, crossing long bare legs.

"Please join me," she said, patting the cushion. "I'm not trying to bed you, Will."

I sat down, feeling my face turn the famous shade of red that Lane and my wife enjoy observing.

"Olivia Brogan," she said, extending her hand. I took it carefully. We shook. She shook more than me. The panels of her dress continued to perform miracles. She caught my eyes falling to her chest. "Oh, this. Yes.

I find that it gives me a cognitive edge. I mean you no harm. But working an event like this, well you can see it has its advantages."

"I can certainly see."

"Make no mistake, I'll be the first to denounce the objectification of women. My eyes are up here. I'm a person, too. Don't treat me as a sex object. Me, too. All that. Of course, that's just delicious indignation that doubles the arsenal, wouldn't you say?"

"I guess."

"Well, as I said, I mean you no harm. You have a lovely wife. What am I saying. She is beyond lovely. As are you. Men can be objectified, too, you know."

"I haven't been able to figure out the male equivalent of cleavage," I said. "There's always the handyman butt crack, but that doesn't seem to have the same appeal."

She laughed. It sounded genuine, but I reminded myself that I had no way of knowing.

"Ask your wife," she said. "Ask her how your broad shoulders cause weakness in certain muscles. How having a man like you stand close, making the woman look up at him, mixes an intoxicating cocktail of fear and desire. Women would be so much better served if they would share these things."

"I'll bring it up at the next meeting."

"Meeting…yes…"

I said nothing.

"She bears a remarkable resemblance to Lydia Bates, your wife. I'm sure you see it. Perhaps less so now, with Lydia's pregnancy. But as sisters, they might have been fraternal twins, especially now that Lydia has gone back to her original hair color."

She paused. I got the impression her approach to our conversation was designed to solicit a response. I tried not to play along.

"I don't know Lydia well. I actually try to avoid her," she said. "Since I had been sleeping with her husband. Women have a sense of that and some things just can't be masked."

"I don't think you were the only one."

"Oh, heavens no! The rumor is that he moved away from blondes and was seeing a redhead."

"Anyone you know?"

"Probably. I know so many people. I understand your wife saw some candidates at our offices yesterday, but more intriguing was the reaction of some of my female employees when *they* saw her. As I said, some things can't be masked."

"Andy mentioned it."

"Andy. That's what you call her? I'll have to remember. She saw it, too. Well, then it's a good thing I avoided meeting her. We all have primal triggers that give us away. Your blush, for example. Oh! There it is again! I'm so sorry!"

She reached out and put her hand on my forearm. That didn't help.

"I'll move on. To be fair, the guilty women your wife met are more recent sexual partners for Davis. I stopped screwing him several years ago."

"Is that why we're having this meeting? You want me to take that information back to my police detective wife?"

She smiled. "Of course, it is. That, and something else."

"Which is?"

"May I share a little history with you?"

"Please."

She retracted her arm and shifted her posture.

"Will, my father founded Brogan Wayne. He had a partner, Allen Wayne, who was like an uncle to me. Family. A fixture in my life growing up. Someone I could count on for Christmas presents and birthday presents. Of course, growing up, I had no idea what my father did for a living. I only knew that he knew everyone. He knew Presidents! Can you imagine? But in this town, in the school I attended as a girl, there was always someone with a better story, a better totem. Still, I was proud. And then I grew up. And I discovered that my father was the Devil. Lawyers. Child molesters. Lobbyists. I think that's the accepted order at the bottom of the morality chain. My father was so ruthless he drove Allen Wayne out of the business and ultimately to an early death. My dear Uncle Allen. My father destroyed him so that he could build Brogan Wayne into a manipulation powerhouse, a citadel of backstabbing and leverage. Coming of age, I learned that Brogan Wayne is that demon on the shoulder of every elected representative on The Hill. Especially now. We're the forked tongue in every ear on every issue where money is to be made."

"Okay." I didn't know what to say. "You make it sound grim."

"I cannot begin to make it sound grim enough. You want to make a few billion for your golf buddies? Sign an order eliminating environmental protections against mining, or safety regulations on oil rigs, or protections for federal lands. Or removing sanctions against private prisons. And if you can't get it done by executive fiat, if you must take it to the hallowed halls of Congress, well then that's where we come in. Pay us enough and we'll find every crack in policy, every growth of mold in a representative's soul, every whore they paid for and every dime they've stolen. And we'll get it done."

I waited.

"It sounds outrageous, but this is a golden age for firms like mine. The genius of the current regime is that they've convinced a share of the public that nothing outrageous is to be believed. What's the old religious expression? The Devil's greatest trick was convincing us he didn't exist? My father once did the Devil's work in darkness. We do that same work now in the light of day and rely on con artists to tell their followers that none of it is real."

"Ms. Brogan, I'm not sure where you're going with this, but politics is not my subject and you're not making a new friend here."

"No," she said. "I understand. You and I grew up thinking that we could reap the rewards of the Forefathers, who crafted this beautiful thing called Democracy in a world that had never seen anything like it. We thought we could let it run, if I may say, on autopilot. Trust those in service to the nation. But then—at least in my case—I inherited the factory that's poisoning the river. I inherited the mine that runs on child labor. I inherited the secret government detention camp."

"Jesus, you're a lobbying firm, not the Third Reich," I said. "What's your point?"

She laughed again. "I'm sorry! I did get a little dramatic, didn't I?"

"Do you think?"

She leaned back on the bench and looked up at the strange artwork on the wall. I expected her to make some point using it as a metaphor or symbol, but she only gazed at it for a moment. Leaning back, the folds of her dress shifted, exposing more than before.

"My point." She considered it for another moment. She turned and faced me. "I know that Davis Bates was murdered."

I worked at keeping my mouth shut.

She shook her head. "Oh, I don't mean I'm privy to some Hollywood-thriller conspiracy. I mean only to tell you that I know the police are now calling it a homicide thanks to your wife. News of any kind travels quickly in this town, but for a firm like mine, it travels at light speed. I have, let's just say, *consultants* on the police force. I know the police have confirmed that the extension cord was custom-made. Like everyone else, up until that moment, I thought Davis was just a colossal idiot."

"Okay."

"All this." She waved her arm at the crowd still milling around beyond the open archway. "My firm. What I inherited. You may not believe this, but I'm trying to change it. I'm trying to fight a guerrilla war. You met my Green Team, the public face of our future. Ten years ago, when my father ran this firm, they would have been unpaid volunteers in a storefront office fighting local ordinances banning books. No firm of this size or billing would have given any of them use of the toilet."

"So, you let them play with the big boys," I observed.

"Indeed. But more than that, I want them to win against the big boys. Beat them at their own game. Lobbying is the tool that is being used to drain this country of its wealth, its integrity and its soul. I plan to use it to fight back." She leaned into me. "Those kids. They're the start of something. We've launched initiatives on fair housing, on gender equality, on LGBT rights, on sensible gun legislation. On economic development that isn't modeled after the robber barons of the last two centuries. We're turning the old school network upside down, using their tools against them on their own damned playing field."

"Commendable," I said. "As long as you can still turn a profit."

"Yes, there is that."

"And what does this have to do with Davis Bates?"

"Davis Bates. He was the establishment. He was the sickness I've been working to eradicate from this firm, from our system."

"Sounds like a motive for murder," I said, thinking how after thirty-some years of watching television and movies, I couldn't believe I had a chance to say that out loud.

"Yes, that's funny. Because after all the horrible things Davis did in his career, to this country, to his wife, and to his children, he managed to close the curtain in a way that levies suspicion on the one person who wanted to bring an end to all of that."

"Did you do it?"

"No."

"That's what you want me to tell my wife? The police?"

"I think it might be a little too on the nose if you rush right out and start proclaiming my innocence. No. I simply wanted to show you who I really am. Not many people know. My Green Team is more of a best kept secret than a brand. I have a long road ahead. People are starting to wake up and discover how they have been conned, and when they do, I will be on the inside for them. But it's a timing issue. If you're a spy posing as the enemy in enemy headquarters, your greatest risk comes when the friendlies overrun those headquarters."

"Maybe."

"That's all. I just want someone to know. You seemed like a better choice than your wife, who has good reason to hate me. Of course, oddly enough, if you go broadcasting this, I'll have to deny it. Ironic."

"Do you buy into the idea that Davis Bates was murdered?"

"The police seem to think so, as of a few hours ago."

"Do you?"

She shrugged. "I think three quarters of the people in that room out there are toasting the extension cord."

I looked down at my hands for a moment. The beauty of being manipulated is never knowing it. Even more elegantly, when you know you're being manipulated, it sows doubt, not just of what you're being told, but of the way you look at facts. All facts.

"Look," I said, "I'm just a—"

"Pilot," she interrupted. "Yes. I know. Just a guy who flies airplanes. Yet somehow, there you are, at your wife's side when she puts an end to Pearce Parks and again when she destroys that grease spot on humanity, Ellery Fulton. There you are. I think you're a bit more than just a pilot, Will."

She abruptly put her hand around my neck and leaned in to kiss me. I managed to turn my head and it landed on my cheek. I know I jerked backward. At least I pray I did.

Because Andy stood in the archway staring at the two of us.

25

I looked for danger signs. For anger. Andy occupied the car seat beside me in silence. She projected a serene aura, even the hint of a dimple at the corners of her mouth. Or maybe I imagined that, out of desperation. I looked for her jaw to lock and her lower lip to gain prominence—never a good sign. When neither happened, I couldn't remain still any longer.

"What?" I asked.

Her eyebrows went up a millimeter.

"I didn't start that!" I protested.

She said nothing. It struck me that she thought this was funny, which made me think I would be okay. Then it struck me that she didn't, which made me think I was in deep trouble.

"Say something!"

She remained silent. The Uber took a strong turn left and I felt myself heaved toward her on the back seat. I stiffened to hold my position. The space between us felt cold.

"Fine, if that's how you're going to be, but you're being unfair."

Her lips did not part.

Goddammit! While we were at the gallery I wanted nothing more than to get the hell out of there and back to the hotel for a private evening with my wife. Now that plan spiraled down in flames.

After pulling away from Olivia Brogan and leaping to my feet, I stammered through a guilt-riddled introduction. Like she owned the room, Andy strolled over to shake hands with one of the women who had destroyed her sister's marriage. A woman who had just put lips on her husband. My wife was cool and calm, and I was starkly aware of the Glock 26 in her handbag. Olivia smiled warmly and traded pleasantries until excusing herself to attend to her other guests. I stood melting in my suit. I have no memory of the small talk that passed between the two women, or of my wife collecting me and leading me to the front door, where she regained possession of her coat.

Next thing I knew we were in an Uber. Riding in lead-lined silence.

"Oh, for God's sake! I know that look! You're trying not to laugh."

Her lips tightened. The Uber made a right turn and Andy braced to remain stationary, slightly turned in her seat, her eyes resting on me.

After an eternity of enduring Andy's silent gaze, the Uber stopped in the center of a block. She released me from her eye lock and opened her door.

"Wait here," she instructed both me and the driver. She slipped out and closed the door behind her.

It took me a moment to become aware of our surroundings. The neighborhood had a boutique commercial feel. A few restaurants lined the street; one featured space for outdoor seating in the summer. Andy trotted lightly between parked cars and disappeared into a set of heavy, brass-fixtured doors. Taking a wider view, I saw she had entered an upscale bar called Negotiation. Low faux-Tiffany lamps glowed in the windows. An underlit bar ran across the back of the room.

"You're in some deep-fried shit, friend," the driver commented.

"Don't I know it."

"What did you do? You don't mind my asking?"

His eyes, set in a mocha complexion, were sympathetic in the rearview mirror.

"Absolutely nothing," I proclaimed, leaning back.

"Uh-huh," he nodded. "I've done nothing many times. Always pay for it one way or another. Wife or girlfriend?"

"Wife."

"'And the Lord God said it is not good that man should be alone.'"

"Most of the time I'm on board with that," I said. "Most of the time."

"She'll come around. She might let you dangle, but you'll be okay."

I watched what little I could see of the bar's interior. Andy remained out of sight.

"I was kissed by another woman. She saw the whole thing."

The driver nodded thoughtfully, gave it a moment, then said, "I take it back. You're screwed."

ANDY SLID BACK onto the seat with her cell phone in her hand. She resumed her angled posture and fixed her eyes on me again. Without looking at the driver, she instructed him to proceed to the Mayflower Hotel. He seemed to wiggle a little lower in his seat. Maybe the seat was armored, or he wished it was. He accelerated in traffic.

I let a couple blocks pass.

"Seriously. Are you not going to tell me what that was about?"

My wife held her phone up for me to see. The screen displayed a photo of me walking with Olivia Brogan as she pulled my arm into her breast. The angle of the photo caught her plunging neckline in a way that thoroughly damned me.

"What? You're going to keep that?"

The driver was right. I was screwed.

Andy's dimples peeked at me. Her gold-flecked green eyes betrayed a glint of light.

She was enjoying this.

"Woman, you are driving me mad," I said. "If you think you can use that to blackmail me into being your household slave boy, well let me tell you, you're absolutely right. But I firmly draw the line at one month, or three. Okay, a year. But that's my limit. Unless you keep that photo forever, in which case I am yours for eternity. But no gardening. I hate gardening. Unless that's what you want."

The smile blossomed. I was saved.

"That was the bar where Davis spent Christmas Day," she said, still holding up the photo. "And your new girlfriend is the woman he was with."

26

Traffic stopped.

"Now, what the devil is all this?" the driver muttered. Glancing past his seat through the windshield, I saw flashing emergency lights. Red and blue light splashed off the Mayflower Hotel and the buildings facing it.

The driver edged forward several car lengths within the stalled traffic flow.

"Don't know if I can get you to the door," the driver said. "That's blocked."

Marked squad cars angled into the traffic lanes in front of the hotel. Andy pulled herself to the edge of the back seat and peered ahead.

"I think you're right. We'll get out here."

She pushed open the back door on her side and swung her legs out. I slid across the seat after her.

"Good luck, pal!" the driver called after me.

I managed to close the door and catch up with Andy on the sidewalk. We weaved in and out of gawkers who stopped to watch whatever unfolded at the Mayflower.

An ambulance pulled up in front of the hotel, completing blockage of all three lanes of northwest-bound traffic on Connecticut Avenue. At the sight of it, Andy picked up the pace. She gave me a glance laced with worry. Her high heels tapped on the cold sidewalk in time to my pounding heart.

We reached the end of the block and crossed L Street only to encounter a new barrier. D.C. Metropolitan Police officers stopped pedestrian traffic, causing a clot of people to form at the corner. Andy weaved around it, slipping through the taxi line still pointed at the Mayflower. She hurried past the driver's side doors, dodging the drivers emerging from their cabs.

"Ma'am! Hold up there, ma'am!" a patrol officer called to Andy. He trotted between cabs to intercept us. "Ma'am, sir, you have to stay back."

Andy almost magically produced her badge and cupped it for the officer.

"Detective Stewart," she said.

The young patrolman studied the badge. He shook his head. "You're not MPD."

"I'm working with Detective Fanko on a homicide. He's meeting me at the hotel. What's going on?"

"Fanko? Third Division?"

"I don't know his unit number. We've been working on the Davis Bates case. Do you know it?"

"Is that the suicide? The extension cord guy?"

"Yes," Andy said. "Look, I need to get in there. Fanko and I were about to question a witness and I have new information. Can you tell me what's going on?"

"Woman was attacked. Started with some screaming and a call from the fourth floor. Reports of someone with a gun. We're trying to lock down the building and sort it out."

Out of the officer's view, Andy's hand clamped my arm, expressing the tension her face hid.

"I need to get in there," she said firmly. "I need to get this information to Fanko—or at least to the scene commander!"

The kid, he couldn't have been far into his twenties, considered.

"Okay. Go."

I thought he might stop me or ask for ID, but he didn't. Andy didn't wait for him to think twice.

. . .

SHE KICKED off her heels and scooped them off the pavement. In bare feet on December-cold concrete, she pounded toward the Mayflower entrance at a dead run. I raced behind her, reminded of last summer's pelvic injury with each step.

Far faster than my feet, my mind shot ahead to images of Lydia, images of Harriet and Elise, images of a horror I fought to bar from my thoughts.

As we closed on the main entrance to the hotel, we saw a stream of guests emerging. Some wore coats. Some didn't. All were hustled out of the building by uniformed police waving and urging them into the street, toward a median filled with winter-dormant vegetation. More police arrived, some in tactical gear, heavily armed. Arriving squad cars blocked the traffic lanes on the far side of the median.

Andy, her dark hair flying behind her, sprinted to the doors. She slowed and searched for a way in past the flow of evacuating guests. As I caught up with her, she spun toward the street.

She took three steps away from the building.

"What?" My breath chuffed out in cold clouds.

"Rahn!" She whirled and faced me with her eyes blazing. "Rahn! I saw him!" She pointed at an opening in the median where police were helping guests climb to the other side.

She bolted forward. Then stopped and turned, torn.

"Will, he's here!" She looked up at the hotel, stricken. "Lydia!"

I took her by the shoulders. "Go inside! Go! GO!"

"Black coat!" she cried out and pointed at the crowd of evacuees. Then shook herself free and darted for the door. She threaded her way inside and out of my sight.

I reversed direction and hurried into the street.

Black coat. It could be any one of a dozen men streaming away from the hotel. The evacuated guests were hustled across the pavement, through the median to the sidewalk on the other side by uniformed officers. The crowd on the sidewalk opposite the hotel continued to grow. Guests milled around, mingling with police.

I trotted past the line, through the median, then angled back in the direction we had come from, scanning the sidewalk from the empty center lane of Connecticut Avenue. I'd seen Rahn's face enough times on my dining room table. But each face I now saw threatened to merge with the prison image Andy kept of Mannis Rahn, the living ghost. I began to doubt. A man standing against the windows of the Gap store across from the hotel seemed to possess Rahn's Every Man features yet wasn't him. A man at the center of a cluster of people drew my attention. Less than medium height. Benign, forgettable face. Yet he clutched a woman at his side, and they chattered excitedly. I didn't think Rahn, making his escape, would stop to camouflage himself with a wife.

The crowd thinned as I moved farther from the epicenter of emergency vehicles. I stopped, turned, and took off in the opposite direction, crossing again in front of the Mayflower, through the stream of evacuees, toward the junction with Desales Street. Police waved cars from Desales onto Connecticut, directing them away from the scene. Cars approaching on Connecticut Avenue were directed into a U-turn to find another way as more police units arrived to block the street.

Most of the evacuees lingered. A few moved away from the scene, glancing back for one more chance to catch the excitement.

One man caught my eye. He limped purposefully up the sidewalk in a black coat. He did not look back. The back of his head showed dark hair above an upturned collar. Something tugged at me, something about the way he moved.

Few if any of the people on the street could stop looking at the police and emergency vehicles. This man never turned his head, never answered curiosity's call. With his hands dug into his coat pockets, he continued forward, now halfway down the block.

I didn't know if Andy was right or not. If she had seen Rahn or just someone who looked like him. Or if the terror welling up inside her caused her to see someone who wasn't there. But if the man who tried to kill Lydia—thinking he was killing my wife—now plodded away from a new crime, melting into busy city night, I stood the only chance of catching him.

I hurried to the sidewalk, then pushed through gawking onlookers in pursuit.

The man picked up his pace despite a significant limp. If it was Rahn, if he did attack Lydia (*please God no!*) maybe she hurt him. Maybe she stopped him. Maybe a pregnant woman alone with two small children met Rahn with ferocity he never anticipated.

The crowd slowed me down. My target bobbed in and out of sight.

More people came toward me on the sidewalk, many driven by curiosity. Rahn, if it was him, opened his lead to at least a hundred feet.

"Screw this!" I said aloud. I darted off the sidewalk into the street, into the jammed oncoming traffic. I crossed in front of a sedan whose driver startled when I cleared his bumper. He pounded out a quick note on his horn. I darted past his mirror before his arm could come up to deliver the universal hand signal for displeasure.

Between lines of cars, I trotted a narrow path, dodging mirrors and sometimes skipping forward sideways.

The man in the black coat turned his head. Unlike other pedestrians who stole glances of an emergency, he looked only at one thing.

Me.

Recognition passed between us.

Rahn!

I broke into a run. He did the same, limping sharply.

My path between vehicles offered no pedestrian obstructions but was suddenly blocked by someone abruptly changing lanes. The grille emblem of a silver Mercedes swung across my knees. I threw my hands out and fell across the glimmering hood. A woman in the passenger seat shrieked.

I picked myself up and danced laterally toward the sidewalk just in time to see Rahn turn the corner at the next street. He escaped my view.

"Oh, fuck this!"

I looked at the woman in the passenger seat and—

Fwooomp!

I vanished. She shrieked again. I didn't hang around long enough to see what she did next. I pushed off the pavement and angled upward toward the bright glass bulb of a lamp post. I made a split-second assessment of the building holding down the corner of the block. Glass and smooth concrete with no grip points.

Connecting with the top of the lamp post, I gingerly gripped the hot, glowing glass and yanked myself on a rising angle toward the next lamp post. This one was higher, with the light cantilevered over a confusing intersection full of traffic and pedestrians.

Connecticut Avenue angled northwest. Another street angled away to the northeast. A one-way street ran from my right to left. This was the route Rahn had taken. As I reached the post, I could see around the corner to yet another street intersecting the one-way street after a very short block.

Rahn had already reached the corner and was now crossing through traffic, against the Walk light.

I hope you get squashed by a bus, asshole!

I had only a moment to mark his position before I turned my attention to the question of navigation.

"Stupid! Stupid! Stupid!" I muttered, thinking of the FLOP units resting in my suitcase. Nothing is as useless to a pilot as the runway behind, the altitude above, and the FLOP units sitting in a damned suitcase!

With one of the power units, I could have easily chased him down, reappeared a few feet over his head and dropped on him like a cartoon anvil. Now I could only navigate from one grip point to the next, or by shooting myself like a pool ball from one building front to another. And there was always the gnawing fear that I might launch at the wrong angle, rising out of control.

I grabbed the high lamp post and marked the fact that Rahn had crossed the next street. He limped on a line forward, glancing back every dozen or so paces. I plotted a new course.

The buildings in this part of town were modern. Abundant glass and smooth grids of concrete. Not much of anything to grip. The lamp posts were spaced farther apart than I would have liked, but they offered the only real choice. On the plus side, I didn't see wires. On the minus side, you never see wires until you hit them.

Taking a moment to aim, I gripped the cantilever portion of the post with both hands, then heaved myself forward. Gliding past the second-floor windows of what looked like a bank building, I covered the short block quickly, skimming above a small Christmas-lit tree at mid-block. My aim was perfect. The arm of the next lamp post came to my outstretched hands in precisely the right position for me to grab on and heave myself forward, aligned on course for the next post and gaining speed. Gaining on Rahn.

He threw a long glance back over his shoulder as he hurried forward, searching for but not finding me—perhaps expecting me to turn the corner at any moment. I think it rattled him when I didn't. Good.

I reached the next post at the corner of the intersection Rahn had already traversed. My aim yielded good results and I caught the post perfectly. I pulled myself forward above the traffic moving from my right to left on another one-way street.

The next lamp post was a challenge. It arched over the street toward me, rather than perpendicular to me, significantly narrowing the target. I let my glide carry me toward it, calculating the intersect point. I would miss the light, but would be high, and have only a limited shot at grabbing the pole's arch to adjust my trajectory. Miss it, and I'd continue high and probably miss the next as well. I'd be headed upward, into empty night and a whole new set of problems.

The light passed under me. A steel arm stretched from the light to the post. I lunged downward and caught it with one hand, pulling myself and adjusting my path at the same time. People with no awareness of my presence streamed in both directions on the sidewalk below me.

Rahn hurried forward at mid-block ahead of me, hustling awkwardly on what I assumed to be an injured leg.

I hope it's killing you.

The one-way street carried busy traffic that returned to normal flow as I got farther from the emergency vehicles blocking the front of the Mayflower. Vehicles hurried past Rahn, just feet from him because the street had no parking lane.

I would catch up to him at mid-block and it would do me absolutely no good. I flew twenty feet above the sidewalk, skimming above leafless young trees, too high to simply drop on him without injuring myself. The next lamp post I would touch stood at the end of the block.

Just as I formed a plan to snag the post and then drop down in Rahn's face, a car abruptly stopped beside him. The left rear door opened, and a man jumped out. He trotted into position in front of Rahn. For an instant, I hoped Andy had managed to call in the cavalry, that she somehow identified Rahn and his escape route, and the police were here to take him down.

No such luck. The man met Rahn with an impatient gesture. Rahn's body language greeted him with what looked like resignation. They seemed to know each other. The man gestured at the car and Rahn hobbled toward it without protest.

"No! No-no-no-no!" I heard myself chanting as I approached.

The scene with the car played out while I glided helplessly overhead, twenty feet high as Rahn ducked toward the open rear passenger door.

The knot that had been my throat since Andy cried out Lydia's name now solidified as Rahn, our ghost, disappeared into his getaway sedan and the vehicle pulled back into traffic. I could do nothing to accelerate. It pulled away from me.

"SHIT!" I cried out. One or two mystified pedestrian faces turned up at the sound.

The light changed to yellow, then red. The sedan, keeping to its lane, showed me brake lights. It stopped.

I recharged a glimmer of hope. Targeting the next lamp post, I caught up after a moment, then passed the stopped sedan. Fixated on the vehicle, I nearly missed landing a grip on the post. Just as I caught it, the light changed, and traffic surged forward.

Shit!

The sedan accelerated into the next block. Once again, the lamp posts were widely spaced, the buildings flat and featureless. Traffic moved slowly, but I couldn't match the vehicle's overall pace and at the same time control my trajectory from post to post. I damned myself again for failing to carry a FLOP unit with me.

To make matters worse, my phone rang. Over the street noise, my old-school jingling ringtone sounded urgent and out of place. Below me, people reached for their phones.

It would be Andy. It would be news, possibly horrible news. Or a demand to know my progress. I was helpless to answer. I could pull the phone from my pocket by feel but I had no way to see the screen and push the right buttons.

The earpiece!

On several occasions recently, Andy made me wear a Bluetooth earpiece allowing us to communicate during my excursions in *the other thing*. She had taken, almost annoyingly, to reminding me to pocket the tiny earpiece. I tapped my jacket pocket and felt the device. Before I could extract it, my lamppost arrived.

I grabbed the pole arm with both hands, pushed back, then hurled myself forward on an angled trajectory that took me out over the street, above traffic, toward the other side. My aiming point was the full front of a building, the broad side of a barn, so to speak. It didn't matter where I hit, because I wasn't going for accuracy and grip. I wanted speed and distance.

My phone continued to ring. As I shot across the traffic-clogged street, I jabbed my hand in my pocket and found the Bluetooth earpiece. Without removing it from my pocket, I fumbled with it until I thought I had it aligned properly. Halfway across the street, I pulled the earpiece out and pressed it into my ear. It slipped into a perfect fit. I hooked the wire over my ear and patted the mic against my cheek.

I was about to reach for the button that opened the incoming call when my target wall loomed. Square windows checkerboarded the concrete wall of a seven- or eight-story building. I reached out and hit the glass with both hands, swinging my knees up and legs in. I pushed off with my hands first, then feet, a sideways leap-frog move. The impact banged the glass and a man sitting in a cubicle on the other side jumped from his chair. He and his startled face disappeared as my ricochet shot sent me back over the lighted street toward the next building face.

I felt panic when I realized that my concentration on the trajectory made me lose sight of the sedan in a river of taillights. Shooting back over the traffic, I found it.

"Chevy Impala," I told myself aloud. "Dark blue Chevy Impala."

I tried to make out the license number, but an SUV pulled up close behind the car and blocked my view. I had time to give thanks that Rahn wasn't in a black SUV. The D.C. streets crawled with them.

Traffic surged forward again. There was no question that the car was faster than me, but the traffic lights played against it and gave me a chance.

My next carom shot bounced off a band of concrete three floors up on another tall office building. Before hitting it, I looked ahead. The opposite side of the street became a row of older townhouse-style buildings. Some had awnings. Some had steps. None had smooth frontal surfaces. Nor were they as high as the office buildings.

I bounced, kicking away on a lower trajectory for what I hoped would be the center building in the row. It had a gray brick façade over a blue awning.

The Impala rolled ahead, through the next intersection. The light at the end of the block was green and if they made that light, I had an excellent chance of losing this race.

I watched the car for as long as I could, then diverted my attention to slamming into and kicking off the gray bricks. At the last second, I rotated my body so that, from my point of view, the side of the building lay beneath my feet, giving my legs a chance to piston against the brick. Like running sideways.

Two things happened.

First, I felt something in my chest. Not the icy grip of fear that came when the young police officer spoke of a woman being killed, and his words sparked horrible images of Lydia. I felt the *muscle* I didn't have. The one that yanked me forward when I had no other way to get Lydia to the hospital. The one that saved Andy and me in Montana, and again in Chicago.

I shook off the surprise and tried to use it.

GO!

I formed the concept in my head like a command.

Nothing happened. I flew forward on the same path, angled across the street toward another pool table bumper shot off the next building.

I tried again.

STOP!

Nothing.

Yet I could feel that grip, that center point, that *muscle* at my center. How was this possible? It frustrated me, more so because there was no time to experiment. The next traffic light remained green long enough for the Impala to roll into another block. I was losing them!

The second thing that happened was that my phone rang again. I reached up quickly and touched the button on my earpiece.

"I'm here!" I said.

"Where?"

"Beats the hell out of me," I said. "Lydia! Is she okay?"

"Lydia and the girls are okay! Thank God! She—"

"Wait! Just wait a sec!"

My trajectory took me across a busy intersection marked with broad piano-key crosswalks. I flew a direct line toward an all-glass building, lit up against the night sky. I hadn't noticed when kicking off the townhouse that my next bumper pool shot took me to a wall of glass nearly perpendicular to me. This sharply reduced my ability to translate a bounce into forward movement. On top of that, I was moving headfirst and facing the wrong way with my back to the building.

"Dammit!" I muttered.

"What?"

"Just...hang on…"

I caught a glimpse of the Impala. It rolled toward the next light, another set of green arrows. This trip was about to come to a sudden halt. It would take me too long to reposition and launch forward again.

I clenched myself around the muscle at my center and was surprised to gain leverage. With it, I rolled to face the building, then curled into a cannonball position. I rotated my body until my feet were aimed at the glass rather than my head and hands.

This had never happened before!

Previously, without a grip on something, without leverage, I simply floated like a gravity-impaired astronaut, unable to alter my position on any axis.

"Will?"

The glass came up fast. My feet hit. I began running, pumping my legs. My leather-soled boots slipped on the glass, and I had to go into a crouch to avoid simply stopping or bouncing back the way I came. Still, the result was more than I hoped for. I shot forward again, past the corner of the glass building, across the street again. It wasn't as much forward momentum as before, but I didn't stop as I feared I would.

"I'm here," I said, slightly breathless.

"Did you find him? Rahn?"

"He got in a car. I'm following it."

"How are you—? Oh!"

"Yeah. What happened? With Lydia?"

"Never mind that! She's okay! Where are you? I'm coming!"

I looked around.

"Again. No idea. Go right out of the hotel. Then first left. I'm on that street going west."

Andy gave instructions to someone. The police? I wondered, but another wall of glass dominated my attention.

Rotate. Curl up.

Around the pivot point in my chest, I repositioned. My feet hit the glass with a stark thump. I pumped my legs and ran several steps, crouching then pushing away. This time I gained speed.

A FedEx delivery van pulled in behind the Impala, blocking my view. I checked out my next bumper pool point on an approaching structure.

"Can you give me an address? A building name?"

"It's all freakin' glass office buildings. There's a MacDonald's on the left."

The fast-food storefront passed below me. The Impala came back into view. I approached more glass. I performed the same move again, feeling it in my chest. My feet hit. I thumped out a few steps, slipped, but then managed to kick off in the general direction of the buildings on the other side of the street. I got careless and the thrust was uneven, driving me on a slight down angle. It took me toward the top of a small tree.

In my ear, I could hear Andy talking about the MacDonald's. Whoever she was with said something back that sounded like "I know it."

Andy spoke rapidly. "Rahn tried to get into Lydia's room. I think he was after me again. He didn't know I changed rooms."

"Wait. Hang on." I bounced again. This building had concrete between the windows and I got lucky. My boots got a grip and I gained speed along with a shallower departure angle. It gave me a longer shot to the next bounce point.

The Impala continued to roll forward. With one or two more good shots like the last one I would be on it. Provided they didn't turn.

"Okay. Go."

"What on earth are you doing?"

"Don't ask. Are you in a car?"

"Yes."

"Police?"

"Uber. Our same Uber. We just turned west on M Street. Is that what you're on? M Street?"

"Beats me. What the hell was all that about a woman killed?"

"I don't know. All I know is that I ran into Liddy and the girls in the lobby. She was sleeping with them when someone came into the room. She screamed bloody murder and he took off. She called 9-1-1 and told them there was a man with a gun in the hotel. I think the response was geared for active shooter. MPD came down hard."

"M Street! They're on M Street! I just saw a sign!"

Andy relayed the message to the driver.

I performed another bounce. This one had me in the same block as the Impala, but they were hitting green lights again and accelerating away from me. The same FedEx delivery truck remained in position behind the sedan and I started thinking of an alternative to bouncing off buildings.

"Move over!" I heard Andy say.

"You talking to me?"

"No."

A moment later I heard a car horn, both in my ear and on the street several blocks behind me. I heard tires squeal.

"CBN News on the right. Pizza Hut on the left. Still on M Street!" I called out. I hit the third-floor windows of the CBN News building and kicked off with a loud thump, drawing the startled attention of half a dozen people sitting around a conference table. One of them dumped a coffee mug.

I tried to angle lower and shot into another intersection that had just given the Impala a green light. On my left, a concrete building with recessed windows. On my right, a building of glass. I tracked toward the concrete building, worried about the way the ridges of concrete between deep windows offered little footing, and a lot of ways to hit wrong.

"Twentieth. Just crossed Twentieth!"

I wasn't wrong to worry about the surface of the building I hit. My feet skidded off the concrete edge and I dropped into the well formed by the window. My boots hit the glass. I threw my hands out to grip the concrete. It bit into my skin, but I pushed off in time to shoot out of the recessed window without slamming my shins on the concrete.

Ahead, the street angled left. Car horns blasted behind me.

"Dee, are you driving the Uber?"

"Yes. Describe the car to me!"

I heard the Uber driver, apparently now Dee's passenger, swear loudly.

"Dark blue Chevy Impala four door sedan. I don't have a license number. Can you see a FedEx van ahead?"

"No. Why?"

"Never mind. They're still on M. Looks like it angles left up ahead."

Construction on this block closed the left lane of traffic, creating a bottleneck, which slowed traffic. That helped. Trees lining this part of the street reached the bottom of the fifth floor. That didn't help. I made a snap decision.

My next bounce point was almost adjacent to the Impala, which sat stalled in traffic. Instead of hitting the building, I rolled myself inverted and reached down. My fingers brushed into the tree. I grabbed. Thin twigs snapped in my fingers. I tossed them free, then closed a grip on a tall branch. The branch bent but held me. I pulled myself to a lower branch, then another, then another. Twig ends stabbed at me. I reached a limb solid enough to give me a pivot point.

Traffic moved again. I took a desperate shot and pushed off.

I flew over the traffic lanes, over the back edge of the FedEx truck. The truck roof was smooth with a translucent skylight. I hooked my hand on the edge of the roof. Working hand over hand, I pulled myself to the open side door of the vehicle. Cars ahead of the truck began to roll. At any second, the truck would accelerate, and I would lose my hold.

My hand caught the corner of the open door just as the driver punched forward, staying glued to the bumper of the Impala.

I held on. Traffic angled to the left. Buildings to my left and right fell away from the street. An open area of trees approached on the left. My practice of bouncing off buildings was finished.

One more stop at a traffic light and I could work my way forward onto the roof of the Impala.

"Will! I see the FedEx truck!" Andy called out to me.

"Rahn's in the car right in front of it. Tell me you're calling in the cavalry."

Traffic abruptly opened up. The Impala accelerated. The FedEx truck stayed in the same lane but lost ground. I held on, praying for a red light.

A block passed. Then another, and another. Green light after green light made the way clear for traffic to spread out and accelerate. The Impala moved two, then four car lengths ahead.

On both sides of the street, the seven- and eight-story office buildings thinned out to be replaced by two- and three-story buildings. The tree population increased. My navigation options decreased.

The next light turned green. The FedEx truck veered into the left lane and I felt it decelerate.

Son of a bitch! He's turning!

I grabbed the roof above the doorway and heaved myself over the side. My legs swung down through the open door.

Fwooomp! I dropped onto the floorboards and appeared beside the driver.

The driver took one look at me and jolted in his seat.

"WHAAA—?!"

The van lurched as he kicked off the gas pedal and went for the brakes.

"NO! No! No! No! Don't stop! Don't stop!" I grabbed an assist handle by the door. "Keep going! Follow that car!"

His foot didn't hit the brake, but it didn't return to the gas pedal either. He glared at me.

"I was carjacked! My little girl is in the back seat! You have to help me!" I pointed at the Impala.

"Will, what are you doing?!" Andy demanded in my ear.

"Please!" I begged the driver. "We can't lose sight of it or we'll lose her! I'm calling the cops!" I plucked my phone from my coat pocket.

The driver, an athletic man with a hard jawline and solid upper body hesitated, then punched the gas pedal.

"That one!" I pointed again to be sure.

He swerved back into the lane behind the Impala, drawing an angry horn blast from a BMW moving up beside him.

"Don't worry, man! I got this!" he cried out. The diesel delivery truck engine roared. "Want me to ram it?"

"NO!"

"What's her name?"

"Who?"

"Your little girl! What's her name?"

"Oh!" I blanked for a moment. "Ethel!"

"Will! Talk to me!"

"Dude, thank you! You FedEx drivers, you're the best!"

"Oh, my God!" Andy said, picking up the hint.

"Call 9-1-1!" the driver hollered above the engine noise. He gestured at my phone.

"Right!" I said. I held up my phone and pretended to punch at the screen. I had no intention of cutting the connection with Andy. I know there are ways to simultaneously make multiple calls. I've seen Pidge do it. But I have no clue how it's done.

"Will, I lost you!"

Both the Impala and the FedEx van had veered left. I glanced at the speedometer. Traffic all around us moved at forty-plus miles per hour, shooting through green light after green light.

"What are we on?" I shouted at the driver.

"Key Bridge. We're going over the Key Bridge!"

"We're going over the Key Bridge," I told Andy. The road widened, and the Potomac River appeared on either side, passing beneath a bridge lighted by twin rows of simple lamp posts. Modern office buildings broke the horizon on the far side.

"Didja gettem?" the driver asked, his eyes alight.

"What?"

"9-1-1! Did you get them?"

"Oh!" I put my phone up to my ear and gave him a thumbs-up. "Just stay with her, okay!" I pointed at the Impala, now moving across the bridge.

The driver pushed harder, closing the gap. He pounded his fist on the wheel. "Hang on, Ethel! We're comin'!"

"Where are you!" Andy called out.

"Middle of the bridge."

"I see you! I'm two hundred yards behind!"

I heard panicked car horns behind us. Andy's work. The FedEx driver glanced at me.

"Tell 'em about Ethel! Your daughter! Tell 'em about your daughter!"

The wind roared past the open door and the diesel engine howled in harmony.

"They know!" I shouted back at him. "My wife is on the line with them!" To Andy I said quietly, "You are on the line with them, right?"

"Little busy here!"

"Dude, they're speeding up!" the driver called out.

The driver accelerated to keep pace with the Impala's taillights. Cars moved in and out of the lane between us.

The bridge ended. Our lanes split off to the right, putting what looked like a park or a vast median between us and the oncoming lanes. Tall buildings that I took for offices and hotels loomed ahead on the left. The Impala turned. We followed.

"Tell 'em we're on Fort Myer, passing the Holiday Inn Rosslyn!" the driver instructed me. I gave him a thumbs-up and repeated the words into my phone. The driver wheeled left. "They're turning in! They're turning in!"

I watched the Impala take a turn onto a driveway that circled in front of a high-rise office building.

"Do I follow? Whaddya want me to do?!"

"Slow down!" I watched to see if the sedan disappeared into underground parking. It didn't. It slowed and followed a curve to the front of the glass tower. "Okay, keep going! Just keep going!"

Mildly bewildered, the driver glanced at me but held his course, passing the driveway.

I tucked my phone in my pocket and slapped the driver on the shoulder.

"You're the best, man! You saved my little girl!"

Without waiting for a reply, I used the door assist handle to leap out of the still-moving van into the night.

Fwooomp! I vanished in midair. The cool sensation replaced the chill of the wind that had been blasting in the open door. Glancing back, I saw the driver's face go slack and his eyes widen.

The momentum of the van plus my pull through the door sent me sailing across a wide lawn fronting a lighted glass office tower. I didn't really think it through. My flight path took an upward trajectory. I estimated impact with the building around the third floor. At best, I might cushion the collision with my arms and stop. At worst I would bounce off and wind up floating thirty feet up with nothing to grip.

As I approached, I watched the Impala stop at the curb beside the entrance. The driver and a front seat passenger emerged. The front seat passenger opened the rear door and Rahn stepped awkwardly out, favoring his left leg. A fourth man slid across the seat behind Rahn. The men looked around warily, waiting for Rahn to get his footing.

The four of them had taken their first steps toward the door when they heard tires squeal and an engine rev. I looked over my shoulder and saw Andy at the wheel of the Uber, racing up the asphalt driveway. The Uber driver sat wide-eyed beside her in the passenger seat with his hands planted on the dash.

Andy wheeled the car around the circle and slammed it to a stop behind the Impala. It hardly ceased moving before she was out of the door with her weapon drawn.

"MANNIS RAHN! HANDS IN THE AIR! NOW! NOW!" she shouted, swinging her weapon to bear on Rahn.

"GUN!"

Rahn dropped into a crouch, stiffly extending his injured leg. The men around him spread out. The man nearest the Impala ducked behind the sedan for cover.

I watched, horrified, as the three men with Rahn jabbed their hands into their coats and produced weapons.

"POLICE!" Andy cried, but her voice mingled with shouts from the three men.

"DROP IT!"

"DROP YOUR WEAPON!"

"DO IT NOW! DO IT NOW!"

Andy froze. I saw her eyes dart from one weapon to the next to the next. The men assumed shooting stances and continued shouting at her. Three black gun barrels locked on my wife.

My heart stopped. I lost all concentration on what I was doing and stared down at the scene.

"Andy, NO!"

"DROP IT!"

"DROP THE WEAPON! NOW!"

Andy tipped the barrel of her weapon to the black night sky.

The man nearest the car hustled around the rear fender. Andy spread her left hand at her side and swiftly lowered her Glock to the pavement with her right. Before she could rise, the man at the car charged her and hit her with a full body block that took her off her feet. She hit the pavement on her side with the man on top of her.

"STOP!" I shouted, but at that moment, fully absorbed in the horror below, I slammed into the side of the glass building. I took a jolt and banged the side of my head.

A second man swept down on Andy. With his free hand, he shoved her face into the concrete. He holstered his weapon and jerked her arms behind her back. A moment later, he clipped handcuffs to her wrists. I heard her try to speak, but the first man put a knee to the center of her back and she lost the air in her lungs, leaving her gasping.

Blind fury flooded my veins. I reached for the levers in my head to reappear and dive to the pavement. I estimated the distance to Andy's weapon. If I could reach it, I decided I would pick it up and empty it.

"U.S. Marshals! You're under arrest!" the third man shouted. He held his weapon on a firing line with my wife's head.

What?

"Puh—puh—" Andy tried to speak.

"She's a cop, you stupid sonofabitch!" I shouted. On the rebound, I floated helpless, thirty feet up, with no momentum in any direction. "Get off her!"

The two men holding Andy down were too absorbed in their own adrenaline-fueled moment to hear me, but the third man turned his head and looked around. He looked at Rahn, who now stood to one side, staring. He looked at the Uber driver who sat holding his hands open and thrust against the windshield.

I estimated the drop to the concrete. It would probably break both ankles.

"Will, no!" Andy cried out suddenly, finding her breath.

I froze.

The two men with Andy pulled her abruptly to her feet, none too gently. I saw blood on the side of her face.

I wanted to scream.

The third man picked up her weapon and approached her.

She struggled for air.

"Puh—police! Mannis Ruh—Rahn, you are under arrest!" she stammered breathlessly.

"What the fuck," the third man said with a note of wonder. "Get her inside!"

The group marched toward the glass doors.

Leaving me hanging.

27

It took me forty-five angry minutes to bring my heart rate back to near normal and find Andy.

Getting down required me to flap my arms and inch my way up against the building. I had to pinch a thin steel frame between the glass windows with my fingertips, then move hand over hand to within falling distance of the concrete. The landing was awkward. I wound up on my ass but managed not to break or sprain anything.

On the way down, I considered my options inside the glass office tower. I expected challenges. Security stations to evade. Cameras. Secure, locked and restricted areas. I made plans to disarm and disable vigilant guards, to steal weapons. I vowed to break Andy out. Handcuffs or manacles would be no problem; I have a trick using *the other thing* that can 'fray' and weaken metal chains to the point of breaking. I anticipated wrapping myself around her and making her vanish, then riding out the confusion that would follow as alarms shrieked and frantic security forces locked down the building. I would get us into an elevator shaft, then we could ascend and then find our way onto the roof or, worst case, break a window, and float free. I hoped to break some heads, specifically the two sons of bitches who threw my wife to the concrete.

None of that happened.

After rising between escalator flights and floating through bland government office space, I found Andy on the third floor sitting in a comfortable-looking lounge sipping from a mug of what smelled like a hazelnut blend. She wore a Band-Aid on the corner of her left eye and her cheek was red. She sat in a fat leather chair with one leg on a matching ottoman and an ice pack on her left knee. Andy wore her badge on a chain around her neck. Her Glock 26 lay in its holster within reach on a coffee table beside her purse.

She chatted amiably with a young woman who seemed to be trying to recruit her to the U.S. Marshals Service.

What the hell?

"…really depends on retirements. I had to accept posting where it was available. I couldn't believe I got D.C. right out of the gate!" the young Deputy Marshal enthusiastically explained to Andy as I gripped the door-frame and floated unseen into the lounge. "Out of ninety-four district offices, I caught the brass ring on the first try!"

"Not bad," Andy said, projecting genuine admiration. "What's the mobility like if you want a different posting."

"You commit to three years at your first posting. After that, it's all based on seniority and availability. But skill sets factor in. Let's say you have a language skill, for example. I'm fluent in Spanish so pretty much any posting except Anchorage can use me."

"Nice."

"And you start off at GL oh seven."

I had no idea what that was, but Andy seemed impressed.

"With your experience," the Deputy leaned closer to Andy, "and being a woman …" She heaved a shrug meant to say anything was possible, then pointed at Andy's coffee mug. "Can I refresh that for you? It might be a while."

"Please," Andy handed over her mug. The Deputy made a path out of the lounge space toward the empty hall I had flown through moments ago.

I pushed off the wall beside the door and floated across the room to where Andy sat. She gazed out the floor-to-ceiling windows at the view across the Potomac. The lighted Capital Dome and Washington Monument dominated the night skyline.

I took a deep breath to calm myself.

"Hey," I said softly, "it's me."

Andy startled, but then smiled. She lifted her hand in the direction of my voice and brushed my arm. I settled in beside her with an anchor grip on the leather chair.

"Are you okay?" I stroked her hand. I wanted to kiss her.

"This?" She touched the Band-Aid. "Just a little road rash. And I banged my knee. It's a little swollen, but nothing serious. I'm fine. Took you long enough."

"Yeah, well this place deploys the most sinister of all security systems."

"What's that?"

"Bad signage. From what I can tell the U.S. Marshal Service occupies three floors of this building. But only one is marked. I've been searching for armed guards, detention centers and secure lockups. If any of that exists, they have diabolically camouflaged their cells as rows of cubicles and their torture devices as copy machines. And to make matters even more confusing, no one is here."

"It's Saturday night, Pilot," she said. "That's why I'm sitting here waiting. They had to call in a chief deputy who lives in Virginia."

"We're in Virginia."

"Well, she's on a horse farm somewhere, and it's an hour drive. The coffee is excellent, however."

"What the hell is going on? Where's Rahn?"

"I don't know. You didn't see him?"

"No. They probably have him restrained in some secret spa on another floor. Torturing him with a crème brulee French roast. Seriously, what the hell is going on?"

She shook her head.

"All I know is once everyone calmed down, and they verified my credentials, it's been apologies and hospitality. But no answers. They said some cops showed up. Called here by a FedEx driver reporting a carjacking. Your work?"

"The guy was a hero. He saved little Ethel."

Andy made a face.

"They weren't very friendly toward you outside. I came in here to kick ass and take names."

"I'm glad you didn't."

"Dee, you almost got shot!"

"Law enforcement gets edgy around guns in public places. I get it."

"Well, it scared the shit out of me! If they won't talk to you, what do you think they're hiding?"

"These guys? Not sure they're hiding anything. I think they just don't want to share any information until the boss gets here."

"But they have Rahn, right?"

"That's how it looks. Don't forget—I sent out queries to all agencies."

"They seemed awfully chummy with him. You got cuffed. He didn't."

"I lost sight of him. They took a different elevator. I asked the rookie who's babysitting me, but she doesn't know anything about Rahn. She's compartmentalized out of the picture. She makes great coffee, though."

"Probably a trick to get you to lower your guard. These people are diabolical."

She couldn't help herself; she looked for me, following the sound of my voice.

"What happened at the hotel?" I asked. "What was that business about a woman found dead?"

"I don't know, but my heart was in my throat until I ran into Lydia and the girls in the lobby. Will, can you imagine? If Rahn mistook Lydia for me again? I couldn't live with myself."

"Well, obviously Rahn hasn't given up. Christ!"

"I guess. It's dumb luck that I saw him on the street."

Andy laid her forearm on the arm of the leather chair. I put my hand over hers. She closed her eyes and hummed a note of appreciation.

The rookie Deputy poked her head in the door.

"I should have asked. We also have French Vanilla and Chocolate Raspberry."

"The hazelnut is very good," Andy replied. "Thank you."

The deputy winked and darted away.

"Bastards," I said. "This treatment is inhuman."

28

Chief Deputy United States Marshal Karen Whitlock arrived forty minutes later. I remained at Andy's side, floating, but couldn't speak because Deputy Marshal Glenda Ortega, the rookie, stayed with Andy as ordered. They chatted, mostly about Ortega's career path. After the rush of pursuit and the adrenaline shock of seeing Andy assaulted, their droning conversation zoned me out. I worried about dozing off and inadvertently reappearing. I desperately wanted some of that coffee.

When Chief Deputy Whitlock entered the room, she gestured for Andy to remain seated. She extended a hand and a warm smile to Andy for the introductions. Compact, slightly muscular, and prone to precise, rapid movements, she looked the part of a middle-school girls' gym teacher. I estimated her age in the early fifties, but if she had gray hair, she kept it in a bottle. Under reddish curls, she carried a round honest face. She showed up in jeans and a flannel shirt and smelled faintly of horse manure.

MPD Detective Mike Fanko followed close on Chief Deputy Whitlock's heels. A moment later, the third man from the unit in the Impala, the one who supervised Andy's takedown, entered the room. He carried a thin file folder.

"How's the knee?" the third man asked Andy.

"It's nothing," she replied.

"The boys feel sick about it. They owe you a dinner. Anywhere in D.C., they said, as long as it serves hamburgers and has a drive-through."

"I'll take them up on that. Please tell them no hard feelings and thank them for not shooting me."

"Oh," the deputy said, reaching in his pocket. "Here's your phone. Sorry. We had to have it cleared downstairs. Protocol for electronic devices."

"Deputy John Merrick, this is Detective Mike Fanko of the MPD," Whitlock gestured between the two men. They traded handshakes. "I asked him to join us."

Everyone found chairs. The room offered seating on a leather sofa, half a dozen padded armchairs, and the fat leather armchair Andy occupied. The furniture was one price point above institutional. It felt like the waiting room at an upscale clinic. The rookie produced a tray containing water bottles, a coffee pot, and several mugs with the U.S. Marshal Service emblem on it. I wondered if I could slip one under my shirt on the way out. Ortega arranged the tray on a side table, then excused herself.

"Can you confirm for me that you have Mannis Rahn in custody?" Andy asked.

"Right to the point," Whitlock observed. "No. We do not."

Andy's expression went cold, but Whitlock waved a hand between them.

"We never did. The man you were trying to arrest is not Mannis Rahn."

"I'm sorry, but I disagree! I've been studying Rahn for over a month and I'm prepared to make a positive identification. Tell me you did not let that man go!"

Whitlock smiled and shook her head.

"We did not let him go. In fact, you're going to meet him shortly. But he is not Mannis Rahn. He is not the man you have been pursuing, Detective. I spoke to your Chief Ceeves. I am aware that Rahn is a suspect in a murder in Essex."

"He is."

"And he mistook your sister for you and tried to kill her."

"Three weeks ago, and again tonight." Andy looked pointedly at Fanko, who sat still, working his rugged-silent-type face for everyone in the room.

"Because of your connection to the Parks case," Whitlock filled in the blank. "I spoke to Attorney General Richardson in Montana. He considers it plausible that Parks may be using Rahn to weaken the case against him by eliminating you as a witness."

"That's right."

Whitlock shrugged. "I'll be frank, Detective. It seems rather pointless, given the evidence they're assembling. A. G. Richardson made it sound like your testimony is not all that pivotal."

"Tell that to Parks."

"I'm not questioning your assessment, Detective. In fact, we take the safety and security of witnesses rather seriously around here."

"If you don't have Mannis Rahn in custody, who am I about to meet?"

"Steggar Rahn. Mannis Rahn's younger brother."

Jesus, I thought, *their parents were sadists. Who names kids like that?*

"I don't understand. There's nothing in any of the files I've seen about Rahn having a younger brother."

"Because we're good at what we do," Merrick chimed in. He patted the folder on his lap.

"How much do you know about Rahn's conviction?" Whitlock asked.

"I have his arrest reports, copies of his prison records from Evergreen, and the transcript of his plea in Oklahoma. Three homicides. He pled out, I assume taking a deal. Life over death. What am I missing?"

"Everything we wanted to keep out of the official record. And ordinarily we would end this meeting right now with some very frustrating language about witness security and need to know and have a nice day. But you are in the unique position of having been the target of Mannis Rahn, and yet you are still breathing. That makes you of interest to us."

"That makes you excellent bait, Detective," Merrick added.

Oh, hell no! I poked Andy in the shoulder with one finger. Instead of acknowledging my protest, she shifted her posture to the other side of the chair.

"I wouldn't go quite that far," Whitlock said.

"Then tell me what I don't know," Andy said.

"Mannis Rahn pled guilty to three homicides in Oklahoma in twenty-twelve. It came as a surprise to everyone concerned because his defense attorney insisted that he could beat the case against his client."

"How?"

"The defense claimed three principle shareholders in an energy company died in a rafting accident on the Arkansas River in Colorado."

"I thought he was convicted of murder in Oklahoma?"

"He was. The energy company was based in Oklahoma. The case was built around a fourth shareholder hiring Rahn to stage the accident on a rafting trip. This is one worthy of a tabloid television show, but I'll skip the lurid details involving two cheating wives, a hundred-million-dollar buyout offer, and all the usual stupidity. Cut to the chase. Strong circumstantial evidence pointed to Rahn being hired to do the deed. It wasn't a slam-dunk case by any means. Like I said, his defense attorney hung his hat on the whole thing being an accident. Until a witness came forward. The witness put Rahn in the crosshairs for a capital offense conviction, and the prosecution hoped it would give them leverage to nail the surviving shareholder."

"Let me guess. The witness was Rahn's brother."

Whitlock touched her nose.

"The prosecution lined up their ducks to flip Rahn. Offer him a reduced sentence—even possible parole after fifty or sixty years. Then suddenly Rahn fired his defense attorney and pled out. He traded the needle for three full life sentences without parole."

"This was before Clayton Lockett," Merrick pointed out. "The one they botched. The death penalty has been on hold in Oklahoma ever since that happened in 'fifteen."

"Rahn refused to roll over on the man who hired him. The prosecutor lost his leverage. And worse, the identity of the witness became known to the outgoing defense attorney, who we think shared it with the man pulling the strings in the first place."

"So, you put Steggar Rahn in WITSEC."

Whitlock nodded. "We anticipated that the principle bad actor in all this would try to make sure the door to prosecution never opens again. Rahn's brother remained a potential witness for a new case. He went into the program in early twenty-thirteen."

"But then Mannis Rahn 'died' in prison," Andy said, fingering air quotes.

"In twenty-sixteen. Then last year, the target of the original investigation, the surviving shareholder, died with four other people when his fishing boat caught fire in the Gulf of Mexico."

"Another accident," Andy noted. "Funny. We just had a couple of those in Essex."

"Your chief told me."

"Why do you think Rahn suddenly pled guilty when his attorney, according to you, was confident he would walk?"

"We didn't know at the time. But now we can guess, thanks to you," Whitlock said.

"Parks."

Whitlock nodded. "Rahn was deemed a high-risk-of-flight, high-security prisoner, it being a capital case, so he was held at an Evergreen facility. Although there are no visitor logs showing Parks directly contacted Rahn while he was awaiting trial, we now know those visitor logs are worthless."

Andy fixed a thoughtful stare on an indeterminate distance. Whitlock waited while Andy did her thinking out loud.

"The prosecutors hold Rahn's feet to the fire with the death penalty, thinking that a deal will get them the shareholder. Parks comes in the back door with a new deal for Rahn, a bold concept that not only gets him out from under the needle but gets him out of prison with a new identity while a box full of barbecue grille ashes gets buried in his name."

"And…"

"And offers the added satisfaction of letting Rahn eliminate his former employer, probably because the guy left him to twist in the wind. Or didn't pay him."

"And…"

"And Parks holds up his end and gains a lethal tool with a perfect alibi. And now Parks may be using that tool to dismantle the case against him."

"I'm beginning to see why you're the darling of law enforcement in Wisconsin and Montana," Whitlock smiled.

"Not so much, at least in Wisconsin."

Whitlock chuckled. "I have no doubt the governor was less than thrilled with your work after you put away one of his big donors."

Andy took a sip of the hazelnut blend. My stomach rolled over. The aroma was killing me.

She pointed at Fanko.

"Why is he here?"

139

I chalked up some smug satisfaction. *Yeah, why is that asshole here?* My triumph didn't last long.

"Davis Bates," Fanko said dramatically. He waited for Andy to prompt him for more. She didn't.

"A bizarre accident, right? That's what we would have put it down to if you hadn't asked one extra question."

"I think your forensic people would have tipped to the extension cord."

"Maybe."

"I called Detective Fanko," Whitlock interjected. "After speaking to your chief, Detective. I learned why you and your sister are here in D.C. For your brother-in-law. My condolences for your loss."

"Thank you."

"Chief Ceeves told me the name and I looked up the Bates case. His case." She gestured at Fanko. "The same MPD detective who showed up tonight at the Mayflower scene where I had a team on surveillance."

"You had a team watching us? At the Mayflower?"

"No," Whitlock shook her head. She opened her mouth to explain but Andy turned sharply to Fanko.

"Wait! You think Rahn is responsible for Davis Bates?"

Fanko said, "Given what I've learned tonight from Chief Deputy Whitlock, I'm open to connecting Rahn to Bates and the Montoya woman."

"Montoya? What woman?" Andy sat up.

"At the Mayflower. I thought you knew."

Andy shook her head.

Fanko glanced at Whitlock. Whitlock shook her head. "I thought she knew as well."

"What woman?" Andy demanded.

Fanko explained. "Another 'accident.' At the Mayflower. The head of housekeeping was found in a service stairwell. It appears she was carrying a box of those little shampoo bottles. Dropped the box, stepped on some of the bottles, slipped and went down a flight of stairs. Preliminary suggests a broken neck. It's a fall that might have been serious but shouldn't have been fatal. An accident. Except—"

"This happened around the same time someone was breaking into my sister's suite."

"Not breaking," Fanko said. "Entering. The initial call was misleading. Somehow it went from intruder to active shooter after a second call reported a woman dead in the stairwell. By the time I got there, the on-scene officers checked the woman's body—to see if she had her master key. It was gone. We re-evaluated. We now think whoever entered your sister's room killed the housekeeper first, then used her master key. We're pulling data from the hotel's key system now."

"Rahn!" Andy said. "Looking for me. Tell me you got video!"

"We have people on it," Fanko replied. "But like I said, things were confused. We had to secure the scene first."

"My family is at the Mayflower!"

"I have a protection detail at the hotel with your family," Fanko said. "Until we can get this sorted out."

"This doesn't make any sense! Why would Rahn go after my brother-in-law?"

"It brought you here, didn't it? Got you off your home turf. Out in the open."

"You can't be serious. You think Rahn came to Washington D.C. and killed Davis just to lure me here?"

"Chief Ceeves told me you were being well protected in Essex. And quite aggressive about bringing other agencies in on the search. Essex—perhaps Wisconsin—couldn't have been comfortable for Rahn."

"That's quite a stretch, Chief Deputy."

"Detective," Fanko said, "you haven't been entirely forthcoming about your situation. Had we known more, we might have put some of these pieces together sooner."

Andy ignored Fanko's accusation. I wanted to punch him in his beard stubble.

Andy turned to Whitlock. "If you're right, then put me out as bait. Let that son of a bitch find me. I can handle him."

"I have no doubt," Whitlock said. "But notwithstanding Deputy Merrick's suggestion about bait, you're a witness in a significant case in Montana. I understand you also have obligations to a case in Chicago. The point is, we're not in the business of putting witnesses, whether in or out of a program, in jeopardy. We're inclined to go the other way. To place you under protection."

"No."

Whitlock gave Andy a moment to settle.

"Detective," Whitlock said, "you do realize that the mandate of the United States Marshal Service is fugitive apprehension. And regardless of a dubious death certificate—and in the light of a possible connection to Davis Bates—Mannis Rahn is a fugitive. He has our full attention. You're far from alone here."

"We saw your bulletins out of Essex about Rahn," Merrick said.

"I won't go into hiding."

A moment of uncomfortable silence settled on Andy's declaration, hardening it.

"I want to talk to the brother," Andy told Whitlock firmly. "You *are* planning on letting me talk to him, Chief Deputy?"

"Provisionally."

Andy turned to Fanko.

"I don't buy your theory, Detective. For one thing, you should know that the woman Davis Bates spent Christmas afternoon with was—"

"Olivia Brogan," he said. "We know. She called me shortly after I saw you earlier this evening. I would be interviewing her tonight, if not for events at the Mayflower and getting pulled into this meeting."

"Olivia Brogan called you?"

"My cell. Direct. The woman is wired. She's meeting me in the morning. Voluntarily. Do you mind telling me how you knew she was with Bates?"

"The bartender at Negotiation identified her from a photo I took at the memorial event this evening."

Fanko crafted an unfriendly squint to let Andy know what he thought of her investigating his case. *Screw you,* I thought. *It's not like you came up with it!*

"Like I said, I'll interview her in the morning. But I'm now looking at Rahn for the Bates homicide. I doubt that having a drink with one of her employees makes Olivia Brogan a person of interest. She told me she had a past personal relationship with Bates. She's probably lucky she didn't go home with him, or she'd be a victim, too."

"And the break-in?"

"Back to Theory One. A drive-by."

Andy wasn't buying it. She confronted Whitlock. "You lost track of

Rahn's brother, didn't you? You had him in a program, and you lost track of him. Until tonight."

"Technically, the program ended when Rahn's employer died in the boat accident. With Rahn certified as dead, with no case, with no threat, there was no reason for us to continue his brother's program. However, we don't let people go back, even if a threat terminates. We told him he had to keep his new identity, his new life."

"But...?"

Whitlock gave Andy a respectful nod. "Yes, there is a 'but.' We felt confident he would be safe. We downgraded our watch on him. We reassigned his supervising marshal. Until a week ago when he failed to respond to a routine check-in."

"But you were watching for him. At the Mayflower. You had people there. Your people picked him up on the street."

"Yes, we did."

I thought about the people hustling in and out of the hotel. And about the people who weren't hustling. People who were waiting. Watchful.

"Why?"

"Steggar Rahn is a schoolteacher. He's no master criminal. Three days ago, he slipped up when he used a credit card for a taxi to the Mayflower. We hoped he might return."

Andy shook her head.

"This isn't making sense. That's before I arrived. How could he know I would be there? If it's true that Mannis Rahn engineered the whole accidental suicide to get me here, that's one thing. But that doesn't explain his brother being there before it happened."

Andy tossed the ice pack off her knee and stood up. She paced the length of the room along the window, brushing a lock of hair from her eyes. She turned, brushed the lock aside again, and returned, deep in thought.

She stopped.

"I want to talk to him. The brother. Now."

The belligerent strand of hair fell again.

29

Andy stared at the man escorted into the room by Deputy Merrick. The tension in her posture made me glance at her weapon, still resting on the coffee table. I thought she might draw the Glock and shoot Rahn.

He strongly resembled the ghost whose face had been gracing my dining room table for the last few weeks. The hair was longer, not cut in a prison style. It sported more gray strands than Rahn's mug shot revealed. The nose seemed different. The expression was warmer, more human, but I wasn't sure that couldn't be turned on and off.

"Mr. Rahn, please take a seat," Chief Deputy Whitlock waved at a chair in our growing circle. She gestured for Andy to return to her seat. Andy did so reluctantly.

"How do you know who I am?" Andy demanded.

Rahn looked at Andy, then Whitlock, whose glance at Andy told him she had the same question.

"You must be Detective Stewart. I—I didn't know who you were. Not until the marshals told me why you were trying to arrest me. They said my brother tried to kill you."

"Then what are you doing stalking me here in D.C.?"

"There must be a misunderstanding. I haven't been stalking you."

"Then explain why you were at the Mayflower!"

Rahn swallowed. His eyes fell.

"My brother contacted me."

"What?!" Whitlock slid to the edge of her chair.

"That's impossible," Andy snapped at him. "You're in WITSEC. There's no way he could have found you."

"I *was* in WITSEC. When they told me Manny was dead, they said the program was ending, but that nothing had changed. I had to keep my new life, my new identity. But I needed closure. There were people in my life, from before, who needed to know. To them I simply disappeared." He looked pleadingly at Whitlock. "I know I wasn't supposed to—and I know now it was a mistake! I didn't think it would matter. I let some people back home know I was okay. I think my brother found out."

Whitlock and Merrick both blew out the same breath in frustration.

"I know! I know! It was a violation. I should have said something! Anyway, I...I got a package. A thumb drive with a Word document."

"From your brother?" Whitlock asked.

Rahn lowered his eyes and nodded.

"When?"

"A week ago."

"I want that drive," Whitlock said. "Dammit!"

"Of course."

"What did it say?"

"He gave me times and dates to meet him. Here. In D.C. at the Mayflower."

"Did he mention me?" Andy asked. "Specifically?"

"No! I told you, I didn't know anything about you! Manny told me to meet him there. I'm sorry. I didn't think anyone would believe me. I had to know. I had to prove it was him. I had to prove it to myself. I swear, if I saw him, I planned to turn him in! I swear!"

"Bull!" Andy snapped. "Why were you at the hotel tonight?"

"It was one of the meeting times he gave me! But when I saw all the police, I left!"

Andy stopped to think for a moment. I looked at the rise and fall of her chest as she drew and released each breath. I looked at the set of her jaw, and the way her lower lip gained prominence. I looked at the way her eyes locked on the man seated before her, the man with the face she had been studying for weeks. I looked at the war flag that fell across her right eye.

Oh, shit!

She leaned forward, scooped up her gun and took to her feet.

"Liar!"

With a move worthy of a magician, she freed the weapon from its holster and swung it to bear on Rahn.

"Whoa! Whoa!" I heard Merrick chant, but he sat frozen along with everyone else.

"I don't believe you," Andy said, steadying the weapon in both hands. "Chief Deputy, I believe this son of a bitch is Mannis Rahn."

"Detective," the Chief Deputy said softly, "please relax and put down the weapon." No one moved. "We can prove this is not the man you think he is."

"Let me," Rahn spoke, also softly. "Let me show you, Detective Stewart."

Andy did not flinch.

Rahn showed her both hands. Keeping his left hand elevated, palm forward, he slipped his right hand into his pants pocket and extracted a small folding knife.

"When I was seven, I thought the sun rose and set on my older brother. I begged him to take me to a set of railroad tracks near our home." Rahn slowly opened the knife. It was scarcely enough knife to trim fingernails. No threat whatsoever. Still, Andy rigidly held her weapon on Rahn. "We were playing. He told me where to stand, near a switch. And the next thing I knew, the switch moved. It crushed my ankle and trapped me. I screamed for my brother. He said he would get help, and he walked away. I cried for him to hurry, but he just kept saying, 'Don't worry. It'll come.' And then he was gone. The pain was excruciating. My foot was trapped between the steel rails. I knew the bones were crushed. I felt them. Grinding."

Rahn took a deep breath.

"And then the train came."

He stopped. He stared.

"I had a choice. I could stand and wait for it…"

For an instant I expected him to say he cut off his own foot with that silly little knife.

"Or I could lean over, sideways and break my own leg on the rail—then let the train run over it."

He closed his fist around the knife with the blade aimed downward. He raised his fist, and then drove it into his left shin. The impact made a dull *Thunk!*

A moment later he released his hand, leaving the knife stuck in his leg, or whatever he used for a leg.

"That's the day my brother took my leg. That's the day I learned he was a monster. And if that monster is coming for you, Detective Stewart, he will go through everyone you love to get to you."

PART II

30

"That was Pidge." Andy tucked away her phone. "Voicemail."

She looked tense and unhappy, about what I expected on my return to the Mayflower Hotel.

Andy stepped past the two marshals accompanying her and pulled me into a hug, reciprocal to mine. I caught sight of Detective Fanko, lingering near the front desk with men in suits, watching. For his benefit I threw a little extra into the embrace, adding a kiss. The marshals used the moment of intimacy to swing their eyes around the lobby and the street outside, searching for threats. Well after midnight, the lobby and sidewalk remained busy. Two MPD patrol units sat curbside along with what could only be unmarked squad cars.

"Trouble?" I asked when we came up for air. She pulled me close again.

"The nurse," Andy whispered. "Later."

Great.

"Ma'am, we would like to get you and your husband upstairs." One of the marshals grinned at us. I didn't recognize him. The team that had knocked Andy off her feet had been replaced by a new duo. The marshal's grin grew lecherous. "Out of public view."

He pointed at the elevator.

They led. We followed.

. . .

"So?" Andy latched the room door.

I stood close and examined her bruised cheek and the small Band-Aid applied beside her eyebrow. I wanted to touch. I wanted to make it better.

"Are you okay?"

"Honestly, it's nothing." She brushed at her hair. The stroke dropped a strand over the injury, as if to hide it.

"The knee?"

"I've done worse gardening. Come on, Pilot! Tell me!"

"Can we get room service? I'm starving," I said, pulling my tie free and tossing it in the general direction of my suitcase. Andy scooped it up, folded it, and put it in a zippered pocket. "Hamburgers. The works. With fries," I said. I pointed at the desk phone. "And you better let the palace guards outside know it's coming or they'll shoot the waiter. I need to make a pit stop." I headed for the bathroom, shedding my suit jacket and tossing it in a heap on the bed. "And see if you can get a couple Coronas with that!"

She crossed her arms and took a hard stance.

"Please?" I added.

A few minutes later, I emerged from the bathroom to find my jacket hung up and my wife sitting on the bed with her legs folded under her.

"The kitchen closed at eleven," she said.

"Dammit. Is the bar still open? We could go down—"

"They're not going to let us go down to the bar." She patted the mattress beside her. "Sit. Talk."

"Really? You think by getting me in bed you can get me to spill my—"

"Will!"

Too soon. I made a note.

I slipped off my boots, crawled up on the bed, propped up pillows for a backrest, and stretched out my legs.

Andy rotated to face me. Her black dress rode a little higher on her legs. She paid no attention and I tried hard to follow suit.

"So?"

I held up a hand.

"First things first. What about the woman? What happened?"

Andy lowered her eyes.

"What do you want to know? It's like they said."

"Andy."

She didn't look up.

"Dee." I reached for her, touched her chin. She met my gaze. "This isn't on you."

"I'm not an idiot!" she snapped. "Sorry. But Will, she was a single mom. Two girls. Not much older than Harriet and Elise. What do you want me to say? Bob. Lydia. Davis. This poor woman...what am I supposed to say?"

I didn't know.

"I know it's not on me," she sighed. "It's on Parks. It's on Rahn. But Parks will never be so much as inconvenienced by any of this. He's locked up in Montana. He won't even break a sweat unless a miracle happens and Rahn sells him out. And even if that happens, Parks will pay all the lawyers in the world to discredit Rahn."

"We'll get Rahn."

"Sure. We will. But—and I know this sounds wrong—but what's the point? If we get him, they'll haul him back to Montana to serve out his three lives. No one will lift a finger on behalf of Bob. Or Davis. Or Graciela Montoya. Worst of all, that poor woman. Even though we know it was him—so far, except for the missing key card, there's not one shred of evidence that it was anything but a bad fall. Not one."

"There's always something."

"Not so far."

"Video?"

"The cameras were sprayed by a man with a baseball cap who knew how to keep his face hidden. He created a path on his way in that got him out unseen."

"Did Lydia see him? Well enough to identify him?"

"No. I don't think he was expecting her there. She said he ran out once she started screaming."

"Ran? As in...ran? Not limped on one leg?"

Andy tipped her head at me. "Yes. Ran. I talked to her. I asked her, specifically. She saw no sign of a limp."

"There has to be something. There's always something."

"Not always. Which means even if—when—we catch the bastard, no one will be trying all that hard to make a case that gives Graciela Montoya justice."

I didn't question. Andy wouldn't make such an assertion without having tapped Fanko and his people for information.

"Will," she said. "I've never faced anything like this."

"He's not a superman."

"He kinda is! Until we can bring him in, Rahn has an unlimited free pass to murder anyone, anywhere, anytime. Because there are only two outcomes for him. Back to prison or evaporate and never be seen again. Death doesn't even count, because he's already dead! There will be no prosecution, no trial, no punishment—because there's no reason for anyone to spend the time or money."

"What's your point?"

"My point." She submerged one hand deep in the waves of her rich auburn hair, as if she could dig her fingers into her own skull and find the answer to my question. Her free hand reached for one of mine.

"I guess my point is...I'm not sure what to do. I feel like I usually know—at least *something*. But this...I'm supposed to be a Detective. It's what I wanted, so much, all this time. And here I am..." Her hand tightened on mine.

Andy doesn't handle defeat well. In any form. And I don't handle seeing her struggle. When she has a problem, I feel a need to fix it.

"Wait here. I have an idea."

Before she could protest, I bolted out of the room. Ten minutes later I returned with a bottle of Moscato and two glasses. The same marshal that suggested we "get a room" gave me a wry eye when I passed him in the hall.

I hopped back on the bed and poured.

"This is your solution?" she asked, goosing the question with a little bravado and a sliver of smile.

"When in doubt, drink, right?"

"I shouldn't..."

"Stop." I handed her a glass and we touched rims. I looked deep into her eyes, and she into mine. We each searched for and found something we needed. "Us."

"Us," she replied. We drank.

My wife is a lightweight and we hadn't eaten. I counted on a few sips of wine taking effect quickly.

"Come on, Divisible Man," she said. Her tone, a thin hair less tense, told me my plan was already working. "Out with it."

"You saw. They hustled Rahn out right after his little speech. Whitlock put a lid on him fast."

"You got my message, though. Right?"

"Jesus, Dee, standing there saying, 'I want to know where you're taking him!'—it was pretty clear that was meant for me, not Whitlock."

"Whitlock isn't telling me anything. They've reverted to lockdown, lockout WITSEC protocol."

"That's because in their eyes, you're a witness and a target, not an investigator."

"Says her. So?"

"No, I do not know where they're taking him."

Andy made a fist and punched the mattress.

"Crap!"

"Whoa there, sailor. Watch the foul language. Because although I do not know *exactly* where they're taking him, I do know *where* they plan to take him." I gave my pronouncement a dramatic beat, but she mustered simmering impatience making me cut it short. "Cedar Rapids, Iowa."

"Explain."

I told Andy that I had to scramble to follow Merrick and Rahn out of the lounge when Whitlock abruptly ended the conference.

"I was afraid they might use the elevator, but they took him to a corner office on the other side of the building. They put that rookie on the door to watch him."

"And?"

"Whitlock and Merrick adjourned to her office, so I followed them. I figured Rahn wasn't going to have much say about things."

"And?"

"And a lot of it was jargon. Shorthand. I didn't understand much."

"How could you not understand?"

"Dee, I'm not sure you get how this works. I can certainly disappear and float in a room to spy on someone, but that doesn't mean that someone is going to lay out their plans in precise detail like the villain in some cheap thriller. Whitlock and Merrick share a lot of common knowledge that's not going to be recapped for the benefit of the popcorn-eating audience."

"What *did* they say?"

"Rahn's current program stays static. Putting together a new program is some sort of financial and bureaucratic nightmare. They're hoping to grab Mannis Rahn first, so they won't have to. They talked manhunt. Here in D.C. The works."

"What else did they say?"

"The brother is being 'returned two-fourteen,' whatever the hell that means. Merrick needs to scramble a 'U-team,' whatever that is. He's going to get Bertram involved, whoever that is. See what I mean? It doesn't come with subtitles."

"Fine. What about Cedar Rapids?"

"Ah! That part I understood. Whitlock told Merrick to make 'it' happen, whatever 'it' is, and he went off to a cubicle. The guy works in a cubicle, Dee."

"As do I, dear."

"Right, but—well, yeah, okay. Anyway, Merrick dashed off to his cubicle, which is much smaller than yours, I'd like to point out. He logged into his computer."

"And you got his login and password!"

I folded my arms and made a face at my wife.

"Really? Did you ever watch someone touch-typing eight digits with random caps and special characters and try to memorize where their fingers landed? It's practically impossible."

"Okay."

"You'd have to video it, then study the video, and even then—"

"Okay! Okay!" Andy took another sip of wine. I did the same.

"But I did look over his shoulder at the screen. He logged into a U.S. Marshals administrative site and pulled up something called a Subject Transportation Order. An online form. He filled out a request for transport from Washington, D.C. to Cedar Rapids, Iowa. Tuesday. One subject, two marshals."

"New Year's Day. Commercial flight?"

"That was an option, but no. He marked it a High Priority with Whit-lock as the senior requesting agent. I assume the request was submitted to whatever bureaucratic Never-Never Land these things go to. I didn't think anything would happen and was about to get out of there, but it must've been hot, because it came back Confirmed in a matter of a minute or two. With an itinerary. They're leaving from the Signature Terminal at Dulles. Private."

"When?"

"Tuesday at noon. And..." I bounced my eyebrows. "I got the tail number."

Andy cocked her head to one side and gazed past me, into a distance, into the future.

"So, we know when and where he will be taken."

"Charlie India Delta. Cedar Rapids. Their ETA is around three p.m. Does that help?"

"Maybe," she said slowly. "They could be returning him to his original program location or to a safe house. I think Whitlock is doing her job. Putting us all under protection while she turns loose the dogs to apprehend Mannis Rahn."

"Good!"

Andy continued. "Protecting the brother. Protecting me as a witness against Parks. But I also think she wants me sidelined..."

"Good. Be sidelined!"

"...her and Fanko, both. That's why she wouldn't let me interrogate Rahn. That's why Fanko camped out here tonight. He's all in on the idea that Rahn staged the whole thing with Davis, but he wants to take charge of it."

"You talked to him?"

"I did. He wanted to know everything about Rahn, Parks, Cinnamon Hills, the works."

"You told him?"

Andy gave me a look. "Of course, I told him. He's a fellow officer conducting an investigation. I called the office to have them send him a copy of the file. Did you see he had company downstairs?"

"The two suits?"

"FBI. Whitlock brought them in. The *federales* are united in their pursuit of Rahn. I suspect Tom will be getting a call in the morning, if they didn't roll him out of bed tonight."

"Excellent! More resources."

"Of course." Andy was never one to mark turf and turn away help.

Being sidelined was something else. She looked up at me and something sparkled in her eye. "Oh, and Whitlock asked Fanko to put out a bolo for you."

"Really? My very own bolo? Cool. What did they say? Be on the lookout for a devastatingly handsome man with an incredibly brilliant mind?"

She cracked a smile and sipped the Moscato.

"Tall, dark and smoldering?"

"I told them we split up when we got back to the hotel. I told them you wanted to see the World War II Memorial and I was tired. Then I lost sight of you when everything hit the fan. If anyone asks, that's where you went tonight." She reached out and patted me on the leg. "As far as they know, Pilot, you missed all the excitement."

"Right." I studied her for a moment. She slipped into her distant look again. "Dee, what are you thinking?"

She shook her head, then lifted the wine to her lips and drew from it slowly.

I waited.

"Pidge says we have a problem with the nurse."

"Yikes! Change of subject whiplash. Did she say what?"

"Only that the Angel Flight nurse called the Essex Air office looking for you. Said it was important but wouldn't say what it was about. Said she needs to talk to you. In person."

"Who took the call?"

"Rosemary II."

"Did she leave a message?"

"No. She told Rosemary II she would find you."

None of this sounded good.

"Don't look at me like that," I said. "I didn't have a choice."

Andy shook her head. "I suppose you didn't. But this worries me. I was afraid this would bounce back."

"Focus on something light and cheerful. Like the multiple-murdering ghost we need to find before he finds you. Because it sounds like you don't endorse the notion of being sidelined."

"I do not."

"Can I take it you have some reason for wanting to know where they're taking the brother?"

"I want to talk to him. And I want to talk to Parks. Something about all this just isn't right. I'm calling Richardson to see if I can get access to Parks this week."

"This week?"

"Helena."

I must have looked stupid.

"Montana? I have to go to Helena. Remember?"

"Damn. That came up fast." I gave a low whistle.

"I know," she said. "We need to get some sleep, then we need to pack up and get out of here." She leaned over and poured the last half of her wine into my glass. "I had three people come up to me at that memorial thing to ask if I knew who was handling Davis's estate. Two of them gave me business cards! The third just gave me the creeps. I do not have time to get tangled up in his unfinished business!"

She made a move to slide off the bed.

I reached for her thigh and stopped her. For an instant, I think she read it as wanting her, wanting intimacy. I did, of course, but that wasn't the matter at hand.

"One more thing," I said. "This isn't great timing, but I think Lane might be headed for trouble."

31

Sunday morning, in the shower, it hit me that this year was nearly over and it couldn't happen a moment too soon. Standing under a hot stream, I cataloged the year's salient bumps and bruises. A broken pelvis. A suspended pilot's license. Job status and career path—indeed, the entire direction of my life—in question. An assassin pursuing my wife. But worst of all, the kicker that caught me where it counts—I just spent a night in a luxury hotel, got Andy lightly buzzed on Moscato, and slept with my wife. And by slept, I mean *slept*.

Andy is many things to me. Wife. Friend. Sounding board. Intellectual challenge. A professional I admire. A force to be reckoned with. A support system I rely on. She is also the woman I could not take my eyes off the day she walked into the offices of Essex County Air Services, or since. It may be a blessing. It may be a curse. But what she ignites in me is never more than an instant away, spawned by the slightest touch, the flicker of a glance, or the spark of imagination. It can be frustrating.

Wine or no wine, Andy was still tense when we turned off the lights sans extracurriculars. I held her close. She kept her Glock close. I drifted off before she did.

I decided, if given the opportunity, I would drop Mannis Rahn off a tall building. I let that thought cure by turning the shower stream from hot to cold.

. . .

ANDY BEGAN her day by telling me to suit up for the private viewing Lydia had arranged. She told me she confirmed that Davis had been delivered to the funeral home by the medical examiner's office as planned. It surprised me. I had expected the medical examiner to withdraw his release of the body, since the police now considered the Davis Bates suicide/accidental death a homicide.

Andy told me to pack my bag. She didn't explain.

At nine forty-five the family clustered in the lobby while Andy and Lydia argued with U.S. Marshal Esther King, a new face, and her partner about leaving the hotel, *en masse*, to drive to the funeral home. King stated she had instructions from Whitlock not to allow anyone to leave. Lydia applied a surly touch and demanded to know what possible authority she had to make anyone stay. Andy proposed a compromise by allowing the protection detail to join the family at the private viewing of Davis Bates' remains. The marshals agreed on the condition that transportation be provided by the U.S. Marshal Service.

That took another thirty-five minutes, most of which Andy spent explaining the situation to Davis's parents, who were still two causes of death behind.

I hoped for a caravan of black SUVs, dramatically trailing bumper to bumper through the nation's capital. Instead, a trio of late-model Chevy sedans arrived, and three new marshals joined King's detail. At the last minute Detective Fanko showed up to conduct his postponed interview with Lydia, only to catch us all climbing into government sedans in front of the hotel. I enjoyed the look on his face when Davis's parents assumed Fanko was part of the transportation plan and hopped in the back of his unmarked squad car.

The caravan wound its way through suburban neighborhoods, eventually finding a street lined with tall old oaks and a funeral home that looked like a Louisiana plantation mansion. The government cars filed onto a loop at the pillared entrance where the marshals circled the wagons. The only other cars on the property sat on a discrete parking lot at the side of the building.

When we exited the vehicles, Lydia's girls spotted me and charged, a storm of lace-accented dresses, hair in ribbons and sparkling tiny black shoes. I took a knee and scooped them up. They threw their arms around me and buried their faces in my neck. I hummed to them softly. Neither they nor I spoke.

Lydia joined us. She wore black, wore dark glasses, and looked pale. I don't know whether the sight of me holding her little girls reassured her or reminded her that they would not have a father in their lives. In any event, she put one hand on my arm for a moment, then moved toward the front door, braced by her sister. I let the girls down and they hurried to form a chain of held hands with their mother.

I hung back, letting Davis's parents and surviving brother follow Andy and Lydia. I gestured for Louis and Eleanor Taylor to proceed ahead of me. Two of the marshals joined the procession. Two more remained with the vehicles. Fanko sat behind the wheel of his sedan. I hoped he was fuming over being drafted into taxi service.

I was halfway up a set of steps when I spotted a woman standing beside a silver Toyota Prius in the parking lot. She watched the abbreviated processional without moving. If the sight of her concerned any of the marshals, they didn't act on it.

Inside the plush funeral parlor, I dropped back. I let Andy and her parents help Lydia with the girls. An open casket had been prepared at the far end of the long, empty room. The family approached it cautiously, silently, with the adults largely focused on the somber little girls.

I chose not to watch. I slipped back out the front doors into the chilly sunshine and worked on swallowing the sore lump in my throat.

The woman in the parking lot had not moved.

I took the front steps to the sidewalk and strolled toward her.

"I didn't want to intrude," she said as I approached. "Private viewing, I was told."

"Hello, Carla. I won't pass the test if you ask me your last name."

Carla of the Brogan Wayne Green Team extended her hand. "Stevens. You weren't told my last name last night."

"I'm sure you'd be welcome to come in."

"I'm sure I wouldn't. Lydia would take it as a sign I was screwing her husband and had come to dramatically mourn the lost future he promised me upon leaving his wife."

"Were you?"

"Gak! Please. Not his type. Do I look like a bimbo? Don't answer that.

No, I did not spread my legs for that meat hook husband of hers. I'm prom clean-up committee, not prom court."

"Okay. You weren't in the rotation. You seem to hate the guy. So then, what? You just like hanging around funerals?"

"The first word in funeral is fun." She folded both hands across the straps of her purse and gazed at the building.

I took the moment to sweep across the front of the building and the street. My survey stopped on a parked SUV with blackened windows. It looked out of place on the otherwise empty street.

"You might not be the only one who thinks so." I flicked my eyes in the direction of the vehicle. She caught on quickly and stole a glance at it during the shake of her head.

"And by the way, no, I actually didn't hate the guy. Everything he stood for, yes. But he was honest about his utter lack of integrity. It's so bad in this town that actually means something."

I gave her a moment she seemed to need. She stole a second glance at the parked vehicle.

"I heard a rumor that Lydia was attacked last night," she said. "But it's your wife that they're really after."

Andy taught me not to fall for conversational prompts. I remained silent. It caused Carla to glance at me.

"Is that why you have the Secret Service protection?"

"U.S. Marshals."

"Ah. Because she's a witness against Parks." Carla nodded her head. The gesture looked like someone tapping an idea into its proper slot. "I also heard a rumor that Davis didn't dumbass himself to death. Is that true?"

"Looks that way."

Again, she nodded her head. Again, I waited.

"Okay," she said abruptly. "Good talk."

She reached in her purse and pulled out her keys, wheeling for the Prius driver's side door.

"Whoa, whoa. Hold up there, Carla Stevens. That's it? You came here to pluck a few pieces of intelligence?"

"That's what makes this town tick."

"Why?"

"I blame Andrew Jackson," she quipped.

163

I folded my arms. It stopped her.

"Let me ask you a 'why?' question," she said. "Why should I answer you? Or talk to you at all? Why shouldn't I cherry pick intelligence from you and then just leave? You're leaving. You're going back to Mayberry and flying your little airplanes while your wife, seriously you call her Andy, plays sheriff. Where you're concerned, whatever happened to Davis is just a chip in the family tree. And from all indications, good riddance. So why should I share anything with you?"

"Because that's what you really came here for. To share. Maybe not with me. Maybe you'd rather talk to my wife. But don't call her 'sheriff' if you want to stay in the conversation. You came here to share something, not gather. You already had confirmation that MPD is treating Bates as a homicide. I'm pretty sure you're about as wired into the police as Olivia Brogan."

She laughed. "Oh, no! That woman knows things before the desk sergeants, and they know everything."

"Okay. What did you come to share? Or should I go get Andy? Or maybe that MPD detective sitting in the Crown Vic over there?"

She cracked a wry smile.

"You'll do."

She took another moment to stare at the building, or perhaps to stare through the walls at the scene of death and mourning inside. I began to wonder, as I had with her employer, how much of this drama was manipulation.

She leaned on her silver Prius.

"We fight," she began, "and fight. Calling staffers. Calling senators. Mustering constituents. You probably picture lobbyists hanging around the halls up on The Hill or putting expensive martinis on our Gold MasterCards, but ninety-nine percent of what we do is in a cubicle on the phone. Begging, borrowing and stealing favors to convince some small-time construction millionaire who decided to run for Congress that wetland protections should not be eliminated so that guys like him can build more condos. We fight, and then we lose. And then we fight some more. And then we lose some more."

"Sounds...frustrating?"

"Anybody who gets frustrated burns out within six months. Frustration is a crutch for amateurs. We simply go on. Like surgeons who don't quit just because someone dies on the table. At least as long as Olivia— God only knows why—stays the course. We're like some sort of crusade to her. She just keeps coming back for more. Taking on new groups. New causes. Piling it on us. We get fired up again, we fight. And then we lose.

"Here's the thing. Lately, even when we have something solid, something we might, in our wildest optimism-drugged dreams, call a sure thing —we've been losing. Congressmen and Senators we thought we had in our pocket, flip at the last minute. Votes we thought we could count on, for show if nothing else, evaporate."

"Are you getting outmaneuvered?"

"Yes. But not the way you think. That wetland example, that was a real issue. And we had it in the bag. Partly because the construction lobby wasn't paying attention. The issue was under their radar. We had a bill, we had sponsors, we had support. We had it all framed up for them, packaged as a win the hypocrites could take back to their districts and wave around showing how much they love Mother Earth, you know?"

"What happened?"

"We lost. They flipped."

"Payoffs?"

"Worse. We lost to The People."

"What people?"

She pointed at me. "We, The People. You. Joe Lunchbox. Mr. and Mrs. America. One after another, the staffers showed us the numbers. Their districts had spoken. We heard the term 'flood' over and over. Like someone waved a wand and The People rose up in droves to beg their representatives to vote in favor of building condos on wetlands, when even Big Construction overlooked the issue."

"Rose up? How?"

"Letters. Emails. Tweets. Facebook messaging. Social media. All those idealists who dream of a pure democracy are getting it, and it's not yielding the utopia they expected."

"Louisville Mass Transit," I said.

She blinked at me.

"My lord, Mr. Stewart! You know how to read!"

"People leave copies of *The New York Times* laying around in the bathroom."

"Well, you're close. But unlike Louisville, we couldn't pinpoint the

PAC pulling the strings. Louisville Mass Transit went down in flames because those two billionaire brothers used their PAC money to pretend to be a grassroots effort. They painted a progressive and well-conceived mass transit plan as a big tax debacle for the hardworking taxpayers. An utter lie. They—"

"I know the story," I interrupted her. "They own automotive companies. Mass transit is bad for the seatbelt business. So, what are you saying?"

"I'm saying that more and more, we're being told that our initiatives flamed out because 'The People' spoke. The People demanded a reduction in clean air standards. The People demanded fewer FDA inspectors. The People demanded legislation that bars litigation for tainted pharmaceuticals. Are you seeing a pattern?"

"Are you coming to me with a conspiracy theory? Because that's precisely how it sounds."

"Of course, it is! Funny, that's what we all think when we're drowning another loss in cheap vodka. Yet Olivia doubles down. She shrugs it off and brings on the next issue, and the next. She adds staff and continues the fight."

"Then put her up for sainthood. She's doing what's right. Sticking to the moral high ground. Picking up the banner for lost causes."

"Yeah. While she keeps cutting the original gene pool. Davis Bates and half a dozen of his kind were all that's left. Old school backroom handshake pumpers taking money from the think tanks and the PACs and the phony foundations. We keep expecting the opposite. That she'll get tired of losing, and losing money, and fire the lot of us."

"I might read *The Times* occasionally, but I'm still that hick from Mayberry, and I have to be honest. I don't have a clue where you're going with this. Or why you think I need to hear it."

"No," she said, shaking her head sadly. "I'm sure you don't. This was a waste of time."

"Because you think I don't understand?"

"Because I think *I* don't understand," she said. "I honestly don't get it."

She glanced at the building again.

"Look. I was one of the few people on our side of the firm who traded a civil word with Davis Bates from time to time, and you know what? He never gloated. He never shoved it in my face when we would lose. But he always had this—I don't know—glint in his eye. Like he knew something none of us knew."

"So?"

"So, if you know something no one else knows...in this town? It can make you rich. Or it can get you killed."

"That's not what got Davis Bates killed," I said.

"What then?"

I didn't want to say it.

My wife thinks she got him killed.

"Any chance I could get your phone number?" I asked.

32

Carla Stevens drove her Prius out of the lot and turned left onto the street, swinging away from the parked SUV. I watched her go with my hands stuffed in my trouser pockets, trying to look bored. Like someone looking for a way to avoid going back into a funeral, I turned and wandered across the lot, away from the street, toward the back of the property. The funeral home thoughtfully provided a meditation garden and path in its backyard and I took full advantage, strolling a narrow gravel path in no particular hurry, until I was sure I was out of the SUV's line of sight.

The path turned nicely between two rows of arborvitae. Abundant shelter from outside eyes.

Fwooomp! As I vanished I pulled a FLOP unit from inside my suit jacket. I snapped the prop in place and thumbed the slide control forward. A low growl immediately pulled me forward. I angled up, between the evergreens that stood a solid thirty feet tall.

The neighborhood had old-growth oaks and an insidious collection of power lines up and down the streets. The funeral home itself rose to two stories. Once I cleared the tops of the evergreens, I reassessed and aimed myself down again. I leveled off a foot or two above the path and back-tracked to the parking lot.

I goosed the power with a shot that sent me gliding toward the street, then silenced the unit. The vector took me past the driveway loop, past the parked marshals' cars and past Fanko's unit, where he sat with his nose down, adopting the common modern pose of being absorbed in a device.

I crossed the sidewalk and floated into the open street, careful to clear for traffic. As if out of respect for the proceedings inside, nothing moved on the street in front of the funeral home.

Easing over the second lane, I pocketed the FLOP and put my arms out to catch the trunk of a tree. I stopped. Trees lined the space between the sidewalk and street, spaced forty or fifty feet apart. Holding position, I reached in another pocket and drew my phone. I found the round button at the base and double-clicked it. I gave it a moment, then found one of the side buttons and pushed.

Click-click!

The camera made its signature sound.

Phone in hand, I worked around the trunk of the tree and launched on a trajectory parallel to the sidewalk, gliding just above the crisp grass to the next tree trunk.

The SUV sat a dozen feet from the tree trunk. A driver mimicked Fanko's pose, head down over a phone or device. The side and rear windows were heavily tinted, but I could see a silhouette in the rear right seat. The face in profile watched the funeral home across the street.

I gave myself a push and floated the short distance between the tree trunk and the black front left fender. Touching it lightly, I adjusted my path. Scarcely moving, I passed the driver's side window close enough to breath on it. I passed the A-pillar and slipped my hand into the left rear door handle.

I stopped.

Camera ready. I closed a grip on the door handle. Fifty-fifty shot, I thought.

I pulled.

The door latch released. Bracing a foot against the rear wheel arch, I pulled the door fully open.

Startled, the rear seat occupant snapped his head around to face the empty door space. In my peripheral vision, the driver's posture went to full alert, and his face filled the side mirror, searching.

Tick-a-tick-a-tick-a-tick-at— The camera chattered out a multi-shot sequence as I held it up, hoping I had the frame properly placed.

"David!" the occupant spoke up.

"On it, sir!" The driver's door snapped open.

I pushed back. The driver swung his legs out and took a stance beside the door, one hand diving under his jacket reflexively. He searched the space beside the open door, then the sidewalk, then quickly pushed the rear door shut.

I drifted backward. The driver dashed to the rear of the vehicle, edging around it like a soldier taking a corner in an urban firefight. Finding nothing, he searched the street again.

The rear seat occupant pounded on the glass of the door I had opened, drawing the driver back into the vehicle. A moment later the engine ignited and the big V8 pulled it away in a harsh hurry.

"Learn to lock your doors, idiot," I muttered, holding up the camera and holding down the shutter button again. It chattered, catching the back of the SUV as it shrank into the distance.

33

"Where did you disappear to?" Andy asked pointedly.

"Tell you later." I held open the big entrance door. Instead of exiting, Andy took Davis's parents aside and introduced them to the funeral director. Without leaving room for debate, she transferred responsibility for Davis's remains to his family. Before they could pepper her with questions, she announced we were leaving. With me still acting the doorman, Andy shepherded Lydia, the children and her parents out of the building to the waiting sedans.

Curbside, Andy directed the marshals to take us to the airport. Marshal King pulled out her cell phone to call up the chain of command for instructions.

Andy's mother protested. "What about our bags?"

Andy gestured at Marshal King. "These kind public servants will ship them home for you."

"I have my things! My—!"

"Mother, there's nothing in your room at the Mayflower that cannot be replaced."

Moving out of earshot of the marshals, Andy pulled her father aside and said softly, "Daddy, when we get to the airport, I want you to take Mom, Lydia and the girls to a certain, magical special destination."

Louis Taylor fixed a serious gaze on his daughter. I waited for patronizing dismissal. He stayed silent, but her mother delivered.

"Nonsense Andrea, we already have our tickets for to—"

"Hush, Eleanor!" Louis said sharply. To Andy, he asked, "Are you telling me to take them—?"

"Don't say it!" Andy interrupted, glancing at the marshals. Her father closed his mouth and nodded.

King leaned into the conversation.

"Chief Deputy Whitlock wants you to return to the hotel."

"I'm sorry, Marshal King, but I'm taking over security for my family."

"This is a mistake, Detective," the marshal warned her.

"No, it isn't."

Andy gave King the choice of driving us or seeing us load up in Ubers.

34

At the airport, Louis Taylor continued to surprise me. After the marshals reluctantly delivered us to the departure terminal, Andy's father handed Andy the keys to his Mercedes and folded a wad of cash into his daughter's hand.

He pulled Andy into an embrace, then turned to me and offered his hand. I took it firmly. He fixed his granite gaze on my face.

"Keep an eye on her," he ordered me.

"I will," I promised.

"Daddy don't contact anyone but me. It won't be easy but see if you can pay cash. All the way. Don't use credit cards—except for a rental car. That shouldn't matter. Remember what I said about phones. Are you okay with that?"

"I am," he said firmly. I stared at Andy's father, scarcely recognizing him. He gave me an unexpected nod and asked Andy, "What about you?"

"Will and I are returning to Essex."

"Is that safe?"

"I hope not."

With his wife still protesting, Andy's father gathered his family and headed in the direction of the ticket agents, a man with an assignment and the determination to complete it.

I stood slack-jawed.

"Jesus Christ, what just happened?"

"Dad and I talked last night. In the bar. While I was waiting for you. I explained to him about Rahn."

"And?"

She watched them go. She waved when Harriet and Elise looked back, each girl clutching her mother with one hand and a favorite doll with the other.

"And he listened." She said nothing more. She looked at me and I caught a glitter in her eye. She wiped it away, then hooked my arm and headed toward a Southwest ticket counter to get us home.

We arrived in Essex eleven hours later.

35

A few minutes before midnight, Sandy Stone met us at the door to her home on Leander Lake. She looked strong and healthy. I felt a flicker of shame for making an automatic comparison to the way I'd seen her when Andy and I found her drugged and near death at Pearce Parks' ranch in Montana. Sooner or later I would have to retire that image.

A light snow had been falling for the last hour of our drive up from Milwaukee. We stomped it off our shoes before entering the elegant house.

"I'm so sorry to do this at this hour," Andy repeated the apology she had given Sandy on the phone as we drove out of Milwaukee.

"Stop!" Sandy commanded. "Give me your coat. I have hot cocoa and cold wine. Or Kahlua for your cocoa if you're inclined. And not another word of apology from you!"

"Hey, Sarge!" Mike Mackiejewski, wearing his patrol uniform, stepped into Sandy's front hall from the direction of the kitchen. He carried a mug in one hand and a department-issue shotgun in the other. "Hey, Will!"

We returned the greeting. Mike spread a boyish grin across his face and drew from the mug. Tough duty.

Andy was not pleased.

"Jesus, Mike! You let her answer the door?"

"I had you covered coming up the driveway, Sarge." Mike waved at a sunroom extension that fronted the house off the dining room.

Andy considered the angles and seemed mollified.

"Is she here?" Andy gestured at the second floor.

"Sleeping," Sandy said. "Poor girl. She's scared."

Sandy's assessment of Melanie didn't surprise me.

"Let's go in the kitchen. It's quieter."

We clustered around a counter height island. In warm, subdued light, Sandy poured cocoa and offered Kahlua. Everyone declined the Kahlua.

Andy jumped right to it. "I want you to pack a go-bag. You and Melanie. Mike, I want you to get them out of here. Take them to the station. The Chief will meet you there."

"At this hour?" Sandy shook her head. "For how long?"

"Indefinite."

"Andy, I can't just take off like that! School starts on Wednesday."

"Sweetie, there is a man coming to kill me, and he would just as soon blink as kill you, too. He's coming. Period. You no longer have a choice."

Mike gave out a low whistle.

"Yeah," Andy said to her subordinate. "It's real. When you drive her to the station, don't stop for anyone or anything. No matter what. Even if it's someone you think you recognize. Situational awareness, Mike. Got it?"

"Got it."

"No, Mike, I mean it. This guy likes to stage accidents. Stop for nothing. You see someone bleeding in the road, you keep going and call it in!"

"Jeez, Sarge, how hot is this?"

"Hot. We left Washington, D.C. abruptly, and it may have taken the man I'm talking about by surprise, but that won't last. I want Sandy gone before he knows it."

"Gone where?" Sandy asked.

"Tom has that worked out. Take enough clothes for a few days. If you need more after that, we'll make all the arrangements. Okay?"

Sandy made a face but nodded.

"There's something else," Andy said. "What's left of the foundation funds from Chicago?"

"Well, if you two board members would show up for a meeting—*ever* —you wouldn't have to ask," Sandy chided.

"How many meetings do I have to miss before I get kicked off the board?" I asked.

Both women ignored my question.

"Of the sixteen million from Chicago, fifteen million, thirty-seven thousand dollars has been returned to the Monroe School District. And might I add that the Chicago city attorney was not very happy about that. You called it, Will."

"Screw 'em if they can't take a joke."

"That means, of the Chicago funds, nine hundred sixty-three thousand dollars remain," Andy calculated. "I want access to the money."

If the request surprised Sandy, she didn't show it.

"That's no problem. I can transfer funds to a different account, or we can add your name to the existing account."

Andy gave it some thought. "What about a debit card?"

"Well," Sandy said, "the bank issued one in my name, which I thought was silly. It's not like I would ever go shopping with those funds. Any formal distributions will be by certified check. I can get a card issued in your name, though."

Andy shook her head. "There isn't time. Can you give me the card you have?"

"Certainly," Sandy said.

"Only for the Chicago funds," Andy assured Sandy. "And you will get a full accounting."

"Honey, it's my opinion that you and Will should take the money and blow it on umbrella drinks in a warm place. Really. I can ask the accountant to work out a lump sum payment and figure out the tax liability up front."

The notion horrified Andy and she said so.

Sandy wasn't deterred. "You seem to forget that, except for Earl, the only people we answer to for distribution of the foundation money are sitting in this kitchen."

"I know," Andy conceded. "But I also know you want every penny of it to be put to the best possible use."

"No matter what you do with it, I consider it good use. We have a quorum here. All in favor of turning it over to Will and Andy, signify by saying 'Aye!'" Sandy raised her hand. I raised mine.

"No!" Andy grabbed my hand and pulled it down. "Absolutely not!

It's just—for once I'd like to cover some outside expenses without having to put in for it from the Department."

"Doesn't matter. The motion passes."

"No," my wife said.

"You're overruled!"

"What kind of expenses?" Mike asked.

Andy looked at me.

"We need to steal one of Earl's airplanes again," Andy said. "Only this time I want to pay him for it."

36

"She's in the fucking lounge."

Pidge met me at the Essex County Air Services front door.

"Who?"

"Christie. The nurse, dumbass. She was here before seven this morning, waiting for you." Pidge thumbed in the direction of the lounge across the hall from the office counter.

I took a deep breath. Partly to stall while trying to come up with a way to avoid the woman. Partly to confirm that Rosemary II had a pot of her superb coffee brewing.

"Why did you bring her here?"

"I didn't! I dropped her in Marshfield when we came back from Bemidji! She came here on her own."

"Why don't you handle her?" I asked Pidge. "You're big old drinking buddies now."

"Don't remind me!"

"Pidge, I can't deal with this now. Andy will be here any minute, and we need to get going. Go tell her—I don't know—anything!"

"Fuck you. She says she's not leaving until she talks to you." Pidge turned her back to me and bounced away, in a direction opposite the pilot's lounge. "I'll preflight One One Kilo." She flipped me the finger before disappearing down the hall toward the main hangar.

I dropped my flight bag next to the counter and unzipped my leather jacket. I could hear Rosemary II moving around the inner office. Earl's car occupied his space in the lot, which meant he was in his office, the next door down the hall. I hurried past the open lounge door to avoid being seen, catching a glimpse of the woman sitting in one of the plush chairs paging through a magazine.

"Hey, Boss," I rapped on Earl's door.

Earl Jackson wasn't in his office chair.

"'Bout time you called me Boss," Dave Peterson said, looking up from an operations binder. He had a flurry of manifest sheets spread across Earl's desk and a look of interrupted concentration on his wide, rugged face.

"I'll call you Sweet Cheeks and sing you a lullaby if you permanently take over filing all the manifests," I said. During my sabbatical from the cockpit, I'd done more than my share of paperwork in the office. "Where's the old man?"

"He and Doc flew over to Chilton to pick up the radios for that Four-Twenty-One. They're supposedly fixed. Again. Third time's the charm, I guess. What's up?"

"Police business. Charlie India Delta."

"What's in Cedar Rapids?"

"If I tell you…"

Dave knew the punchline.

"I heard you and Andy are on a tear. You taking Pidge?"

"Until Uncle Sam blesses me with my damned license again."

"I don't know why you bother. Nobody's going to ramp check you."

"It's Andy's thing. A cop thing. Being legal when on police business, for some reason."

Dave nodded but graciously didn't pursue discussion of my license. I felt like I'd been talked to death about when the FAA Aeromedical Branch in Oklahoma City would get off its ass and reissue my medical certificate.

"You have a visitor."

"I saw."

"She doesn't seem to want to talk about whatever she wants to talk about. Is she having your love child?"

"Twins. Don't tell Andy. Speaking of whom, I need to go. Are you booked out today?"

"Pontiac again. In the King Air. Getting to be a regular route."

"Nothing wrong with that. Later!"

I started to duck out the door.

"Hey!" Dave waved at me to come back. He lowered his voice. "Close the door."

I did.

He picked up a pen and tapped it on the binder, a nervous tick I'd seen him perform during checkrides I'd given him.

"I want to ask you something."

"Shoot."

He swallowed, looked past me to make sure the door was closed, and tapped the pen a few more times.

"Dude, out with it."

"Okay," he said. He swallowed again. "Andy's friend. Sandra. Is she...? You know. Is there...?"

"An ex-fiancée and momentary husband who recently tried to kill her on her honeymoon? Um, yeah."

"I know that! I just wondered if there was anybody..."

"New? Are you asking if Andy can set you up with Sandy Stone?"

"I—uh—I dunno," he stammered. "I guess not. I suppose that whole bad business was pretty recent."

"Oh, do you think? And do you think she might hold it against you that you were on the flight crew that delivered her to her near death?"

I immediately wished I hadn't said it.

"Yeah, you're right." He flipped the pen up onto the desk. "I just thought, maybe—I don't know what I thought."

Crap. He looked like the kid who didn't get picked at the dance. I felt low for reminding him of his role in the worst experience of Sandy's life. None of that was Dave's fault.

I shrugged.

"Give her a little time, bud. She's been through the wringer. She's outta town for a while, but maybe in a few months, when we have one of those damned foundation meetings she's always scheduling, who knows? Maybe I can take you along as my valet."

Dave looked at me like I just announced Christmas.

"I gotta go."

"Thanks!"

. . .

I AVOIDED the pilot's lounge and took the long way around to the main hangar where I expected to find Pidge preflighting the Piper Mojave that Andy booked for the flight to Cedar Rapids.

I found Pidge leaning on the leading edge of the wing with her cell phone to her ear.

"What are you doing? Andy will be here any minute!"

She pushed the phone toward me.

"Talk to your wife."

I took the phone.

"Hello?"

"Will, we have to delay."

I didn't understand. It had been Andy's idea to rush off to Cedar Rapids today and spend the night to ensure we didn't miss the team of marshals delivering Steggar Rahn to his destination. If we missed the arrival, we missed any chance of finding out where they were keeping him.

"Why?"

"I need to help Lane buy a dress."

"A what?"

37

She was older than I remembered. In my mind's eye, she had been in her mid-twenties, blonde and possessed of a grim professional presence. Seeing her again, I upped her age into early attractive forties and attributed the professional affect to Angel Flight circumstances. I also, absurdly, expected to find the Angel Flight nurse sitting in the pilot's lounge wearing scrubs. She wore jeans and a heavy sweater, and the blonde hair I remembered was reddish gold and tied back.

I closed the door quickly behind me.

"Hi," I said. "We never formally met. I'm Will Stewart."

"Christie Watkins." We traded an awkward handshake.

"Did you get coffee? It's surprisingly good, for an airport FBO."

"I'm fine." She gestured at a mug holding down a coaster on the coffee table. She stared at me.

"Look," I said, "maybe we should get something out of the way."

"Maybe we should."

She held her eyes on me.

"Okay."

Fwooomp! I vanished. She jumped and then threw her hand over her mouth, the same gesture I last saw in the plane over Marshfield.

Before the weightlessness could lift me too far off the carpet, I reappeared.

Fwooomp!

She shivered. I reached out and put a hand on her forearm.

"Let's sit down, okay?"

She bobbed her head and backed into one of the leather chairs. I took a seat on the sofa to her right.

"I had this whole speech in my head," she said. "Now I can't remember a word of it."

"I get that. It's weird. This thing. But I really need you to—"

"Oh, I know! I know! Don't worry, I made a promise and I intend to keep it. I don't want you to worry! Also, I spent a very long night with your friend, Pidge. She made clear what she would do to me if I blabbed about all…this. My word! That girl has a mouth!"

"She does." I laughed.

I let her pick up the laugh and we both used it to ease the tension. She settled in her seat.

"So, you're wondering why I'm here."

I tipped my head back and forth. "Not that much. I get that you needed to know it really happened. But before you ask me a lot of questions, I have to tell you that I can't answer them."

"It's secret?"

"Yeah." It was. It was a giant secret, particularly from me. "I can't say anything more than that."

"Sure. Yeah. I get that. Um—but I have to ask about the side effect. I really need to know. Will, that's the only reason I came here today. I swear. And I swear I will never tell a soul. Not after what you did. And I never would ever, *ever* have bothered you again, but medically speaking…"

It never occurred to me that she would look at me as a medical professional. Dr. Stephenson had his questions. Dozens of them. But thinking back on my consultation with him, the question of side effects never came up.

"It's not something I worry about," I said. "Hasn't affected me, if that's what you're asking."

She blinked, uncomprehending.

"No, I—uh, I mean—I wasn't asking that. Oh, I see!" She shook her head vigorously. "I was talking about Emma Parrish."

I drew a blank and spread my hands to show it.

"The little girl! On the plane!"

"Oh," I said. "Sorry. I never got her name."

It suddenly struck me.

Side effects...

"Is she okay? She was okay when I dropped her off! I mean, I handed her off to a nurse and she was awake. I didn't think the—you know —*flight* hurt her."

The dawning look of wonder and confusion on her face took me aback.

"You don't know," she said. Her hand went to her mouth again, and tears came to her eyes. For an instant, I saw her in the Mojave cabin again, crying.

Oh, God, no.

Like a cold steel punch to the gut, I realized what she was asking. Side effects. In my arrogance and over-confidence, I had taken an action without thinking through the consequences. I had thought only about delivering the child to the hospital.

I felt sick.

"She—" My mouth went dry. "She didn't make it?"

"Oh, my God! No! I mean, yes! But, no, that's not what I meant. I— she's fine. She made it just fine, thanks to you!"

I blew out a breath. My skin felt cold and my mouth arid. "Jesus Christ!"

"Oh, I'm so sorry! I didn't mean to—" She stopped. She reached out and put her hand on my knee, a practiced and professional gesture of tenderness. But the dampness in her eyes was genuine. "You don't know, do you."

"Know what?"

"Her condition."

"Christie, you're killing me. Spit it out. Are you telling me that this child is now—like me?"

"No! No, I don't think so. No, that's not it at all."

"So?"

She sat back again.

"What do you know about Polycythemia Vera?"

"That I should take childhood diseases for one hundred, Alex."

"Polycythemia Vera is a condition that results from a mutation of a gene called jak2."

"Jack-too?"

"J-A-K-T-W-O. It's a—"

"Whoa. Stop the train. You're looking at a genuine high school graduate, and instead of biology, I took chemistry. And all I know about chemistry is that I have it with my wife. You're going to have to dumb this down for me."

Christie held up two hands in surrender.

"Okay. Polycythemia Vera is when the bone marrow produces too many red blood cells. It leads to a thickening of the blood."

"Is that what the girl has?"

"Yes. Polycythemia Vera cannot be cured. In most cases it's treated with phlebotomy, which is the transfer of certain amounts of blood."

"Transfusion."

"Uh-huh. But in certain cases, and I'll skip the details—"

"Please."

"In certain cases, because of blood clots and other issues, phlebotomy doesn't work. In those cases, a regimen of chemotherapy is prescribed to stop the excess production of red blood cells. But it doesn't always work."

I pictured Emma Parrish. Her thin skin. Her wide eyes looking up at me.

"And?"

"And it can turn into Acute Myeloid Leukemia."

Certain words have power. Leukemia was one of them.

"Our little passenger was well on her way past Polycythemia Vera into Acute Myeloid Leukemia. She hasn't been responding to treatment. In a way, she got behind the treatment curve." Christie let the point stick the landing.

I felt my pulse throbbing in my temples.

"Christie, we did everything we could! I may have called it a Christmas Miracle, but I only meant the part about getting her down. There was no way—"

"Will!" She put up a hand like a stop sign. I froze. She reached in her purse and pulled out her phone. After thumbing the screen, she flipped it around and held it up for me to see.

Emma Parish, the angel from my Angel Flight, smiled brightly at the phone. Her flesh looked pink, her cheeks had color. Her eyes had light. She clutched one of the ugliest stuffed monkeys I've ever seen as if it were the Christ child himself. Love and a fierce grip on life met the lens of the camera.

"Look at her."

I did.

"She made it? The therapy worked?"

"No," Christie said. Her chin quivered. Her voice broke. "They never performed the therapy. This is the girl you handed over to the nurses on Christmas Eve."

Smiling. Alive.

"She—I thought—I—"

The image reminded me of Harriet and Elise. I looked at Christie the Nurse for answers, but all she could give me was rain. It ran down her cheeks to her quivering chin.

"You did this. It had to be you! Did you know?"

Holy shit!

CHRISTIE COMPOSED herself drawing from a box of Kleenex on the coffee table. I took to my feet and paced the length of the pilot lounge.

"Her red blood cell count was elevated, but no more than you would have if you were dehydrated. And there is no sign of leukemia. None."

I paced. Stopped. Repeated.

"They didn't treat her, Will. They didn't know what to do with her, except give her ice cream and wait for her mother. They practically drained her, taking blood samples. There's no explanation. Except…"

I waved my hands in protest.

"Look, I have no idea what her deal is," I said. "And I have no idea what my deal is either, to be honest. I can do this thing, okay? That's as much as I know."

"You've never had anything else like this happen? Any medical effect that—I don't know—had no explanation?"

"No."

A lie.

Lydia.

Lydia drowned.

Lydia starved of oxygen. Lydia showing up in a hospital with blood oxygen levels that made no sense.

"You're jumping to a conclusion here, Christie. It's coincidence. That's all. The kid went into remission."

"Oh, so now you're the oncology nurse? Please. And I may have almost destroyed my liver with your friend Pidge, but I am a remarkably lucid drunk with a good memory. I know what I saw. I know what Pidge told me. You're the wild card here, Will Stewart. When I handed that girl over to you—*God! What was I thinking!?*—she was *this close, this close* to shutting down. Do you think for a moment I would have let you do what you did if I had any other option?"

I stopped pacing. I stared at her.

"Nursing is science. It's my chosen field. I'm not a bimbo in a pointy hat looking to marry a rich doctor. I know what I saw. I know what followed. I might be the only one who knows, but *I know.*"

I let it sink in, then strolled to the couch and sat down beside her.

"What's your point?"

"I'm not here to out you."

"Thank you."

"I'm grateful. For that girl's life," she said slowly. "But I want to know if what you did...if that's...*something you can do?*"

"I have no idea." She looked at me for more. "Really. I have no idea. I had no idea that would happen. And to be fair, I have no idea it did happen. I have no idea or proof that what you're saying has anything to do with me."

"Then let's find out!"

I blinked at her. This was going way too fast.

"Let's find out! Will, if you can do this for children—think of it!"

"Do what?"

"Do what you did! Cure them!"

"Hang on! You're making a colossal assumption based on what may have been a huge coincidence."

She pushed herself to the edge of her seat.

"Yes! I am! Why do you think I came here!"

I started to rise again, feeling a renewed need to pace. She grabbed my hands and stopped me.

"Will, please! I agree with you, there's no proof one way or another.

Maybe it was you, maybe it was the Little Lord Jesus. All I know is what I saw in that plane, and what I saw in Marshfield. That girl is the Christmas Miracle you said she would be. I spent two days drunk out of my mind because I didn't want to believe what I saw. I'm still hung over. But I need to know. And I think you need to know."

My mind reeled.

"What do you want?" I asked.

She clutched my hands.

"Come with me. To Children's. In Milwaukee. Come with me and do it again!"

"No."

It wasn't what she expected.

"No," I repeated.

"You would let children die?"

"Wow." I pulled my hands free.

"I'm sorry!" She pulled them back into her grasp again. "I'm sorry! I didn't mean that!"

"There is so much here you don't know," I said. "So much here I don't know."

"You're right."

"And what happens if it doesn't work? Or just as bad—what happens if it does?"

Now she let go. She sat back in her chair. She took another Kleenex and wiped her eyes.

"That's not what you're asking. You want to know if I'll keep my promise."

"Damn right!"

She fiddled with the Kleenex. Folded it. Tucked it in her purse. She stalled.

On the ramp outside, someone ran up an aircraft engine.

When she spoke, her voice dropped. I had to strain to hear her over throbbing piston engine roar.

"I've been an oncology nurse at Children's Hospital for twelve years, Mr. Stewart. You can't imagine what I see. What I've seen. After a while, you want to believe that you'll get used to it. Or you want to believe that it's some sort of cycle of life. Or you want to believe in God, or Allah, or Shiva, or whatever the fucking flavor of the day is! But they just keep coming. Those little faces. Clutching their little monkeys and bears and dolls...and you pray for something to happen. Like Emma Parrish. You pray..."

She emptied a breath into the air between us and fought to control her voice.

"Yes. I'll keep my promise. No matter what happens. Your secret is safe. I also promise you that no matter what happens, I will only ask this once. After that... after that it's up to you."

38

I found Andy in her cubicle at the Essex Police Department. She waved me in to sit, holding her phone to her ear. Seeing her absorbed in something eased my clouded mind. I took a risk, driving to join her at the station. She reads me well, and at the moment I didn't want to be read.

"That's not—"

She did not look happy.

"I understand, but—"

I could hear the voice on the other end. Not the words. But the tone. My wife locked her jaw as someone became more and more strident.

"Yes, sir."

"Yes, I'll be there."

She lowered the phone and stabbed the screen. I gave her a minute to bury her fingers in her hair and finish the conversation in her head.

"That was Richardson. He won't let me see Parks."

"Why not?"

"He doesn't want us asking about Rahn."

"Why?"

She shook her head. "He knows Parks won't see us without his attorney present, and he thinks Parks' attorneys will jump all over it, all over us. Richardson thinks they'll use Rahn to lay on a whole new pile of motions and misdirection. Such B.S."

"Did you tell him that Rahn is trying to—" I stumbled on the words "—you know?" My emotions were raw after talking to the nurse.

Andy flipped one hand back and forth.

"He knows. He still thinks Parks is capable of an 'eliminate the witness' gambit."

"But what?"

I gave her a second.

"He now thinks Parks might get off."

I was speechless. Andy read my expression and explained.

"He fully agrees that Parks is capable of sending Rahn—or someone —after me. But now he's saying he doesn't think Parks is actually doing it because I'm not that pivotal to their case. I'm just a cop who uncovered the evidence. It's not like I was a witness to Parks committing a crime, except for Sandy—but remember, they're laying all that off on Todd."

"Parks was in on it! Christ, he was behind it all!"

"That's hard to prove. Especially when Todd claims Parks wasn't involved."

I slumped in the plastic chair. "Oh, this just keeps getting better. Why would Todd cover Parks' ass?"

Andy gave me a look that told me I should know. And I did.

"Of course. Parks has all the money."

"Richardson says that the same firm defending Parks has now taken on Todd's case. Which means Parks is picking up the tab. Richardson also said he's getting some political heat."

"I don't get that. I thought this case was political gold for Richardson."

"Well," Andy said, "it's just a guess, but Parks was a big donor— across party lines. Not just here in Wisconsin. If he's in prison, his assets are frozen by the government. They might even try to take some—since this whole business could be construed as breach of contract. Point being, that's a lot of money locked up that would otherwise be funneled into PACs for people who were depending on it."

"Jesus Christ." I thought about Bargo Litton's billions. "Is he giving up? Richardson?"

"No." Andy shook her head vigorously. "But he now feels like he's on thin ice and doesn't want to go off on tangents. He thinks he can make a case linking Foyle and Parks, but that Rahn is a tangent. He thinks if we go down that road, the defense attorneys will make it all about Rahn and then show that there's no proof the man even exists. Or that he worked for Parks. And by stretching that elastic logic, they'll say the case involving Foyle and Parks lacks foundation. They'll try to make it about Rahn, which, of course, it isn't."

"Three people dea—" I stopped. The look on Andy's face told me she didn't need to be told. "Well, this just sucks."

"Maybe. The case against Parks is far from lost. And I get that Richardson is being cautious."

I caught a glimmer in her eye.

"Wait. What do you mean 'maybe'?"

She glanced around the squad room. Mae Earnhardt, the regular evening dispatcher, was doing a day shift for some reason. She stood at the copier. Andy used her eyes to tell me to hold my questions. I felt like holding someone's throat instead.

"What dress?" I asked, looking for a relief topic.

Andy had dropped "dress shopping" on me then needed to take another call, leaving me hanging.

"For Friday. The Freshman Freeze." I must have looked bewildered. "The dance? The Freshman Freeze dance?"

"Okay. What the hell is that?"

"A big deal. A big after winter break social at the high school. Put on by the new freshman class. It's more of a winter formal, but they allow freshmen to attend. To—I don't know—get them more integrated with the upperclassmen now that they've had a semester to relax. Or as a reward for showing up again after the holiday. I don't know. It's a long-standing winter tradition here. Comes right after the holidays."

"Lane's going?"

"Oh, you have no idea. This is big drama. Lane. Sarah. All her friends are going. And there will be boys. Our little Lane is going to a dance and she wants me to help her pick out a dress tonight after work. And I think it's because there's a boy."

"What boy? You mean that junior Nazi?"

"No. A crush. A *boy* boy," she said with mild exasperation. "And yes, it has to be tonight, because we're going to be gone for a few days."

"Jesus, Andy, did you tell her you're in the middle of trying not to be —you know—murdered?"

"I already let her down once. I can't do that to her again. I'm not going to let Rahn destroy my life!"

I stared at her. Hard.

"It's just some shopping, and then we'll go. Did you tell Pidge to be ready?"

"Yeah." Pidge wasn't thrilled about a night flight on New Year's Eve. She had other plans. But I could also tell part of her liked the idea of teaming up with Andy and me again. "I repeat, what boy?"

"What do you mean?"

"At the dance. What boy?"

"She was tight-lipped about it, but it sounds like someone is interested in her. Someone's been sending her notes. She hinted it might be an upperclassman."

I gave her a sharp look.

"What? You mean Braddock?" Andy asked.

"Ever see 'Carrie?' Pig's blood? This isn't some kind of setup, is it?"

"No, no." Andy brushed the idea aside. Then stopped to think about it. Then shook her head again. "No."

"Where are you going dress shopping? I'm a little worried about you being out and about by yourself."

"She wants to go to the Goodwill Store."

"No. Really? For her first dance? Can't you take her, I don't know, where the rich girls go?"

"I would love to, but she saved up her own money for this and you know Lane. She has to do this on her own. She won't take help. If I make a *thing* out of it that only makes it worse. I'm not going to make a *thing* out of it. And there are some nice dresses at the Goodwill Store."

"You're sure the Braddock kid isn't going to pull some shit?"

Andy gave me a long stare, eyes narrowed, lower lip strong.

"No," she said. "I'm not sure."

We looked at each other for a moment.

"Maybe you and I should go on a field trip," she said after thinking about it.

"Maybe we should. Do we have time?" My watch and stomach were both suggesting lunch.

"Have you got some of your little propeller-thingies with you?"

I smiled and patted the breast pocket of my leather flight jacket. I started to speak, but Andy put up a flat hand to stop me.

"No, you're not calling them that."

"Calling them what? You don't even know my new name."

"I don't want to know." She stood up. "Let's go."

ANDY DROVE UNIT TWENTY-THREE. In the car, I rehashed the Internet research I asked Lane to perform.

"The old man posts a lot of stuff from right-wing sites, conspiracy sites, and what looks like white supremacist stuff. He's also cherry-picking tweets from the Tweeter-In-Chief. The incendiary stuff. Lane followed some of the links to some pretty nasty pages. She said there are a lot of quotes from that Internet nutball, Josiah James. White nation poli-cies. Conspiracy crap. Doomsday theories. Survivalist bullshit. That guy sells a lot of survivalist merchandise."

"He was at the memorial. I saw him." Andy squinted.

"You're kidding me!"

"No. He was there. Isn't that the guy who says the Democrats are running extermination camps on the dark side of the moon? That all the shuttle missions were to haul away true Americans resisting the Deep State?"

"It would be funny if not for the fact that idiots believe him."

"What about the kid? What's he posting?"

"Not so much," I said. "He has a Facebook page, but most of it is devoted to comic books. Er, graphic novels. He's apparently a fan. Lane said she didn't see his racist stuff there. He seems to be doing that for her eyes only."

"Maybe he still has some shame. I worry about him being a loner," Andy said. "That's not good."

"No. Not if the old man is pumping his head full of poison. One thing the kid did have on his site, and the old man had a lot of, too, was guns. The old man had some rants about the Second Amendment. The kid posted pictures of himself at a range, shooting off an AR, various handguns."

"Anything else?"

"That's not enough?"

"Well, it's not good. Believe me, we take this stuff a lot more seriously now, obviously. But there are limits. Never good limits, because we get second-guessed if someone actually does go out and commit an atrocity. Or we're made out to be the secret police if we jump too soon. Can't win."

"I don't have the same limits." Not long ago, my wife might have protested. She stayed silent. "But are you sure about this? About going off on a wild goose chase when you have Rahn to worry about?"

"I have other cases, Will. I have a job." She glanced at me. "Besides, this feels good. To be doing something besides obsessing about Mannis Rahn."

"If you say so."

A quarter mile from the Braddock home, she slowed the squad car.

"Better do it," she said.

I reached in my pocket and pulled out the Bluetooth earpiece and slid it into my right ear. I unhooked my seatbelt.

Fwooomp! —I vanished. My weightlessness prevented the seatbelt warning from sounding.

Andy eased onto the property and rolled the squad car to the back of the house. Nothing appeared to have changed since my visit. My eyes immediately went to the cameras.

"You see 'em?" I asked. Andy leaned forward and looked through the windshield.

"Yup." She made a note of the cameras as she slipped her fingers into a pair of leather driving gloves.

She opened the car door and emerged slowly. To someone watching, she simply paused and surveyed the property as any professional in law enforcement would. I floated out the door and maneuvered behind Andy, careful not to let my feet touch the snow. I grabbed the belt at the back of her coat.

She closed the door and walked carefully across the rutted driveway to the back steps, towing me. At the top of the concrete stoop, she paused, took one more look at the camera above the door, the one that spooked me badly, and then pressed the doorbell. We heard a muted chime inside.

Andy stamped her feet on the stoop.

A latch snapped. Then another. The inner door opened.

Ben Braddock cast a guarded look at Andy, at the squad car parked in his yard, then at Andy again. He pushed open the storm door.

"Mr. Braddock?" Andy asked politely.

"Yes?" He had a nice baritone. He was clean-shaven and tidy. I had only seen him in coveralls. Today he wore a knit shirt over jeans. Just a shade taller than my wife, but double her weight, he looked the part of a suburban homeowner. I expected greasy hair and dirty fingernails. Maybe a Nazi tattoo. I expected bald contempt for the police car and its driver. He displayed nothing but blank curiosity.

"Detective Stewart, Essex Police Department."

"I know who you are."

"May I come in?"

He gave her a steady appraisal, up and down, then pushed the storm door wider. Andy took the door and swung it fully open. Braddock stepped back, allowing Andy into the house.

I held on as closely as I could without tripping her. Once inside, I pushed away to the right, giving her a tap in the small of her back as I drifted clear. I floated toward an arch that opened on the family's living room. The piano with the photos I'd seen on the last visit anchored the room.

"Thank you. It's a bit nippy out there," Andy said cheerfully. She produced a business card from her coat pocket and handed it to Braddock. "We're visiting all the homeowners in the area. There have been several break-ins. Have you had any trouble here?"

Braddock shook his head. "No."

"I noticed your cameras. Quite a setup. Are they active?"

"Uh-huh."

"I wonder, has anyone been on the property—anyone you didn't recognize? Maybe when you were not home?"

"No," he said.

"Do the cameras record?"

"Yes."

"And is that something you review?" Andy asked. "I ask because we think whoever is doing this is posing as a delivery person. Like Amazon. Trying the doors to see if someone is at home. Are you at home during the day?"

"I work."

"Oh. Where do you work?"

"Is that relevant?" His first pushback. Andy smiled and shook her head.

"Just neighborly curiosity. Do you get deliveries here, Mr. Braddock?"

"Once in a while."

Andy launched into a one-sided conversation about how when she grew up it was so exciting to get a package from the JC Penney catalog, but now it seems like every house has an Amazon box on the front step by the end of the day.

I moved deeper into the house.

A stairway rose from the front foyer to the second floor. I pushed to where I could reach the railing. I pulled myself up, leaving Andy to chat with Braddock, although his contribution to the conversation seemed limited to monosyllables, consistent with his conversational tendencies at The Silver Spoon. Andy spun the tale about fake deliveries and told him that several people reported that when they answered the door, the driver told them he had the wrong address and left.

I reached the top of the stairs and connected my memory of the rooms I'd seen through the windows to the doors on either side of the upstairs hallway.

I pulled left and let myself float. I passed a bathroom. I passed a closed door which I remembered as the boy's room, where I'd seen NASCAR posters and die-cast toys. I listened as I floated by, but I heard no telltale music or video game noises. Middle of the day on New Year's Eve. He could be there, hunkered down under headphones, or he could be anywhere, with school being out of session. I decided to come back to that door.

I continued to the end of the hall. The last door opened on a master bedroom with a queen-sized bed, unmade. I reversed direction. I found the room I was looking for in the other direction beyond the stairway, behind another closed door. I tested the knob. Locked.

The house was old. The doorknobs were as old as the house. This didn't require anything fancy. I pressed my thumb against the key cylinder and rotated—it turned without a key. A useless lock. I wondered why anyone would bother.

I turned the cylinder silently. When it stopped, I turned the knob until it stopped as well. Holding pressure on the knob, with the latch clear of the jamb, I pushed the door open, expecting to find Corey Braddock at the desk I'd seen through the window, working the laptop I'd seen.

The room was unoccupied.

The desk sat as I expected. The laptop remained in place, alight. The screen showed a Google welcome page, with the cursor blinking in the search box, beckoning a user. Clutter on the desktop included a bottle of gun oil and gun cleaning supplies. I didn't see any weapons or boxes of ammunition this time.

From the first floor, I could hear Andy's voice, carrying the conversation. At one point, I heard her laugh. Disarming and charming.

Holding one hand on the jamb, I pushed the door open and eased off the knob. I used my handhold on the jamb to push across the room to the desk. The desk chair had wheels, so I avoided contact. I caught the edge of the desk with my left hand and fixed a grip to remain in place. I put my right hand on the wireless mouse.

I clicked the browser history pulldown.

First listing: A communication electronics forum.

I opened the site to a page that answered questions about wireless electronics. I clicked my way back to Google.

Second listing: Josiah James. An editorial called The Coming Storm.

I skipped it.

Third listing: The cast of Marvel's *Iron Fist*.

Two more listings related to Marvel comics.

The sixth listing stopped me cold. I pulled out my cell phone. By feel, I found the round button on the face and pressed it twice in rapid succession. After a moment, I held it between me and the laptop screen. I found the side buttons and pressed. The device made the old school camera shutter click sound, entirely meaningless to the digital electronic camera in my phone. I moved the phone left and right and shot more photos. Unable to see the phone screen, I couldn't be sure I got the picture, so I hedged and shot four more.

A door opened in the hall behind me.

The kid!

Footsteps in the hall.

I looked over my shoulder to see Corey Braddock passing the doorframe. He glanced in the room, as if expecting to see something or someone. He stopped. He listened to the conversation coming from downstairs.

Thin, compared to his father, he had long hair, swept back from his forehead and over his ears. He had a handsome, slightly delicate face. He wore a black t-shirt and black, tight jeans. He wouldn't be mistaken for muscular by anyone at his school. I tried to read something in his eyes, then realized I was seeing way too much of his face.

He fixed his attention on the screen behind me.

A look washed over his face. Panic? Worry? I couldn't tell. But he hurried toward the laptop still displaying the page I'd found.

I kicked the floor with my toes and launched for the ceiling. Too late. My long body was never going to clear in time.

I felt for the muscle in the center of my body. Finding it, I used it to rotate, swinging my legs up and into a horizontal position just as the kid reached the desk. I bumped into the plaster ceiling. I have no idea how the kid missed hitting me.

At the desk he reached for the mouse. Taking one more worried glance over his shoulders, he clicked to close the browser. The image I photographed changed to a desktop wallpaper scene of a tricked-out SUV bursting over a sand dune.

The kid blew out a breath. Relief. He turned quickly and left the room, closing the door behind him.

I bumped against the ceiling, listening to his footsteps. They clumped down the uncarpeted hall. I heard his bedroom door close.

I pushed away from the ceiling and aligned myself with the desk once more. Sliding the mouse, I opened Google again and dropped the browser history. I shot more pictures. After closing it, I took one last look at the laptop and thought about the page I'd seen. I thought about opening it again but decided I had seen enough.

More than enough.

39

"Look at this!" I held my phone up for Andy to see.

"Hang on." She focused on driving but pulled a plastic Ziploc bag from the console between the seats. "Take the wheel for a sec."

I reached over and began steering. This part of Paradise Road ran straight as a steel ruler.

Andy tugged her gloves off and carefully dropped them into the bag. She secured the zip closure and put the bag in her coat pocket.

"I got it." She took the wheel again.

"That's a really good idea." I gestured at her pocket and held up the phone again. "Look at this."

"I'm driving, Will. Just tell me what it says."

"Common household chemicals used to make plastic explosives. This is some kind of recipe."

She glanced at the screen but didn't comment.

"You need to call someone. The FBI. ATF. Somebody."

"And tell them what?"

"What do you mean? This is damning!"

"Every survivalist and white supremacist nutball in the country downloads that crap. Most of it is bogus. Mix it up and you get a smelly paste that removes mildew from your shower."

"C'mon, Dee! You're not dismissing this—really?"

"No," she said firmly, "Of course I'm not. What else was on there?"

I read them off.

"Survivalist site. Learn to process expired food after the apocalypse. Yuk. A white nation site. Something about cleaning supplies—which I'm guessing has more to do with chemicals for making bombs. Um. Amazon. A couple more graphic novels, I think. This kid really ought to delete his browser history."

"Let's be glad he didn't. Aside from making explosives, I'm not hearing anything surprising here, based on what you told me about Lane's research. We know the father is a racist, a Nazi sympathizer, a white supremacist. Lane may be right about the kid growing into it."

"Okay. So you do take it seriously."

"I never said I didn't. Why do you think I will get those gloves tested? Even if it's a bogus formula, the intent is not. And if he's progressed to the point of making explosives, it might show up as residue. I touched the door knob and parts of the banister."

Andy drove, thinking.

"I wonder if Greg LeMore would mind taking a look at this list…" The Milwaukee PD detective had a nerdy side and had recently applied it to help Andy on a case.

"And how do you explain where you got the list?"

"Send me those photos. Explaining them is not my biggest concern."

MY WIFE REFUSED to drop me off at home. She considered it unsafe. I argued. I told her I would vanish and float around the house until she got home. She said no. She let me choose between staying with her at the station or returning to the airport if I would promise to sit tight until she finished shopping with Lane. It surprised me that she planned to uphold her commitment to Lane after what we'd seen, but I didn't question.

I chose the airport. Andy dropped me in the parking lot and wheeled out in a hurry.

As I entered the flight office, Rosemary II told me she planned to close the front desk early to pick up Lane and wanted to know if I'd like to tag along on the dress-shopping trip.

"Not if I can schedule some dental surgery," I said. I realized by the look on her face I'd been had. She laughed and disappeared into the inner office.

I strolled down the hall, noting the empty pilot's lounge. The nurse was gone but her presence lingered. Her phone number, written on the torn corner of a magazine business reply card, whispered at me from my wallet. She asked that I call her to set up a time to meet at Children's Hospital in Milwaukee during one of her shifts. She wanted to experiment. I didn't.

I had a lot to think about. And like most occasions when I had something weighing on my mind, I looked for a way to avoid thinking about it.

"Hey, Boss," I said, leaning on the doorframe to Earl's office.

This time Earl Jackson, not Dave, looked at me from his desk chair. The weathered skin on his forehead furrowed and he gave me a look that said Go Away. A stranger would have retreated. I knew his face always looked that way and ignored the message. "Got a minute?"

"Not when every Tom, Dick and Harry sticks his head in here taking up my time," he growled.

"Good." I slid onto the Army surplus metal chair next to his Army surplus metal desk. Earl leaned back in his chair, tipping it to a point that defied both engineering and gravity. Old springs in the chair warned of doom.

"You hear anything from Stephenson?" he asked.

"A week ago. Doc said he called OK City and they told him they got everything. It's been radio silence since."

"Government couldn't find its own ass with a map and ten Sherpa guides," Earl muttered. "What's the latest on this dead man coming after Andy?"

Rosemary II knew about Rahn, which meant Earl knew about him, too.

"U.S. Marshal Service is making it a priority, and they brought in the FBI. They're on it."

"Bullshit. You tell your wife to pack a bag and I'll fly the both of you somewhere that motherfucker will never find you. Someplace where the sand is warm, and the beer is cold. I got a couple spots I've used myself— on occasion. Private airstrips. I guarantee that shit won't find you, and if he does, he'll regret meeting a few of my friends."

"You must know something about Andy that I don't if you think she'd ever run and hide."

Earl glanced at his watch and something dawned on him.

"I thought you would be wheels-up for Iowa by now."

I shrugged.

"My wife has a dress-shopping appointment with Lane and her mother. Big dance this weekend and Lane's charged up about it. We leave after the ladies have satisfied the need to spend money."

Something warm and human flickered across Earl's face. The effect was disturbing. He quickly shook it off.

"Going up to Helena, then? After Iowa?"

"That's the plan. Listen," I said, "I was wondering how the monthly numbers have been tracking. I mean, with the new aircraft on the line."

"And without you holding up my end," Earl reminded me.

"Yeah, that."

"Which is just about killing me, I hope you know. Means I gotta put up with Pidge double the usual."

"But you've got Dave back on, and the King Air starting to catch on with some of the regulars."

"If you're asking if your seat is still open, you know the answer, buddy."

"I appreciate it, but that's not what I was asking. I was wondering about the fleet. You replaced both Navajos with higher-end aircraft. Are they fitting in?"

Earl reached up and laced his fingers behind his head. The chair springs protested as he tipped farther toward disaster.

"Okay," he began, "I'll confess that I thought we were overextending. Didn't think we could support 'em. And we might drive away some of our customers with the higher rates. Maybe it's just a honeymoon period, but so far, I think there's more demand *because* of the changes. If I didn't expect you back any day now, I'd start looking for two more pilots."

"Do you think we could use another Navajo?" The Piper Navajo had less power and performance than the pressurized Mojave but was more economical to run. "Maybe let go of one of the Barons?"

"I might add one, but I wouldn't replace a Baron. What's on your mind?"

"Well, it might seem like I slept through that last meeting we all had with Sandy," I said, not counting the one Andy and I had with her at midnight last night, "but when she got to talking about the logistics of vetting applicants for grants, she started talking about site visits at small-town schools all over the country. Travel. My first thought, of course, was of Essex Air Service, being the crackerjack salesman I am."

Earl squinted at me, then said, "Nine hundred sixty-three thousand dollars."

I must have looked surprised.

"Sandy told me. While you were gone. That's how much is left from that bastard Chicago Irishman. I helped her work out the details of returning the money to that school district in Monroe and helped her fight off some of those sharks from the City of Chicago. Two of those assholes came up here looking for her. Did she tell you?"

I shook my head.

"I intercepted them." He curled up a lip. "They lost interest. But I know about the leftover cash. Nice chunk of change."

As usual, Earl Jackson was a step ahead of everyone else in the room.

"I was thinking the foundation might buy an airplane, and maybe lease it out to Essex Air when it's not being used. Gives her a good way to get around to little school districts. Gives us a relief valve if business keeps up the way it has. And maybe generate revenue for the foundation."

"And maybe keep you and your wife from hijacking my fleet all the time."

"That too."

Earl cocked an eyebrow at me. "Sandy thinks we should give all that dough to you and Andy."

"I'd take it in a heartbeat, but it would never pay for my divorce. I was thinking—as part of all this—maybe the foundation could buy the O'Reilly Hangar—once Six Nine Tango is out of there. If we can track down the current owners. They don't seem to be coming back."

"The bank is the current owner," Earl said. His eyes became thin slits, a sign of thoughts lining up for takeoff behind them. "And Six Nine Tango is gone."

"What?"

"I don't know why I thought you knew, 'cuz you ain't showed your face around here much in the last week, but a big-assed truck pulled in here while you were in D.C., along with a van with half a dozen guys in coveralls. Not so much as a howdy-do from any of them. They unsealed the hangar, backed in, and were gone in less than an hour."

"Don't they have to ask you first?"

"It's not my airplane anymore. Belongs to the insurance company."

"Was it them?"

"What the hell would they want with a bunch of scrap aluminum?"

I had no idea.

"Feds?"

"Same question. Nobody collects the wreck unless it's for a lawsuit or a major investigation, and last I heard nobody's suing anybody. I called that woman from the NTSB—"

"Walsh?"

"Yeah. Her. She didn't know anything about it."

"What about the report? Are they releasing it yet?"

"She said it was still listed as pending. She sounded pissed about that."

Gone. The airplane I shared life and death with was gone.

I felt like something had been taken from me. I visited the hangar containing the wreck of the Piper Navajo that came apart under me only once. Last summer. With Earl. At the time, I hoped it might whisper to me, share its secret and tell me why it died but I didn't. Connie Walsh, the investigator from the NTSB met us there, unofficially, and walked me through the remains of a once graceful flying machine. She spent close to an hour translating the incomprehensible damage in cold mechanical terms. At the end, I was no closer to understanding what caused the accident, or its aftermath, than when I first laid eyes on the twisted remains. But knowing that the wreckage remained in the O'Reilly hangar instilled a certain comfort. It let me think I might go back again someday and learn the secret.

Not anymore.

"Did they say where they were taking it?"

"Didn't say squat to anyone. Didn't check in with us at all."

I didn't know what to say. Or if I would ever know what to say.

40

"Here," Andy held up her phone for me to see.

"One second," I said through the intercom. I adjusted the trim and engaged the autopilot. The Mojave hummed through a cold, clear night sky pinpricked with stars above us and small-town clusters of light below.

Andy occupied the co-pilot's seat. Pidge took a seat in the back and propped her feet up on the facing seat with her attention buried in her phone.

"Okay," I said. Andy held up the phone again.

The image showed Lane Franklin adorned and glowing in a close-fitting red satin dress that left one shoulder bare. The dress was simple, surrendering all attention to the beauty of the figure within. As stunning as she looked, her face stole the scene. Her expression mingled wonder with surprise and childlike anticipation. As if she'd never seen herself like this, or ever considered it possible. The astonishment radiating from her eyes was breathtaking.

I felt an uneasy mix of awe and worry.

"Wow."

"I know," Andy said. "She was bursting. She had that dress picked out weeks ago. She asked them to hold it for her, but I don't think she believed they would until she actually put it on. God, she was so nervous!"

Awe and worry. I let the worry dominate.

"What are you doing about Braddock?"

"Everything. I couldn't reach LeMore, but I emailed the list to him. I talked to the Chief and he agreed we should notify ATF and Homeland. We put a rush on the samples. We're taking it seriously, Will, if that's what you want to know."

"Did you tell Lane?"

"Of course not!"

"I'm worried about this dance," I said. More so now that I'd seen the photo.

"Already on it. I called Chet Allison and told him we were looking at a possible issue with Corey Braddock. He knows the boy. He knows the family, and what they've been through. And he knows of the father's... proclivities. Tom's bumping up our presence Friday night from auxiliary to active duty."

"Meaning?"

"Meaning instead of some of our police auxiliary volunteers doing dance duty, we'll have on-duty officers there. We'll have a general lockdown and limited access. You and I will be there."

"We will?" Under different circumstances, I thought it highly unlikely Andy could drag me to chaperone a high school dance unless handcuffed.

"Yes," Andy confirmed. "We will."

"I don't think Lane will be happy about that."

"Wrong. Aside from whatever has her heart racing about Friday night, Lane really wants you there. She must have asked me five times if we would be back in time."

"It's not that crush thing, is it?"

"I think it's more a dad thing. First dance. Becoming a young woman. You're as close as she has to a father figure. She needs you to be a part of it."

A dad thing or a crush. I didn't know which was worse.

Chicago Center interrupted and handed us off to the next sector. Andy knows the drill and remained silent through the exchange.

"I notice you're not protesting," Andy said when the radio frequency fell quiet again.

"That little Nazi son of a bitch does anything to Lane and I'll kill him."

"I think you'd have to take a number," Andy said.

"CHRISTMAS EVE IN BEMIDJI. New Year's Eve in Cedar Rapids," Pidge said dropping to the tarmac. "My fine fucking social life! So, what's the plan?"

She looked up at me, then Andy. Andy glanced back at me. We both hesitated.

"FUCK!" Pidge snapped. She dropped her overnight bag to the pavement and folded her arms. "Goddammit, I'm not moving an inch unless you two tell me everything! And I mean fucking down to the short hairs EVERYTHING! I've done this song and dance with you two and I wound up in a barrel last time. I'm here. I'm part of this team. Andy, you can fucking deputize me if you have to, but you can't freeze me out."

I could pick up Pidge and carry her bodily to the FBO office if I had to, but planted on that tarmac, her posture adopted all the mobility of Mount Rushmore. Arms folded across her chest. Feet apart.

"We're here to locate a suspect," Andy said.

"Bullshit."

Andy sighed. "And..."

"And?"

"And you're right, Pidge. There's more to it. Let's get in out of the cold, get a hotel room—"

"—and a couple cold beers," I suggested.

"And then we'll tell you the whole plan. Okay?"

Pidge picked up her bag, grinning.

"Okay. Three muska-fucking-teers! Let's do this!"

THE SIGNATURE FLIGHT Center facility had a nice feel to it, one that a pilot could appreciate. Reasonably new. Good furnishings. A comfortable pilot lounge for those of us who sit around airports and wait while the clientele motors off to keep the wheels of commerce moving.

It was also empty. New Year's Eve. In a little over three hours the calendar year would retire here in central Iowa. I hoped to be celebrating with my wife in a quiet hotel room, once we got through the preliminaries.

Pidge leaned on a countertop where someone should have greeted us.

"Hello!" she called out.

"I'm going to the ladies," Andy said. She dropped her bag beside mine.

"Everybody's out partying," Pidge observed.

"Not quite." I pointed. A fuel truck rolled to a stop outside the broad glass windows facing the ramp. A young man wearing heavy coveralls and a reflector vest hopped out of the cab and jogged around the back of the truck. He glanced in our direction and stopped. Pantomiming, he pointed at himself, then us, then his watch, then held up a hand with all five fingers splayed.

"He must be the welcoming committee," Pidge said. "Be here in five. I'm gonna hit the head, too."

She trotted off after Andy. I waved at the fuel truck driver. He scooped up a set of chocks from the edge of the ramp and hooked them over his shoulders, then jogged back to the driver's side and reached in for a pair of lighted wands.

I've been in his shoes. Shorthanded. Handling customers in the office and marshaling airplanes on the ramp. Showing him some patience took no effort on my part. I leaned on the counter to watch his ballet.

Wands in hand, he jogged to an open area on the ramp closer to the terminal than where I had parked One One Kilo. In position, he turned and held both arms up with the wands lighted, facing the field. I shifted my attention.

Flashing strobes and navigation lights moved behind light thrown forward by a set of taxi lights. After a moment, I heard jet whine accompanying the light show. The pilot flicked his lights to tell the lineman he'd been seen. In response, the lineman waved his wands in a beckoning motion, dipping them to show the pilot where he expected the jet to end up.

The jet moved into light cast onto the ramp by powerful spotlights mounted on the building. A Cessna Citation twin-engine business jet, gleaming white with thin blue stripes accenting the glossy finish. It moved quickly into the position indicated by the waving wands. The lineman held the wands up over his head and brought them slowly together. The jet stopped when the wands touched. Nicely done, I thought, by both parties.

I was about to reel my attention back into the office to see if my wife had emerged from the restroom when the jet's tail number caught my eye.

I read it.

It took a second.

Shit!

"Andy!" I shouted across the empty lobby at the restroom door. "He's here!"

The jet stopped forty feet from the glass wall of the office. The nose pointed to my left. I saw the cabin door seal break and the door drop. A uniformed flight officer stepped down, followed by a man in a dark suit. From his demeanor and the intense examination he made of his surroundings, it was easy to pin the U.S. Marshal tag on him. Even easier when he pulled a small com unit from his pocket and spoke into it.

A set of headlights ignited. A dark sedan rolled out of shadows on the far side of the ramp to my left. The vehicle headed for the jet.

"Andy!"

All doubt evaporated as I saw a man descend the short jet stair with his left leg extended stiffly before him. Once on the tarmac, holding the stair rope, he turned back to the cabin. Someone inside handed him a cane.

Steggar Rahn.

The ramp officer spoke to the com unit, then gestured for Rahn to move forward. The sedan swung toward the jet, scribing an arc that brought it to a halt across the jet's nose. The marshal offered to take Rahn's arm, but Rahn brushed his hand away. The sedan's rear left door opened and swung out. Rahn hunched toward it on his signature limp.

"Shit!" I cried out. I glanced at the restroom door. It remained closed.

I dropped to one knee and threw my carry-on case on its back. I found the zipper and jerked the case open. Jamming my hands into my socks and underwear, I probed until I felt my ski goggles wrapped in a black balaclava. I pulled them out and stood up. With my left hand I patted my left breast pocket, identifying my cell phone in my shirt pocket, and a pair of propulsion units in my jacket pocket.

"What's going on?" Andy appeared. I pointed.

"He's here! They came in early!"

"What?! We don't have a car!"

"I got this!" I said. I pulled my Bluetooth earpiece from my coat pocket and slipped it in place.

Rahn maneuvered himself into the open sedan door. He turned around and lowered himself onto the seat, holding out his artificial left leg. As he awkwardly managed his cane and the leg, the marshal jogged back to the plane. Someone handed an athletic bag out the door of the jet to the waiting marshal, who hurried it to the sedan. Rahn secured both the cane and his leg. The marshal handed him his bag and closed the door. He patted the roof of the sedan twice, and it lurched forward, swinging away from the parked jet.

"Got your phone?" Andy asked urgently.

I touched my shirt pocket.

"I'll see if I can get a car! I'll call you. Go!"

The sedan showed taillights as it moved away from the jet on a track parallel to the building.

A car on a ramp at a Class C airport meant it had to pass through a security gate. It wasn't hard to imagine the U.S. Marshals having permission and gaining access. But such access is limited. I figured it would be a gate at the end of the building, or between hangars. The sedan's taillights were already moving out of my view. I could try going after it via the ramp, but it would be a tail chase. Easier to intercept, I thought, than to chase.

Goggles in hand, I bolted for the doors on the side of the building opposite the ramp. Behind me, the marshals were already buttoning up their jet and preparing to move out. The sedan disappeared from my sight.

Pidge emerged from the restroom as I dashed for the glass doors that opened on an access road and parking lots.

"Where are you—?"

I ignored her and pushed through the doors. Even before clearing the building overhang I began accounting for street lights, parking lot lights and other aerial obstacles.

A moment earlier, the deserted office had been a problem. Now I was thankful for the absence of witnesses. I ran across a sidewalk into an empty roadway. I looked right, the direction from which I expected to see the sedan.

Nothing.

They had to come out somewhere. Beyond the nearest hangars, the ramp sprawled around the commercial passenger terminal. There had to be a security exit on this side of the terminal.

A set of buildings with a DHL sign blocked my view. Commercial cargo. That meant trucks coming and going. That meant a gate.

I pulled the balaclava over my head. It pinched the Bluetooth earpiece in my ear and microphone against my cheek. I slipped the goggles on and adjusted them over my eyes.

Checking the airspace above me, I pulled a propulsion unit and small propeller out of my pocket. I snapped the prop in place and thumbed the slide control to make it whirl briefly. Check.

I glanced over my shoulder and caught Pidge grinning at me.

Fwooomp! I threw the levers in my head forward and felt the cool sensation take its place around my entire body. Before I could float free of the pavement, I tapped my toes and launched straight up.

Rising, I felt my heart pounding and the strange muscle aligned down my center. Using it, I pivoted slowly to my right to face the control tower and the ramp beyond. As I rose, the Cedar Rapids airport spread out around me. The departing Marshal Service's Citation jet rolled steadily across the field between blue taxi lights.

I rose above the Signature Flight Center roofline. A line of hangars lay between me and the main terminal, which spread its spider leg jetways onto the empty tarmac. No waiting jets nuzzled the jetways. The windows to the terminal showed empty spaces.

Nothing moved on the ramp. That meant the car had to be passing behind the hangars below and before me.

I tipped the propulsion unit and aimed for a point at the end of the row of hangars. Everything I knew about airports told me the security gate stood on the other side of those structures.

As I approached a point over the last roof in the row, a set of headlights probed the darkness. The lights waited a moment. Then twin cones of light pulled the sedan onto the airport service road.

Gotcha!

The car turned left. I angled left to intercept. It accelerated on the service road. I pushed the thumb slide forward. The propulsion unit growled, and relative wind strengthened against me.

A parking lot studded with light poles swept below me. I subconsciously angled my flight path higher, clearing the poles by a healthy margin. Power lines ran parallel to the service road. I climbed to a point well above them, roughly three hundred feet above the surface.

The sedan traced a line from my right to an intercept point I determined on the service road. Most airport service roads limit traffic to twenty-five miles per hour. It looked like the marshals weren't concerned about being stopped as they accelerated along the road to well above the limit. I pushed for more power and began to wonder if I had enough.

The road curved right. Looking ahead, I saw where the service road formed a junction with a wider highway. The highway ran west into dark countryside, and east toward the lights of Cedar Rapids. I hoped for west, thinking the car would be easier to follow if it ran alone on a country highway.

It turned east. Worse, as it passed under lights at the intersection, I saw the car's color. Scarlet.

That's not right! I would have sworn that the sedan was dark. Black or deep blue. Maybe a gunmetal gray. But not red!

On impulse, I pushed the power all the way forward and dove toward the highway. The sedan accelerated, now moving to my right. Like a fighter pilot taking aim, I fixed an intercept on the sedan. If I could get close enough to fall in formation with it, I might see in the windows. I had a horrible sinking feeling that I wasn't going to find Rahn sitting in the back seat.

I angled in from the sedan's flank. I pushed the power hard. If this wasn't Rahn, if I screwed up, I needed to backtrack fast to—

SNAP!

The wire caught me across the chest. In a split second I went from a relative vertical position to spinning backward, head and heels trading places rapidly. A sharp pain announced that the air in my lungs had evacuated. My chest burned.

Sky and earth flipped over and over. I threw my arms out, but it had no effect, other than losing my grip on the power unit. I heard it hit the pavement that was racing toward me.

Red taillights passed below me.

I tumbled over the median.

I hit pavement near the westbound centerline and had time to thank God there were no headlights bearing down on me. I slammed down hard on my back. I tucked as best I could to prevent my head from hitting the pavement. My shoulders took a hit and I skidded, then bounced.

STOP!

The muscle in my center locked up and all motion ceased. I hung horizontal over the right lane of the westbound highway, gasping to replace the air that flushed out of my lungs. My chest felt like it had taken a bull-whipping.

Tipping my head back, I could see the wires, the poles, and one wire violently waving up and down between the poles.

Idiot! I thought. You dove right into a wire!

I cursed myself and slowly rotated to an upright position.

Distant taillights marked the growing space between me and the departing red sedan. Still gasping for air, I probed my chest to see if anything felt broken,

It wasn't him, I told myself. Or tried to convince myself. I had little chance of catching up.

What a screw up!

In the far eastbound lane of the four-lane road, the propulsion unit screamed. The prop had shattered. Unladen, the power unit howled like a dental drill, which seemed an appropriate accent to my misery.

Now what? Andy might not kill me but having lost Rahn meant this trip was over and her chances of interrogating him were finished. She might not express disappointment in me, but that wouldn't stop me from levying it on myself.

I looked at the wire, heaving up and down between the poles, transmitting the impact energy to the next segment. Telephone. Not power. If it had been power…I didn't want to think what might have happened.

"Christ!" I said aloud between heavy gasps.

Just as I reached in my jacket for my reserve power unit, fresh headlights appeared on the airport service road. Taking into account their position and speed, I applied some wishful thinking and calculated that they might have come through the same security gate as the red sedan.

Maybe…

I snapped a new prop in place and tested the power unit. Leaving the first unit to scream itself to death on the side of the highway, I began a slow vertical climb. The headlights swung through a curve and approached the highway where I now made a very specific point of rising above the wires and poles.

Reaching the highway, the car stopped under a street light.

Dark sedan. A Lexus. My hopes sank. It seemed an unlikely government vehicle. Still…

I made a two hundred and seventy degree turn and stopped facing the highway, set up to see the driver's side of the car.

The Lexus turned left, swinging its headlight beams into the dark countryside, away from Cedar Rapids. I let it pass.

In the left rear window Steggar Rahn's face caught light from the last streetlight.

I aimed the power unit at the western horizon and started a new chase, trying hard to ignore the burning pain across my chest, the throb in my shoulders and the expanding bruise to my ego.

I CLIMBED HIGHER, needlessly seeking an extra margin of safety above any other wires that might attempt my assassination.

The sedan's taillights guided me. The Lexus had the road to itself. The speed limit on this stretch of highway must have been fifty-five, because I had to push the power unit to its maximum to keep up. Height and perspective gave me an advantage, so that even if I lost ground, I could maintain contact with the vehicle. Provided they didn't pull into a tunnel or a parking garage. I considered that unlikely here in the dairy cattle countryside. Farms passed below me, some with large lighted cattle lots. I smelled cow manure. Winter dormant fields spread away on both sides of the road.

After a long run straight west, the car slowed for a four-way stop. A flashing directional signal predicted its right turn onto a perpendicular highway. I took the opportunity to cut the corner and closed the gap. I swung in behind the vehicle holding an altitude of roughly five hundred feet. No wires up here.

The speed limit on this road must have been lower and the marshal seemed to obey. I guessed forty-five. Keeping pace was easier.

They rolled north through farm country. Lighted farm yards and dark cattle pens passed on my right and left, separated by wide snowy fields. The starlight and snow combination gave the countryside a moonglow, even though the moon itself showed only a sliver hanging barely above the distant lights of Cedar Rapids, as if it had just risen from a sparkling pool.

My Bluetooth earpiece announced an incoming call. I switched the propulsion unit from my right hand to my left and touched the button through the thin black fabric of the balaclava.

"Where are you?" Andy asked before I could speak. She sounded out of breath.

"Damned if I know," I said. "Where are you?"

"Stuck! We couldn't get a car at Signature, so we ran all the way over to the terminal, but Hertz and Avis are both closed. There's a National desk with an after-hours phone, but all we get is a recording."

"That's alright. I got this," I reassured her. "They went west. Now they're going north. Out in the country. Once they stop somewhere, I'll light up my phone and figure out where I am. We just need to know where they stash the guy, right?"

"Affirmative," she replied with a sigh.

"What the hell's the deal with showing up a day early?"

"Witness security," she said. "I should have expected it. The marshals are being unpredictable. Smart. Be careful, okay?"

"What day is this?"

"Oh, shut up. Just be careful!"

"Affirmative."

I assumed the connection ended when she said nothing more.

The car continued to roll through the night. I confronted a new worry. I had limited battery power and no reserve. What if they were on a longer road trip? What if Cedar Rapids wasn't the destination, just the nearest airport that could handle a U.S. Marshals jet? What if I puttered to a halt twenty miles up the highway?

I suddenly regretted leaving the dying power unit on the road back at the airport.

I pushed the worry aside and focused on the moment. Night flying is often my favorite. There's serenity in the black smooth air most often found at night. Without red cockpit lights affecting my vision, I became aware of how acute my night vision had become. Starlight, thin moon-light, yard lights and the reflective character of the snow painted a dream-scape spreading to vast distances below me. The road ran black between white fields. Buildings whispered their colors. Red barns. White farm-houses. Blues and tans thinned out by the absence of light. Here and there holiday lights added riotous colors to the night, but those were merely accents. Absent sunlight, the light of the night around me was more like a scent in the air, something that had to be detected but which once found was remarkable in its strength.

The red taillights followed high-beam headlights on an unwavering line through the night. At one point, something black passed between me and the sedan. An owl? A large bat? I had no idea, but its passing told me I wasn't alone in the night sky. And reminded me that, pulled by my whirring propulsion unit, I was the intruder.

Time ticked by at a rate I couldn't determine. My mind wandered. I tried to think up ways to tell time and resolved to look up methods used by blind people. Perhaps a Braille watch. Or something that could speak to me through the Bluetooth earpiece. Andy is an expert at finding things on the Internet. This might be a task best assigned to her.

"I need a utility suit!" I blurted aloud, thinking I could use a few more pockets and devices. The words were lost in the forty-plus-knot relative wind roaring past me.

In time, the Lexus drew me out of my thoughts by showing brake lights. Its speed diminished. This wasn't the first time. Twice before, four-way stops brought the car to a halt. But this time there was no crossroad. I slid the power to neutral and assumed a glide that gradually slowed as wind resistance pressed against me.

Below me, the car turned beneath a leafless hardwood tree. The head-lights swept across a snowy yard, then illuminated a large old house. A farmhouse fronting several outbuildings including a barn. A glance told me this wasn't a working farm. The house stood on a lot cut from the fields around it, but I guessed that the fields were rented or owned by someone else, because the farmyard and outbuildings showed no sign of machinery or livestock. The house sat in the center of the lot, square, with two stories and porch across the front. An attached garage joined it in the back. The car rolled up a driveway past the house, then performed a U-turn and paused while the garage door opened, spreading warm light on the snow as it rose.

I pushed the slide for more power and swung into a sweeping curve around the property, using the house as a pivot point while descending and diligently watching for wires. I reversed the power once I had a downward track established, slowing myself. I came in low over the barn at the back of the lot just as the vehicle pulled into the garage.

No sooner had the taillights turned to brake lights and the vehicle stopped when the garage door reversed and began to drop.

Dammit. I would not get to see the passengers emerge.

I slowed my descent. I checked for wires again (and rubbed what was going to be the mother of all bruises forming on my chest) and eased lower and lower. Pulsing the power, I let myself float toward the structure until I could reach out and anchor myself to the peaked roof above the garage. A square of light on the snow at the side of the garage told me where to find a window. I tucked away the power unit, hoping to save what energy remained.

Hand over hand, I pulled myself along the roofline to the corner of the garage, then along the eaves to a point above the window. I pushed myself down until I could see inside the garage.

Steggar Rahn limped past my point of view, ushered into the house by two serious, solid-looking men.

Bingo!

AFTER WATCHING the marshals escort Rahn into the house, I began a peeping-Tom survey of the safehouse through the windows. Once inside, the marshals spread out and conducted a perfunctory search of the house. Rahn lingered in the kitchen, shedding his coat and starting a kettle of water on the stove. He opened a cabinet and extracted what I guessed to be tea. After setting up a cup with a tea bag, he went to work on a coffee maker, pulling coffee from another cabinet. He pulled two mugs from another cabinet and set them up for the marshals. His movements were deliberate and practiced.

When the marshals returned, their demeanor eased. Coats came off, revealing the weapons each carried. They were nearly identical men. My size. Athletic. Short business-like haircuts and sharp, appraising eyes. One of them walked to the window where I hovered and gazed through me at the landscape. They chatted, and the sound of their voices reached me through the glass, but not the words. The one nearest me said something and grinned. Both Rahn and the other marshal laughed. He seemed comfortable with his bodyguards. Rahn pulled a loaf of bread from a breadbox on the counter, then went to the refrigerator for jam. He knew which drawer to open for knives. He knew which cabinet to open for plates. He set the plates around a small kitchen table and then waited for the kettle to boil.

Steggar Rahn aged himself with his limp and a slight stoop he applied when handling the cane. I would have guessed him to be in his early sixties, but the limp and stoop prejudiced me. Without them, I might have gone as low as mid-forties. I should have paid more attention when Andy sat at our dining room table and muttered facts about her quarry aloud. Watching his brother maneuver around this kitchen, I got the impression of a man prematurely aged, or an actor playing an older role.

After the kettle boiled and the coffee brewed, the men sat together at the table and assembled jelly sandwiches. The marshals didn't remove their weapons. They remained vigilant as they chatted over this late-night snack.

I left them and pushed myself to the roof.

USING MY PHONE REQUIRED REAPPEARING. The marshals were no dummies. The house sat alone on a stretch of country road, with broad sight lines in all directions. A few old trees dotted the property, but for the most part, anyone observing or taking aim from in the house would have a clear shot in all directions. Lighting up a cell phone, even a few hundred yards away, didn't seem like a good idea.

The roof solved the problem. The marshals, if they looked outside, would be looking out, not up.

I found a thin circular chimney at the roof peak and angled up to get a grip on it. I swung myself into a seated position with the chimney between my legs. No heat or smoke came from the pipe.

Fwooomp! My butt and legs settled onto the shingles and cold immediately seeped through my jeans. I pulled out my phone, which was remarkably bright. From my cold perch, I called Andy, glad that the screen winked out once it touched my cheek.

"Where are you?" she demanded.

"About twenty miles west. I've got the location marked. It'll be easy to find. You should know...the brother knows his way around this house.

I don't think it's some random safehouse." I told her about his moves in the kitchen.

"They took him back."

"Back where?"

"To his witness relocation residence."

"They said he was blown. Why would they—?"

"Bait. Whitlock is using him as bait. Because Rahn now knows where to find his brother."

"Why would Rahn come here? When he's after you?"

"There's nothing to say he would. But look at it from Whitlock's point of view. Setting up a whole new identity and location is a costly headache. Grabbing Rahn is a priority. If there's even a chance he tries to make contact with, or go after, the brother, she's got him covered."

I told her about the two marshals, whose purpose now seemed clearer.

"There's no guarantee Rahn will show up there, but he'll get a surprise if he does," she said.

"Well, this changes things a bit—as far as you interviewing the brother."

"No, it doesn't."

"You're not planning on barging in on them tonight, are you?"

Andy muttered something about wanting to do exactly that. Then she backtracked and said, "No, not tonight. In fact, it can wait until after I talk to Parks."

"Richardson said you can't talk to Parks," I reminded her.

"Uh-huh."

I waited for her to explain. She didn't.

"Well, may I just point out that I'm freezing my ass off up here?"

"Can you get back to Cedar Rapids?"

"I have a better idea."

I told Andy that I had Rahn's location locked in my phone, and that the map in my phone put the small town of Vinton just under a mile away, and with it, Victor Tango India, the Vinton Veterans Memorial airport.

"I've flown charters there. I think I have enough power to get there. Have Pidge fly you to Vinton and pick me up. Rahn's not going anywhere anytime soon. We fly up to Helena and take care of business, then hop back here. Vinton has a crew car we can use."

Andy agreed. I added a request.

. . .

FIFTEEN MINUTES LATER, sitting on the roof, I watched the Mojave's landing lights approach. They seemed to hang in the sky, hovering. An illusion that told me Pidge had the airplane headed straight toward me.

"Ten degrees right," I said.

"Ten degrees right," Andy repeated.

Pidge applied the course adjustment. The landing light grew brighter.

"You're on the right line. I'm lighting up,"

I touched my phone screen and opened a flashlight app. I selected a strobe effect that immediately tried to blind me. Checking the yard once more to make sure I didn't have a marshal wandering around, I held the phone up, aimed at the approaching aircraft.

"We see you!" Andy announced, excited.

I let her feel the triumph and didn't point out that the strobe from my phone was probably the brightest light for a mile in any direction.

Pidge held course. A moment later the plane roared overhead.

"Okay. Target marked."

"I love you when you sound all military. I'll see you on the ramp at Vinton," I said into the Bluetooth microphone.

"Love you, too."

I killed the strobe and ended the call. I pushed the phone into a zippered pocket and drew my propulsion unit.

Fifteen minutes later I climbed aboard the Mojave. Pidge kept the pilot's seat. I took shotgun and Andy crawled under a blanket in the cabin. We launched for Helena, Montana.

41

Accounting for a light headwind, it took four hours and twenty-eight minutes to reach Helena. Pidge flew left seat as far as Pierre, South Dakota. I took over as we passed over Pierre and touched the wheels to the numbers on Runway 27 in Helena at seven minutes after four in the morning. I had doubts about finding services at that hour, but Exec Air Montana was open, offered us a courtesy car and a heated hangar for the Mojave. Snow, we were told, was expected later in the day. Andy scooped the courtesy car keys off the counter before Pidge could get her hands on them. Pidge called shotgun and graciously offered to use one of the company iPads to guide us to the motel Andy had named.

It was a short drive.

"Pidge," Andy said, making the turn under a lighted sign, "this isn't the motel I asked for. This is the Doubletree."

"Oh? Is it?"

"We can't stay here! We're on a budget!"

"No, we're not," I chimed in from the back seat.

"Yes, we are!"

"It has a pool," Pidge said. "But if you insist, then just drop me off here and you guys can go camp out at the Roach Motel. Maybe you can catch the bedbug rodeo."

"Or something else," I muttered. "Andy, you're getting a stipend from the Montana AG's office. We can tap the foundation for the overage."

Andy heaved a sigh and pulled up to the hotel. Pidge leaped out before the wheels stopped, hedging against the possibility that Andy might keep going.

The desk clerk found us rooms.

"Technically, I'm supposed to charge you for the night, but I'm listing you as checking in today." He handed us key cards with a smile. Pidge plucked hers from the clerk's fingers and spun for the elevator.

"Wake me for dinner only if you must!"

"Lunch!" Andy called after her.

"Fuck!"

I DID the trick with the key card. The lock snapped. I held the door open and Andy slid past me with her roller bag. She checked the room, I presume for lurking murderers. Finding none, she shed her coat and found a place for her shoulder bag and her service weapon within.

"Why don't you go first," she gestured at the bathroom. I had been prepared to play the gentleman and defer, but my bladder appreciated her suggestion. When I emerged, she slid past me with her roller bag and closed the door.

I checked my watch. Four-forty. I walked to the window and pulled the room-darkening curtain back far enough to examine the low-rise city from the fourth floor of its only high-rise hotel. Helena nestled below low hills, but with sunrise still only a suggestion, it was impossible to see beyond the night glow of streetlights.

I kicked off my boots and propped them together under the room's simple desk. Wallet, room key, car keys and aircraft key—all went to the desktop. I have a routine in hotels and follow it religiously. If I don't, things get hard to find. I turned on the desk lamp and turned off the main room lights.

I'd seen better rooms, but not many on duty as a charter pilot. I thought about the Pineview Motel and counted myself lucky to be at a Doubletree, although I had low expectations for use of the bed. Neither Andy nor I had banked much sleep.

I resigned myself to once again accepting basic functionality for the bed when the bathroom door opened. The light winked out and Andy emerged.

My breath caught.

The single soft light from the desk illuminated my wife the same way a malfunctioning flash bulb illuminated Rita Hayworth and made her the most famous pinup of World War II. Light and shadow. Curves and contrast. Andy's sculpted long legs rose above high heels on the striped hotel carpet, then teasingly disappearing into a short hemline that defied geometry on an angle across the highest points of her thighs. Her dress glimmered, silvery white, kissing her figure across every inch of its scant fabric. Her light caramel-colored shoulders set off white spaghetti straps that held up twin points of pinched fabric rising over the beckoning compound curves above her hips and narrow waist. The dress had no neckline as such, but a span of empty space plunged to a point well below her diaphragm. The fabric, if it was fabric and not simply a coating of shimmering light, hid nothing. My wife's body was embossed on that simple tiny dress, a gown I probably could have balled into my fist and shoved in a pocket.

"Where did you get that?!"

Under a playful fallen lock of her auburn hair, she let dimples peek from her cheeks. "This old thing? I borrowed it from my sister's closet. And may I say, what a slut!"

"One man's slut is another man's goddess. You look—"

I had no words.

And Andy knew it.

She began an excruciatingly slow and highly arousing stroll toward me. From somewhere—I admit I hadn't been looking at her hands—she produced her phone and held it up toward me.

"We need to discuss this." Olivia Brogan tugged at my arm in the digital photo between Andy's outstretched fingers. Olivia Brogan had nothing on my wife. "Would you like to hear my list of demands?"

"More than you will ever know."

She approached. Her signature perfume, suggesting fresh breakfast fruit in summer, seduced my senses. My pulse throbbed behind my eyes and elsewhere.

"I do not appreciate my property being touched by another woman,"

Andy said softly, yet with commanding deliberation. Her rich lips begged me to kiss them.

I had to swallow to speak.

"Does this mean you consider me yours? Because I never got around to the asking for your hand thing with your father."

"You are most certainly mine. Whether or not I am yours remains to be negotiated." She now stood close to me. Parts of her touched me. "As for my demands, we can start with—"

Her phone rang.

The two of us looked at the device as if it just launched the attack on Pearl Harbor.

Andy checked the screen. "It's Greg."

I opened my mouth to suggest she drop the phone in the toilet when she interrupted me. "Don't move!" She pointed a slender finger at my chest for emphasis, then touched the same finger to her phone and held it up between us. "Hi, Greg! You're on speaker with me and Will."

"Hi, Will!"

"Greg."

"Hey, I know it's stupid o'clock in the morning, but I wanted to get back to you ASAP on these browser histories." Greg LeMore, the Milwaukee PD detective who helped rescue Lane and who more recently traveled to Essex to lend his technical expertise to a case, would have been a welcome outside resource at any time—except this moment.

"What did you find?" Andy cast apologetic eyes my way.

"Well, you saw the obvious. Your boys are into home-brewed plastique. A lot of these sites are phony, but I'm sorry to say the one they're looking at is the real deal. I forwarded the URL to Homeland, and they're moving against it as we speak. But if your guys have this, they may be well on their way to cooking up some very nasty and noisy shit."

"We were afraid of that," Andy said.

"Yeah. How actionable is your intel on this? Do you have cause?"

Andy looked at me and I rolled my eyes.

"That might be a problem."

"It usually is with you two. Just sayin'. No judgment. That doesn't make the information any less valid. You need to find a way to develop probable cause on this and raid this place. Andrea, are these the same bozos you ran into over that Cinnamon Hills case? Those Nazis?"

"Might be connected," she said. It was dizzying, seeing her in detective mode, standing with her phone in her hand, wearing that—dress. I didn't know whether to close my eyes or ask her to put on this act nightly.

"Well, then that might not be the bad news."

"I hesitate to ask," Andy replied.

"Look, I'm not going to ask where or how you got this browser history, okay? But holy shit, if you can get your hands on this computer, and I know that might be a big ask, but if you can..."

"You said there was bad news."

"Yeah, oh yeah. The photos you sent—"

"We never sent any photos, Greg. Do you understand?"

"Right. You never sent any photos. But if you look a little farther down a certain browser history you'll find a story from JSOnline."

"What's JSOnline?"

"*The Milwaukee Journal Sentinel.* Online. There's a story about the search for a site for the Democratic National Convention."

Andy adjusted her posture on her high heels. I stared at her. It was killing me.

"So?"

"Milwaukee is in the running, and the story on their browser search history is all about when the DNC team is coming to town. As in this week. Friday."

Andy's elegant fingers slipped up into her hair. She stared down at the phone, fully invested in the police business at hand.

"Oh—my—God."

"Yeah. A lot of really bad scenarios come to mind. In this political climate, with the kind of messages that are getting put out by you-know-who, I'm sorry, but some of his hard-core followers think they're hearing tacit approval to pull off some really bad shit. Andrea, seriously, are you able to develop something actionable?"

Andy shook her head slowly. Fingers still buried in her hair.

"We'll try. I'm in Helena right now."

"Montana? Christ, it must be cold there."

"Let me get off the line and call Chief Ceeves. I'll pass along everything you said. Can I tell him to call you if he needs to?"

"Absolutely! Hey, good that you sent me this, Andrea. Really good. I took it to Chief Schultz. He's on it here. He's working with the DNC security people. Andrea?"

"Yes?"

"This is going to ramp up the pucker factor here. If you guys in Essex can't move on this, you might find yourselves overrun. Just sayin'."

"I get it. Thanks, Greg."

She touched the screen. She looked up at me with sad eyes.

"I need to call Tom."

I turned around, pulled the desk chair away from the desk, sat down and propped my feet on the bed.

"Fine with me. As long as I can watch."

THE CALL PULLED Tom Ceeves out of bed. He quickly conceded that it warranted the sleep interruption. Andy spelled out what Greg LeMore gave her. She handled this call without speaker-phone, but I could still hear his baritone side of the conversation. I watched the dress fabric dance on her skin as she paced. It shocked me that Davis Bates would have allowed his wife out in public in a dress like this. But God bless Lydia for owning it, and Andy for borrowing it.

Andy finally ended the call and ceremonially dropped her phone on the desk beside my keys. I was about to slide my feet off the bed and get up out of the chair when she lifted one leg over my thighs and straddled me where I sat. The move hoisted her hemline and I got the distinct impression she wore nothing under the dress.

"Now," she planted a flat hand on my chest, "where were we?"

"Something about a list of demands."

Dimples appeared. She leaned down, letting her hair fall in a frame around her face. Her green eyes glittered. The architecture of the front of her dress changed deliciously.

"And it's a long list," she whispered, coming close. Her hand remained planted firmly on my chest as she lowered her lips to mine.

My phone rang.

"Dammit!" she said. Still straddling me, she leaned over and stretched her arm out to pull my phone from the desk. She looked at the caller ID. "Carla? Another new girlfriend?" She handed me the phone and fixed a look on her face that suggested I better put this on speaker. I did.

"This is Will."

"Hey. It's Carla Stevens. Is this a bad time? It's morning here. I forget what time zone you're in."

Andy's dour look cracked slightly as she suppressed a smile.

"No, hey, not at all," I lied cheerfully. "I have you on speaker with Detective Stewart."

"Uh—okay, that's how you refer to your wife?"

"Hello, Carla," Andy said.

"Oh, hi! Okay, well, then it's good I got you both. I'm sorry it took me so long to get back to you." Andy gave me a quizzical look. I shook it off. "Those pictures you sent, Will? You know who that is, right?"

"If I knew, I wouldn't have sent them." The images shot of the man in the back of the SUV parked across from the funeral home were almost a bust. I need to practice shooting photos without being able to see the phone. My framing nearly missed him entirely. Only the last few shots offered a serviceable look at this face. Caught with an expression of mild shock, the SUV occupant stared at an inexplicably open rear door.

"Luca de Maurier."

Andy and I both looked at the phone.

"Right," Carla said, "you have no idea."

"Enlighten, please," Andy prompted her.

"Luca de Maurier is a fixer. D.C. is full of them. Lawyers, mostly. Some of them are money guys, you know, pseudo venture capital guys. It gives them a way to throw around a lot of cash. Some of them are home-grown. Some of them are international. Like de Maurier. Rumor has it he helped the Russians push the Union for a Popular Movement in the last French general election. But there's another rumor that said it was the MPF."

"MPF?"

"Movement for France. Another party. Could've been both. That's how de Maurier plays things. All angles. One against the other. He was also looked at by the Brits over a sex deal with one of their MPs. I forget who."

Andy's knit brow telegraphed her next question. "What's an international fixer doing hanging around at Davis Bates' funeral?"

"Good question," Carla replied. "Let me know what you come up with. But I can tell you this…he was on Davis's personal calendar two weeks ago. Took me a while to access it. That's why it took me so long to get back to you."

No, it wasn't, I thought. *You just wanted to see what value the information had for you first.*

"They met?"

"Can't say for sure. The appointment is in his office calendar. I don't have access to his personal calendar. Maybe that D.C. Metro detective can get his hands on it."

"You should share this with him," Andy instructed.

"If it was something nefarious, why would he have it in the office calendar for everyone to see?" I chimed in.

"He didn't. He had it down as a dental appointment. I had to make a few promises to his personal assistant to decode that. Don't ask."

"Is it nefarious? Him meeting with a guy like this?"

"Oh, I don't know," Carla said lightly, "would you see anything suspicious if the President of the United States had a private undocumented meeting with a former KGB agent? Oh, wait. That happened. Anyway, yes, it is fucking thunderbolt nefarious! The question is, what was Davis up to? And now I wonder if this might have gotten him killed!"

I glanced up at Andy to see if she might embrace a theory that diminished her self-imposed guilt. She didn't.

"I don't know anything about this de Maurier," Andy said.

"Unless his great grandmother is named Daphne," I threw in.

"Different spelling," Carla replied. "And I suggest you do a little digging, Detective. This is not a good person."

"Okay. Um, thank you."

Carla Stevens didn't answer. The call had already ended.

Andy stood over me for a moment, then lifted the phone out of my hand and slid it back onto the desk. She froze in deep thought, still holding her position above me with her legs locked on my thighs. I was about to let her off the hook by dropping my feet from the bed, so she could back away, when she abruptly shook her hair over her shoulders and dropped her face to mine.

The kiss ran deep and felt hungry.

When it ended, she slid her lips around to my ear.

"For heaven's sake, take this dress off me before the phone rings again."

42

"What's the plan, man?" Pidge asked between bites into a hamburger half the size of her head. She held it with both hands, like it might get away.

Andy and I slid into the booth across from her. Andy glanced at the approaching server and held up one finger to stall Pidge.

"Can we get one of those, but split?" Andy pointed at Pidge's plate, then at the two of us. "And an iced tea?"

"Coffee for me," I said.

The woman tucked the menus she carried back under her arm and strolled away, jotting the order on her pad.

We turned our attention back to Pidge who had inexplicably stopped in mid chew with a big grin on her face. She looked at me, then Andy, then me again.

"What?" I asked.

The grin expanded. "You two got busy last night! Happy fucking New Year!"

I thought Andy might blush or brush the topic aside, but instead she leaned close and pulled my chin into a kiss.

"I almost forgot! Happy New Year!"

"Amen to that!" I kissed her back.

"Okay, okay. Enough. I'm trying to eat here. And I want to remind you both that I didn't get a New Year's boning last night because some-body hauled my ass all the way to fucking Montana." Pidge lunged into the burger again. "Mo mwhuh uh plun?"

"The plan," Andy replied, "God, I can't believe I'm not only doing this, but bringing a civilian into it, too. Pidge, you have got to swear by all that you hold dear you will never reveal any of this to ANYONE. I'm not just talking about what Will can do. I'm talking about what we're about to do. Swear to me!"

Pidge bobbed her head, hastily swallowed, and laid her half-eaten burger on her plate. She sat upright and solemnly placed her hand flat on the toasted bun.

"I swear on the soul of this dead bison I will never reveal that which passes between we three muska-fucking-teers. All for bun, and bun for all."

"That's bison?" I asked.

"Yeah, and it's fucking amazing! So, spit it out, Andy!"

Andy heaved a deep sigh.

"We're going to break someone out of jail."

THE IDEA WAS ANDY'S. She laid it out for me after she laid me out. We held each other sharing a light sheen of sweat under a single sheet. Sunlight pried at the seams of the room darkening curtain, although I couldn't guess the time. We had been at it for a while.

She explained her idea as I brought my breathing and heart rate back down to normal. That she could discuss this so soon after making love made me wonder how long the idea had been marinating.

When she finished, I had questions.

"You? This is coming from you? Detective Andrea Katherine By The Book Stewart?"

"I need to find out how he communicates with Rahn. That's not some-thing he'll give up willingly. I don't have leverage through Richardson or his office. I don't have the luxury of time to wear him down. Even if Richardson would let me near him, Parks will wrap himself in lawyers. He won't say diddly. Plus, if I throw a lot of Rahn questions his way, it only tips off his lawyers. I don't have another choice."

"Doesn't something like this mess up their case?"

"How's he going to explain it? If we do this right, how can he possibly explain it?"

"Don't get me wrong! I'm all in. It's just—after the nurse, I thought you took a dim view of letting anyone else witness *the other thing.*"

"I do. But this is different. He won't know it's us. It'll be like Litton. The way you did it with Litton, except without letting him see you. You said that's what you wanted. You know, to do with *it.*"

I did. The idea sent an electric charge through me.

"Okay, but there are some tricks. Things like getting through doors. How am I supposed to get to him?"

"It's practically impossible. Even for you."

"You're not being encouraging."

"Oh, I mean it. It is practically impossible. Richardson told me he's being held in the county jail. Visitor access is out of the question because I can't be seen there, and neither can you. If it's like every other county jail I've ever seen, staff access is through key cards or key pads, but that won't open doors. It just registers identity. Every door has a camera—even the inner doors—and must be released by a guard. Even the staff areas. Plus, we can't just piggy-back on some staffer going in. There's no guarantee they would take us to him. Richardson also told me he was sequestered. He's not in general population."

"Solitary?"

"No. There's only one way to do that in a county lock-up. Special observation cells or medical. But that means Parks will be watched twenty-four seven. Some places use heavy glass instead of bars."

"It will get a little obvious if someone suddenly appears in his cell, then. Or if he disappears."

"Completely. That kind of observation is usually in a bull pen. Guards in the center at work stations. Cells all around. Or dual access. Bull pen on one side. Medical on the other. But you're right. No matter how you slice it, even if we could get to his cell, and get in, they can see him. Also, remember how you couldn't do that metal-melting trick in Chicago? Because the door was magnetic, not bolted?"

"I don't actually melt the metal."

"Frayed. You said it gets frayed. But it doesn't work on magnetic locks, right?"

"Right. I suppose I could try it on bars, or hinges, but…"

I felt her head shake against my chest.

"We don't want to damage anything. And whether we went in through visitor access—which is a whole different set of problems including having to provide ID, which means Richardson would know I was there—or we go in through staff access, either way there would have to be half a dozen magnetic locks to deal with. And cameras. They're sure as heck not going to buzz me in on my badge. We need to get to him without being seen."

"And go at him like I did Bargo Litton? Full on gun in the face?"

"No gun. But yes."

"Well, just how am I supposed to get to him?"

"We."

"We? Oh, this gets better and better. How do we get to him?"

"He comes to us. And then we break him out."

Pidge listened as Andy laid out the details, sopping up ketchup with her diminishing supply of steak fries. I worked on my half of the bison burger. It was as good as advertised. Andy spoke in clipped sentences as if briefing a squad of patrol officers. She hardly touched her lunch.

"One question." Pidge finished the last fry and licked her fingers. "What if I get caught?"

"Why would you get caught? Doing what? All you're doing is driving around, making a phone call."

"Which they can trace to my phone, which links me to you."

"No. There's a CVS up by the college and it's open today. Pick up a burner phone." Andy turned to me. "You said you need fresh batteries anyway. Just wear a hat and keep your face down when you go in there. Just to be sure."

I did need batteries.

Pidge considered the task, measured the risk and shrugged. "Cool. But I get to drive the getaway car."

43

"Batteries?"

"Check." I goosed the slide switch on my FLOP unit to confirm. I touched the two spares in my jacket pocket.

"Pidge ready?"

"Born ready!" She glanced at me and grimaced. "Cheesy, right?"

"Yeah."

Nevertheless, Pidge flexed her gloved fingers on the wheel of the Chevy Impala crew car on loan to us from Exec Air Montana. The old sedan probably couldn't outrun a Postal Service jeep, but it could blend in.

"Okay, let's go," Andy said. She tapped Pidge on the shoulder from the back seat. Pidge levered the column shifter into Drive and gave the car gas. It ambled away from the curb.

I flipped open the iPad and gave Pidge directions to the Lewis and Clark Justice Court where Andy would be meeting with Richardson and his prosecutors in less than eighteen hours. The short drive from the Doubletree was made shorter by light New Year's Day traffic. The snow we had been promised by evening had already begun dusting parked cars.

Pidge turned the sedan onto East Broadway Street. On my right, Fire Tower Park displayed its namesake tower. The parking lot, as Andy hoped, was empty.

"It's smaller than I thought," Pidge said as we ascended a shallow slope and the stone courthouse buildings approached on our left. "Pull over here?"

"No! Keep going. If they have cameras picking up street views we don't want to be seen stopping. This is all residential up ahead. We can let Will out in somebody's driveway." She glanced at her watch. "It's two-fifty. Ten minutes."

Pidge drove on. I craned my neck to look at the brick buildings beyond the older courthouse. I had studied the layout on Google Maps, the everyman air reconnaissance resource. Now, at street level, I checked for trees and wires. There were plenty of trees, but except for the small radio tower behind the building, it looked wire-free. I couldn't see the exercise yard behind the Lewis and Clark County Detention Center but knew its location and dimensions. Despite images from Google that suggested it was a meager space, it boasted a guard tower at the corner farthest from the building.

Pleasant-looking homes fanned out beyond the government-domi-nated block. Pidge drove through two intersections, then turned into a driveway and pulled up behind a parked pickup truck. I glanced at the house to see if anyone was looking, but the front windows wore closed curtains.

Andy pulled out her phone and touched the screen. After a moment, my Bluetooth earpiece jangled. I touched it to open the connection.

"We're on." I leaned over and gave her a kiss. "See ya!"

Without hesitating, I opened the car door. I stepped onto the driveway.

Fwooomp! The familiar sound, somehow growing more reassuring each time I heard it, thudded between my ears. I vanished. I gripped the top of the car door and pushed upward.

The car and driveway fell away quickly. I saw Andy's hand reach for and close the car door. Pidge backed out of the driveway and reversed direction, accelerating back toward the court complex.

"Can you hear me?" Andy's voice spoke in my ear.

"Loud and clear."

"Running commentary, dear."

"Roger that."

I aimed the FLOP unit at the court buildings, now becoming visible beyond the neighborhood trees. I pushed the slide forward, heard the prop whine and immediately accelerated.

I couldn't help the grin that spread on my face.

Flight!

"This is just freaking amazing," I said.

"No, it's fucking scarier than shit, Will!" Pidge called out to Andy's phone from the front seat.

"What kind of attitude is that for a shit-hot pilot?"

"When I fly, I want an airplane strapped to my ass!"

"Just drive, honey," Andy told her.

I leveled off just above the treetops, largely because it's more fun skimming above the winter-bare branches. The roof of the courthouse approached. I pulled back the power and let myself glide.

"Coming up on the courthouse."

The light snow in the air, a white gift from gray obscured skies, added to a quilt of snow resting on the old building's roof. I reversed the thrust and reduced my glide to a slow walk.

"Time check."

"Two fifty-seven," Andy reported. "Will, you need to be in position before they bring him out."

"I know." Andy had emphasized the point.

She'd done her homework and from that I gained a better understanding of how firmly she had become fixed on this plan. From the moment Richardson denied her access to Parks, her course was set. She talked with the Montana prosecutors about her interview schedule, slipping in coy questions about Parks' location, his facility, his routine. She called the county jail in the role of an officer planning a visit and learned that, rain or shine, the county required its guests to maintain good physical fitness. Every pod of prisoners in the jail took to the yard daily during an allotted time. Parks was no exception, but being sequestered, his allotted time wedged between periods when general population prisoners used the yard. Andy told the officer on duty she expected to interview Pearce Parks. He told her not to plan the interview between three and three twenty-five, the time slot reserved for Parks to exercise.

I passed over the edge of the courthouse roof, over the asphalt lane between the courthouse and the jail, and over the twenty-five-foot high brick wall surrounding the exercise yard. Trampled paths of snow hugged the yard's perimeter. Even if the sun had shown its face on this New Year's Day, the low winter angle would have denied the prisoners warmth in the high-walled yard.

"Two minutes," Andy said.

I pulsed the power unit to stop my forward glide. Hovering over the long, narrow yard, I felt for and used the muscle running down my center. I rotated to examine the guard tower rising above a corner of the wall opposite the jail building. Constructed largely of the same red brick as the jail complex, it sported three hundred and sixty degrees of glass. I spotted the guard through the glass, silhouetted against the gray and darkening sky. I expected to see him with a rifle at port arms, but then recognized a long object rising above the bottom edge of the glass between us. He kept his weapon secured yet easily within reach. A narrow door opened from the small tower onto an iron grated catwalk that ran the full circumference of the tower.

The guard faced the yard, waiting.

"One minute."

I rotated and studied the exterior wall of the jail, which featured a single steel door with a small observation window at face height.

The tower guard moved closer to the glass. He lifted and cradled the rifle.

"Thirty seconds." Andy's warm, soft voice contrasted starkly with my surroundings. For a fleet instant I imagined myself trapped here, hungry for the sound of that voice.

Thirty seconds. Just enough time to take care of one last detail.

I pulsed the power and floated to one of the high corners in the exercise yard rectangle. There, a boxy and rather dated closed circuit television camera hung permanently aimed at the space below. Easing up to it, I leaned close and opened my mouth. I huffed a long, warm breath on the cold lens. It instantly fogged up, then the fog turned to frost.

It must be colder than I thought.

I made the short flight to the opposite corner of the yard and repeated the action. It was a gamble. One camera fogging over might not cause alarm. Two, on the other hand, was apt to invite investigation. By then, however, it would be too late.

My skin crawled as I pulsed the power unit to drop down into the yard. The walls rising above me on all sides not only diminished the light but served to extinguish hope for those within.

The light in the observation window changed. Figures moved toward it. A face filled the window. Young. Intense. Not Parks. The face examined the yard and his eyes lifted to the guard in the tower. The guard raised his hand and signaled.

The face backed away from the wire-meshed glass. The door emitted a mechanical buzz, then a harsh snap as the magnetic lock released. The door swung open revealing a muscular officer in tan. Behind him, in blaze orange, Pearce Parks stood loosely at attention, hands respectfully pinned to his sides.

The guard stepped back from the door, out of my sight line. After a moment, Parks nodded. Carefully keeping to his side of a line painted down the center of the corridor floor, Parks stepped into the yard.

Still tall, still thin, Parks had nevertheless changed since I encountered him at his Ranch in Sioux Valley. Any tan evidence of jetting to sunny places had faded from his skin. His complexion hung pale and drawn. His once arrogant facial bones now seemed hollow and desperate. His white hair was past due for a trim. Over the standard orange jumpsuit, he wore an orange outdoor coat. It draped his shoulders to excess. No personal tailors here. No cowboy shirts or boastful belt buckles topping western jeans.

Yet this was not a man defeated. If anything, the look in his eyes and the set of his face projected something beyond the I've-got-my-lawyer-on-the-phone arrogance I had encountered before. Something more dangerous.

Seeing it reminded me that this man had unleashed Garret Foyle, the instrument of death that killed Bob Stone and a woman and her two children whose fallen bodies still rise up behind my closed eyes—all too often.

This was the man who sent Mannis Rahn to take Andy from me.

I hated this man. It made what I was about to do all the easier.

Parks trudged forward, angling right, following the path worn in the fallen snow. He didn't look up at the guard watching him from the tower as the door to the jail closed behind him. His eyes fixed on the dirty footprints he followed.

He passed me, unaware.

I pressed the slide control on the FLOP far enough to get the prop turning with a subaudible growl. Propwash flowed over my hand and I inched in trail behind Parks. My eyes flicked from his shoulders to the face in the tower. The guard watched, immobile. Not optimal.

"Is he there?" Andy asked in my ear, her own voice dropped to a near whisper as if she floated alongside me.

I said nothing. She signaled receipt of the message by not asking again.

Parks drew closer to the wall below the tower. The tower glass angled outward, giving the guard full view of every square foot of the yard. No blind spots.

The guard maintained his statue-like stance, his eyes fixed on Parks. If this continued, it meant I would have to make my move while being watched.

The only difference the guard's presence would make was in the timing. Making my move while the guard watched just meant the alarm would go out sooner, assuming he believed what he saw.

Just as I readied myself and sent a nerve message to my thumb to push the power unit slide control forward, the guard turned away. He moved out of my sight. Perfect.

I hit the power. Less than six feet ahead of me, Pearce Parks alerted to the alien sound. His head turned just as I collided with him from behind. I felt his entire body jolt in surprise. He tried to twist away from his attacker.

I threw my left arm and both legs around his torso and all my concentration into the levers in my head.

Part of me expected this to fail. Possibly with very ugly consequences.

I know I can pull someone into *the other thing* by embracing them and then vanishing. I never tried pulling someone in after I already disappeared. Would it work the same way? Would it fail? Or worse, would it work partially, causing a portion of the body to disappear and slicing the person apart the way metal frays and breaks when it hangs both in and out of *the other thing*?

If so, I decided it couldn't happen to a nicer guy.

FWOOOMP! I pushed hard. He staggered forward and lifted his arms to shake off the phantom that now clung to his back. *The other thing* snapped around him.

He vanished.

Gravity released him. His feet lost their grip on the snow. His forward momentum took us to the wall below the tower. We collided with the stone.

"Gah!" I think his face caught the brunt of it.

He began to fight and squirm, but his feet no longer touched solid ground. The ricochet off the wall sent us backward in the yard. I kept my right hand behind me, clear of his swinging arms. I shoved the power slide fully forward and aimed the prop skyward.

We launched like a rocket. He screamed.

"Shut up!" I snapped in his ear. "Shut the fuck UP!"

The startling sound of words and a voice had the desired effect. He fell silent. We cleared the top of the wall, passing the guard tower. Inside, the guard lowered a phone from his ear, alerted by the sound of Park's scream. He moved to survey the yard, then I lost sight of him.

Parks squirmed. "Hold still or I drop you! Understand?" He tensed.

The ground fell away. The trees fell away. We climbed into falling snow. Helena sprawled around us. I wasn't about to enter the low cloud ceiling, so I twisted my wrist to level off and accelerate away from the jail complex. Knowing Andy could hear my commands to Parks, I said nothing more to confirm success.

Riding on his back, I pointed Parks along our line of flight. I kept the power unit out of his reach. Being weightless made it surprisingly easy to maintain a one-armed, two-legged grip on him. His body felt bony and sinewy. I stayed on alert. The last person I carried like this was a teenaged girl who beat the crap out of me in the process. I half dared him to adopt the same tactic. I had no qualms about letting go.

My wrist strained to hold the power unit so that it would give us forward flight until I realized I could simply flip it around and reverse the thrust like a pusher propeller. After that, directional control became easy.

Fire Tower Park appeared ahead. A single dark sedan sat in the parking lot. Andy and Pidge waited for me to arrive.

Parks found his voice, strained and squeaking. "WHAT IS THIS!?"

"I told you to shut up. Open your mouth again and you take a long fall. Got it? Don't answer that."

He didn't. The rigid muscles in his body began shivering.

The park slid beneath me. A flick of the power unit would put me on a downward vector, taking me to the spot where Andy waited to interrogate Parks.

I kept going.

The park—and the sedan—passed underneath us. I aimed us upslope over a scattering of homes on the ascending hillside terrain. Beyond the homes, rugged hills rose under untouched snow.

"Are you close?" Andy asked in my ear.

I glanced down. The sedan receded. "Change of plan," I said.

I got silence. My wife doesn't argue. She processes.

"I'm going off the air." I killed the power unit long enough to use my right hand to touch the back of the Bluetooth earpiece and break the connection with Andy before she could protest. I felt bad about it, but a cold calm pushed regret aside.

I felt that calm before.

A very dark door opened deep in my heart. I struggled to analyze whether the impulse to murder this man was calculated justice or vain revenge. Either way, cutting Andy out of the debate, though it may have consequences later, was essential.

My destination appeared out of visibility that had grown more and more opaque as the snowfall intensified. Bulbous and gleaming with what looked like a fresh coat of paint, the giant mushroom stood alone on the rising hillside, high above the city whose name had been painted on its smooth sky-blue panels. The water tower occupied rough, undeveloped terrain above a small pump house. Both structures stood within a footprint defined by chain link fence. A service road ran down the hillside toward civilization, but the land around this tower held nothing but rugged slopes and snow-covered trails.

I adjusted my flight path, aiming for the top of the bulb. The low ceilings had not yet obscured it, though I could see clouds touching the tips of the hills beyond. The water tower stood over a hundred and twenty feet high. A winter skullcap of snow covered the top like a white kippah professing reverence to God. I aimed for the center and cut the power.

It was awkward, holding Parks and trying to fly an intercept course for the top of the water tower. I adjusted the power to reduce my glide to a crawl, drifting slowly toward what I estimated to be dead center. I thanked the weather gods for a light wind.

The snow cap lay less than a yard beneath my feet when I arrested my forward motion. I considered the next moment carefully. The bulb of the tower was huge, but being almost spherical, everything from top center formed a slope that eventually dropped off to nothing. The steel was smooth and would be slippery under the thin layer of snow.

If this bastard panics he'll start something I can't stop.

Tweaking my position slightly, I held a hover over what I believed to be the apex of the tower. Now or never.

I released my hold on Parks. An electric snap, not far from the kiss of static electricity from a dry winter's touch, broke through to my arm and legs where I had been holding him.

His orange form appeared. He fell. His arms pinwheeled immediately. I prepared to grab him again if he did something stupid, like try to stand. He didn't. His feet hit the snow and his legs shot out from under him. His arms went out and he dropped to his belly, hugging the snowy top of the water tower, face down. His hands flexed and grabbed. His arms and legs scrabbled and jittered. Like bergs breaking from an ice pack, big flat pieces of the snow cap broke and slid toward oblivion. Parks quickly realized that the slightest slip in any direction would be unstoppable. He froze.

He lay panting.

I let him get hold of himself. I used power to move forward, taking up a position a few feet from the top of his head.

For a moment, I thought I heard a malfunction in the power unit, or a distant wind rising. Then I realized it was a guttural mewling sound coming from Parks. His body shook, and the high-pitched sound grew louder.

"Hey!"

He shivered.

"Hey asshole! Look at me!" I realized as soon as I said it how stupid that was.

"WHAT IS THIS!? WHAT'S HAPPENING!?"

"Get a grip. Lift your head. Look."

"I c-can't!"

"Look up, or I'll give you a swift kick in the ass."

His face came up slowly. Snow clung to his cheeks. His eyes were bald orbs of terror. His mouth hung open taking and expelling air in helpless gasps.

"I—I can't take heights!"

"Good."

"Please! Get me off here!"

A huge slice of the snow cover broke off and slid away. He shrieked.

"I wouldn't move if I were you," I suggested when he ran out of air.

"*Please!*"

I let him settle down.

"Who are you? What do you want?!"

"I am your end. This is where you die. Up here where you can scream all day long and no one will hear you."

"*You can't do this to me!*"

"The evidence suggests otherwise."

He held his face up out of the snow but couldn't move.

"Move one inch in any direction, and you slide off this thing. You will hit the ground at close to terminal velocity and it will be over quick, but I can tell you that the ride down will take fucking forever. You'll have all the time in the world to think about what's coming, and what's waiting for you on the other side. Got it?" I had no idea if that was true. It sounded pretty good to my ear.

His head shivered up and down.

"Please! Please get me down from here!"

"Nope. But hey, maybe a couple years from now some helicopter pilot is going to fly over and wonder about the orange bag of bones up on this tower. They're going to find the claw marks you left in the paint. They'll take bets on whether you starved to death or died of stark terror."

The look on his face inclined me to bet on the latter.

"PLEASE!"

I touched the cold, black spot deep inside myself and took a moment to think about how easy it would be to simply fly away and leave him here. I was probably wrong about the starvation thing. He'd freeze to death by morning.

"PLEASE GET ME DOWN!"

"Listen to me."

"PLEASE!"

"Listen to me!"

He clamped his mouth shut, but his chin quivered out of control.

"Do you believe in God?" I asked.

It took a moment for him to process the question. His head bobbed.

"Good. I work for Him. Got it? He's listening to every word you say. So, I'm going to ask you some questions and you can lie all you want, but I wouldn't recommend it. You can stick to whatever story you and your money and your lawyers have been telling, but when it's all done, He knows. Judgment is coming. The only hope you have is in the truth. Got it?"

"You're not—! How is this—?"

"Are you doubting me? Look around you! You got a better explanation? Do you think you got up here in that Falcon 20 you used to hop around in? Yeah, I know all there is to know about you."

"This isn't happening!"

I laughed. "Do you think you're still in that exercise yard, having the mother of all hallucinations? Let me give you a little push and see how that works out for you." I flicked the power unit and floated up alongside him. I stretched out my foot and tapped his hip. He stiffened and more snow broke and slid away.

He screamed. If he could have dug his fingertips into that steel casing, he would have.

"NO! PLEASE! Anything—I'll do ANYTHING!"

"That's a good first step. Here's a test question. Did you send Garret Foyle to kill Bob Stone?"

He hesitated.

"Pearce," I said. "Shithead. Do you really think you have options here?"

He remained hesitant. I touched my boot toe to his hip again. He repeated his shriek. Then said, "I did. I d-duh-did send him!"

"You're getting the picture. Did you send Anthony Beauregard Tyrell to rape and murder a girl in Tulsa, Oklahoma?"

"He wasn't supposed to kill her!"

I let his words hang—and hang himself.

His body shook. It might have been a sob. It was hard to tell with his face twisted in a terrified knot.

"I'm suh-suh-sorry!"

"Apologies are not my department. I hear Satan uses them as white noise when he sleeps. Next question. Mannis Rahn. Did you send him to kill Detective Andrea Stewart?"

"Who? What? No! NO!"

This surprised me. I rotated for a better view of his face. I had no idea what kept his eyes from bursting out of the sockets.

"God knows I'm telling the truth! HE KNOWS!" Parks raised his head up higher and terror turned to anger. He let off a feral shriek. "You're full of shit! This has nothing to do with God!"

"You got a better explanation?"

"I don't know how you did this, but don't bullshit me with blasphemy! If God wants me, take me now! DO IT!"

He had me there.

"Strike me down! Dammit, strike me down! Because there is no God! This is drugs! Or technology! Or whatever the fuck it is, but it's not the Old Testament and you're nothing but a manipulator like me!"

I felt my blood rising. "If I'm like you, then your chances of getting off this dome just dropped to zero, asshole!"

"FUCK YOU!" he cried. He shot his head from side to side, looking around for the first time. Looking for an out. "A deal then! I'll make a deal! Whatever you want. I've got money! Just promise to get me down!"

"Mannis Rahn! Tell me!"

"Fine!" he snarled. "Yes! He was one of them. He was the first! He was my biggest mistake! I made him the offer and he took it, but I had no idea what he was. He had no fear and I had no control!"

"Why is he going after Detective Stewart?"

Parks stared. He worked his jaw, but no sound emerged. For the first time since landing, he seemed to quell his terror.

"That bitch!" He dropped his face into the snow. "That fucking bitch!"

That cinches it. I'm leaving you up here, you worthless piece of shit.

My phone jangled in the earpiece.

Not now.

"How do I connect with Rahn?" I asked. "How do I find him?"

His head came back up, shaking.

"I have no idea! I don't want him anywhere near me! Don't you understand?! He's fucking insane. The last time I ever saw him, he came to me in the night! He raped the woman I was with and then put a fucking knife in my face! He fucking touched the tip to my eyeball while she watched!" Parks spit the words out and the snow near his face flew like spittle. "GET ME DOWN!"

"You let him go?"

The sound coming from Parks could have been a scream. It took imagination to realize it was laughter.

"Me? I let him go? HE LET ME GO! He's the fucking devil and I made my deal with him!" His voice fell to a whimper. *"please-please-please-please-get-me-down-I-can't-take this..."*

I thought about it. I thought about how firmly made up my mind had become. In counterbalance, I thought about Andy. As if following my thoughts, Parks continued begging.

"Please get me down! I don't know how to reach him, I swear, I don't! I don't ever want to reach him! Please get me down..."

I pulsed the power unit and drifted down, closer, until I could reach out. I clamped my hand on the back of his skinny neck. The touch electrified him. His whole body stiffened. He cried out. His hands clawed at the smooth, rounded metal beneath the snow. A fresh slice of the snow cap in front of his face broke loose and slid away. He began sobbing.

"Listen to me," I said in a low voice, forcing him into silence. "Listen to me." He cocked his head to hear me.

"I put you up here. I can do it again. At any time. Do you understand?"

His head bobbed. I tightened my grip on his neck. Spread eagled and clinging to the water tower, he made no move to resist me.

"DO YOU UNDERSTAND?"

"YES!" He screamed, fierce and full of desperation. Despite that, the sound was quickly swallowed by the muffling snow and his voice fell to a rasping whisper. "...yes..."

"I should leave you up here," I said, more to myself than him.

I lowered myself to within inches of his ear. "I'm going to tell you what you're going to do. And you're going to do it. Or I will be back. I'll bring you up here. I'll take you down again. Over and over. Until the sheer terror of anticipating my next visit stops your black, rotted heart. Got it? Over and over. Any time I want, I can do this to you. And you can do nothing to stop me. Got it?"

He couldn't answer. His mouth stopped working.

44

Getting Parks off that snow-capped water tower was hard. After I explained what I expected of him, and what it would take for me to leave him alone, he sank into a kind of catatonic fugue. His bug eyes never blinked but I think he stopped seeing. I worked my way around on top of him, spread myself out and pried his body up to get my arm under his chest. He whimpered—or screamed with his mouth closed. He couldn't seem to close his eyes.

God bless the City of Helena for their shiny new water tower.

I stopped feeling concerned that I might cut him up like a cantaloupe by making him disappear.

Fwooomp!

Against my expectations, he vanished. I peeled him off the tower. He remained rigid, but all sound and strength drained away.

My phone rang again just as we cleared the tower.

I touched the earpiece. "It's done."

"Dammit, Will."

She was not happy.

"It's done," I repeated. "We'll talk about it when I get down. Go to Phase Two." That was Pidge's name for it.

I think my wife hung up on me.

. . .

I RETRACED MY ROUTE. By the time I reached Fire Tower Park, the crew car with Andy and Pidge had gone, leaving twin tire tracks in fresh snow. At least they were sticking to the plan; more than could be said of me.

Over the courthouse complex, I watched drama unfold in the streets. Squad cars with lights blazing rolled up on all sides of the block. Officers in uniform, some carrying rifles, trotted outward in every direction. I wanted to hear a siren wailing like some old chain gang movie, announcing the prison break. Apparently, a siren wasn't protocol. Squad cars moved to take up positions at intersections around the complex. The perimeter expanded fast. Possibly too fast.

I goosed the power to pick up speed. Keeping an eye out for the fringe of the expanding search, I flew over downtown Helena. The western city seemed subdued under new falling snow. Traffic was light. The few police vehicles I saw hurried toward the courthouse epicenter.

If Parks saw any of this, he didn't flinch. Maybe he finally closed his eyes. He hung rigid in my grip.

We had estimated correctly that any search would expand from the jail, and that roadblocks would appear on the arterials going out of town. There weren't enough officers yet to seal the town, but that might not take long. It didn't matter all that much. Andy told me that most escapes are prosaic, hardly the stuff of dramatic films and novels. In one recent case, an escaped criminal turned himself in to the police because mosquitos infesting the woods he sheltered in were eating him alive.

The spot we picked for the end of this drama was not far from the Doubletree. I talked Andy into having Pidge drop her at the hotel where she could engage in a lengthy discussion with the desk clerk, putting herself on video with an established timeline, in case Richardson got suspicious. Despite my instructions to Parks, there was no guarantee he wouldn't spill to Richardson the kind of questions he was asked, especially about Rahn. Richardson didn't seem like a dummy to me.

After dropping Andy at the hotel, Pidge's instructions were to drive southwest on Cruse Street. I found the street by finding the hotel and flying the same path. My phone jangled again. This time it was Pidge.

"Almost there," she said.

"Okay, you're running ahead of me. Pull over and wait." I saw brake lights ignite and our loaner sedan wallow to the side of the road. "Hold up. I see you. Coming up on your six now. Stand by."

I lowered the angle of my trajectory, spotting the curve in the road ahead and the open, rising terrain to one side of it. This was the spot we selected. Any good escaped convict knows to get off the roads and into rough terrain. At least in the movies, they do.

Mindful of wires (Andy had been shocked by the red welt across my chest) I descended toward a point where the road divided. The ground rose on my left. I spotted a sign that said Dale Harris Park and angled toward it.

Good enough.

Passing over the twin post sign, I let Parks fall onto snow-covered grass. An electric tingle rode through my hands as his body reappeared. He felt gravity snag him and pinwheeled wildly. He only dropped a few feet, but it caused him to screech.

I would have savored that screech fading away as he slid off the glossy dome of the water tower.

"Don't kill him." Andy said those words to me on the way to the jail. Not strident. Not flippant. Simple and serious, and with a steady gaze. Words shaped in the stone structures of her beliefs. I heard the words again in my head and saw the flecks of gold in her eyes.

"I didn't," I said aloud as Parks flopped into the snow. He lay whimpering and for a moment, I thought he was finished, but he pushed himself to his feet and staggered forward, up the slope toward low brush and trees. Perhaps some instinct told him to run. Maybe he genuinely thought he could escape.

"Didn't what?" Pidge was still on the line.

"Nothing. You're up."

I let myself ascend slowly above the park sign. I kept an eye on Parks. He gained steam and the dark rising terrain offered him hope. Then I heard sirens. I looked back at the highway to see a dark sedan parked by the side of the road. A squad car pulled up and fixed its lights on the petite blonde standing by her open driver-side door with her cell phone in hand, pointing at the man in the orange jump suit headed for the hills.

45

"He said he didn't send Rahn."

"He's lying." Andy made it sound more critical of me than Parks. We sat at the end of the hotel bar. The room was a riot of brown and tan. A row of flat screen TVs blazed with college bowl games above lighted glass shelves glittering with liquor bottles. Half a dozen patrons watched without much fervor for one team or the other. The bartender hovered near her touchscreen cash register at the other end. The sound of the games and the light banter in the bar covered our subdued conversation.

"I don't think so. The man was terrorized."

"He's playing you. That's why torture doesn't work. They'll say anything to make it stop. Will, we had a plan!"

"We did. And it worked."

She didn't look at me. "The plan was for me to interrogate him."

"Dee, what were you going to tell Richardson when a half-crazed Parks unloads his weird tale and the only element that rings true is that it was Detective Stewart doing the interrogating—after you've been demanding to question the man."

"Between babbling about disappearing and claims of flying through the air?"

"Doesn't matter. Put yourself in Richardson's shoes. It's a crazy story but there's just one little piece that you can't let go."

"Which is?"

"How would Parks know you happened to be here? Today?"

Andy locked her jaw and I knew I had her. She would never allow me to think that she couldn't have done a better job of prying the truth out of Parks, but she knew I was right.

"You could have argued this earlier, you know."

"And you would have cancelled the entire plan."

"No." She frowned. "Okay, yes."

I glanced at the snowfall outside the hotel thinking it would do nicely should anyone take a helicopter or drone up to the water tower to confirm Park's story by looking for a panicked snow angel impression on the dome. It seemed unlikely, but the devil is in the details.

Andy wasn't prepared to let go yet.

"He's lying," she said again, "because there's no other reason for Rahn to come after me." She drew a healthy gulp of Corona from the bottle on the bar.

I shook my head. "Parks admitted to Foyle. He admitted to Tyrell. But he freaked out when I brought up Rahn. He was *scared* of Rahn."

"Can't be. It has to be the other way around. Rahn is scared of him. Parks has something on Rahn."

"No. You're going to have to trust me, Dee. That's not what happened. That's not how Parks reacted."

She turned to face me. "Then why? Why is Rahn doing this? He's out. He's free. He's anonymous. Why isn't he on a beach in Mexico? Why am I his damned hobby? Why is he murdering innocent snowplow owners in Essex? Why is he ramming cars into icy lakes?!"

"I don't know."

"Well, I intend to find out. Screw Whitlock, I'm going to talk to the brother. As soon as I'm done with Richardson tomorrow, we go to Iowa."

"And have you determined how you're going to get through two U.S. Marshals?" I asked, thinking I knew the answer. I was wrong.

"Waving my badge," she snapped. "Or my gun."

She huffed at me and went back to her beer. I eased into mine beside her. We drank in silence for a moment.

Someone scored a touchdown on the flatscreen. The network covering the game replayed it from seven different angles.

"Where the heck is Pidge?" Andy broke the silence, glancing at the entrance.

"Last I saw, she had a hunky deputy sheriff writing his number on her palm out where they were chasing Parks up the hillside."

"Great getaway driver. So much for anonymity."

Having found a new way that her team betrayed her, Andy reverted to sulking, leaving me to try and find interest in the game suspended above the bar. A tall order, since I never went to college and had no interest in college football.

After a few minutes she abruptly finished her beer and stood.

"Pay the lady."

"Where are you going?"

"Upstairs. I'm angry with you. So, I'm going upstairs to have angry sex with you. Assuming you show up."

She stalked toward the exit without looking back.

"Oh."

OVER THE NEXT COUPLE HOURS, I gained an entirely new perspective on the experience of having my wife mad at me. When we finished, I hoped that more than just my physical energies were spent, but instead of slipping under my arm and into an embrace that signaled peace in the family, Andy twisted away and moved to the end of the bed. She sat with her naked back to me, her body outlined by cold street light slipping past the curtains.

"What?" I asked.

Her head went down. She sat in silence for a moment. Then I heard her voice, small in the hushed room.

"You're going to leave me behind."

I sat upright.

"What are you talking about?"

"What you do. You're going to move on. There's no room in what you do for what I do. For me."

I gathered the sheet and slid over to her. I put it around her shoulders and her hand rose to take mine, but she didn't turn to me.

"This is Litton all over. The desert. You went off on your own. You said it's what you want to do. With…you know."

I did say that.

"I tried to be you." She gave that a long sigh. "Today, against everything I believe in and work for, I tried to be you. A jailbreak! Torturing a suspect! Me! I tried to be like you, Will. And it didn't work. You still did it alone."

My mind shot down half a dozen different response avenues. None of them led to anything but affirmation of what she was saying.

Except one.

"I can't do anything without you."

Her hand squeezed mine. She sniffled. I reached, touched her face, turned her to me. In the darkness silver tears streaked her cheeks.

"Not anything."

ANDY'S PHONE rang in a dream that had me gliding across a winter landscape with a student pilot. We entered the airport traffic pattern, lining up for a landing. In the dream I assessed whether the student was ready for solo or not. That decision by most certified flight instructors is made largely with the gut, not the head. One more good landing, I dreamed, and this student—it suddenly became Lane Franklin—is ready for solo. The student, Lane, lined us up on final. *She's got this. She's going to put it down perfectly, right on top of that water tower. She has to. If she's off, even by inches, we'll both slide off and die.*

The phone rang again and the student next to me shoved my arm away and rolled off the bed. Not Lane. Andy. Not flying. Tangled in the sheets.

Andy grabbed her blinking phone from the nightstand. It threw a surprising amount of light into the darkened room.

"Who is it?" I asked, stupidly trying to sound coherent.

"D.C. area code." She jabbed the screen to take the call. "Detective Andrea Stewart."

"Detective, this is Chief Deputy Whitlock." Andy held the phone to her ear, but in the silent room I could still hear both sides of the conversation. "There's been a development."

"Go ahead," Andy said, swinging her legs off the bed. She sat with her back to me but made no move to cover herself. I looked past her at the clock radio on the nightstand. Seven forty-eight. Between D.C., Essex and Helena with its Mountain Time, and with an all-night flight thrown in, my rhythms were shot to hell. Lingering effects of the sleepless night at the Pineview Motel joined the mix.

"Rahn has reached out to his brother."

Andy's hand went up into her hair.

"How? What did he want?"

"His brother won't tell us."

"I'm sorry, Chief Deputy, I don't understand. How could Rahn reach out to his brother? Don't you have him in custody there with you?"

"No. We returned him to his program location."

"You said his program was compromised."

"Yes."

"You're using him as bait."

"Yes."

"And now you have a bite. This is what you wanted, isn't it?"

"It is."

"Then you're about to arrest Rahn."

Whitlock let the line fall silent for a moment, then said, "Detective, you're a lot sharper than you're pretending to be at this moment. Can we cut through the shit here?"

"You first. Why are you calling me?"

"I told you. Rahn reached out to his brother. His brother reported the contact, but he won't tell us how or what was said."

"Why?"

"He says he will only talk to you."

Now it was Andy's turn to let silence fill the line. She turned to me, but her face remained in shadow, her body an outline. I couldn't read either.

"I understand you're in Helena," Whitlock said. "You're scheduled for meetings at the prosecutor's office in the morning. I need you more than they do. I'll speak to their office about rescheduling."

"I'll take care of that."

"One more thing. You need to tell me where your sister is."

"Not a chance."

"Detective, you may want to reconsider. The one thing our subject told us is that your sister and her family are in his brother's sights. Do I need to remind you that I have vastly greater resources for protecting your family?"

"And do I need to say out loud what I know you have been thinking? That maybe you have an internal security problem which would explain why Rahn knew where his brother was? And knew where he would be in D.C.?"

"Not possible."

"Right. Forget it, Chief Deputy. My family stays where they are." Andy nodded at me, then spun away and stood. "I'll come. Tell your marshals to meet us where your jet dropped off Rahn in Cedar Rapids. I'll be there at eight a.m. local time."

Andy waited. She gave Whitlock a moment to catch up.

"How did you know he's in Cedar Rapids?"

"You said it yourself, Chief Deputy. I'm a lot sharper than I pretend."

46

"Police! Open up!" I pounded on the door. The metal door had a hollow core. My fist produced a lovely, resonant thunder.

"Fuck you! Go away!"

Andy gave me an impatient we-don't-have-time-for-this look.

I slammed the door again. "City of Essex Police! Open up or we're breaking it down!"

"Stop it," Andy muttered.

I heard the latches release loudly, harshly. The door jerked open.

I stand over six feet tall, with something extra from my western-style boots. I don't often look up at faces, but the young man who filled the door had a good three inches on me. He was shirtless, and more impressive for it.

"I hope you have a good fucking reason for impersonating an officer," he said. I peeled my eyes from the tree trunks he called arms and glanced at his trousers, at the stripes down the side.

"Uh, Detective Stewart, do you want to take this?" I stepped aside. If the look on Andy's face suggested anything, it was that I might be having more angry sex with my wife.

"I'm terribly sorry to disturb you, deputy, but we really need to speak to the occupant of this room." Andy didn't pull her badge like I hoped she would, but something in her tone informed the half-naked deputy that she was a fellow officer.

"The fuck you do!" Pidge called out from somewhere in the room. "Go away!"

"Wheels up in sixty, Pidge!" I called out, then took an abrupt step back, out of range of the long arms of the law filling her room door.

"No fucking way!" she called out. After a moment, she countered. "Two hours!"

"An hour and fifteen. I'll do the preflight and file. Get your friend here to give you a lift. Lights and sirens. That'll give you a few extra minutes."

"Pidge, honey, it's serious." Andy contributed.

A set of car keys belonging to the old Chevy came flying out of the darkness. They landed on the hall carpet. "Oh, you fucking people suck!"

I picked up the keys and headed down the hall trailing my roller bag and my wife.

47

They tried to grab Andy while I settled the bill for the two rooms using the debit card Sandy Stone had provided. Andy handed me the card and said there was coffee across the hall from the front desk, and did I want any? I told her most assuredly Yes and stepped up to the empty check-in counter.

There were two of them. One sat in a brown leather wingback chair facing the check-in desk. The other stood inside the alcove of the coffee and snack room. Both positions commanded a view of the hotel entrance. They must have been waiting on the assumption we were out to dinner, not already in bed.

I think of my situational awareness as being well honed. The few seconds my back was turned suggested otherwise. For starters, I missed the man in the coffee room entirely. I also missed the fact that the man in the wingback was wearing a suit worth more than I make in a month. The first suit I'd seen since arriving in Helena. Andy told me later she went on alert the moment she saw it.

I missed how the first man swung up out of the chair behind Andy as she went for coffee. I also missed the blow Andy delivered to him when he tried to clamp his hand around her bicep. By the time I turned around, he was already doubled over with both hands belatedly protecting his groin, gasping for air. He folded back into the big brown chair. Before his trouser seat hit the leather, Andy had her weapon drawn and pointed at the second man, also expensively dressed. He stood with a cup in one hand and the other hand holding back the left side of his suit jacket to reveal a large semi-automatic hand gun tucked in a shoulder holster, a gesture he had initiated to convince her to go along quietly.

"Hands!" Andy snapped, taking a step backward to equalize the line of fire between both men. The one in the chair groaned and lifted his hands. The one standing released his jacket flap and raised his. "On your knees, hands on your head. Both of you! Right here!"

She waved her weapon at the patch of floor in the center of the hallway facing the front desk. Both men moved into position. The one with the groin injury moaned as he lowered himself to his knees. Andy took two more steps back, securing a position well out of reach.

"On your bellies. Now!" I expected commentary, but neither man spoke. Both looked capable enough. I assumed if one was armed, so was the other. They eased themselves to the floor. "Hands behind your backs! Carefully!"

They complied.

Andy glanced at me. "Will, outside pocket. The zippered pocket. Would you mind?" Keeping her weapon trained on the two men, she lifted one shoulder to indicate she meant the shoulder bag from which she had drawn her weapon.

I found the pocket and pulled the zipper. My fingers found a tangle of dual loop zip ties.

"Handy." I pulled out two and stepped around her to bind their wrists. Both men had manicures. When I finished, I stepped away from them. Andy handed me her weapon.

"Try not to shoot me, dear," she said. She gingerly removed handguns from both men, sliding them across the floor toward the front desk where a young woman holding my room bill summary stared at Andy. Andy ran her fingers up and down their bodies. She found extra ammunition magazines on the smaller of the two men, the one still gasping for air and trying not to throw up. Andy slid the magazines across the floor.

"Something he said?" I asked.

"He got a little handsy. And this one got a little gunny." She took back her weapon, crouched facing the larger of the two men and addressed him, probably because of the two, he was the only one capable of speech. "Care to explain?"

"Sorry, ma'am. I think you have mistaken our intentions," he said. I detected a touch of British in the accent.

"And I think you've mistaken the intent of concealed carry laws in Montana. Then there's assaulting a police officer. Attempted kidnapping."

The man on the floor lowered his face to the tile, suggesting the conversation was over. Andy stood up and studied the hotel doorway, and the lighted parking lot beyond. Snow continued to fall, although lighter than it had been when we evacuated the bar. A gunmetal gray SUV sat outside collecting falling flakes. White exhaust swirled around its tailpipes.

"Miss," Andy said to the girl at the front desk. "Would you call room four-oh-seven and ask the deputy sheriff there to get dressed and come down to the lobby." She gathered up the two handguns and magazines and placed them on the counter. "And please put these somewhere out of sight and out of reach. Carefully!"

"My dad and I shoot every weekend," the girl said with a hint of smile. "No worries." She picked up the weapons fearlessly and disappeared into an adjoining office.

"I don't think Pidge is going to be very happy," I said.

"Hold down the fort. I think someone wants to have a chat with me."

"Whoa! You're not going out there!"

"I am."

"Dee! These goons just tried to abduct you!"

"Goons?" The big man spoke again. "Sir, you injure me. Your wife has nothing to fear. My employer would simply like a word with her. We may have been a little...zealous. Apologies."

"Shoot him if he gets...zealous." Andy turned and walked out the front door. I watched her march purposefully across fresh snow and open the right rear door of the SUV. She stood back as she swung the door, then leaned forward to check the interior, front and rear. A familiar face sat in the back seat. Andy seemed satisfied with the situation and slid onto the leather seat. She closed the door.

I stepped closer to the front door, trying to be ready. I had two FLOP units in my jacket, but one was all but dead. I cursed myself for not replacing the batteries sooner.

"Miss, do you have any C-cell batteries back there?" I asked the girl when she returned. She shook her head and glanced up and down the hall looking for Andy.

"Is your wife a cop?"

"Detective. City of Essex Police."

"She kicked his ass!" She pointed at the smaller man, whose face wore a sweaty sheen over bright red skin. He seemed to be practicing a breathing technique designed for childbirth. "I mean, wow!"

After about ten minutes, Andy stepped out of the SUV and walked back inside just as the deputy, in full uniform, emerged from the elevator. I looked for Pidge and uttered a silent prayer of thanks when she didn't appear, thinking one assault in the lobby was more than enough for the evening.

While the two men lay on the floor listening, Andy spelled out the situation for the deputy. The conversation in the SUV had done nothing to soften her stance toward the men on the floor.

"Do you want to pursue this?" Deputy Ron Stoltz, according to his name tag, asked after drawing Andy out of earshot of the two men.

"The assault, no. But you may want to examine their standing with regard to the two concealed weapons I confiscated. If either of them has a record, that's serious. At the very least, they broke CCW law. I wouldn't mind if they were kept occupied for a solid twenty-four hours." The way Andy said it made clear her wishes. Deputy Stoltz had no trouble understanding.

"Can do."

"Thank you, Deputy," Andy extended a hand. "I'm sorry about interrupting...you know...she's a lovely girl."

He smiled. "I dunno. I might have been in over my head."

Andy fished out a business card and traded with Stoltz. "It's Detective now," she said, pointing at the card which carried her former rank. "Let me know if you need anything. Oh! And, are you still able to drive Pi—er, Cassidy out to the airport?"

"Sure, no problem."

Heaven grants small favors.

48

On the drive to the airport, Andy started to explain the men in the hotel and the conversation in the SUV. I put up a hand and asked her to pause. As much as I wanted to hear it, if she really wanted to be wheels-up as fast as she had asked, I had a lot of work to do. While she drove in silence, I used the iPad to get a weather briefing, map a flight route and file a flight plan. I was still scrolling through icing reports and forecasts for the route between Montana and Iowa when she parked the crew car outside Exec Air Montana.

Pidge arrived shortly after, not under lights and a siren, but in her deputy's Subaru. She caught up to us in the heated, lighted hangar just as I finished the preflight. I braced for anger, but she arrived with a grin on her face and a bounce in her step, possibly because her deputy strolled with her. His height made her look like a child. Their parting was two degrees past friendly. I glanced at Andy, who watched with a look of approval. At least it wasn't wham-bam, thank you deputy.

Pidge and I finished prepping the Mojave and supervised the ground crewman that towed her from the hangar. Andy chatted with the deputy, who told her that colleagues from the City of Helena Police Department arrived at the Doubletree and all three men we met were now enjoying the hospitality and reduced efficiency of Helena law enforcement, such as it was on a short-staffed holiday. He suggested it might be more than twenty-four hours before they saw daylight.

Andy seemed satisfied. We boarded and soon climbed out through the snow-laden clouds. After Pidge leveled off *en route*, I slipped out of the co-pilot's seat and joined Andy in the cabin.

"Was she drinking tonight?" Andy gestured at Pidge in the pilot's seat.

"She said no. She and Deputy Horn Dog were having an intimate appetizer before going out to dinner."

"Because you had a beer. Before."

"That's why she's flying. Plus, I can drink and fly all I want. They took away my license, so I don't have to obey the rules."

Andy broke a small smile. Hardly more than peeking dimples. "You talk a good game, but I know you. You would have told me we had to wait."

"If Pidge wasn't along, I wouldn't have had the beer. You know I don't drink on overnight charters. You never know when the client is going to shake you out of bed and tell you to warm up the plane."

She shimmied herself down in the seat, slipped her shoes off and put her feet on the facing seat next to me. We both wore intercom headsets, which I had switched to cabin only so that we could talk and not interfere with Pidge's radio work. Not that there was much ATC communication over the wilds of Montana tonight. Pidge and the autopilot guided us through smooth air at nineteen thousand feet, well above the cloud cover that was sifting snow onto Helena and its surroundings. The engines sang a one-note lullaby.

"Lemme guess," I said pulling my phone out. I stroked through some photos until my finger landed on the one I wanted. "This guy?"

"Yes. Your other girlfriend's friend, Luca de Maurier."

"She's not my girlfriend. For one thing I would never let her do that thing you—"

"Nuh-uh!" Andy pointed a finger at her headset and then at Pidge.

"She can't hear us."

"Still," The same finger now waved a warning at me. "If you would like a repeat performance, we won't be discussing it in public."

I wanted a repeat performance. "What's an international fixer from D.C. doing in Helena, Montana?"

"Looking for me."

"Now I'm jealous." I put a possessive hand on her leg and stroked the back of her shapely calf. She didn't seem to mind.

"Actually, he was looking for Lydia. Rather desperately, I gather. That's why he followed her to the funeral home. But, he said, he didn't feel it was his place to approach her to discuss business under the circumstances. More likely, he didn't want to show his face with a squad of U.S. Marshals hovering about. I think the mysterious de Maurier prefers to keep his distance from law enforcement. He said he waited for us back at the Mayflower, but obviously we didn't return."

"Waited for what? What's so urgent?"

"I didn't ask, not directly. It was a weird conversation. He didn't want to tell me anything, but also seemed like he needed to confirm that I knew what he was after. I wanted him to think I knew what he was looking for but didn't want to tell him anything either. We were like two people playing Pictionary with no sketch pad. What I got was that he had some sort of deal with Davis—and that meant he now had to deal with Lydia. Remember those people at the memorial who were asking who would be handling Davis's affairs? I think he was behind at least one of them. I told him I was handling everything for my sister. He got coy with me and said, 'Then you surely know what I'm discussing.' And I told him I was aware of Davis's business, but that things have changed."

"What things?"

"How would I know? I was trying to get him to hear what he wanted to hear. Saying that hit a nerve. He got angry. Money has already changed hands, he said. Certain things have not been delivered that were promised. I told him that money may have changed hands, but I only recently obtained my sister's power of attorney—"

"You did?" The last thing I wanted was Andy tangled in Lydia's life.

"No. But I want him to think I hold all the strings. I told him I haven't personally confirmed payment, and now that I was taking over the price might change. That really got his blood pressure up. I think if we hadn't waylaid his minions and they had scooped me up, that would have been when things got ugly for me. Instead, I decided to rattle his cage. I told him other parties have now expressed an interest."

"An interest in what?"

"How would I know? But I can tell you this, it did not please the man. He demanded proof that I had the material."

"What material?"

Andy's eyes flared. "Will, try to keep up here. I have no clue what material."

"I was prompting. It's how we do it at the Silver Spoon."

"And I was flying blind. God only knows what kind of side business Davis was running. In all honesty, it's not my biggest concern right now. This is probably something Olivia Brogan should be handling."

I shook my head. "I don't think so. This sounds off-book."

"Yeah, well I'm a little busy right now to be cleaning up after my brother-in-law."

"So?"

"I told him I didn't have it with me, but it's safe. And then it got weirder. He asked me if the redhead has it? But the way he asked me, I don't think he knows who this redhead is. I think he's fishing. Like it's something he heard, and he wanted to know if it was true. And maybe he could get around me."

"The redhead?"

"It's something we heard, too. Remember? That Davis had switched from blondes to redheads?"

I didn't remember. "What did you tell him?"

"I told him no. Not anymore. Whatever this is about, he sent men with guns to get my attention. For heaven's sake, I don't want to send him off after some poor girl with red hair who either has what they're looking for or worse, has no clue."

"Whatever it is, it's important enough that he came all the way to Helena to find you and close the deal before too many people get wind of it."

Andy let her eyes wander to the side window. The cabin lights were low, allowing us to see the way starlight ignited a glow in the cloud tops below us. They moved with the deliberation of a relentless river.

"Well, you probably haven't heard the last of it. Maybe Lydia has a clue. Have you talked to her today?"

"Yes. She said it's hell." Andy chuckled. "But they're doing fine, and the girls are loving it." I felt a shift in topic. When Andy does that, she often does it to allow her thoughts to marinate. I went with it.

"Your parents are good with them."

Andy's sigh was wistful. "Way better than they were with us. With me. But I guess that's the whole 'grandparent' thing, right?"

"They say it's more fun." I ran my fingernails up the back of her calf and down the back of her thigh. Not erotic. Soothing. The touch caused her eyelids to lower for a moment. "So, what about it?"

"What about what?"

"Kids."

We've had the conversation before. Many times. It always goes the same way. One of us asks the question, usually over Coronas on the porch or nachos at Los Lobos. The other one says, "Nah." End of conversation until the next time.

I waited for her to hold up her end in the usual way, which, of course she would, what with us chasing through the night sky in search of a psychopath trying to murder one half of our future offspring's parents.

Her lower lip pushed out, slightly, begging for a kiss the way it sometimes does. "I dunno. What do you think?"

Holy shit.

I avoided answering by turning the cabin lights off, pulling a blanket from the seatback and spreading it over her knees, administering a kiss and escaping to the cockpit.

IT's a secret well-kept in aviation circles. Small airports often have a one-room flight office, usually unmanned, unless there's a maintenance operation on the field. Those one-room shacks often keep a sign-in book and hang a set of keys to some old clunker parked in back. Visiting pilots are welcome to make an entry in the book and take the keys. Make sure you bring the car back with a full tank.

In the case of Vinton Veteran's Memorial Airpark, the shack belonged to Iowa Air and Rotor, and the crew car was a Chevy Astro van. We arrived at one forty-three a.m. and rolled up to the self-serve gas pumps. I sent Pidge and Andy to get the car (fingers crossed that it was there and would start) and warm it up while I refueled the Mojave, keeping in mind that we might need to depart in a hurry.

The outside air temperature read in the single digits and the cold was eating at my bones as I pulled the gas hose from the reel. Screw it. The field was deserted at this hour. After positioning the ladder by the wing, I laid the hose on the ground and—

Fwooomp!

I vanished. The cool sensation that came with disappearing pushed away the biting cold. I picked up the hose and proceeded to fuel up, using the hose to keep my feet anchored on the tarmac and the fuel ladder. I thought it looked funny and half wished someone was around to see it—a whole new concept in self-service fueling.

After I finished the fueling operation, I reappeared, climbed in the cabin and fired up the engines for a short taxi to a set of tie downs on the ramp. The old Chevy van pulled up alongside the cabin and sat idling. I tied down the airplane and retrieved our overnight bags, then locked up the airplane.

"Thanks for the help!" I threw the bags in the back of the van and climbed in. Pidge had the wheel. Andy took shotgun.

"Fuck you, it's colder than a fed's heart out there!" Pidge threw the van in gear. "And if the heater in this piece of shit doesn't start working, I'm going to light it on fire!"

"So, what's the plan, Detective?"

"We drive up to the house and knock on the front door. If the marshals inside have a problem, they can take it up with Whitlock."

"She thinks you're meeting her team in Cedar Rapids six hours from now."

"Perfect."

49

The farmhouse spilled light from the kitchen window at the back of the house. All other windows framed mute darkness.

"You said there were two marshals," Andy commented as we climbed the front porch steps. "At least one will be up and on guard." She hammered the front door with her fist. I rubbed my shoulders and arms and minced my feet in the cold. Pidge remained behind the wheel of the van. The old, yellowing headlights sprayed uneven light on the gravel and snow-packed driveway.

Andy checked the window in the front door. A hallway connected the front door to the kitchen at the back of the house. She watched for movement.

We waited. She hammered the door again.

"Not the best guard," I said.

"What's he doing?" Andy gestured for me to look over her shoulder.

At the end of the hallway one of the two marshals I'd seen during my reconnaissance of the property moved slowly across the kitchen linoleum. He held one hand up in front of his face as he trudged in what I could now see was a slow circle. The hand wavered as if palsied.

Andy slammed her flat hand into the door three times. It should have awakened the dead. The marshal looked around the kitchen for the sound but did not respond. He trudged out of our line of sight.

"Something's not right," Andy said. Her hand went to her satchel and she performed the magic trick of filling her grip with her service weapon.

"Let's go around." I spun and hopped down the steps. Our footsteps made the cold snow sound like Styrofoam. Andy tugged on my sleeve and scooted ahead of me with her gun raised.

"Are you sure you want to be skulking around a U.S. Marshal's safe-house with a gun in your hand?" I asked.

"Better than the alternative if Rahn is doing the same thing."

We couldn't help but be caught in the headlights of the van as we trotted up the driveway alongside the house. Our shadows became giants on the barn at the back of the property. In black pantomime, the shadows moved urgently.

The first floor of the house was at least three feet above the yard level, built more than a century ago by homesteaders who must have feared flood among God's many wraths. The height put the lighted kitchen window too far above our heads to see through. We hurried past and cut around the corner of the house where the garage joined. A smaller set of steps climbed to a porch and back door, which probably opened on a mudroom and then the kitchen. Andy started up the steps when I reached for her arm and stopped her.

"Listen."

She froze and tipped her head. She heard it too. "Is that…?"

She reversed and dropped back onto the lawn. She jogged to a window on the side of the garage wall, a twin to the one on the other side through which I watched Steggar Rahn and his protectors arrive. She leaned her ear to the window.

"The car is running!"

I ran around the corner to the back of the garage. The big door hung closed. It had a keypad. I flipped up the cover and confronted the standard arrangement of ten numbered buttons and an ENTER button. I tried the ENTER button. Nothing. With the door down and connected to the motorized opener, there was no way to manually raise it from the outside, and no chance I'd come up with the right code.

Andy found me and made the same assessment in an instant. I asked, "Did that marshal look coherent to you?"

"C'mon!" She darted toward the back door, taking the steps by twos. She jerked open a storm door and let it swing wide, out of the way. She tried the knob. Locked. Snow on the porch boards made the footing slippery. She tried a shoulder against the door, but her feet absorbed the equal and opposite reaction and nearly shot out from under her.

"Wait!" I stepped up beside her. "Stand behind me and brace my back!" The porch had a railing running between posts that supported an overhang.

Andy secured her weapon and took up a position with her spine to the post. She pressed her hands into my back just below the shoulder blades. I planted one foot and raised my right leg. I kicked, leading with the heel, as close to the knob and latch as I could, hoping we weren't dealing with a heavy deadbolt and old hardwood.

My boot heel slammed into the door. My left foot skidded out from under me and I went down hard to the sound of snapping wood. I landed on my left butt cheek and the jolt transmitted up my spine to snap my head. Stars danced in the corners of my vision, but the door swung away.

Andy started to step over me. I grabbed her leg.

"We have to get them out of there!" she snapped at me. I pulled myself to my feet.

"Dee, that house may be full of carbon monoxide. Lethal levels. Even short exposure can cause permanent damage."

"I'm going in!"

"No! I'm going in." *Fwoomp!* I vanished and grasped her hand. "I'll be protected. Give me a push and wait here! Call for help! I'll get them out. I can carry them! Push!"

"What makes you think—?"

"PUSH!"

Andy groped, found me, and shoved me into the dark mudroom. "Hurry!"

The door between the kitchen and mudroom wasn't locked. I hit it with both hands and grabbed the knob to stabilize. Bracing one hand against the frame, I pulled the door open. Yellow kitchen light flooded the mudroom. Behind me, holding position in the cold, safe night air, Andy drew her phone.

The marshal we'd seen in the kitchen stood against the kitchen table, one hand braced on the table, the other fluttering in front of his face. I don't know what was keeping him on his feet. His head was bowed. I pulled myself through the doorframe intent on hitting him from behind and wrapping my arms around him. Midway through the flight, he abruptly leaned over the table and vomited. His body heaved twice, then lost all structural rigidity. He flopped into the mess on the table and immediately slid away to the floor. His shoulders hit my legs as he went down, almost flipping me. I caught the edge of the table with both hands. His head hit the floor with a thud.

Out of the corner of my eye, on the far side of the kitchen, I saw the door to the garage. It hung halfway open.

"Andy, he could be here!"

"I know! Just get them out!" she called out to me. Then I heard her speaking to her phone. Officer down. Medical emergency. Carbon monoxide. She ran through the steps needed to establish her credibility to the operator.

I pulled myself down and grabbed the marshal's belt. I needed to get a grip on him, but the front of his shirt and his face were wet with vomit. My throat spasmed in solidarity, but I fought it.

"Screw this!" I muttered. *Fwoomp!*

My feet hit the floor as I reappeared. I closed my mouth and nose, bent over and grabbed the marshal's shirt collar. Belt in one hand, collar in the other, I pounded a path through the mudroom and out the door. Andy stepped aside quickly. I dragged the limp body down the steps and onto the snow. Without ceremony, I dropped him and hurried back inside.

"At least two marshals plus the brother!" I called to Andy over my shoulder. As I hit the interior doorframe to the kitchen I vanished again, giving myself a hard pull on a trajectory toward the front hall.

I had to breathe. Trying to hold my breath was not an option. My hope was that whatever *the other thing* did when it wrapped itself around me, it might filter out the colorless, odorless carbon monoxide filling the house. Once before, it seemed to have that effect in a room filling with deadly smoke.

If I had that wrong, I would know soon enough.

"Hello! Hello! Anyone here! Emergency! Wake the hell up!"

I sailed down the hallway. If one marshal was up and on guard duty, the other might be resting, but at the ready. If it were me, I'd take a first-floor couch over a second-floor bedroom. Readiness over restfulness.

A living room opened on my right. I found a light switch on the wall as I glided and reached out to flick the switch On. The front hall light glowed. Lumps of blanket and human form filled a sofa against the opposite wall.

"Hey! Wake up!" I called out as I hooked one hand on the framed entrance to the living room. "We have to get out of here!"

The figure did not move. I shot across an intricately patterned green carpet that reminded me of U.S. currency. My outstretched hands hit the back of the sofa and I stopped. I reached down and jerked a blanket off the man in jeans and a t-shirt lying with his back to me. I grabbed his arm to avoid floating away and hit him on the shoulder with my other hand.

Nothing.

He seemed young, strong and healthy, but he did not respond. There was no point in checking for a pulse. If he was alive, he wasn't waking up soon. If he wasn't, it didn't matter. What mattered was getting him out of the house.

I found the new muscle running down my center and used it to rotate my body above him, parallel to his. I pulled myself down into an embrace, arms and legs around him as best I could. I pushed *hard.* Static charge struck out wherever I touched him. *FWOOOMP!*

His body vanished beneath mine. Gravity let us go. I pulled him tight against me as we lifted from the sofa, then rotated again until my feet touched the wall above the sofa. I kicked. We shot across the carpet, out of the living room, into the hallway. We crashed into a banister rising alongside the stairs to the second floor. I took most of the hit with my shoulders.

"Shit!" I released one hand and grappled with the banister, rotating again, now aligning with the long hallway. If I got this right, I could make the shot all the way through the mudroom and out the back door. "COMING THROUGH!"

I pulled hard. I had it mostly right. The doorframe between the kitchen and mudroom clipped my passenger and sent us on a bad angle for the outside door. I had to catch it with my hand and adjust. I pulled myself through the door and aimed for the open lawn behind the house, near the prone body of the first marshal. Pidge was on her knees beside him, frantically rubbing snow on his face. I shot past Andy who stood anxiously to one side, still snapping instructions to the emergency responders. I heard her say "helicopter" and "hyperbaric chamber" as I flew by.

Once over the lawn, without any finesse whatsoever, I reappeared.

The marshal and I both dropped to the frozen ground. He hit first. I landed on him. It punched the air out of me.

"This one's still breathing!" Pidge cried out.

I scrambled to my feet and wheeled for another trip inside. "Check this one, Pidge!" She crawled across the snow and began work on the second marshal, touching her fingers to his carotid artery, leaning down to press her ear to his mouth and nose.

I jogged back up the steps and sucked in a lungful of air, racing past Andy into the house. This time, I stayed visible, pounding a path to the stairs. I hooked one hand on the banister and reversed course, taking the steps by twos.

At the top of the stairs I found another light switch and ignited a pair of incandescent fixtures at each end of the hall. Four doors, two on either side, offered me choices. My lungs began begging to draw breath. Something I read once said carbon monoxide is slightly lighter than air. If the first floor was bad, the second floor might be utterly lethal.

Fwoomp! I shoved myself away from the top of the banister, aiming for the first doorway. On reaching it, I locked on the frame and pawed the inside where a light switch should have been found. My pawing caught the switch and a desk lamp on the far side of the room illuminated. The room had a bed, neatly made and unoccupied.

Using the doorframe, I shoved myself toward the next door. I got the same result.

The third door opened on a bathroom. Only one option remained.

The moment I grasped the doorframe, I found the light switch. The room was another bedroom and this bed was occupied. I pulled hard and flew straight to the foot of the bed. Bracing my legs against the mattress, I jerked off the blankets and sheets that covered Steggar Rahn. He lay on his side, eyes closed. He wore a t-shirt over sweatpants that covered both legs to the ankle. One foot wore a heavy sock. The other had a flat, plastic look in the shape of a foot. It seemed large and clunky. I had already decided that the only way to get him out of the house was to make him weightless and fly him out. Now I wondered if *the other thing* might slice off his artificial leg.

I pulled myself over him, repeating the maneuver of clutching his arm and pounding on his shoulder.

"Hey! Wake up!"

He moaned but didn't lift his eyelids. I noticed that the window near the head of the bed was slightly open.

I grabbed him, pushed hard, and made him vanish. I pushed off the bed, applying angular force that floated us to the doorway. I rotated and assumed an upright position. I had too much distance to cover to rely on grips and pushes. Reaching into my flight jacket, I pulled free a FLOP unit and propeller. I snapped the blades in place and slid the control forward. The unit responded faithfully. We launched down the hall. At the top of the stairs, I angled the unit down. At the bottom of the stairs, I cut the power, hooked my hand on the railing and pulled us around. I goosed the power and we shot through the hallway, through the kitchen, through the mudroom and into the cold open air.

I maneuvered to a spot near where Pidge was giving mouth-to-mouth to the downed marshal that had been sleeping on the first floor. Andy knelt beside her, still holding the phone to her ear. I lowered Rahn to the snow and let him go. He snapped into view and dropped. The landing forced a clipped moan from his lips and I saw his eyelids flutter.

Fwooomp! I dropped onto the snow beside him. He blinked up at me.

"Whuuh..." he tried to speak. He smacked his lips and began to squirm. "Ssss-cold!"

"Relax!" I put a hand on his chest as he pushed at the ground with his elbows struggling to rise.

"Whaahappened?" he muttered. "I feel sick!"

"Carbon monoxide. Try to get some air in your lungs. Try to flush them out. Breathe!"

He heaved in a breath, blew it out, heaved in another and began to cough. He abruptly turned his head and leaned toward me.

"Don't you puke on me!" I blurted out and skittered backward on the snow.

He gagged, heaved for more air, and coughed.

"Dee, what's the word?"

"Helicopter is coming from Cedar Rapids. They said twenty minutes out five minutes ago."

I looked at Pidge who continued pushing air into the marshal. I looked at Andy.

"His heart's beating. She's trying to get clean air into him. What about him?"

"He sleeps with the window open. Might have saved his life."

Steggar Rahn pushed himself upright, heaving air in and out of his lungs. "Detective Stewart? Is that you?"

"Yes."

"This—" he gasped "—this was—my brother! This was my brother!"

Rahn said it to Andy, but he stared at me, wide-eyed.

50

I pulled the van ahead and we lifted the two marshals into the back. Steggar Rahn worked his way to his feet, then promptly fell over. Pidge lifted him from the snow and helped him into the front passenger's seat. The heater was anemic, but better than nothing. I made a run back into the house and brought back blankets. After everyone was wrapped, I made another run into the house.

Out of sight of the van, I vanished and pulled myself into the kitchen. After the fresh winter air, the scent of vomit rolled my stomach and threatened to trigger my gag reflex. I hurried through the air above the table to the open garage door. Inside, the Lexus I'd seen deliver Steggar Rahn to the safehouse hummed at idle.

I found the garage door switch and hit it. The door rolled open. I backed out and closed the kitchen door. Then I floated back to the front hallway and opened the front door. I tried several windows. Two of them opened. Others were either painted shut or I missed something about the latching mechanism. I wasn't anxious to hang around and figure it out.

At the back door, I reappeared and walked out. I dropped down the steps and went around to the garage. With the door open, the car exhaust puffed out into the winter air in a faint white cloud. Avoiding the cloud, I went to the driver's side door, opened it and slid onto the driver's seat. I punched the start/stop button and the obedient V6 went silent. The steering wheel hummed up and out of my way for my convenience.

Rescue took twenty-five minutes to arrive. Before the big Bell helicopter announced itself with its characteristic whomping blade sound, a Benton County Sheriff's unit arrived. Andy, responding to the flashing lights of her trade, jumped out of the van and met the uniformed officer at the end of the driveway, badge out. The two of them huddled, then the officer returned to his unit and backed out onto the road in front of the house. He flicked his headlights to bright and illuminated a landing zone for the medevac chopper. I noted that the road had no wires hanging above the two-lane.

After that, it was an official evacuation. The chopper landed. Andy backed the van out of the driveway and the medics from the helicopter took over. The two marshals were loaded on stretchers. Steggar Rahn made his own way.

Blasting snow skyward and cold rotorwash over us as we watched, the helicopter lifted off and became a set of blinking lights in the night. I watched it go with a pilot's eye, thinking how strange it was that the ship was quieter leaving than when approaching. That might not have aided the mission of this model's forefathers in Vietnam.

Andy walked up to me at the end of the driveway where I stood in the burgeoning silence. She slipped in close and accepted my arm around her shoulders, but her face remained upturned to mine, etched with concern.

"Are you okay? Do you feel okay?"

"I'm cold."

"No. I mean, you were in there a lot. Any headache? Anything?"

I pulled in a breath of cold air and shook my head. "I wasn't sure, but now I really do think *the other thing* filters the air somehow. I feel fine."

"How did he do it?" she asked the winter silence as much as she asked me.

"He's a goddamned ghost."

51

W hitlock found us at the hospital in a general waiting area. The comfortable space contained plush furniture in small clusters. The worried and the waiting had a choice of sitting near flat screen TVs or an eternal flame gas fireplace. A pseudo-kitchen offered coolers with complimentary beverages. A coffee station presented a wide variety of boutique blends. I helped myself to several cups.

Pidge found an unoccupied sofa, pulled it away from its cluster, turned it to face a wall and climbed over the back to curl up and go to sleep.

Andy either paced or waited with me. When we sat together, she idly traced the lines in my palm with her close-cropped fingernails. Eventually she let her head rest on my shoulder.

Chief Deputy Whitlock walked in at almost nine a.m. with two accompanying marshals.

"They relayed the news to our pilots," Whitlock said without preamble. She pulled off her gloves and unwound a scarf from around her neck.

Andy stood, prompting me to take to my feet as well.

"I'm so sorry," Andy said.

Whitlock opened her mouth to speak but the words caught. She clamped her mouth shut and nodded. It told me she knew what we knew, and that it hit the woman hard.

Forty minutes earlier a somber doctor found Andy in the lounge and invited her to sit with him. He spoke of the carboxyhemoglobin levels revealed by testing the blood of the two marshals and Rahn. He speculated on the lethal toxicity of the air in the house. He detailed percentages that would give you a headache, percentages that would make you vomit, percentages that would put you in a coma and percentages that would induce death with only a few breaths. Then he told Andy that the marshal who had been staggering around the kitchen when we arrived had died. His partner from the sofa in the living room had been taken to a hyperbaric chamber and was being treated. He was expected to live, but the question of long-term damage would only be revealed with time. Steggar Rahn, the least affected, occupied a standard room where he was receiving pure oxygen. Of the three, his carboxyhemoglobin levels were the lowest. Andy told the doctor about the open window, and he agreed that it likely spared Rahn's life.

Whitlock knew all of this when she found us.

"I'm sorry," Andy said again. "I don't know their names."

Whitlock, looking tired, sat down.

"Marshal James Radovan. He—um, he didn't—" she stopped and collected herself. "Marshal Peter Williams, he's in the chamber." She reached out and took Andy's hands. "He owes you his life, Detective. He has a family. They both do."

Andy shook her head. "I wish we had been there sooner."

"You were there soon enough to save two of them. That counts. There's nothing I can ever do to thank you enough for blatantly disregarding my wishes. These were my people. These were…" She fell silent.

"There is one thing you can do," Andy said softly. Whitlock looked up at her. "Let me speak to the brother."

STEGGAR RAHN GOT a private room with an armed Cedar Rapids police officer at the door. He lay in a bed wearing a tight-fitting oxygen mask. When we entered, his eyes were closed, but he wasn't sleeping. He blinked at the sound of us bumping the door open.

Initially, Whitlock restricted the visitation to Andy alone. Andy told Whitlock that it was me who carried all three men from the house, risking my own health and safety. She pointed out that Rahn might want to thank me, and we might use that debt of gratitude to gain information he may otherwise withhold.

Andy also insisted that the marshals leave the room. She promised to share whatever she learned but demanded to see him without Whitlock or her subordinates. After a brief stare-down with my wife, Whitlock reluctantly agreed and waited in the hall.

"Are you going to point your gun at me again?" Rahn pushed his oxygen mask aside to speak as Andy entered the room. I closed the door behind us.

"You asked for me," Andy said curtly.

Rahn pursed his lips in a shallow smile, then shifted his gaze to me. He let it linger for a long appraisal. I wondered if he was trying to determine whether to trust me or not. Or if he was simply trying to remember what happened. He had the look of a man fitting pieces of a puzzle in place.

"This is my husband, Will. He carried you out," Andy said.

"I'm sorry, I don't remember much. But—of course—thank you."

"Let's never do that again," I said, hanging back.

"I need you to tell me everything you know," Andy said without preamble. Rahn lifted his gaze from me.

"Good," he said, turning back to Andy. "You need something from me. I need something from you."

"What do you want from me?"

"I want you to get me out of here and away from these U.S. Marshals."

"Why?"

"Because that's how my brother found me! His information came from the Marshals Service." Andy had suggested the same thing to Whitlock. Her reaction surprised me.

"That's ridiculous!" Andy shook her head.

"Is it?! When my brother contacted me—before I went to Washington —I was stunned. I was terrified. But not just for me. I realized the mistake I made in contacting people from my past. I was horrified that I may have brought harm to those people! I had to know!" He reached up and pulled the oxygen mask over his head. It tangled, and his hands shook as he struggled with it. "Dammit!"

Andy stepped forward and helped him clear away the plastic tubing.

"There were only two people who knew where I was. Teachers I worked with. After Mannis reached out to me, I called them. Both said they never heard from anyone. You have no idea! I thought—I thought Mannis may have—may have hurt them! But that's not how he found me. That's why I know he's getting information from within the Marshals Service."

"There's no way. What possible connection could a convicted murderer, an escaped convict and a dead man, make or have with the U.S. Marshals Service? And even if he had a connection, what are the chances that connection would be in the right position to have access to your files? Crap stories like that are the reason I can't watch TV dramas about cops!"

"There's no other explanation, Detective!"

"Look, I don't know you. I'm not violating half a dozen federal regulations to help you on the basis of a wholly unsubstantiated accusation."

Rahn sank back against his propped-up pillows, diminished but not defeated.

"I guess it doesn't matter. That's not why you will help me get away from them. Detective, I will tell you everything I know, just as you asked, and it will help you find my brother. And you will help me get out of here and away from the U.S. Marshals, whether you believe me about them or not."

"Why would I do that?"

"Because I know where my brother is going, and I want you to take me there. I want to be there to stop him. I have a right, after all he's done to me! You need me! I know things you need to know!"

Andy put both hands on the rail of his hospital bed and leaned toward him. "Tell me. Tell me where he's going. I will stop him."

Rahn broke his eyes free of her intense stare.

"I can't."

"I didn't think so. You don't know where he's going."

"No. I don't. But you do." He said it with renewed strength. "You know."

"That makes no sense. I have no idea where he's going."

"Oh, but you do. He's going to kill your sister and her children, and not in that order. He told me. He was gruesomely specific."

"That's impossible!"

"Are you willing to bet their lives on that? I don't know where your sister is, but you do. And somehow, so does Mannis. You don't have much time. You need to take me with you, because I know how to stop him. I know what you need to know—when the time comes. And I'm not saying another word until we get there."

52

"Okay, here's what we do. We have Pidge steal a helicopter—"

"I don't know how to fly a fucking helicopter!"

I tried to look incredulous. "How hard can it be? Lift up the lever on the side. Pull on the stick between your legs."

"You go pull the stick between your legs!"

"Will you two hold it down, please," Andy said. She glanced around the lounge. Whitlock had gone back in to speak with Steggar Rahn, but one of her marshals strolled through with a pair of coffee mugs in hand. He went to the coffee station for refills. We waited. On his way back out, he gave Andy a respectful and professional nod.

"Why don't you just have him do his magic disappearing act?" Pidge poked a thumb in my direction.

"No." Andy would have none of it. Earlier she took me aside and asked if Rahn had been awake and alert when I flew him out of the house. I said no, but I wondered if something subconscious gave him a memory he could never reconcile. A dream in which he could fly.

Andy fidgeted. Rahn insisted that his murdering brother was headed for Lydia and her girls. Driving or flying? Andy wanted to know. Driving, Rahn assumed. Andy told Rahn that we had an edge. Before leaving the room, she told him she would either be back for him or she wouldn't—she had not yet decided.

Outside the room, I took Andy aside.

"You're not seriously considering this, are you?"

She lowered her head. A thick lock of hair fell across one eye. She brushed at it and breathed deeply.

I pressed. "That bullshit about a leak in the Marshals Service? Really? Plus, the guy has one leg and he's recovering from carbon monoxide poisoning. Not exactly someone you want at your side if you really are going face to face with his psycho brother."

"I know."

"But?"

She looked up at me. "All of that is true. But there's something else."

Her jaw locked. Her lower lip gained prominence beneath flaring eyes. The combination warned me that she would not be swayed from a path that was already etched in her mind.

"What?"

She glanced at the officer standing outside the room door, chatting with one of the marshals that arrived with Whitlock. She pulled me away. We began strolling back toward the lounge.

"How did Rahn get from Bob's garage to his shop?" She didn't wait for me to offer a guess, which I did not have. "That's been bothering me from the day it happened. Will!" She hooked one hand on my arm and pulled me close. "What if he's in on it?"

"Him? Dee, he offered to testify against his own brother! That's what put Rahn away in the first place!"

"I know. I know. But—things change. People change. Who knows what's happened between these two? Maybe Rahn and Rahn reunited and bonded again. Maybe this guy has a variation of Stockholm Syndrome. Do I trust him? No! But nobody—not Lydia, not the girls, not my family —not me or you—will be safe until we end this."

"You mean arrest...right?"

She looked away. "That will be up to them." She stopped and glanced back at the hall, at the closed door. "I'm not sure how much time we have, but if we take him with us, and he is in on it, they may think they have the upper hand. They may think they're reeling me in."

"Jesus Christ! How is that a good thing?"

"It means they're not out hurting anyone else. C'mon."

. . .

WE HUDDLED IN THE LOUNGE, trying to come up with a way to make it work.

Andy's phone rang. She read the screen and said, "I have to take this."

She stood and stepped a few paces away, far enough away that we could only hear her side of the conversation.

"Hello."

"Why? What happened?"

"When? How?"

She listened to a long explanation.

"No, sir, it's no problem."

"I understand. I can certainly come back again."

"Right, no I understand. I'll have our office put in the paperwork."

"Yes, sir. You're welcome. Please keep me posted."

The call ended. Andy slipped a smile free from a face that had increasingly worn tension and worry. She slid back onto the chair beside me.

"That was Richardson." Pidge and I perked up. "Pearce Parks has been hospitalized."

"My heavens!" I said grandly. "Whatever happened?"

"It seems he escaped yesterday. No one is quite sure how or why, but he was recaptured—"

"Thanks, no doubt, to a heroic concerned citizen!" Pidge injected.

"And has suffered some sort of psychotic break. They're not sure what. Richardson says he's incoherent. He claims someone forced him to escape and is trying to kill him. His lawyers tried to get in to see him this morning, but he told the guards he's firing them all. They pulled some strings and had him hospitalized, and they're claiming the people in the jail attacked him for the purposes of gaining a confession. It's all a bit of a mess, so my meetings with the prosecutors are postponed—indefinitely."

"Shocking," Pidge said.

"Is he pleading out?" I asked. Because that's what I told him to do. Or he could expect another trip to the water tower.

"Not sure yet. Richardson said he'd let me know. He cleared me to leave Helena."

"Good to know, since we're long gone. Let's get back to the one-legged man in there."

Andy held up one hand. Whitlock entered the lounge and walked to where we sat.

"My team and I are going out to the scene. I'm going to ask you to remain here, in Cedar Rapids. I know I gave you access to the witness, but that was a one-time access, Detective. That's now rescinded. There's no reason for you to remain here at the hospital. The officer with Mr. Rahn will not be allowing any visitors. Please don't take this as a lack of appreciation for what you did. I'm just trying to get control of things until we can sort this out."

"I understand," Andy said. "It doesn't matter. He had nothing helpful when I spoke to him. We're getting ready to go back to Essex."

Whitlock shook her head. "I'm sorry, but I need you to stay here. For now. I assume you flew in?" She glanced at me, then Pidge.

"Yup! We're parked right where you guys came in. That kick-ass MU-2 sitting on the ramp," Pidge chimed in. "Can't miss it. But if you're going to keep us here, I better call the office and make sure the plane isn't booked out on charters."

"Well, I'm sorry for the inconvenience," Whitlock said, "but I'm sure you understand." She looked at Andy for confirmation of the last part.

"Of course."

Without another word she hurried out.

"MU-2?" I asked Pidge.

"Yeah, there's a gorgeous MU-2 sitting on the ramp out at Signature. Saw it the other night when we came through here. I always wanted to fly one of those."

"Jesus, Pidge! You just lied to a federal officer!"

"Is that why I feel all tingly?" She wiggled in her chair.

"I'll bet you anything Whitlock puts someone out there to watch that airplane and make sure we don't leave. You better hope it's still there!"

"It is. The ramp rat told me it's for sale. Been there since summer."

Andy, who had only been half listening, sat staring at the hallway after Whitlock. She held the pose for a long minute, then turned to me as she pulled out her phone. "I need to call Tom."

As she dialed the City of Essex Chief of Police I looked in the direction Whitlock had gone. Andy asked, "Something bugging you about her?"

"Did you notice? Whitlock has red hair."

53

Abducting a federal witness from a secured hospital room under the nose of an armed police officer was disappointingly anti-climactic. Andy waited an agonizing twenty minutes after Whitlock's departure. She fixed her badge to her belt so that it was visible under her open coat. She then filled a tall coffee cup and walked down the hall to Rahn's guarded room and offered the patrol officer the coffee. He declined, admitting to her that his bladder already ran above flood stage. She laughed and told him there was a restroom around the corner, and she would hold the fort while he relieved himself. He scooted away, professing thanks. He was only gone a few minutes. He returned to find Andy still on guard, still holding the coffee. They chatted a few minutes. She insisted he take the coffee, then she left.

"He's going to get dinged," she said with some regret, joining Pidge, me and Steggar Rahn in the lounge. "I feel bad about that." She looked at Rahn, dressed in the same t-shirt and sweatpants he wore when I found him. Pidge stashed his discarded hospital gown under a sofa cushion. "We better get you a jacket."

"I'll need a cane, too," Rahn said. "If there's much walking this thing can get pretty sore." He patted his left leg.

"I can imagine," Andy said. "Let's go."

54

F lying for a living teaches you to see time as a constantly moving ribbon. Putting yourself, or your airplane or your passengers at a specific location at a specific time on that ribbon means segmenting the ribbon. A piece for getting out of the hospital and into the old Chevy van. A piece for driving the van from Cedar Rapids to Vinton and from Vinton to the airport just north of town. A piece for refueling the van along the way, paying the price for its use. A piece for returning the van and its key, loading the Mojave and conducting the standard preflight rituals. A small piece for taxi, runup and pre-takeoff checks. And then you hit a marker point, the moment when the wheels lift off. From that point you become part of the flight plan, and the numbers assigned to the moment of landing are fixed. After landing, the ribbon is measured again, allowing for taxi, parking, unloading, securing the aircraft, securing ground transportation and travel to the ultimate destination.

Do it often enough and time management becomes a sixth sense. My sixth sense told me we would stand in the Essex County Air Services office, wrapping cold fingers around a cup of Rosemary II's near-perfect coffee at just after four p.m.

I took my first sip at three fifty-seven.

Rahn asked to use the restroom. Andy watched him hurry down the hall on the cane we bought him at the hospital gift shop, along with a hooded fleece and a ball cap. She took up a position to keep watch until he stepped out. During the flight, I expected her to interrogate the man, but just prior to departure she asked me to stow the passenger headsets. She put Rahn in a forward-facing seat on the left side of the aircraft. She took a seat on the opposite side facing aft, directly behind my co-pilot's seat. It felt like she was protecting me. I noted that she kept her shoulder bag tucked in beside her. I gave her a look that asked if she wanted me to join her, but she gestured for me to sit up front. Near as I could tell, Andy did not exchange a word with Steggar Rahn during the one hour and seventeen-minute flight.

Entering the office, Andy never let her eyes leave Rahn except to check her phone. She showed me. "Five missed calls from Whitlock."

Pidge leaned over the counter and rotated the monitor on Rosemary II's computer to check the schedule for Thursday and Friday.

"Where's Earl?" she asked.

"Gone," Rosemary II replied with a pointed glance at Andy. Rosemary II had been uncharacteristically quiet during our arrival. She reads people as well as her original namesake did. I sensed her reading of Andy told her my wife was both on alert and on the job.

"Good place for him!" Pidge said happily. She slid away from the counter. "You need help?" she asked Andy. Pidge rolled her eyes in the direction of the hallway. "Someone to kick some ass?"

"I think we've got this. Go home. And thanks."

"Any time. I'm going to sleep for the next twenty hours."

"You've got an eight o'clock tomorrow, honey," Rosemary II reminded Pidge.

"If I'm not here, start without me!" She breezed out the front door.

Andy went quickly to the counter. "Did—?" Rosemary II put up a hand before she could finish. She reached under the counter and pulled out a zippered pouch, something once intended for a small set of tools.

"Earl picked it up. He said he triple checked it. You be careful!" Rosemary II slid the pouch across the counter to Andy, who slipped it under the flap of her shoulder bag.

"Is Pidge gone?" Dave Peters cautiously poked his head out the pilot's lounge door. He looked in both directions. "Oh, hi, Andy!" My wife waved but didn't engage. She returned to her station, watching the hallway. Her hand hovered near the flap of her shoulder bag.

"You're hiding from Pidge?" I asked, mostly to draw Dave's attention away from Andy.

Dave made a face. "She got her undies in a bundle because I covered her schedule today."

"That sounds like you did her a favor."

"I made her take Saturday as payback. I think she was going skiing, but I really need the time off. I gotta pick up the rest of my stuff from my parents' place." Dave had moved back to Essex in a hurry after losing his job as a pilot for Evergreen Reform, Pearce Parks' private prison company. "Hey, you wouldn't want to help a buddy move shit, would you?"

"Love the idea, but Andy's got me on a short leash this weekend, with her family in town."

"And the dance Friday night!" Rosemary II reminded me.

"And the dance."

Dave lowered his voice and turned away from Andy. "Dude! In-laws? You seriously gotta blow that off. I pay movers in beer!"

"Can't, man. She's got deeply incriminating material on me. I'm going to be toeing the line for a long time, right honey?"

Andy held her position, watching. Without turning, she said, "Your pal was a very bad boy in D.C., Dave."

"How bad?"

I shrugged.

"Really, how bad?" Dave grinned at Andy. I could see that she could do without this distraction, but that she knew Dave wasn't going to let it go. "What kind of incriminating material?"

"Photographic evidence," I said. Without taking her eyes off the hallway, Andy fished her phone from her pocket and extended it to me.

There's no window in the men's bathroom. What's he doing in there?

I took Andy's phone and opened the screen to her camera gallery. She doesn't shoot many pictures, unless it's for work. Since she hadn't been at the office for a couple days, the most recent photos were from D.C. I found what I was looking for at once. Dave hovered at my shoulder.

I held the phone up to show Dave the photo of Olivia Brogan that would playfully enslave me to my wife for some time to come. Dave's grin widened as his eyes locked on the part of the photo that most men would zero in on, but then he expanded his view and a questioning look clouded his face.

"What?"

"I think I know that woman!"

Andy glanced sharply at him.

"Yeah! I know that woman. Wow, Will! You are in some deep—!"

"How do you know her?" Andy marched up to Dave. She took the phone from my hand and held it up. "Dave, how do you know this woman?"

"Uh—she was one of them! You know, one of the women we used to fly into Sioux Valley, for Parks to take up to his ranch. Jesus, Andy!" Dave tried to back away, but my wife pressed him.

"When?"

Dave raised both his hands and his shoulders. "Couple years ago, I think. Right after I started flying for Evergreen. I remember her because —well, I mean *look at her*—and because he took her to the ranch, but one time he up and left without her. A big soap opera blow-up. One of the other guys said she hooked up with someone else who was at the ranch and it really shook up the boss. I don't know!"

Andy stared at Dave without really looking at him.

"What?! What did I say?"

The door at the end of the hall opened. Andy put the flat of her hand on Dave's chest and pushed him backward into the pilot lounge. He opened his mouth to speak but she put a finger to her lips.

Rahn hobbled toward us, cap on, hoodie flipped up. He limped with his face down, concentrating on the path ahead, looking old as he planted his cane with each step. Rosemary II watched him from behind the counter. She cast Andy a curious look.

"Let's go!" Andy said, hurrying to the door and holding it open for Rahn.

I threw Dave one last flare of the eyes trying to tell him I had no idea what just happened.

I trotted to the door and followed Rahn out into winter's early darkness. Andy followed, three paces behind.

55

"Did they tell you I taught high school social studies?" Steggar Rahn twisted in his seat beside me. I focused on driving. We took my car. Andy sat directly behind me, which prompted Rahn to turn toward her. "Sixteen years. Loved it. Don't know if I'd love it so much these days, though. How do you explain to kids what's happened to the American idea?"

"Tell me about your brother," Andy said.

Rahn heaved a sigh. "What a waste. What an absolute waste of intellect, of mind. My brother Mannis was—is—I don't know—the smartest person I ever knew. You know how they say ESP is actually the subconscious extraction of cues from things like atmospheric pressure, skin tension, pheromones? I think he has that. I think he can read minds. I don't mean like science fiction, but I mean read intent, just by reading body language, maybe carbon dioxide from people's breathing—something like that."

I followed my headlights away from the airport into farm country. Snow-covered fields lined the narrow road. The black sky hung above us, starlit and cold. I cruised roughly fifteen above the speed limit.

"Maybe I have a little of that. Like right now, Detective, I sense you don't trust me."

"Let me clear that up for you," Andy said. "I don't trust you. I told you before, I don't know you. That doesn't mean we don't have a common goal. But that's as far as it goes. You've been holding out on me. It's time. Let's talk about your brother…you testified against him in Oklahoma."

"No! I didn't. It never came to a trial."

"Right. But you came forward as a witness and made the prosecution's case."

Rahn gazed out the window. His breath fogged it lightly. "Hardest decision of my life. I know it sounds strange, but a little brother never loses his love for big brother, no matter what happens, no matter what he did. That core love is ingrained. I guess it's the reason abused women don't leave. They love the idea of love. I never stopped loving *the idea*— you know? The idea of a big brother. Right to the end."

"Do you regret doing it?"

"I regret having to do it."

"Brotherly love notwithstanding, Mr. Rahn, your big brother, as you aptly put it, is a monster. He took your leg. He's coming for me. And you say he's coming for my sister and her children. It's time you told me. What, exactly, did he say to you?"

"He knew where I was, of course. I told you the marshals are compromised, but you refuse to believe me. I don't trust that woman, that Whitlock."

"She told me that your brother contacted you, but you wouldn't tell her how. Tell me. Now."

"I will. And here's further proof that you cannot trust the marshals. Mannis not only knew where I was, he knew how to call that marshal's cell phone. He waited until the marshal was in the bathroom and I was in the kitchen. I picked up the call. He spoke to me. He could see me through the window. He said so."

"Did you tell Whitlock about this? About this leak?"

"I told you, I don't trust her. What if she's the leak? That's why I insisted on seeing you. I don't know who in the Marshal Service to trust. They nearly cost me my life!"

"Why did he come after you? Why not go straight for my sister?"

"He said he saw me in D.C. and knew I betrayed him again. He said I should be punished for it. I didn't know, of course, what he was about to do—with the car exhaust. That's what he does, though. He punishes. Just like he plans to punish you, Detective, by harming your sister and her children."

"How? How does he intend to get to my sister?"

"He said he knows where they are."

"Punish me for what? I thought he was sent to eliminate me as a witness against his benefactor. Why would he make it personal?"

"Oh! Oh, this is my brother we're talking about! With him, every motive is personal."

"Why is he doing anything at all for Parks? Parks is in jail, and probably will be for the rest of his life."

"My brother may be a monster, but he is loyal. He is devoted to Parks. I suppose for setting him free."

I tried to see Andy's eyes in the rearview mirror, but the angle was wrong.

"You really think he's that smart?"

"Detective, I was supposed to die last night, but did you see how he did it? Carbon monoxide! An elaborate accident! That's what he does!"

"Didn't look like much of an accident to me," I said.

"You're obviously not familiar with the growing number of fatalities caused by keyless ignition in late model vehicles, Mr. Stewart. It's an epidemic. People pull into their garages and forget to turn off their cars because there's no key. The cars are silent, it goes unnoticed. Tragic. Almost thirty people dead in the last ten years. Many more suffering permanent ill effects from carbon monoxide poisoning. It's just the sort of thing my brother would know about and use."

"How fortunate that you sleep with the window open," I said.

"Yes. A childhood habit. I need to hear the night sounds. Birds. The wind. I feel...cooped up if I can't. But if you had not come when you did, even that wouldn't have saved me."

Andy didn't reply. I turned onto Sunset Circle Road, the road that circumnavigated Leander Lake.

"My brother would say he's not a brute. That he's not a killer. He would hold up these accidents as testament that he allows fate to take the ultimate hand. I suppose fate *did* take a hand for me. Perhaps that proves his point."

"He's a psychopath. He gets off on describing how he plans to murder children," I said.

"Unless that was only intended to motivate your wife, Mr. Stewart."
He turned to Andy. "It strikes me, Detective, that even if he is caught,
there will be no way to prove he tried to kill me last night."

"Murdered a U.S. Marshal," Andy said.

"What?"

"He murdered a U.S. Marshal last night. Attempted murder, in your
case. Murdered, as regards Marshal Radovan."

"Yes, of course."

"Who had a family."

"That's so sad," Rahn said. "Terrible. Are we close? You haven't told
me where your sister is hiding."

"We're quite close. In fact, just ahead, do you see where the road
curves sharply to the right? That's where your brother tried to kill me."

"Your sister," Rahn said, staring through the windshield. I flicked the
lights to bright, but they failed to penetrate beyond the road ahead. A wall
of black hid the lake.

"But it was me he was after."

Rahn said nothing as we swung through the curve. After a moment, he
spoke again. "I don't understand. Does your sister live in this area?"

"She does," Andy said.

"And she's here?"

"What better place to hide someone than in their own home, after their
pursuer has come to believe they've been driven out."

"Ah! That's creative, Detective."

We drove the short remainder of the trip in silence.

I PARKED my car in Lydia's driveway in the same spot it occupied the
night I met Andy's parents. Andy hopped lightly out of the back seat and
hurried around the car. I thought she might help Rahn, who struggled to
get his artificial leg through the small dimensions of my compact car door,
but she bypassed him and went straight to the front door. A motion-
sensing light detected her presence and cast bright light onto the sidewalk
and snow-covered gardens bordering the front of the house. Andy touched
the keypad beside the front door. A snap released the lock. She opened the
door and gestured for us to wait. She disappeared, then reappeared.

Andy held up her hand and gestured for us to be quiet. She listened.

After a moment she said, "Something's wrong." She looked around the yard, at the house, at the roof. "You said he was driving? Your brother? From Iowa?"

"Yes," Rahn affirmed.

"We spent too much time at the hospital. He had too much head start on us." She reached for her shoulder bag.

"Are you saying he's here?" I asked. "Inside?"

"I don't know…" She turned to Rahn. "Moment of truth, Mr. Rahn. You said you could help me stop your brother. How?"

Rahn looked at the house, at the dark wooded lot around it, at the two of us. He drew a long breath.

"Let me approach him. My brother would never believe me capable of confronting him. He would never fear me. He believes whole-heartedly that I worship him. That I would never harm him. Or fight back."

"Christ! He tried to kill you last night! He probably thinks you're dead!"

"All the better. And he won't think I have the strength to stop him, Mr. Stewart."

Andy said, "Then that may give us an advantage. Do you know how to handle a handgun, Mr. Rahn?"

"I own several. I enjoy shooting, Detective. But shouldn't you call someone from your department?"

"My department, and every other law enforcement agency, won't be happy that I kidnapped a federal witness. Sorting it out will cost us too much time. We may already be too late!" She pulled the small zippered pouch from her shoulder bag and opened it. She extracted her Berretta M.92, a weapon I liked and once used to persuade a corrupt old billionaire to adjust his attitude in life. Andy offered the weapon to Rahn. "It's loaded."

Rahn regarded the gun suspiciously. He looked at Andy, then me.

"Don't look at me, man. I hate guns," I said, presenting both palms in surrender.

"Why don't you take this?" Rahn handed me his cane. "I can hobble without it. I presume this means you trust me, Detective?"

"I trust that you want to stop your brother."

Rahn examined the Berretta. With swift, practiced moves, he dropped the magazine in his palm and thumbed a round free. He held it up to the light and examined it. Satisfied, he pulled back the slide and slid the round into the chamber. He released the slide with a snap, then palmed the magazine home like a pro. Weapon loaded and live. He flicked the safety off and applied a two-handed grip. He looked at Andy.

She nodded acknowledgement of his expertise. I silently prayed she knew what she was doing. "Muzzle awareness, Mr. Rahn. I'm counting on you," she said. "Although for a social studies teacher, you seem to know your way around a gun."

"Lead the way, Detective."

SHE APPROACHED the open front door. Rahn bumped and scuffed his prosthetic leg up the sidewalk behind her, both hands on the Berretta, muzzle pointed at the concrete. The interior loomed, dark and silent.

"Is there a light?"

"Wait!" Andy whispered. "Don't turn the lights on. Let your eyes adjust."

We entered in trail, Andy first, Rahn behind her, me a reluctant tail-end Charlie. Andy stepped behind us and closed the door. Squares of light streamed through the windows, lending shape to the rooms and furnishings.

"You lead, Mr. Rahn." She gestured at the big sitting room with the view of the lake. The curtains had been pulled open and the white starlight on the quilt of snow over the ice on Leander Lake provided ample light.

"Where is everyone?" Rahn limped forward slowly, eventually pausing in silhouette at the center of the room.

"My sister has a safe room directly below us," Andy whispered. "She must have retreated into it. It has cell service. I can call her to tell her we're here, but it might not be a good idea just yet."

"Are you sure she has the children with her?"

"Yes."

"I suppose that's best. To be in their own home. With their own things…"

Andy stopped. She let Rahn move deeper into the room. "What does your ESP tell you? Is your brother here?"

Andy's question met with silence. After a moment, the voice that answered in the darkness changed.

"Why do I get the feeling you already know the answer to that?"

"Will, please turn on the light."

I moved sideways and found the light panel by the entrance to the room. The panel had several on/off switches, and a row of sliders. To avoid a rapid assault on the eyes, I selected two of the sliders and eased them up. High around the room, recessed lighting blossomed into a warm glow.

Rahn stood at the center of the room with the Berretta pointed directly at me. He gave a rueful snort. Holding the gun on me, he spoke to Andy. "I had no expectation you would make this so easy. Lower your weapon, Detective Stewart, or I will kill your loving husband where he stands." He spoke calmly. His voice deeper and resonant with authority.

I took a step back. "Andy don't!" I warned her.

She didn't listen. She eased her weapon's muzzle slowly downward.

"Drop it, please. Carefully."

She bent her knees and opened her hand. Her service weapon clattered to the hardwood floor at her side.

"Step away from it."

She took one step back, never taking her eyes from Rahn. She said, "It was never about me."

Rahn stood a little taller. His face shed its veneer of humanity. I began to see the merciless undercurrent that ran beneath the photos my wife spilled on our dining room table. The nose was different, but only because it had been recently broken. A painful but effective way to change appearance. "My God, woman! You were full of yourself, clinging to the idea that Parks would go to the trouble of eliminating you as a witness. The man is a pompous fool, but even he would have trouble justifying the effort."

Andy completed the thought. "There was no mistake. It was Lydia all along. The lake. You were following her, not me. You were following her to the lake. There was nothing spontaneous about it. But things went a little sideways when she stopped at our place and drove over our mailbox." Rahn didn't answer. "But then in D.C., at the Mayflower, something changed. That night, you knew we were all supposed to be at Davis's memorial. You didn't expect Lydia to be in the hotel room, but she was—only you also didn't try to kill her. You ran away instead. I didn't understand, until I factored in Davis's murder. You were looking for something.

Something Davis Bates had. This is all about him. About something he had. Something other people want. Something that you now think Lydia has."

"The children. Where are they?"

"They're not here, dumbshit!" I snapped. My nerves were popping like loose power lines. I steadied myself, flexed my fingers, and let electric tension run down my arms. In my head, I closed a firm grip on the levers that make me vanish.

Andy was calmer than me. "What do you want with the children?"

Rahn rolled his eyes. "Please. It was enough that I had to put up with this whole charade. I'm not going to stand here and tell tales to a dead woman. And frankly, what I wanted from your nieces is nothing compared to what I now want. This situation has become far more interesting." He adjusted his aim from the center of my chest to my face. "You're my new shiny object, Mr. Stewart. Tell me—what was that you did last night?"

"Don't know what you're talking about."

His arm moved again, shifting his aim to Andy. "There are fifteen rounds in this Berretta, counting the one in the pipe. I bet I can fire fourteen into your once lovely wife without actually killing her. She will live, but she will be very hard to look at. Very hard to live with."

"You were awake? When Will pulled you out of the house?" Andy asked.

"Fully. Did you think I would let myself fall asleep in that gas chamber?"

Andy nodded. "Of course. Your intention was to be rescued alive—the sole survivor. And then to persuade me to help you escape from the supposedly corrupt and compromised U.S. Marshals. I told you that was a crappy story."

"Perhaps. It doesn't matter now. I *certainly* never expected to be carried out of the house like that! *Incredible!* Tell me, Mr. Stewart."

I said nothing.

"Really? Fourteen rounds, Mr. Stewart, with one left over for you. Amazing what the body can survive. And what a lifetime of horrors follows. Reconstructive surgery. Colostomy bags. Paralysis." He pointed the Berretta at Andy's face. "I want to know what you did and how you did it!"

"I'm from another planet, asshole."

Rahn gave me a cold look, then pulled the trigger.

Despite the dry snap of the Berretta's hammer falling, I flinched. "Jesus, Dee! I told you I'd hate this part."

Rahn looked at the weapon and pulled the trigger again. Again, the hammer snapped down with no effect.

"I never said it was a working weapon." Andy bent double like a dancer and swept up her gun. She pointed it at Rahn, who held his useless gun on her nevertheless. I half expected him to throw it at her.

Rahn snorted and shook his head. "I should have asked myself, what police office, especially one of your caliber, Detective Stewart, would give a loaded weapon to a civilian?"

"They'd have to be an idiot."

"That may be the case. My brother is still here, somewhere."

Andy gave that a thoughtful moment. "That was my initial assumption. I called my department. I asked them to look at the files again. Parks made a mess of things by mixing Steggar Rahn's DNA and fingerprints with the Mannis Rahn prison file. No one is certain which set is which. Which means I'm not sure if you're the adoring little brother who is a lot more like his big brother than he would have anyone believe…or if you really are Mannis Rahn and you killed your brother for his betrayal, and to make his life the perfect hiding place. Of course, there's a very easy way to establish whether you're Steggar Rahn or Mannis Rahn. In fact, you suggested it."

She lowered her weapon and fired. The report hit my unprotected ears like sharp slaps to the head. Rahn whirled and went down hard on the wood floor. Bits of something exploded from his left leg below the knee.

"OH YOU ROTTING BITCH!" he screamed, grasping at his left leg. "YOU MISERABLE CU—!"

"Hey!" I shouted. "Shut it!" I jogged to the center of the room and pulled the Berretta from his grasp. Even without a firing pin, I didn't want it anywhere near him. He curled himself and clamped his hands over his leg.

"Your wooden leg is bleeding," I said, backing away.

Andy stepped forward. "Mannis Rahn, you're under arrest for the murders of Robert Thanning and Graciela Montoya and Marshal James Radovan. You're under arrest for the attempted murder of Lydia Bates, and for the murder of Davis Bates. And as of this moment, I'll take a leap and say you're under arrest for the murder of your brother, Steggar Rahn." Andy took another step. "Now, I want to know why you're so interested in my sister's children."

For one deeply uncharacteristic moment I thought she might plant her foot on his bleeding, bullet-blown leg. She refrained.

"FUCK YOU! AAAAHHH! IT HURTS!" He clawed his sweatpants up over his knee to reveal plastic in the shape of a lower leg. Midway up the calf, the plastic had shattered. He began pulling the bloody pieces apart. "GET ME SOME HELP FOR FUCK'S SAKE!"

Andy didn't move. Blood soaked Rahn's fingers. He pulled the fake prosthesis apart. It was little more than a sheath over his own pale leg.

"YOU BROKE THE BONE, BITCH!" he screamed. He twisted backward and writhed in pain, then curled forward again. He tore at a set of leather straps at the top of the device, near his knee. He struggled to get his remaining good leg under him, kneeling like a child tying a shoe. "HELP ME! GET THIS OFF ME!"

"Will, there are towels in the kitchen," Andy said calmly. I hesitated, preferring to watch the bastard writhe. Andy glanced at me. "Before he bleeds out."

I reluctantly started to move when Rahn flew out of his crouch. Something thin and shining whistled through the air. I heard a *Snick!* The sound of metal striking metal. A slender blade hit Andy's gun and knocked it off target as she fired. Rahn dodged the opposite way and the shot missed. He staggered on one leg toward Andy. His right arm swung through an arc as she brought the gun to bear again. The blade in his hand whistled and caught Andy on the forearm. She fired directly into Rahn's body, then cried out in pain, clutching her right forearm with her left hand, once again taking her gun off target. Rahn shrieked and lunged at her. He wound up for another strike and she tried to lift her arm to fire.

Two steps. My feet pounded on the floor and I lowered my head and shoulders. I hit him in the gut, punching as I drove him backward. He smashed his fist down on my back, but the blade had been raised. Only his fist caught me. Badly. Slamming one of my kidneys. I kept going, driving and lifting. He hammered me with his fists. I stomped across the floor. We hit the windows behind him. Glass shattered. Rahn screamed and there was blood. Gravity grabbed us. I tried to remember what lay on the deck below the windows overlooking the lake, because we would hit it hard and bones would break.

Andy screamed my name. Cold and shattered knives of glass touched us.

I pushed *hard*—

FWOOOMP!

Rahn, a black mass blocking my view, vanished and Leander Lake spread across my vision. Instead of dropping, we sailed outward. Lydia's patio slid beneath us. Then snow-dusted steps leading to the lake. Then a small dock. Then nothing but white as we drifted over the frozen lake, tangled and wrestling.

Rahn smashed his fist into my back, then stopped. I felt him adjusting, changing posture. I knew what was coming. The blade drawn from his false prosthesis—he could only be working himself into a position to drive the blade down into me.

FWOOOMP!

Two struggling bodies reappeared in the night over the ice. Gravity took us, startling Rahn. The stabbing blow never came. The immediate sensation of falling swallowed us and we dropped. I estimated twenty feet. There was no time to wonder whether the ice had thickened enough to hold us or not.

I struck the ice feet first. The *Crack!* could have been a gunshot. In the split second before we plunged through I heard the sound chase across the still surface of the lake, explosively creating fissures and veins.

We broke through and splashed into frigid darkness.

For the second time in my life I felt penetrating cold beyond imagination. Knives cut to every bone in my body. I clenched, and in doing so, tightened my grip on Rahn. He kicked and screamed, the sound of his terror muted by the black water. Pressure built in my ears as we dropped, deeper and deeper. He clawed at me with both hands, which told me the blade had escaped his grasp. I held on and pulled him down.

There was no air. There hadn't been when we began the plunge. Whatever air I started with had been blown out by the crash through the ice. My lungs burned. I wanted to hold him until we hit bottom but too soon I had to let him go. I feared he wasn't finished, that he could still make it to the surface. I tried to kick him, but in an instant, the writhing, mewling black mass thrashing the blacker water in front of me ceased to exist.

I sank, alone.

Only one way out and it was going to hurt.

Fwooomp!

The instant I vanished, I rocketed upward. Weightless space in the water, nothing but buoyancy, I shot up, folding my arms over my head and praying.

We had drifted away from the hole we made going in. Hitting the solid undersurface of the ice nearly knocked me out. Brilliant lights exploded across my vision. Hard edges gouged my arms and shoulders, then tore down the length of my body, finally scraping my legs.

Then nothing.

I floated above a new, jagged hole.

I blinked to clear my eyes and saw the tiers of Lydia's wood and glass house. I saw an explosion of red and blue lights in the treetops on the far side of the house. I saw light across the main level, and in that light the shape of my wife frozen in the glassless window frame. Behind her, racing into the room, the dominating shape of Chief Tom Ceeves and then two more Essex PD officers. I heard her crying out my name, over and over as I floated above the snow-covered ice.

Then I heard something else.

Pounding. Weak thudding. A heartbeat with no rhythm. It came from below me. I looked down and saw the hole where I had burst out of the lake. Farther away, another hole where Rahn and I went in. Outside of those two blemishes, the lake surface looked creamy and smooth. Unbroken.

The pounding and thumping grew frantic. Then hesitant.

Then it stopped.

I watched for several minutes. Nothing disturbed the frozen surface of the lake.

Andy's voice reached me. She'd been calling the whole time, but now she reached me.

"Will! WILL!"

"WHAT?"

The silhouette threw her hands to her face. Her shoulders shook.

Through cold, dense winter air, I heard her laughter.

Or crying.

Or both.

56

They kept us at Essex County Memorial so late that the ER nurse offered us a room. Utterly fatigued, I opened my mouth to say Yes, when Andy cut me off.

"If I don't sleep in my own bed tonight, I'm going to die."

"I get that," the nurse said. She adjusted the sling around Andy's neck and the way it cradled her right arm. "I'll be right back with around three pages of instructions for you, dear. The doctor will give you a prescription for the pain."

"No," Andy waved her off. "I have ibuprofen at home. That will be fine."

"You're sure?" Andy said yes. The nurse slipped out.

Andy sat against propped up pillows on an examination bed in the ER bay. She looked comfortable with her long legs crossed. I sat next to her on a stool. My right arm matched hers, but to a lesser degree. Bandages over fewer stitches and no sling. The blade that Mannis Rahn sheathed in his phony prosthetic leg had sliced a three-inch gash to the bone on Andy's forearm, but thankfully didn't damage critical nerves or tendons. Sam Morrissey, who I greeted as "my favorite ER Doc," applied fourteen stitches and told her she would have a lovely scar to make up lies about. I had a gash on the outside of my forearm and another on my right thigh, both the result of exiting Lydia's home through a plate glass window, which didn't shatter harmlessly like the ones in the movies. I also had a cut in my scalp where the ice caught me, along with countless bruises on my arms where I had tried to shield myself. My kidneys felt like they'd been worked over with a meat hammer. I passed some blood during a stop at the toilet.

"Are you under the impression we pass out reward points to frequent visitors?" Sam Morrissey had asked while he tortured me with his needle and thread.

"You're not even trying to make this hurt less, are you?"

"Well, I suppose I could, but when you have a patient who is not fully forthcoming…where's the incentive?" I like Sam, but between surviving the in-flight break-up of an airplane and delivering a drowned woman to the ER alive without explanation, I think he held my mysteries against me. He confirmed my suspicion when he smiled at me and gave the thread a firm yank.

At least I only got nine stitches. Five on my forearm. Four on my thigh. For the second time, I arrived in the ER soaked to the bone. Morrissey added to my humiliation by putting me in one of those flimsy backless hospital gowns while the nurse took my clothes to a dryer. My consolation was that Andy found the gown amusing. The smile that danced on her lips warmed me.

All smiles vanished when Tom Ceeves showed up.

"We're going to have to send a dive team in to find him. Or wait until next summer and have some water skier wipe out after hitting him. I think it better be a dive team." The chief loomed over Andy on her bed. "You two need to stop putting shit in Leander Lake."

"I'll let you law enforcement types talk official business," I said, rising to take to the door.

"Siddown, Will," Tom said. It wasn't a request. I planted myself on the stool, wishing it was taller. Tom loomed over me, too.

He looked at me and then Andy.

"Are you a hunnerd percent that's our guy for Bob?"

"Yes, sir. That was Mannis Rahn. There's going to be trouble identifying him when they pull the body, because Parks messed with his records. But it was him. He was posing as his own brother. I sent a text to Chief Deputy Whitlock in Cedar Rapids and told her to get a cadaver dog out to that farm where they had Steggar Rahn in a WITSEC program. I think they'll find the brother there. I also told her to examine the marshal's phone. I'm certain it will show there never was any call from outside."

The chief absorbed her report, then said, "How's your sister? Is she okay?"

"It's been a nightmare."

"I spoze."

"Oh, I don't mean the threats and all that. I mean where they've been hiding."

"What did you do with them?"

Andy laughed. "My father. When we were kids he had this idea that a family vacation should be a road trip. Just hit the road. See America. He kept talking about when he was a kid and there were these commercials on TV with a jingle that said, 'See the U.S.A. in your Chevrolet!' Dad made us take a couple trips like that. No planning. No itinerary. Flop in whatever motel came along that had a pool. When we asked where we were going he said, 'a certain magical destination.' We all thought he meant Disney World, but he meant the trip was magical because the destination kept moving—and in the end it was home sweet home. All I remember is being stuck in the back seat with my brother and sister and fighting half the time."

"That's how you hid them? You had your dad hit the road?"

"Uh-huh," Andy smiled. "Liddy was furious. Right now, they're somewhere between Pensacola and Springfield, Missouri, Liddy thinks. She also admitted that Dad is in his glory and the girls are loving it. They've been to every amusement park in the south, she thinks."

I couldn't picture it.

"I told Dad no credit cards. Cash only. No plan. And keep the phones turned off except for the first five minutes of every even hour."

Now Tom grinned. "Jesus, Andy, that's diabolical."

"Uh-huh," she said proudly. "What about Sandy?"

"Oh, she and Melanie are with my mother in Beaver Dam. Mama wants to adopt them both. She's going to be disappointed when I send them home tomorrow. Can I assume it's safe?"

"Yes, sir. I believe Rahn was the threat, not Parks. I don't think this was ever about Parks or Todd Jameson. In fact, nothing about any of this is what it seemed."

Tom abruptly turned to me. He stared at me and I felt acutely aware of the size of his hands. I automatically put a grip on the levers in my head that make me disappear, thinking it might not be a bad idea.

"What am I supposed to do about you?" he asked. His deep voice seemed to induce a harmonic vibration down my spine.

"Put me down as an innocent bystander? Or buy me a beer and put me in for a medal?"

He was not amused. Out of the corner of my eye, I thought I caught Andy suppressing a grin. Witch.

"Every time you're around one of these I gotta write up goddamn reports with holes in 'em. Like when you fished her sister outta the lake a few weeks ago, and drove her here in—what was it—an F-22? Going how many hunnerd miles an hour?"

"Sir, I think Will—"

"Uh! Uh!" Tom put that big slab hand up for Andy to hold her tongue. She locked her jaw obediently. "Now I got two guys going out a broken window and landing forty feet out in the ice. What? Didja fucking bounce, Will?"

"Kinda…?"

"Well, lemme see your shattered leg bones. It's twenty feet down to that deck up there and there ain't no disturbed snow. Or footprints."

"Um, maybe it snowed?"

"In the eight seconds between when we heard the first shot and when we got in the room? And just how the hell did you get outta that ice again and come up on the south end of her property?"

I had a favoring wind to thank for that, although it took ten minutes to get to shore and reappear.

Tom veered his anger back toward Andy. "And that's the last time I let you give a murder suspect a loaded gun, Detective!"

"Yeah!" I said firmly jumping on his bandwagon, which earned me a searing look from both.

"Although it was pretty goddamn smart," Tom muttered. He started to speak again, but his jaw hung up for a moment. When he finally snapped it shut, he simply shook his head. "Whatever you write up, Andy, make sure it sounds plausible! I gotta get back. Thanks to you, I've got ATF and Homeland all over my office."

"Sir is that about Braddock?" Andy sat up. "I want to be there. I want to be part of that."

Tom's head shook before she finished speaking.

"Not with one clipped wing you're not." She protested, but he gave no ground. "It's all going to turn out to be a snipe hunt. Braddock's a brainwashed ass, and he may be cooking up home-brew plastique out there, and worshiping the memory of the Third Reich, and it may land him in a world of hurt, but that's all will come of it. Jesus, the feds think they're hunting Bin Ladin again."

"My gloves—they tested positive?"

"Can't tell you that."

"They're going in? When?"

"Can't tell you that either, or I get my own furnished cell at Guantanamo. Or some shit like that. It's all hush hush. I'll let you read about it after those government suits declassify it in fifty years. Don't lemme see you around the office until Monday!"

He took one last long look at me.

"See ya' at breakfast, Will."

"Roger that."

He brushed his way through the pale blue curtains between us and the open center of the ER. I turned to Andy, who stared after him. When our eyes met, I could see wheels turning.

I said what she was thinking. "He's going to kill you when you show up at the station tomorrow..." I checked the wall clock. "...er, today."

"Yeah. He will."

The curtains parted. Sam Morrissey appeared.

"Okay, frequent fliers! I have tetanus shots! Will, turn around and bend over."

"What?"

57

The light that pried open my eyes wasn't dawn. The bedroom Andy and I share is on the northeast corner of the second floor of our rented farmhouse. Dawn light has an unmistakable angle and intensity. This light, and an immediate gnawing hunger, said midday. Given that we hit the pillows after three a.m. I felt some satisfaction in logging solid sleep.

I stretched a flat hand across the mattress expecting to find Andy's warmth, but met with nothing but cool sheet. It came as no surprise.

The note I found on our kitchen table told me to text her when I got up.

In a meeting. Call you soon. Love you! Her reply chirped my phone almost immediately.

"Well, I guess Tom didn't kick you out of the station," I replied aloud.

I'm not one for lazing around the house in sweats, but an army of small and large aches slowed me. After making coffee a priority, I sat at the kitchen table contemplating Mannis Rahn, a ghost who had haunted our lives. I thought of what he called me. His "new shiny object." Here was someone who learned my secret and immediately wanted more. I thought about Christine Watkins, someone else who learned my secret and wanted more. Their motives may have been at opposite ends of a morality scale, but the result for me was the same.

When the coffee suggested to my stomach that it could use some company, I fixed myself a nutritious lunch consisting of a tube of Pringles with peanut butter. I poked at the heap of mail on the table, but without much interest beyond the *AOPA Pilot* magazine. Andy, as tired as we were last night, had gone through the pile, which had been accumulated by Rosemary II in our absence. Andy seemed to be looking for something and showed disappointment in not finding it.

I checked the answering machine. There were seventeen messages from robots and scammers, three from Al Raymond wanting to sell Andy a car, and two hang-ups listed as Private Caller. I vowed to renew my campaign to eliminate our land line.

Andy called, of course, when I was in the shower. I killed the stream, scrambled to rub the shampoo out of my hands and picked up my cell phone, which I had placed on the toilet tank in anticipation of her inevitable timing.

"Stewart Shower, visitors welcome," I said.

"How long are you open?" she asked.

"Oh, we're a twenty-four hour a day operation."

"Well, then, I may swing by later."

"How's it going?"

"Spooky. These guys don't mess around when it comes to possible domestic terrorism. Listen, can you square away an airplane later? We'll use the foundation money to pay for it."

"I can check the schedule. Where to?"

"A certain magical destination. I don't want to say more than that on the phone."

Andy's paranoia made me feel a little more naked than I had a moment ago, which is saying something. "Then we're in agreement that it's not over?" I brought up the possibility on the way home from the hospital. At the time, she hedged. She did again.

"Maybe. I called Helena to see if they would hold onto Luca de Maurier. But his D.C. lawyers came down hard and he and his crew are already gone."

"Wow. I guess the fixer fixes. Are you thinking—"

"Let's not talk about this on the phone. Text me when you know about the airplane."

"For when? When do you want to fly?"

"This afternoon. I think I can be at the airport by four."

"I'll check it out."

"Will?"

"Yes?"

"Don't let your guard down."

ROSEMARY II HAD NOTHING AVAILABLE. Dave was out on a charter in the King Air. Pidge had the Mojave. Both Barons were on charters. I suggested taking a single-engine Cessna Skyhawk, but one was booked for a Private Pilot Checkride; the other was in the shop for an annual inspection. I wasn't interested in taking one of the Cessna 152 trainers.

"I can get the Mojave tomorrow afternoon," I told Andy when she called me back.

"We have that dance," Andy said.

"Really? Don't you think this situation takes priority?"

"For what I need, it won't matter if it's late Friday night or early Saturday morning. We're *not* letting Lane down. Will, you have no idea. The girl has been texting me nonstop."

"About what?"

"Her dress. Her hair. Her accessories. Other girl things. No, it can wait until Saturday morning. Life goes on, darling. But lock it in on the schedule, okay? Early Saturday morning."

"Can do. Destination TBD. What about Ly—"

"Later, Will. We'll talk about all of this later. I gotta go."

She left me wondering who she thought had the power to listen to private cell phone conversations.

LATER ENDED up being much later. Close to nine p.m. Andy found me asleep in my recliner. I emerged from a dream I couldn't remember to the sensation of warm lips on mine. The warm lips parted, and the tip of a tongue tickled my lips. Without opening my eyes, I reached up and found the ponytail at the back of her head. I pulled her in for more.

"God, I hope you're my wife," I said, eyes still closed, when we parted.

"And I hope you would know the difference."

"That was nice."

"I always wanted to do that. To see if you turned into a frog." She stood up and began working her ponytail free. "You hungry? I brought Chinese."

"As soon as your father gets back here, I'm asking for your hand in marriage."

"Dad and the entourage are in the deep south." She shook her hair loose and stepped toward the kitchen.

I snapped the recliner down, stood, stretched and followed. "How much longer do you think you need to keep them under cover?"

I heard the refrigerator door open. Bottles clinked. Andy handed me a Corona. She touched hers to mine. "Us."

"Us," I said.

"I want to bring them home on Saturday. That's what the airplane is for."

We put out plates. My nutritious lunch hadn't carried me as far as I hoped. My love for my wife grew as she pulled little white cardboard boxes out of a bag. I opened them and served, what with Andy maneuvering one-handed.

"What was the one thing Rahn seemed obsessed about?" Andy prompted me between initial bites.

"The children."

She pointed a finger at me. "And do you remember the break-in? Anything peculiar?"

"They went through the kid's room. And—" I struggled with it for a moment. "And their toys! Some of their toys were taken."

"Give the man an eggroll!" She literally gave me one. "Now let's look back at this whole thing. Big picture. Lydia dumps Davis. Hard. She packs up the kids and hauls her life here, to Wisconsin. She cuts him off from his kids. So, why would someone send Mannis Rahn to kill my sister? Because I was entirely wrong. They were never after me. Parks was never after me. Why, then? Why go after Lydia?"

"Mmgrmph?" The eggroll was delicious. "Revenge? Divorce by homicide?"

Andy shook her head. "You mean Davis? I don't think so. Not specifically, anyway. But you're close. What's the result if Lydia dies in the lake?"

"Davis gets…holy shit! Davis gets the kids back!"

"Yes! But when that failed, we come to Act Two. In which the angry, drunk, asshole ex-husband, facing financial disaster, decides to send his wife a Bitch-o-Gram pretending suicide, but flubs the whole thing and accidentally kills himself, or so our ghost made it appear. Which had the net result of what?"

"Drawing the wife *and children* back to D.C." I replied. "But hold up there, Sherlock. Why go to all the trouble? If the kids are the target, why not come after them here?"

"They were too well protected here."

"Why not just go with suicide? For Davis?"

"Because he was an angry asshole, not a despondent divorcé. The accident played beautifully. Pretending to bitch text Lydia. Minimal police investigation. Fits the victim. Brings the wife and kids back. And it would have worked if we hadn't measured the extension cord."

"Kudos to you."

Andy acknowledged me with a sweet, demure nod. Rare acceptance of a compliment. "The break-in was *pro forma*. Making sure they covered all bases. I doubt they really expected to find what they were looking for. The real objective was to bring Lydia and the girls back. Once that was accomplished, they needed to get to the children. It keeps coming back to the children! And it wasn't driven by Davis."

I worked over a bit of General Tso's chicken, thinking about the incident at the Mayflower. "Everyone was supposed to be at the memorial. Or cocktail party."

"Except the children."

"But they wouldn't be left alone, for heaven's sake!"

"No. In fact, there's every reason to believe that if Lydia had gone, she would have taken them with her—you know, if it was really a memorial service. Who knew it was a cocktail party? And if she didn't take them, they would have been with my parents."

"Then is it the children themselves? Or something they have?"

Andy leaned back and searched an indefinite distance for a moment, shaking her head. "Honestly, I have no idea."

"Saturday morning," I said, "there's a catch…"

"Which is?"

"No Pidge. Just me. Stone cold illegal."

Andy looked at me and tipped her head back and forth. "What the hell. I've always wanted to fall for a bad boy."

ANDY REFUSED to give me any details about the planned raid on the Braddock property. Not even our Usual Disclaimer opened the door to her sharing. The federal authorities allowed her to sit in on the plans and briefings under strict terms of secrecy. If it had been her secrecy, she would have shared. Someone else's secrecy was to be respected. All I knew about the effort on Friday was that it required her to leave home at four a.m., which is damn dark and damn cold in early January. I insisted on rising to make her breakfast, although she ate lightly under a cloud of distraction. She accepted a hurried kiss and departed in the trusty Unit 23 ahead of a trail of cold engine exhaust.

I contemplated grabbing a couple power units and taking a flight to the Braddock property to watch events unfold.

I went back to my warm bed instead.

"NOTHING!" Andy slid off her heavy winter patrol officer's jacket. I notice that she had ditched the sling. She winced, however, pulling her arm from the sleeve. "A complete bust."

She looked at me, standing in my suit, a white shirt and the blue tie.

"I know! I know! I'm late!" She hurried past me for the stairs. "There's a corsage in the 'fridge! Would you get it, please?"

I found the flower in a plastic box. "Where did this come from?" I called after her. Too late. She was upstairs.

She returned less than fifteen minutes later, looking stunning in a dark blue dress made of something shimmering. Unlike the last dress I'd seen her in, which I swore I would never allow her to wear in public, this dress had sophisticated style and a formal touch. How she managed to put up her hair in record time, I had no clue, but she captured it in a swirl at the back of her head, with teasing strands that curled from her temples.

As I have often done, I watched as she descended the old wooden stairs like a princess.

"Wow." My simple compliment brought dimples and a smile.

"You remember this dress, right?"

"Of course, I do."

"I wore it to Matt and Trisha's wedding." She descended the last couple steps reading my blank expression. "You don't remember it!"

I pulled her into my arms. "Every time I see you is like the first time."

"Oh, you are so full of crap!"

I did the only thing I could to derail my demise. I kissed her.

"GONE. That's what. The place was deserted. And if you think that didn't set off the alarm bells! My God!" Andy drove Unit 23, playing catch-up with the clock. I wondered, given her speed, if she would turn on the lights and siren.

"Both the kid and the old man?"

"Uh-huh. We have BOLOs out on both of them, and on Braddock's truck. The kid didn't show up at school today and the old man didn't show up at work."

"Where does he work?"

"He works for the railroad. He's a maintenance supervisor. And yes, that's a whole new set of alarm bells. TSA is involved now."

"Did you find anything at the house? Explosives?"

"No...and yes. No, we didn't find any finished product. Yes, we found signs of production. Electronics. Chemical traces. The dogs reacted in the house and in the garage. No question that something was there."

I pictured the Braddock garage as I had seen it. I could almost smell the workshop, the hints of welding smoke, oil and grease. The musty smell of the old tarp covering the second vehicle.

"What's weird is that they've had the place under surveillance for the last twenty-four hours. There were lights on overnight. All we can figure is they left before the surveillance was set up."

"Nothing in the second vehicle?"

Andy glanced at me. Then at the road. Then at me again. "What second vehicle?"

"In the garage. The second vehicle. The one under the tarp."

She looked at me again. Her eyes grew wider.

"Shit!" She pumped the brakes and brought the squad car to a halt, then lifted the gearshift into Park. I automatically checked over my shoulder to see if we were about to be rammed, but the road was empty.

Andy scrambled for her phone, one handed. She dialed. "Pick up. Pick up. Pick—Chief! It's Andy. Did anyone run a DMV registration check on Braddock?" I heard Tom Ceeves speaking but Andy had the phone close to her ear. "Right. He has the truck. Any other vehicles registered to him?" She waited. She tapped her foot and checked the mirrors as I had. After a moment, she slid the phone away from her lips and said, "Will, put the car in gear for me, please."

She held her phone in her left hand. She cradled her bandaged right arm in her lap. I wondered just how much pain she was feeling. I reached over and pulled the column shifter into Drive. Andy lowered the phone from her ear and switched to speaker. Holding the phone and the wheel in her left hand, she hit the gas and we shot forward.

"Just the truck," Tom said. "Why?"

"There was another vehicle. In the garage. Under a tarp."

"Okay...and we know this, how?"

"Hi, Tom!" I said.

"Aw, Christ!" I started thinking I might not make the chief's Christmas card list next year.

Andy covered for me. "Let's just say that I just remember seeing a second vehicle when I was there last week. Under a tarp. Okay? Did he ever have a second vehicle registered? He was married. Chances are good they were a two-car family. The wife is deceased, but maybe it was registered in her name. It would be a few years ago."

"I'll call you back."

The call ended. I reached over and lifted Andy's phone from her fingers, I slid it into her handbag.

"What does this mean?" I asked.

"It means we missed something."

58

Andy parked in the fire lane outside the district offices that adjoined the high school, less out of convenience and more to make the parked police unit sit at the curb as a statement. She drew a few looks as she stepped out of the squad car in high heels. We followed a stream of kids toward the field house entrance until Andy glanced at my hands.

"The corsage!" I jogged back to grab it from the front seat while she continued through the doors. I caught up to her just inside the entrance, a lobby the size of a house with walls lined by trophy cases. The standard lights were dimmed. A decorating committee had strung holiday lights overhead like stars. The field house was dark, but through the doors I could see more star-like strings of light.

Boys in suits, many of them looking awkward in ill-fitting coats and ties, milled around or hurried to or from something. Girls in near-formal dresses looking vastly more mature clustered together, chattering energetically, stealing glances at the boys. A few couples moved through the space together holding hands. The noise overwhelmed my senses. A handful of adults hovered at the edges or behind an open snack bar occupying one side wall. Kids and adults behind the snack bar counter doled out soft drinks and treats. Music pounded its way through the doors to the field house.

Andy searched the crowd. "Do you see Lane or Rosemary II?" She had to lean into me and shout to be heard.

I joined the search, then tapped Andy on the shoulder and pointed.

Lane and her mother approached across the plaza outside the field house entrance.

I stood transfixed.

Lane Franklin walked alongside her mother projecting beauty, warmth, explosive anticipation and suppressed fear all at once. Andy saw her and squeezed my arm like a proud parent.

They entered the field house lobby and Lane hurried into a hug with Andy.

"Honey, you look amazing!" Andy gushed after she slipped out of her coat. Lane beamed, as if Andy's words were the blessing she was waiting for.

Lane turned to me. "Hi, Mr. Stewart!" Before I could ask who she would one day fly for, she fell into a hug against my chest. I could not stop a flood of memories. I had held this girl before. We prepared for death together. We escaped it together.

"Hey!" was all I could muster up. She squeezed and I squeezed back.

"Pictures!" Rosemary II chimed in. "Come on!"

"Let me take your coats," I offered to Andy, Lane and her mother.

"I'm not staying," Rosemary II announced. "I promised I wouldn't, and I'm jealous of you two! But I get it. Now, come over here and let me get pictures!"

We moved out of the crowd to a corner by one of the trophy cases and began a photo session. Lane by herself. Lane with her mother. Lane with Andy. Lane with Andy and me. I was about to attend to checking the coats, which we had piled on the floor, when Lane grabbed my hand and pulled me back into position for one more photo. Andy handed me the corsage to give her, and you would think I'd given her the moon, the stars and all the shine in the sun.

Rosemary II took the shot, then put her fingers to her lips. Her eyes glistened.

"Lane Franklin! You look fabu!" Sarah Lewis, blond hair bouncing, ran up to her friend and traded hugs. "Hi Detective Stewart!" She embraced Andy, then shared hellos with me and Rosemary II. The capacity for energy in the two girls seemed to double.

"Can we go inside?" Lane, bursting yet ever obedient, asked her mother.

"Go! Have fun! I'll pick you up at eleven! I love you!"

The girls hurried away. I picked up the coats and looked for a place to check them, mainly to avoid the inevitable teary moment between Andy and Rosemary II.

It took a few minutes to figure out that coat check was simply the cafeteria down the hall, where garments were unceremoniously dumped on tables. I found space and made a note of it for later, anticipating a rush at the end of the evening.

I found Andy on the phone at a far corner of the lobby, trying to hear over the din. It was impossible to catch the words she formed. I waited, watching a cloud of worry descend over her face. She ended the call and tucked away her phone, then took me by the arm.

"We need to find Mike. He's here somewhere."

"What's up?"

"The mother had a car. I want Mike to do a run around the parking lot."

"You think the kid is here?"

"Maybe. And if he is, maybe he's just here to dance. And maybe not."

Andy hurried through the gathering crowd. I followed. We tried the field house first, passing from the lighted lobby into the dark, mood-drenched atmosphere.

I immediately noticed clusters of kids dancing in spotlights cast on the floor. It took me a moment to realize the spotlights formed the shape of a star, roughly twenty feet across. The beams descended from the field house ceiling, where spotlights had been mounted. Six beams hung like pillars. Six stars drew kids away from the throng near the DJ, creating luminous evenly spaced stencils of light on the big floor. They danced in groups within the stars.

A light show exploded around a DJ at the far end of the massive field house. Swinging beams of light illuminated the bouncing crowd. Boys and girls danced to a throbbing beat, sometimes with each other. The music had been distilled to thundering bass. Kids streamed past us to join the throng. Others streamed toward us. Still others hung at the periphery, waiting to see someone or to be seen. Adolescent drama played out all around us.

I pointed at a uniform. Andy looked, then leaned in close.

"Auxiliary!" she shouted into my ear. I nodded. Essex PD trained and used volunteer auxiliary officers for events like this and for parades and summer festivals. The uniform without the sidearm identified the auxiliary officers. That and the fact that most were older and noticeably less fit. The one standing on the edge of the bleachers watching the crowd was, on closer examination, not Patrol Officer Mike Mackiejewski.

"I thought you were going to—" Andy waved me to stop talking. She pulled me back toward the lobby where the sound went from intolerable to simply awful. "I thought you were going to use regular officers here tonight!"

"We were, but the whole raid thing today was supposed to make that unnecessary. Now it feels like the opposite! C'mon!"

We hurried out into the lobby and scanned the crowd. Andy grabbed my arm and pointed at the snack bar. Mike stood to one side.

"You want me to what?" he asked loudly when Andy tried to explain. She looked around. Not wanting to alarm anyone, she had kept her voice low. Now she gestured for Mike to follow her.

We stepped outside into cold night air.

"I need you to get in your unit and check the parking lot for a vehicle."

"What vehicle?"

"Call base. Get the particulars from the Chief. It belongs to Braddock but was registered to his wife." Mike nodded. His face darkened. He was fully informed on the day's action. "Might be here. Might have been driven by the kid."

"Do you think he's got—you know?"

"I don't know. Don't take any chances. If you spot the vehicle, or if you spot the kid, call it in. And Mike," Andy put her hand on his arm, "if you see him wearing a long coat, or carrying something, or holding any kind of device...stop him. Call for help if you can. But if you can't...stop him!"

"Jesus, Andy!" Mike gaped at her, then spun to jog away.

"Hey!" Andy called after him. "Give me your portable!"

Mike handed her his radio, then took off again.

We hurried back inside. The goose bumps rising on my arms weren't just for the cold.

"We need to see if he's here. You saw him in person. I've only seen pictures. Let's split up! Call me if you spot him!"

"Got it!" She threaded through the milling crowd. I went in the opposite direction.

Countless high school kids passed through my field of vision. I tried to remember the boy I'd seen in the Braddock home. I tried to gauge his height and factor that into a process of elimination. I worked my way around one side of the lobby, arriving at the entrance to the field house. I moved inside and tracked along the front of folded bleachers thinking it would be ridiculously easy to miss Braddock in this darkness. Kids less than a dozen feet from me were nothing but silhouettes. Still, in most cases I could eliminate. Too short. Too heavy. Short hair. Rugged features. And fifty percent of the crowd was female, reducing the challenge. I started to nurture hope I might spot him.

The hope faded when I reached the end of the floor where the DJ performed his set on a raised platform under racks of moving lights. The dance floor bounced, a constantly changing, throbbing mass of bodies under a light show. Faces flashed around me. Bodies were intermingled and all but indistinguishable. A few of the older kids danced erotic moves against each other. I wondered if chaperones were instructed to separate the ones that got too expressive.

Not my assignment.

I sacrificed my hearing and worked across the front of the DJ platform, then around the other side. I covered the length of the field house, then cut across the broad floor, skirting the stars cast on the basketball court and the kids dancing in their light. No luck.

The lobby had thinned out. Most of the crowd clustered against the snack bar. A few latecomers entered, hurrying to shed coats and join the fun.

I spotted Andy in a sharply animated discussion with one of the heavy-set, gray-haired auxiliary officers. He pointed up a hall. Both of them hurried out of my line of sight. I jogged across the lobby, made a left and followed them into the cafeteria where I'd dropped the coats. They moved ahead of me toward the center, where a food court, silent now, expanded off to our left.

They stopped. I caught up with them.

"I've seen two so far," the officer said. He pointed.

A cardboard box sat on the floor against the wall. Roughly twelve inches high and wide, it had no markings on the sides. Heavy black lettering ran across one top flap. READ TRUTH.

"Where's the other one?" Andy demanded.

"Hallway. Back by the side of the field house." The officer pointed. "It's got the same message on it."

"Okay," Andy jammed the fingers of her right hand into her hair, paying no attention to the bandaged wound on her right arm. "Okay. You go that way." She pointed at the opposite end of the cafeteria. Make a circuit around the center quadrant. I want to know if you see any more. And *don't touch anything!* Got it?"

"You don't have to tell me twice!" he said. He hustled away.

"Are you thinking—?" I hurried after Andy, who charged in the direction the officer had pointed.

"Yes. Dammit." She broke into a run.

We reached the end of the cafeteria. A hallway formed a junction with the short hallway that led to the field house lobby. Andy broke right and two steps in spotted the second cardboard carton. She slowed to a trot and stopped fifteen feet from the box, which nestled against the wall.

READ TRUTH.

"Dammit dammit dammit!" She lifted the radio in her hand, but I caught her and stopped her.

"Transmitter," I said. I pointed at the handheld radio. "Use your phone!"

"We need to..." she didn't finish the thought. She pulled her phone out and punched the screen.

I looked around and saw something I didn't want to see. Beyond the box, two girls emerged from a restroom. They talked excitedly as they approached the position of the box.

"Hey! HEY!" I started toward them. They stopped talking and looked at me. "Who else is in there? Is anyone else in there?"

Both girls shook their heads. They approached me cautiously. I was happy to see them stare at me and pay no attention to the box on the floor.

"C'mon! We need to clear this hallway. Hurry up!" I waved at them like a traffic cop. They picked up the pace and hurried past, then resumed chattering once past me.

"Chief! We have a problem!" Andy pressed her phone to her ear. She described the discovery, threading her fingers through her hair.

I caught her side of the urgent conversation.

"Yes! Yes, I'm calling it. Evacuate."

"Is Maybridge still there with his dogs?"

"Good! Can you get them here asap?"

"And those ATF bomb guys, too!"

"No, I'm calling it. Mike is checking the lot, but I'm calling it."

"Right. Got it."

She hung up. "The chief is calling Chet Allison. He's here somewhere. He's telling him to meet me in the lobby. Let's go!"

I hadn't seen the high school principal but wasn't surprised that he was here somewhere. If a protocol existed for an orderly evacuation, he would know it. We hurried. Andy moved with remarkable speed in her high heels.

Halfway to the lobby the portable radio came to life.

"Sarge! You there?"

It startled me. I would have dropped the radio. Andy calmly lifted it to her face. "Go ahead, Mike."

"I got the vehicle. In back, by the football field. And more bad news. We have an open door. I'm going in."

"Mike! Hold up!" Andy stopped to think. "Hold up for a minute. Two minutes. Hold up for two minutes, got that?" She let the mic button go and said to me, "If he goes in and startles the kid—and the kid has a detonator... We need to get this evacuation going *now!*" She pressed the mic again. "Mike, give me five. Five minutes! And when you go in, approach Code Serious. Code Serious."

"Got it. Five." I could almost hear Mike swallow through the radio transmission.

"What's Code Serious?" I asked.

"Exactly what it sounds like." She resumed her dash to the lobby. When we arrived, we gave it half a minute to try and spot Chet Allison. Not seeing him, Andy declared the emergency. She pulled out her badge and held it up to the nearest group of kids.

"Listen up! Listen up! We have a situation. We are evacuating the building! Now! Grab someone and go. Leave your coats! Go out the lobby and all the way across the south parking lot! Go! Go! Go!"

They stood and stared at her.

"You heard the lady!" I barked at them. They scrambled.

The auxiliary officer jogged around the corner out of breath. He spotted us and raised his hand with four fingers up, mouthing "Four more."

Andy acknowledged, then raised her arm in a spinning motion, and pointed at the doors. The officer got it. He began to work the crowd. He cornered several adults and enlisted their help.

Andy and I spread out, repeating the evacuation instruction.

This is going to take too long.

"Andy! I'm going in!" I pointed at the field house. I didn't wait for her to protest.

I broke into a run, dodging kids who were coming and going. Twice I collided with someone. One, a girl, went to the floor with a shriek. I skidded to a stop and pulled her to her feet, then broke into a run without a word. I knew exactly where I needed to go, but getting there, the last fifty feet, meant threading through the dancing mob at the foot of the DJ's station. Bodies crushed against me, bouncing to the beat. I quashed mild claustrophobia and pushed through. The lights bobbed and flashed in my face. I smelled perfume. Body spray. It grew thick around me.

I reached the platform and jumped it. Rows of amplifiers surrounded the tables where the DJ worked his soundboard. I hopped over them, catching his eye and a startled what-the-hell look. I hurried up to him, gesturing my fingers across my throat. His what-the-hell look morphed into a screw-you look.

I leaned into him and pulled his headphones away from one ear. "CUT IT! NOW!"

He had time to blink before I reached for his panel. I didn't have a clue, and he knew it, so he slapped my hand away before I could mess something up. He pulled a slide lever back to the stop. The music abruptly died. Stomping, dancing feet carried on for half a dozen beats. "Microphone! Now!"

"What the fuck, man?" He didn't move, but I spotted a microphone on the table and snatched it.

I spoke into it. "Is this on?" It wasn't.

I turned to the DJ. "Turn this goddamn thing on!" I put some menace into the words. He reached over and flicked a small switch on the stem of the mic.

I lifted it to my lips. "Hey!" My voice boomed through the field house.

A few voices cried out at me.

"What the fuck!"

"Turn the music back on!"

"Asshole!"

"LISTEN UP!" I drowned them out easily. "Listen up! This will only take a minute. You're not going to freaking believe this, but we just got word that the official tour bus for Beyonce Knowles is passing through Essex. Yeah! That's right! And she has a connection to Essex High, a friend here, who persuaded her to swing by! Yeah! I kid you not! I kid you not!" An electric murmur ran through the crowd. "This is once in a lifetime shit, people! So VERY CALMLY, I want you all to WALK, and I mean WALK out of the field house and exit the building. If you want a chance to see the lady in person, her tour bus will be pulling into the south parking lot in about five minutes! This is for real, people! This is for real!"

A few voices rang out. "Bullshit! Put the music back on!"

But the wave had begun. Kids turned and bolted.

"STOP! DO NOT RUN! Somebody's going to get hurt! You won't miss her. She'll be here long enough for you all to see her. WALK PEOPLE! WALK!"

It worked.

"Are you shitting for real, man?" the DJ looked at me with bald wonder.

I flicked the mic button Off and leaned close to him. "No! There's a fucking bomb in the building and we need to get every one of these kids out of here. I want you and your assistant over there to help me. Fan out on that side and make sure no one stays behind. Stick to the Beyonce story if you can! If not, call it a police emergency! Now GO!"

His wonder turned to white-eyed panic so I flat-hand slapped him on the chest. "GO!"

He wheeled and waved at his assistant. The two of them hurried off the stage. I broke in the opposite direction.

A short-haired blonde caught my eye. Sarah Lewis moved at the back of the crowd now herding themselves toward the lobby exit. I jumped the amplifiers and hopped down from the stage. I ran after her and pushed through the crowd around her.

"Sarah! SARAH!" I caught her shoulder. She whirled to face me. "Where's Lane?"

She blinked and looked guiltily around.

"Where is she?"

"Mr. Stewart, she's meeting someone!"

"What? Who?"

"I don't know." Sarah's face struggled between truth and lie.

"Sarah, you need to tell me! Now!"

"She's been getting notes. From someone. He wanted to meet her tonight." She spoke hesitantly at first, then picked up steam. "He put notes in her locker. Totally old school. He said he rejects technology because it masks the soul. He's so romantic! And he wanted to dance with her! Tonight! But away from all this!"

Cold fear ran a blade through my chest. *Braddock! How could she fall for this!*

"Where? Where are they meeting?"

Sarah read the fear in my face and froze up for a moment. I gripped her shoulders as the crowd pushed past us. "WHERE?"

"Uh—the note—he said—under the Seventh Star!"

I blinked at her. "What?"

"He said under the Seventh Star."

"Sarah, what the hell is that?!"

She pointed. As the crowd moved out of the field house, the vast basketball court floor became vacant. The spotlights in the steel rafters projected huge luminous stars on the glossy wood floor.

"There are only six!"

"No. There's one more. In the black box theater! That's where they tried it. The light. There's one more! Mr. Stewart, what's going on? Is she okay?"

"Where's the black box theater? Where is it? Show me!"

"What's going on?"

"Show me!"

She scooped up my hand and pulled me on an angle away from the flowing crowd. We cut across the floor toward a lighted exit between walls of folded bleachers. Breaking into a run, she released my hand and dashed to the door.

"Through here!" She hit the door bar and threw the door open. A short hallway led to a junction, then left or right. Sarah went right. "It's down here! At the end!" She started to pull ahead. I accelerated and clamped a hand on her shoulder to make her stop. She tried to pull away, panting.

"Wait! Listen to me!" I stopped her. "The theater lighting crew. Is Corey Braddock on that crew?"

Her eyes widened.

"He is! Do you think he's—oh my God!" She tried to pull away, but I stopped her.

"No! I got this. You need to get out of here. There's no Beyonce tour. It's a bomb threat and they're evacuating. I want you to do something for me!"

Sarah continued turning to look for Lane. I tightened my grip on her arm.

"Listen, Sarah! I want you to go back to the lobby. Find my wife! Tell her what you told me! Tell her where to find me! Got it? Can you do that?"

Sarah fired a worried look down the hall. "Lane!"

"I got Lane! I got this! Just get to my wife! Hurry!"

She hesitated, then nodded and bolted away, her high heels clicking in time with my pounding heartbeat.

Dammit! Dammit!

I dashed forward, covering the remaining length of the hall. As I approached the end, I spotted it. Another box. READ TRUTH.

A set of double doors hung open to my right. The interior looked dark. I heard a sound. Music chords. A guitar, heavily amplified, strummed once. Then twice. I stopped at the doorway and edged forward until I could see inside.

A huge white star, painted in light, lay on the floor. As if floating in the light at the center of the star, Lane stood facing him.

Braddock.

He stood close to her. Another cardboard box sat at their feet. This one had been split open, with the words READ TRUTH now inverted on the box flap. Beside the box, a smaller object lay on the floor. A wire ran from the object to a cell phone on the floor at their feet.

A girl's voice sang out, the start of a song.

Lane's head tipped downward. She held something in her hands. Pages. She turned them, concentrating. He watched. The plaintive sounds of the girl in the song filled the darkened space. The song flooded the hallway where I stood. The singer sounded wounded. The words, heartfelt.

I pulled a propulsion unit from my suit jacket—the only one I had. I found the propeller and snapped it in place. Lane turned another page. Absorbed.

What was it? A manifesto? The collected expression of the kid's blossoming hate for her? For her skin? He stood staring at her, but his posture seemed out of tune with the image in my mind. Something wasn't right. He looked like a breath held. Like someone locked in the silence between heartbeats. He looked—expectant.

I thumbed the slide control and the prop spun. *If I can reach him before he detonates...!* I checked his hands. They hung at his side, empty. His phone lay on the floor.

The girl singer filled the air with the first lines of a song about having a great night, about a first accidental touch. It sounded sweet. Adolescent.

If I can reach him—

Fwoomp! I vanished. I gripped the doorframe and pulled myself into the room, a space the size of a theater stage. Feet now gliding above the black wood floor, I gave the power slide a push. The prop growled unheard below the overpowering music. I accelerated across the space between the open doorway and the floating white star.

The song broke into a powerful, slow beat. Lane lowered the booklet in her hands, then gently dropped it to the floor. She seemed hypnotized by his relentless gaze. The singer and her song gained momentum.

I wanted to scream at her. She moved slowly forward and put her arms out, closing them around him. He lifted his hands and placed them on her back.

They began to sway, absorbed in the tidal motion of the deep beat filling the room. Heavy reverb on the singer's solo vocals wrapped the words around them. They shifted on their feet, leaning back and forth. He stood a full head above her. She stared up at him. He at her.

They danced.

I watched his hands. Empty. I watched his eyes. Locked on her. I searched his face, looking for the hate. Looking for the betrayal that was surely coming to destroy her. He had lured her in with anonymous secret notes and the dreams of romance that bloom in a girl's heart. And I knew of no more innocent or open heart.

When the moment came, I would kill him.

As I approached, I looked down at the box. I looked for wires and containers and signs of explosive death.

Glossy artwork and dramatic lettering peeked from between the box flaps.

The song lyrics spoke of pure adoration. The words merged with my image of Lane. A girl whose first step on an adolescent journey landed at this moment of hope and desire. This had been her secret. This had electrified her.

The singer became Lane.

As I approached the illuminated star, I searched the pages of the open booklet Lane had dropped. I expected to find the hate, the venom broadcast from Josiah James' web pages, the spittle flying cries for a white nation and supremacy.

Instead I saw Lane, drawn heroically. The figure on the pages had her face, her skin, her eyes. They blazed. I was close now. Close enough to reappear and charge them. I could take them both to the ground and get my hands on his hands before he could act.

It didn't fit.

A box full of glossy booklets. Drawings of Lane. There were other figures on the page, and now I found what I expected. Vicious faces contorted in rage. A muscular white male in a Confederate flag t-shirt. A Nazi armband.

A graphic novel! The kid self-published a graphic novel!

I reversed the power unit and pointed it up so that it would drive me down to my knees. Not caring what it looked like, I reached for the comic book. I turned the page.

Lane as heroine. Lane fighting snarling racists. Lane triumphant.

I flipped pages. Not only was Lane drawn with remarkable accuracy, the kid had rendered his father as one of the vicious racists. His father cooking chemicals in a garage. His father building devices and packing them into coolers. His father loading the coolers onto a pickup truck.

The kid had drawn and published his father's plans. I flipped the book to the end, where Lane the Heroine confronted the father who stood cursing her, detonator in hand.

"Holy shit!" I said aloud.

We had this all wrong.

There is a bomb! But not here.

I looked up at the boy who had not betrayed a girl, but who had been smitten by her. A kid who turned on his own father. He danced. He embraced her, my Lane, with his eyes closed and his breath held, perhaps wishing the moment might last forever under this luminous star.

The lyrics said what he couldn't put into words, telling Lane he adores her.

Beneath the music, I heard steps in the hallway behind me.

Andy!

I picked up the graphic novel. It didn't matter to me if they saw it float inexplicably through the air or not. The weight of it planted my feet on the floor. I turned and took giant steps toward the door, like an astronaut hopping across the moon. I reached the door quickly, at nearly the same moment as Andy. She pressed her back to the wall and held her weapon high, in front of her face.

She could hit him from here. She could if she had to.

"Dee! It's me! Stand down! Don't shoot!"

She blinked, startled, seeing the graphic novel float into the hallway.

Fwooomp!

"Is that Braddock?" She gestured with the muzzle of her Glock.

"Not the Braddock we thought! Look at this!" I held the book up for her to see. "It's a graphic novel! Look! This is his father. This is the bomb-making. The kid is exposing his father! And look! He drew Lane as a superhero. This—all this—it's a romantic gesture! *It's a goddamned romantic gesture!* Jesus, Andy, he's got it bad for her!"

Andy stared at the pages. She glanced into the room at the couple still swaying to the deep and desperate lyrics. Lost in each others arms.

"What?"

"There's no bomb! Not here. Those boxes are full of these graphic novels. He wrote it to expose his old man! He's denouncing his old man!"

"But Lane said—"

"I know! She said he looked at her like some kind of bug. He showed her offensive sketches. I think she had it wrong. He looked at her like a boy smitten. I think he showed her—here! This!" I held up a page with a burning cross, but in the foreground a furious Lane held an angry mob at bay. "And here—" I flipped a few pages and found a Nazi SS symbol. Lane the superhero held a terrified Nazi by the throat. The heinous symbols flapped on a collar beneath her clenched fist. "The kid has it bad for a girl of color and his old man is dumping his racist shit on him! The kid knew what the old man is doing! He set this all up to rat him out."

It was a lot to absorb. Andy scanned rapidly, switching her alert gaze back and forth between the comic and the couple in the beam of the star's light.

The song came to an end. Plaintive last chords were struck. The two kids slowly swayed to a halt. Silence fell around them, but they didn't part. Lane reached up and put her hand behind Braddock's head. She pulled and he bent forward, letting her lips find his.

"Oh my God!" Andy whispered beside me.

We slid sideways to the edge of the doorframe.

"How could we get this so wrong!" Andy said softly. "So wrong!"

We watched. They sustained the kiss, long and tender. When they parted, they shuffled away from each other, and the inevitable awkward moment came.

Andy stepped into the doorframe and the movement caught their eyes. Lane took an abrupt step back.

"Andy?"

"Lane, can you come here please?" Andy didn't mean to make it sound like a reprimand, but it did. Lane hurried out of the light toward us, her head lowered.

Andy dropped her gun to her side and slid it behind her hip.

Corey Braddock watched Lane go, lowered his own head and shuffled his feet uncomfortably. They were just two kids caught in a moment that should have belonged only to them.

Dammit!

First kiss, full of secrets. All the drama. No wonder Lane had been over the moon about her unknown suitor.

I looked at the artistry in the graphic novel. This kid didn't just possess skill. He had that extra element beyond skill that injects life into pen strokes on a page. He had heart. If he was slipping anonymous notes into Lane's locker, leading her to this moment, it had to have been intoxicating for her.

What a mess.

Lane picked up the pace and hustled toward Andy, who now put out her arm and put it around Lane's shoulder. They turned into the light.

Inside the luminous five points of the spotlight star, Corey Braddock began picking up his things. He scooped the speaker off the floor and put it in the cardboard box. He reached for his cell phone.

The moment froze.

"DON'T TOUCH THAT DETONATOR! HANDS WHERE I CAN SEE THEM!"

At the back of the black box theater a door swung wide. Mike Mackiejewski filled the backlit frame of the door, striding into the dark room. Etched by light from the projected star, I saw the department-issue shotgun raised as he charged forward.

Corey's hand closed on his cell phone. He rose to look for the source of the voice. The cable dangled between the phone and the box.

"Mike, NO!" Andy screamed.

FWOOOMP! I vanished—

GO!

—an explosive grip yanked me across the black floor, past Braddock. I threw my hands out and reached for the dull black barrel of the shotgun.

White light blinded me. The blast slammed my ears. The shotgun recoiled into Mike.

FWOOOMP!

Full bodied, I slammed into Mike. We went down. He reacted violently, twisting away, gasping. I rolled to one side, fearing he would take aim on me, but I discovered the shotgun in my hands. I had torn it free.

We sat on the floor gaping at each other.

That's when Lane's voice rose in a scream that tore into my heart. No words. A scream from deep within her filled the black space.

I saw Mike, his face bloodless, his eyes wide.

I saw Andy, in the doorway with Lane, arms wrapped around the girl, holding her back.

I saw Lane struggle, screaming, hands outstretched.

Lying in the center of the white star.

Arms thrown out.

Corey Braddock.

59

No amount of light, red, blue or white, flashing or static, could take away the fact that above all, the night had gone black.

I thought it might remain that way for a long time.

The evacuation took on a life of its own. Protocol, procedure and a small army of officers, many of them federal, became an engine that would not be stopped. Cordons were set up. Emergency vehicles descended on the high school. Ambulances rolled in. The fire department arrived. Paramedics.

A huge crowd comprised of the shivering evacuated were driven from the school building to the south parking lot. Many diverted to their cars and tried to leave. They were stopped. Someone, thinking fast, opened the elementary school next door and a migration began. Boys in thin suits and girls in sleeveless dresses marched across the snowy schoolyard, hunched and freezing, watched by armed officers.

A team arrived with bomb-sniffing dogs. The assessment came quickly. The boxes that had been placed around the building were contaminated with explosive residue. A new level of threat and protocol descended.

Andy, holding Lane as if she would never let her go, was ordered to leave the lobby where they sat on a bench and I stood helplessly by. Andy refused. The ATF officer in black tactical gear threatened to escalate the issue until Tom Ceeves appeared and stepped between them.

"There are no bombs," Andy told Tom.

"Doesn't matter! I want you three out of here!" the officer demanded.

Tom leaned over and looked down at the red-faced officer. "She said there are no bombs. There are no bombs."

The officer looked up at a wall of man and took a step back. "Fuck you. It's your neck." He hurried away.

My phone rang. I pulled it from my pocket. It was Rosemary II. I had texted her and told her she may hear of an incident at the high school, and that Lane was fine and was with us.

"She's fine," I repeated, taking the call. "She's with Andy and me."

"What happened? Should I come and pick her up? What's going on?"

I considered the consequences of truth and lie. I chose both. I told her there was a bomb threat, and the dance was evacuated, and we would bring her home as soon as the parking lot cleared out and things settled down. I told her if she drove here, she would not be able to get in. We'd see her soon.

Looking at Lane as I put away my phone, I decided returning the girl to her mother couldn't happen soon enough. Andy sat on a bench with Lane sobbing against her chest.

Tom looked at Andy. "Where's Mike?"

She nodded her head across the lobby to where a cluster of Essex PD officers and auxiliary stood around Mike Mackiejewski. Mike's head hung. He stared at his feet. At his side, his hands shook. Like an irregular spasm, his head jerked back and forth, trying to deny what could not be denied.

"Jesus," Tom said. He turned and walked slowly toward his deeply wounded officer.

Andy looked up at me with bulbs of tear hanging from each eye. "This is going to kill him, Will. This is going to kill him."

I jammed my hands in my pants pockets and stood watching, helpless.

I had been too late. Nothing, not prayer, not the levers in my head, not the fact that I shot across the room powered by a thought, would change what happened. The ribbon of time that brought Mike into the room looking for a kid with a bomb—a kid who picked up a device with a wire running to it—had already flowed past. And it brought black night.

As I stood watching, two men wearing bomb suits appeared from the direction of the cafeteria, pulling a heavy padded barrel on wheels between them.

"What are they doing?" I asked.

Andy assessed. "They're going to detonate the boxes."

It was too much. I thought of the artistry, the flying colors, the brilliant way in which Braddock had captured Lane the hero, the savage expressions he embedded on those who ran on hate. I thought of the sacrifice. The loss. The monumental stupidity.

"Where are you going?" Andy called after me. "Will!"

No one stopped me. I made a line from the corner of the lobby to the doors. Everyone gave the two bomb techs a wide berth as they emerged into the night air, and I had a clear path. I reached in my jacket for the carbon fiber propeller. It would do.

I caught up to them as the first shouts came from cops watching from a safe distance. The bomb techs' suits limited their visibility. They never saw me coming.

I leaned over and grabbed the box from the bottom of the heavy barrel. One of the techs turned and began shouting. It was muffled, coming from within the suit.

I dropped to one knee and heard heavy boots approaching. Somebody thought they should take me down before I blew myself up. One swipe of the blade did the trick. I pulled open the flaps of the box and dumped it.

Glossy graphic novels spilled across the concrete.

"There." I pointed. "There's your bomb."

We all stood looking at the heroic cover image of Lane Franklin.

EPILOGUE I

60

Going from the dry cold of January in Wisconsin to the warm damp air of South Carolina felt cleansing. I paused on the steps of the Mojave to draw the moist air into my lungs. I wanted it to wash me from the inside out. I wanted the sunshine to burn away lingering sorrow. I turned my face toward it and let the warmth work its magic. Around me, the airport ramp sang hurried engine songs that suggested life would go on, busy would remain busy, and time's ribbon had not stopped flowing.

It had been hard to feel that way in Essex.

Andy was right about Mike. The shooting destroyed him. A young man whose only dream in life had been to wear the uniform of law enforcement, he now found himself shattered and lost. His colleagues tried to help him see that he had no choice. They told him the signs were all there. Momentum drove his every move and the facts at hand justified his action. But from the instant the shotgun blast hit Corey Braddock in the heart, Mike understood his mistake. I feared for him. Whatever road lay ahead for this once energetic, confident young man, it offered no peace.

BEN BRADDOCK TRIED to blow himself up along with the committee conducting a search for the next Democratic National Convention. He had been told to do so by countless Internet voices, supported by innumerable urgent pleas from political pundits who filled screen frames on relentless cable news. The future of the nation stands at stake. Demons are destroying America. A conspiracy of epic proportions is crushing the American dream and driving good, hard-working, tax-paying Americans to despair and ruin. They must be stopped. Braddock, it was later learned, had traveled across the country several times to attend rallies, listening carefully for instructions in the subtext of energizing speeches from the man he saw as his commander-in-chief, his *leader*.

A full day before the police raid, Braddock left his pickup truck at a railroad maintenance substation and loaded his homemade plastique into the back of a railroad service truck, the kind with retractable steel wheels that allow it to ride the rails. With the highways crawling with state and local police searching for him, the ride to Milwaukee on the Wisconsin Central rail line was by contrast unimpeded. He might have made it all the way to the hotel where the committee was staying, if he hadn't panicked at the sight of a cordon of MPD squad cars. He stopped in mid-street, reversed and backed onto a Prius. He then regained his resolve and decided he wouldn't be stopped, except the steel railroad wheels caught the Prius and dragged it down the street behind the truck. When officers in a Milwaukee Police squad car, one of a dozen stationed around the hotel on orders from Deputy Chief Don Schultz, spotted this rolling wreck, they swerved into position and cut Braddock off from his target. The alert officers recognized what and who they were dealing with, and the scene on North Jefferson Street less than a block from the Pfister Hotel quickly turned into a standoff. Shouting slogans sold as bumper stickers on Josiah James' website, Braddock jumped from the truck with his detonator in hand and mashed the trigger. In coolers carried in the pickup bed blasting caps snapped and the homemade plastique ignited. The explosive fizzled and sputtered, emitting noxious smoke and leaving Braddock to wonder what went wrong as men in blue drove him to the pavement.

Cell phone cameras caught it all. Video flooded the media and Internet within minutes.

Battle lines were drawn at once. News organizations reported on a failed bombing by a domestic terrorist. Voices from the fringe decried the brutality of the police against a hero simply attempting to alert good Americans to the demon threat. T-shirts of Braddock standing boldly alone on the street were available within hours. Pundits would soon announce Breaking News that the police had also shot the man's unarmed son.

AFTER SOME SHOUTING by Chief Ceeves, it was determined that none of the boxes placed around the school by Corey Braddock contained explosives. The residue detected by the dogs was simply that. Residue. The boxes were confiscated by the federal authorities on the scene, but in the days that followed, rumors ran wild that Principal Chet Allison himself hid one of the unopened boxes. The rumors were driven by dozens of copies of the graphic novel circulating around the school. The rumors proved false. Corey had published his graphic novel on Amazon. Anyone could buy a copy. Thousands did. Corey Braddock and Lane Franklin became tragic heroes.

ANDY and I escorted Lane to Unit 23 and drove her home. A new round of tears broke out when her mother met us at the door. I hung back, feeling guilty and heartsick, thinking of all Lane had been through. Andy explained what she could to Rosemary II, then parted and let mother soothe daughter. She closed the front door behind her. I met Andy on the sidewalk and she let me close my arms around her. We held each other in silence.

Just as we parted, the front door blew open. Lane bounded down the steps coatless and in bare feet. She collided with me and threw her arms around me.

I don't know how long we stood there.

She cried. I couldn't speak. I could only press my face into the child's sweet-scented hair. When she finally spoke, the words were soft, halting.

"I know—what you did—I know—you tried!" I wanted to answer but something hard and sour caught in my throat. "I just want you to know I know. I hope you'll be okay!" She squeezed me once more and ran back into the house.

Well, dammit.

Andy needed to get back to the scene quickly and saw no point in me having to be there for the endless debriefing and paperwork avalanche descending on her—or to face the ire of the visiting bomb squad. From Lane's house, she drove a couple blocks toward the high school, then stopped to let me out.

Neither of us moved.

"I had this wrong," I told her. "I had the kid all wrong. I saw what I was expecting to see."

"We all did, Will. Lane did. We all did."

We sat in the idling squad car, letting the heater whisper regrets and recriminations. Andy would be more critical of herself than anyone. I owned my guilt, but with time I would find others to blame, and I resolved to extract payment for their crimes.

"Go home," she said, taking my hand. "But wait up for me, okay?"

"I will."

"And don't drink. We're flying in the morning. You're flying in the morning. We're going to get Liddy and the kids."

Which we did.

THE NEXT MORNING, on a flight plan filed in Earl Jackson's name, I illegally flew Andy to a rendezvous with her sister and the two little girls in Springfield, Missouri. The children were thrilled by the idea of going for an airplane ride. Lydia declared if she had to spend another night in a motel she would burn it to the ground. Louis and Eleanor Taylor politely declined a ride home, saying they would like to continue their road trip. Andy confided in me later that her father would be found in a "little airplane" only if it carried his coffin.

We loaded Lydia and the two girls, their assorted luggage and the souvenirs of their road trip into the Mojave and launched into cold winter sunshine.

Before sunshine turned to sunset, we had them home, along with the item that Mannis Rahn had been sent to murder for.

IN THE CAROLINA SUNSHINE, Andy stepped out of the cabin behind me and put her hand on my shoulder.

"How did it feel?"

"What?"

"Flying. From where I sat, you looked pretty good."

"Got a thing for bad boy pilots, do you? Will Stewart, air pirate!"

She warmed up a smile. It was nice to see. It had been a week since the black night at the dance. The light on her face had been slow in returning. "You're not quite the bad boy you think you are."

I stepped off the airstair onto the tarmac and turned around to lift her by the waist to join me. "Whaddya mean! I just hijacked one of Earl's planes, stole the princess, and flew halfway across the country without a pilot's license! That's some bad-boy shit!"

She hesitated. "Yeah, about that…" She reached in her shoulder bag and pulled out a folded envelope. "I thought I would give this to you when we opened our Christmas presents, but that's been, you know…" The holiday spirit was long gone, and the few times I brought up our little tree and the unopened gifts, she evaded the idea. "It's not really from me, but I've been wanting to give it to you. It came yesterday, but you were so excited about breaking the law today, I decided to wait…oh, heck! Here!"

I took the envelope and flipped it over. I read the return address.

"Well, open it!"

"I see you already did."

"Of course, I did! Are you insane?" She bounced on the balls of her feet. "I've been waiting for this ever since we saw Stephenson! I wanted to put it under the tree for you, but it didn't come, and it didn't come. I was getting worried, especially after you said they came and hauled away the…you know."

"The wreck." I could say it. She couldn't.

"So, open it!"

I cracked the top of the envelope where she had already sliced it open. I looked inside, then lifted out the letter with the FAA symbol embossed in one corner.

"You're not quite the pirate you think you are," she said. She hooked me by the back of the neck and planted a kiss. "But you're my pirate."

"Well, shoot," I said, mildly flummoxed. I looked over the brief and officious letter that told me my application for a First-Class medical certificate had been approved, and that suspension of my pilot's license had been lifted. "Damn. And crap! I didn't bring your present!" Her Christmas gift still sat under our little artificial tree at home, untouched since Christmas Eve. She gave me a coy caught-in-the-act look.

"What?"

She lifted her hands and plucked at the buttons on the top of her blouse, eliciting an immediate thrill in me. She undid one, then two, then slowly pulled the halves apart. Hanging from her neck, just above the swell of her ever-so-lovely breasts, the heart pendant with the tiny diamond sparkled in the Carolina sunshine. "Thank you! I love it!"

We reveled in the moment. Like the sunshine warming us, it felt cleansing. I would have been happy to let time freeze then and there.

It never does on the good moments.

WE RENTED A CAR. Andy thought a convertible might be nice, but there were none to be had. I appreciated her attempt to adopt a sunny spirit, given the discussions we'd had all week, and the dark decision that brought us here.

We off-loaded no luggage. There was no plan to check into a hotel. The flight to Hilton Head had been two-legged. The flight plan for departure remained undetermined.

We navigated the rental car out of the Hilton Head Airport following the blue line on my iPad. Andy drove, but set a sedate pace for a change. I wondered if she wasn't as resolved as she claimed.

The landscape surpassed beautiful. Extravagant homes peeked from behind walls and gardens. Wealth hung in the air like high clouds on a summer day. Attractive. Intriguing. Out of reach.

We didn't talk much during the hour-long drive. About a mile from our destination, Andy found parking in a lot intended for visitors of a national wildlife refuge.

"I'm going to ask you one more time—"

"Don't!" she said sharply.

I studied her, searching for a hint that she had changed her mind, or a clue that refusing to discuss the question signaled a change of heart. She pressed her lips together, giving the lower lip prominence that told me to go no further.

I couldn't help myself. I had to say it again. "It's just...I don't ever want your badge to mean less to you than it always has. You're right to believe in the law."

"I always will. But you're right too, Will. Sometimes..." She didn't finish.

"Yeah."

We stepped out of the car. I opened the back door and lifted out the only small piece of luggage we carried. From an old backpack, I extracted my fishing vest and slipped it on. Digging into the pack, I found three power units and matching props. I loaded them into the vest.

"Did I tell you? I'm calling them—"

"No, you're not." She grabbed the front halves of the vest and pulled me into a kiss. We held it, long and determined. When we parted, she spoke breathlessly. "I can live with this. Whatever happens."

She reached in the bag and handed me the final piece I needed.

"Right."

OLIVIA BROGAN SUNNED herself on a vast deck behind an even more vast house. My first thought, on approaching, was that I had made a mistake in assuming she would be alone. A house this size on precious coastal real estate—why wouldn't she fill it with admiring guests? At the very least, she had to have servants.

Her text message said to come alone. *I know. Let's talk. Come alone.*

I expected she would want the conversation to be private. But now, flying inbound along a beach that stretched to the horizon, looking at the size of her house, I worried that I miscalculated. What then? Abandon the mission?

I felt the package pressed against my vest pocket and thought about Harriet and Elise, who now knew me well enough to say "I love you" every time we parted. And who I loved right back. I thought about Andy, and the price she paid to play a part in this. I thought of Lane Franklin and the role Olivia Brogan played in crushing her heart.

No. I wasn't about to abort.

I flew a circuit around the property. An expensive coupe sat inside one open bay of a six-car garage. Except for the blonde stretched out on a chaise lounge on the deck, I saw no sign of people. A healthy off-shore breeze drove rows of waves, like an invasion force, onto sand the color of Olivia Brogan's hair. Colored flags mounted on poles every few hundred yards on the beach flapped and snapped loudly.

I made a stop, low, in the weeds beneath the deck that overlooked the beach. Then I kicked off, adjusted for the wind and lined up to approach the deck on a path parallel to the beach. A swimming pool glittered in the center of the deck. It seemed funny to me, to have a pool beside the ocean.

She lay with her suntanned legs crossed, holding a magazine. She had tied her blonde hair in a ponytail to govern it in the breeze. Oversized round sunglasses masked her eyes. A cooler sat on the deck beside her, open. Small bottles nestled in ice pretending to be giant diamonds in the sunshine. As I descended, I checked the back of the house. Broad patio doors opened to a huge casual sitting room. No sign of companions, security or servants.

I had to goose the power unit to hold my approach line in the salt-scented breeze. She alerted to the sound and lowered her magazine. I touched down near a round table with highback chairs and fixed a grip on one of the chairs. For some reason the idea of appearing with a battery powered propeller thingy in my hand seemed unsophisticated. I took a moment to remove the prop and stow the parts. The fishing vest felt a little backwoods to me, but there was nothing to be done about it. I needed the pockets.

She cocked an ear, hunting the source of the sound. I waited until she turned her head in my direction.

Fwooomp!

She startled and cried out, then gathered her composure quickly. "Good Lord!" She couldn't reign in the look of wonder on her face. "That is remarkable!"

Less than one hundred feet away, Atlantic waves slapped the sand loudly. I wondered if living in a place like this was worth the stratospheric price tag. This wasn't exactly peace and quiet.

She folded the magazine and swung her legs off the lounge cushion. I initially thought she wore a robe over a bathing suit, but it was a simple one-piece short sleeve white dress. A row of buttons ran down the front to a hemline that gave most of the stage to her golden-tan legs. She wore white sandals with heels.

"You do know how to make an entrance!" She stood up. "Can I offer you something? Water? An excellent and rare private stock vodka?" She gestured at the cooler.

"Are you alone?" I asked.

"I am. There's no point in being here unless I'm alone. This view demands solitude. And I refuse to tolerate the interruptions of an attentive staff. They can clean and restock when I'm gone." She walked closer and put out her hand. "Thank you for coming, Will." I think she expected me to shun her handshake, but I didn't. I took her hand and she took mine and it turned into something more than a handshake as she pulled me across the deck to where she had been sitting. She slid back onto the lounge seat and patted the cushion beside her. "Please. Sit."

"What? No promise not to bed me?" I turned and pulled a chair from the table. I sat down facing her.

"Do you feel you need one?"

"My wife was not entirely pleased by our last conversation."

"That's understandable." She lifted off her sunglasses and looked me over with dark eyes. She leaned back on the cushion, lifted her legs and stretched them out again. "May I be direct? Did you come here to kill me?"

"The thought crossed. You look fairly defenseless here."

"Oh, I am. I am entirely at your mercy. I don't have a gun in the house. I don't keep a stiletto strapped to my inner thigh. Look! See?" She pulled her hem up to show off.

"Seems a little careless."

"What's the point? With someone like you, and that entrance you just made, what would be the point of extravagant security measures?" She applied sudden intensity to her gaze. "You know...people in my economic bracket, we're a small population. We keep tabs on one another. I have an acquaintance—a very wealthy man—who, it is rumored, recently suffered a serious security breach. It changed him. Made him a recluse. No one knows his location. He dropped off the political scene overnight. You wouldn't know anything about that, would you?"

"Telling tales out of school might lower your opinion of me. As would lying."

Her smile broadened. "Oh, my! Then I'm all the more anxious to know the answer to my question. Are you here to kill me? Or can we explore a mutually beneficial relationship?"

"Do you mind dying? Because I think I have good reason to make it happen."

"I mind terribly! And I can give you millions and millions of reasons not to make it happen."

"A bribe? Or desperately buying your life?"

She laughed. "I don't do anything desperately. I wouldn't know how to put a value on my life. And I don't bribe. I'd like to discuss a partnership."

"I'm listening."

"Yes, but who else is? Would you please stand up? And please remove that vest." As I stood, she stood. I pulled off the vest and handed it to her. She removed the package, still wrapped in brown paper, examined it briefly, then set it aside. She removed the power units and smiled at them. "Now that's interesting! I am dy—well, let's say anxious—to learn more." She set them aside. She ran her fingers up and down every seam and then examined each button closely. When she finished, she turned to me.

"This is going to get personal," she said.

It did.

"Satisfied?" I asked when she finished.

"I believe I could be," she said. "But wait here."

She strolled across the deck and disappeared into the house. I took the moment to go to the railing and look at the Atlantic as it continued its million-year effort to erase this island. Looking left and right, the nearest homes were visible, but stood several hundred yards away. I marveled that she appeared to own so much beachfront on a coast where expensive homes stood shoulder to shoulder.

"What are the flags?" I asked when she returned carrying a small device.

"Warnings. The riptide is deadly along this stretch of beach. Swimming is not advised."

"Do you?"

She stepped up to me and held up the device, which matched a cell phone in size, but had three times the thickness. She touched a screen. It emitted a rising, high-pitched tone. She began waving it back and forth across my head, up and down my arms.

"Never. I'm not a good swimmer."

She scanned my body down to my toes. Rising again, she scanned the vest and the wrapped package. She turned the device off and set it aside.

"You couldn't just do that to begin with?"

"Where's the fun in that? Now sit! Let's decide if you're here to kill me or to open a door to a world you could never imagine."

She returned to her lounge chair. I took to the deck chair again.

"Notwithstanding the demonstration you just got, you know what I can do. You could only have learned that from Mannis Rahn."

"Manny, yes. He was astonished. He called me from the hospital in, where was it? Cedar Rapids? Anyone else, I wouldn't have believed. But Manny was nothing if not pragmatic. I would thank you for saving his life, but you seem to have balanced the account. Yes. He told me. Next question?"

"I don't have that many. We have most of it figured out. The connection between you and Rahn would have eluded us entirely. Except we ran across someone who knew you visited the Parks ranch right about the time Parks began his experiment with Rahn."

"Yes, I met Manny at the ranch. A bit of a failure for poor Pearce. Manny had higher aspirations, and Pearce did not adequately consider his leverage over Manny."

That bitch. "He called you a bitch. Parks. I thought he meant Andy, but it was you. Now I understand. He said Rahn raped you."

"Deliciously. We made Pearce watch."

"You hijacked his pet assassin."

"Yes. Though I understand he did much better with those Nazis. I saw potential in Manny. And Manny loved fucking me."

"Nice perk." I reached for the package on the table. I slipped the tape free and unrolled the brown paper Andy had crafted from a grocery bag. I held the item up. "This is what you sent him after."

Olivia couldn't help the smile. "The redhead!"

"Ellie's favorite doll."

"Probably not a good representation of the female form, but little girls have dreams." The head was too big, the legs too long, and the waist too thin. The doll was a character from a cartoon series about a high school populated by teenaged monsters. This one was either a cute ghoul or a charming vampire.

"She loves this thing so much that her mother bought two more just in case she ever lost it. The spares were stolen from the house in D.C. But you already knew that." She chose not to confirm.

"Is it there?" Olivia gestured at the doll.

"What? Oh, this?" I pulled the head off the doll and extracted a flash drive from inside. I held it up. "Yes. It was there, right where Davis put it. I assume he did so shortly before Lydia packed up and left him. The miserable shit didn't care about getting his children back, but he was willing to kill his wife to get this back."

Olivia made a face. "Well, not entirely."

"No. Of course not. Rahn was your instrument, not Davis's. You sent him to kill Lydia."

"This is where I am reluctant to share, Will. May I have it please?" She held out her hand.

I laughed and stood up. "Reluctant to share? That's funny! You know what? I think we're done here. Time for me to fly, as it were." I picked up the vest.

"Wait!" I caught a flash of panic on her face, there and gone in an instant, like heat lightning in summer. She smoothed a veneer of warmth in its place. "Wait, please. I thought we were getting along well."

"And I thought you wanted to discuss a partnership." This brought new excitement to her eyes.

"Let's! I'd like nothing more, because clearly with your abilities and my position, there is *nothing we cannot do.*"

"You mean get away with."

"Without doubt." She slid closer on the lounge cushion. "What's your price? If you didn't come here to kill me for my sins, and I really didn't think you had it in you, then what's your price? Do you think there's a price I can't meet?"

Looking up at me, she reached out and put her hand on my thigh. "Will, there is *nothing—nothing* you can't have. When Manny told me about you, I thought of you running around with your wife playing at solving crimes when you could be destroying whole crime syndicates! Flying around in your little airplanes when you could own and operate your own 747! Think about it! I deal in power. You *have* power! Untapped power! Talk to me!"

"I don't know my price for partnership. Yet. But I'll tell you my price for the job interview. You want a shot at making me your new shiny object? You pay up front."

"Anything."

"An explanation. Sans bullshit. What is this?" I held up the flash drive.

She stood and walked to the railing. She turned around and leaned on it. "Data breaches. Millions of records."

"That's not what we found."

She shook her head. "No. What you have in your hand gives data breaches meaning. Have you ever seen a list of data breaches? You can find them on the Internet. Of course, those are only the ones that have been made public. The ones that have not are far worse. Hundreds of millions of records. Social security numbers. Addresses. Credit cards. Telephone numbers. Personal information. Medical records. Voter registration. Anything and everything. You hear about them all the time. But did you ever stop to ask yourself what good is all that data? And to whom? Data has no value, Will, except to someone who assigns it a purpose."

She waited. I chose not to be prompted.

"It's not for stealing Blu-Ray players from Best Buy, I can assure you. And it isn't fodder for phony credit cards in the hands of swarthy mobsters in Slovenia either. The breaches are almost universally Russian. What's funny is how the whole world knows that Russia is waging war and conquering entire nations online, without apology—yet most people, some at the highest level, choose to look away. Astonishing!"

"Go on."

"Will, Russia is not a nation. It's a crime family. Some members of the family seek wealth in mining, some in cyber theft. Some buy, some sell, some kill each other off. It's quite fluid. Opportunities arise. Farsighted individuals recognize that products—and data is a product—have a shelf life. They apply it for their own purposes, of course, but eventually put it on the market. Other individuals—like me—find value in things that seem to have run their course. A fire sale comes along. Gold mines can be had for pennies on the dollar."

"Okay. Data. Then what?"

"Yes, 'then what?' is the key question. I told you, I grew up in a world where money buys political influence. Votes on the floor of the House of Representatives and the United States Senate. Lobbying. My market is anyone with an angle, an objective, a desire to rule, or make the rules. My father did it old school. But that's not working quite as well as it once did. I needed a new approach."

"You can't mean your Green Team?"

She laughed. "Please. They're merely curtains. No, I'm talking about how a pharmaceutical company expects results when they pay to have certain laws governing liability revised. They're not comfortable with Congressional representatives who insist on taking the will of the people into account. It's disappointing to see millions spent and then have a vote go the wrong way because some Congressman is scared to go back to his town hall meetings."

"I think it's called representative government. That's what they called it in fourth grade civics, anyway."

"They lied to you. What you hold in your hand is the will of the people." I thought about Carla Stevens lamenting her losses. *We The People.* "When that vote comes up, and the senator I own is uncomfortable because his state leans against the proposition I'm paying for, I make certain he can show that his state *wants* him to vote the way he's supposed to vote."

"How?"

"Data breaches. Which yield data. Which yields names, addresses and emails. Which can be fed into machinery that pours hundreds of messages into the offices of that senator so that when he votes the way he's paid to vote, he can point with a straight face at the number of emails he received. The number of Instagram messages, Tweets, and yes, even handwritten snail mail letters, all from real people with real addresses. All clamoring to support *my client's* position. Like favoring less federal protection for wilderness lands. Like making sure there's an assault rifle in every closet. Like making it illegal to sue a pharmaceutical company when they poison your children!" She picked up speed. "Mountains of data are useless! Unless you know how to make them useful! *I make them useful!* When someone pays me ten million to make the restrictions on their environmentally murderous mining practices go away, I don't waste it begging for votes! I have *The People* do it! I give a piece of the pie to the senator —you know, make sure the donors fill those re-election coffers—but more importantly, I give him the peace of mind to vote the way the money tells him to vote!"

I gave her a moment. Her chest heaved up and down. She caught her breath, closed her eyes and shook her head. "I get a bit animated."

"Take your time."

"Servers overseas. Print shops that can churn out custom, handwritten envelopes, handwritten letters. The technology is amazing. It's machinery with literally hundreds of moving pieces, Will!" She laughed. "I have to tell you—there is one link in this chain where millions of dollars are stuffed in plastic garbage bags and carried by camel to my vendors. By camel! It is a great, complex enterprise, and that fucking son of bitch Davis Bates did the worst possible thing he could do!"

"Expose it?"

"No! Copy it!"

"And put you out of business."

"Worse! Compete! I don't want competition. I *own* this market!"

"Luca de Maurier. Was he in it with Davis?"

She laughed. "That pimp? It shows you how small-minded Davis was. How little he understood the magnitude of what I built. Davis pitching my creation to de Maurier was the equivalent of a GM assembly line worker approaching a gas station owner about starting a car company."

"And James? Where does he fit in?" She cocked her head. I took it to mean she wasn't expecting me to know about Josiah James. Frankly, I wasn't sure. I took a shot. "He's your tool in this, too, isn't he?"

She tipped a nod in grudging concession. "When you want to make a minority look like a majority—when you want to push people along a scale—you need a voice advocating, no shrieking, far beyond your target point. If you want stronger drug sentencing guidelines, you get someone to scream that pushers should be summarily shot and thrown in a ditch. If you want to bottleneck cheap labor coming in to the United States, you launch a rant about how some immigrant in Stockholm stabbed a white schoolteacher. Teach people to contemplate the extreme and they'll stand by and accept the merely outrageous."

"Do you finance James?"

"Among others."

I struggled not to hear Lane's scream in my head. In the week since the dance, her agonized outcry haunted me. Corey Braddock lying in the center of the seventh star, arms thrown out like the cross he had drawn, haunted me.

"I'm being transparent here, Will. I want you to understand that. Some of this is distasteful, but I'm being honest with you. I want that to mean something to you."

She had no idea.

"Were you there? When Rahn killed Davis?"

"Nowhere near," she said confidently. "If I had been, I would have gotten something a little less cryptic from him than 'the redhead has it.'"

"But you set Davis in motion. Drinking with him. Goading him into the fake suicide. The calls to Lydia. The idea of texting. You got him up on the chair. Rahn finished the job. Applied the creative touch."

"Manny was a genius. Davis was desperate to get his children back. He had no idea that I knew what he really wanted."

"When you sent Rahn to kill Lydia—he had help. Was that you?"

"You flatter me, but no. I have other resources."

"And Bob Thanning?"

She blinked at me. "I don't know who that is." She continued without missing a beat. My fists clenched. "Let's not dance around a key question here, Will. Nothing, and I mean NOTHING has my fingerprints on it. Should we fail to come to an accord, and should you foolishly wander off telling this tale, none of it traces back to me."

"Maybe."

She shook her head. "Oh, trust me. More than that, I am hailed as a crusader. I've been called a modern Joan of Arc. *Vanity Fair* asked to do a piece on me. *The Atlantic* wants to interview me. My image is clean. Dynamic. Admired. Almost saintly. The left loves me. You would have an uphill climb against my spin." She waved her hand in the air between us, trying to erase the past. "But enough about me. Your turn. What is it? How does it work? I have a million questions. Can you really *fly*? Do you have any idea what that's worth? For heaven's sake, what are you doing with it besides chasing your wife around?"

"My wife does a lot of good."

"Will! Your wife has no imagination! We could topple governments! You want to fight crime? We could destroy government-sponsored crime syndicates! You want to play hero? We could assassinate every drug cartel kingpin in Mexico! This? What I've been doing? Yes, I'll take a bow! It's creative! The money pours in. But my God! Together with you—*there is no limit!*"

I stood up. I lifted the vest off the table and slipped it on. I returned the power units and the doll to the pockets.

"I think I told you. Politics isn't my thing."

"Will, you can't be serious! You can't walk away from this! There isn't a soul on this planet that would turn away from this kind of wealth and power!"

"Oh, I can think of one." I held up the flash drive for her to see, then slipped it into my jeans pocket.

Her expression darkened.

"You may think you're untouchable," I said, "but if this goes to the right people, if they dig deep enough, I'm sure they will find you. At the very least, it's going to expose some people in Congress who will have some serious explaining to do."

"Make the wrong choice here, Will, and it will expose much more than that." She said it evenly, deliberately. She stood staring, and in the same way Steggar Rahn's face melted into the face of his murdering brother, her face shed all warmth. I sensed the polite conversation was over.

When she spoke again, her voice was low.

"Your wife. She's a cop. That must worry you." She fixed a half-lidded stare on me. "So many random police shootings across this country. People are stirred up. White. Black. Left. Right. And the children, those little girls. So precious. It stops your heart to hear about abductions. Kids disappearing. Sex trafficking. Children. Josiah James has entire web pages devoted to the horrible sex trafficking the Democrats are doing to fund their Deep State. Absurd, but still frightening."

"Are you threatening me, Olivia?" I asked coldly.

"Yes! If that's what it takes to awaken you! Yes! I am *without question* threatening you! And your wife! And your family! And your friend Pidge. And Earl Jackson. Do you think Mannis Rahn is the only resource I can bring to bear on a problem? Walk away with that flash drive, Will, and you won't see me coming." She read my stiffening body language. "What? Are you going to give me the 'touch my wife and I'll...' speech? By definition, you won't even get organized until after the funeral. Is that a price you're willing to pay?"

I looked at her, then looked around. "Just to be clear. You're here. You're alone. You're threatening *me*?"

"Will," she said, issuing a long sigh, "that's not who you are. Can we just take a breath here? Rather than look at the downside... me murdering your friends... you murdering me...let's look at the upside. I'm a 'one percenter.' All the talk about how the one percenters in the world are untouchable, is—frankly—true. Why stand outside the wall pounding until your fists bleed, when you can be on the inside with me? Where you don't even hear the pounding? You came here with a mind that was more open than you think. *Let's work this out.*"

"There would be no stopping you, would there? If I walk away?"

"Don't think of it that way! Think of how there would be no stopping *us*!"

I said nothing.

"Look. Let's suppose for a moment that I could be comfortable with the two of us simply parting as friends. You take the silly thing with you. No one will make any sense of it or connect it to me. It's a blueprint, not a smoking gun. You go your merry way. *But you'll always wonder.* Living on your wife's salary and the peanuts you make flying little airplanes. Struggling to pay off your hospital bill—yes, I know every detail about you. You'll always wonder what might have been." She crossed the wood planks and stepped close to me. "Live life! I do. I waited here unarmed, unprotected, knowing you would come with ample reason to kill me. I took a calculated risk and it's fucking exhilarating! Come on! Show me! Show me what you can do! And then let's do it together! Can you really fly?"

She touched my chest. She moved closer.

I looked away. Thinking. Measuring the cost. Measuring the truth Andy and I had wrestled. There was nowhere to go within the legal system. Andy ultimately surrendered to that fact after we talked it into the night, night after night. Justice. The law. Lawyers and courts. The frustration, layered on the tragedy we both witnessed, brought Andy to the brink of questioning her deeply ingrained belief in the law. And eventually accepting the alternative.

Olivia Brogan was untouchable.

And if I walked away, nothing would prevent her from dismantling my life by destroying everyone I love. Starting with my wife. Could I risk letting her strike first?

I looked at her.

"How much money are we talking about?" Her eyes lit up.

"Will," she said breathlessly, "I have *Saudi princes* in my client list! Russian oligarchs!"

I lowered my eyes and gave the moment its due consideration.

"If I do this, there's one thing that has to happen."

"Name it."

"Take off your clothes."

Everything changed. As if her very bone structure shifted, her entire countenance changed. Confidence. The assurance of victory. It ran like electric current under her skin. Her lips drew back in a seductive smile. On this path, she knew she had full control.

She knew better than to jar the moment with words. She stepped back, a woman adept at putting on a show. She brought her fingers to the buttons on her dress and for a dizzying moment I remembered Andy making the same move. The buttons slipped free. One after another. After another. She never took her eyes from me, watching my eyes trace a path down her skin as I am sure she had done for men countless times.

She unbuttoned the dress to her navel, then shrugged out of first one sleeve, then another. The dress fell to her feet. She stepped out of it, closer to me. She wore nothing beneath the dress.

"Pick it up."

Flashing a hint of playful curiosity, she complied.

"Fold it. Leave it on the cushion." She watched me watching her. I tried to let my eyes wander just as she expected them to. It was not easy. My pulse pounded, but not for a reason she would have approved. "The shoes, too. I want you barefoot."

This made her smile. She slipped out of her sandals and placed them neatly beside the folded dress on the lounge chair.

She turned to me, offering me everything, most importantly the illusion of control.

I stepped closer and slid my hands around her waist, pulling her body against mine.

"Hang on."

Fwooomp!

She shrieked. I pushed off the deck and she shrieked again. Her hands dug into me. "Not so tight," I said. "You have no weight. Gravity has no effect. You won't fall as long as I hold you."

"Oh, dear Lord!"

I pulled a power unit from the vest. Behind her back, I snapped a propeller onto it. We continued to rise. She laughed. I could smell her hair.

"This is so much more than I thought! Will! If I can do this, too! Do you realize what we can do? Where we can go?"

"Let me show you," I said. I slid the control forward and the power unit buzzed. We sailed over the house. She continued laughing, almost as if she needed to remind me she was there. I angled my wrist and we curved toward the beach. I dove until we skimmed six feet above the golden sand with the waves lapping to our left.

"Would you really have killed my wife?" I asked.

She breathed heavily, gulping the air. I felt her turn to watch our path. "As my partner, I can promise nothing will ever happen to your wife."

She didn't have to explain the flip side of that.

I curved left, over the water.

"Why did you go after Lydia?"

"Because Davis asked me to. Will, let's not go there. You're making the right decision. When we get back, I will start by transferring a million —No!—ten million dollars to an account in your name! How does that sound?"

"Why did Davis ask you?"

"The man was about to have his balls cut off." She fell silent. We sailed above the wet sand. "He knew I had...resources. He didn't know that I already knew what he'd taken from me. It was my first hint that he'd hidden it with his children. He panicked because his children were suddenly out of his reach. He needed to get them back and tried to use me to do it. When I realized it..."

"You sent your assassin with benefits to put an extension cord around his neck."

"Can we please discuss this later?" She wiggled against me suggestively. "You're taking my breath away, and I don't just mean this—*Oh Lord!*—incredible thing we're doing!"

"One more question. You're certain? You're certain that what you're doing, with all the forgery and counterfeiting, and the murders—"

"I murdered no one! Mannis Rahn was an escaped psychopath."

"Right. All that. You're untouchable?"

"You have no idea! The beauty of this! It's too big! Steal ten dollars from a gas station and spend ten years in prison. Cheat the government out of half a billion in taxes and they make you president! I'm untouchable! It's so big, so diverse, it's impossible to see anymore! No one can ever put any of it together with me—with us! Even if what's on that drive got out! Even if someone tried to expose me, I have layers of protection you cannot begin to imagine."

I eased my flight path out over the water. The shore receded, two, three, four hundred yards. The water color changed from a pale blue-green to a deeper blue. Streaks in the water below told of dangerous currents beneath the surface, cause for the warning flags on the beach. I stopped the power unit and allowed us to glide. It was quieter here. Away from the shore. We floated ten feet above the uneven surface.

There have been times since *the other thing* happened to me when I touched murder in my heart. Watching innocent people harmed. Facing dark and evil people. Some were ugly and unabashedly vicious. One wore symbols of hate etched in his skin. One hid his rot and corruption behind adobe walls and paid security guards.

But what if dark and evil had a flawless smile and beauty? Smooth skin and a firm body? Golden hair? Olivia Brogan counted on her beauty as a bodyguard.

In that moment, I understood two absolute truths.

Olivia Brogan would never be touched.

And she would never allow me to refuse her.

I slipped the power unit into my pocket. I ran my hands down the length of her arms and found her wrists. She had a firm grip on me. I closed my hands on her wrists and pulled her grip free.

I spoke softly over the silent waves.

"She folded her clothes neatly and left them on the deck. No one knows why she walked out into the ocean that day."

"What?"

I let her go.

61

All I had to do was land on Olivia Brogan's deck and reappear.

Then return the deck chair to its place at the table and wipe the metal back bar with my shirttail.

Then pick up her electronic scanner and put it in my vest pocket.

Then take off my boots and socks and walk down a set of stairs to the sand below and hike on a line straight to the water. My larger foot size wouldn't matter. The sand would dribble into the telltale footprints, obscuring their size and shape while leaving a clear trail.

Then stand where the water lapped at my bare feet and throw the scanner far out into the waves.

Then vanish. Simple.

62

She didn't have time to scream. The instant I felt the electric snap of
release, she reappeared and dropped into the gently heaving ocean
less than ten feet below us. The surface took her, leaving an irregular
puddle of bubbles that bobbed on the waves. She sank, swallowed by
silence. With no beach to break on or hull to lap against, the sea does not
speak. It would never tell this tale.

I looked at the distant horizon. Not west, where the land marked the
border between sky and sea. East. Where the Atlantic lived up to its name
and seemed to go on forever. Murder in my heart had been a cold and dark
object. I touched it—embraced it—in the name of a guy who plowed the
snow from my driveway and a woman I never met who worked long
hours in a Washington D.C. hotel.

To the world, Olivia Brogan slipped off her clothes, folded them
neatly and walked into the ocean to let the riptides take her. Justice could
not be cleaner.

It might not be Andy's justice, but it could be mine.

She broke the surface gasping and clawing.

"PLEASE! HELP ME!"

The riptide pulled her away from me. From here to the beach even a
powerful swimmer unimpeded by riptides would be challenged. She had
no chance. She moved seaward, heaving and spitting, arms flailing. I

pictured her becoming smaller. I pictured letting the offshore wind push me toward land, watching her shrink to nothing.

"PLEASE! DON'T DO THIS TO ME! PLEASE! I'll—" The salt water silenced her for a moment as she slipped under. When she broke the surface she stopped calling out in favor of gasping for air.

She struggled, floating farther away.

I touched it one last time. Murder in my heart. Cold. Black.

I could live with it, when I thought of what this woman had done. Not just to Bob or Graciela Montoya or Lane. But what she promised in a future I could all too easily imagine. Andy tragically shot in the performance of her duty. Harriet disappearing into horrors unimaginable.

Olivia Brogan could do these things without a single golden hair falling out of place.

Let her sink.

I released the thing I touched in my heart knowing it would remain there and sensing that we would renew our acquaintance.

I felt for the muscle that ran down my center, the one connected to the all-but-tactile levers in my head that made me vanish. Flexing it, I rotated my body until I was parallel to the surface. Flicking the propulsion unit, I eased forward, slowly catching up to where she worked her arms in a relentless effort not to sink below the waves. Her hair had broken free of its ponytail tie and floated around her bobbing head like a spill of liquid gold.

It is harder when the evil is pretty.

She tried to tread water but could hardly keep her face clear of the surface. Half of her gasping breaths took in salt water, which she spit and coughed away.

She stopped calling out, either because it took too much air or because she couldn't see me. For all she knew, she was alone at sea.

I eased closer. Her naked body wiggled and shimmered as the surface of the water played optical tricks with everything below. She regained a degree of rational thinking and searched the surface around her, wild-eyed. Maybe she thought she could find out which way to swim, but as I dropped closer to the water, even I could only see the land in flashes. It looked like something floating in the distance, seen between swells.

Her arms worked the water furiously. Her legs kicked. She wouldn't last long.

Like a fisherman trying to snag a fat dinner skimming in shallow water, I fixed on one arm. I waited until the moment was right, then plunged my hand into the water. I met resistance in a way I felt once before, but I stabbed my hand downward and clamped a grip on her bicep. I wasn't sure this was enough and flashed on the same fear I had with Pearce Parks, that I might not push *the other thing* far enough, that it might slice her apart and stain the water as the pieces sank.

Would that be so bad?

FWOOOMP! The sound in my head exploded like thunder against the silence of the open ocean.

Olivia vanished and flew out of the sea in a cloud of spray. She continued wiggling and fighting as if she now thought rising into the air might somehow drown her, too. I swung upright and threw an arm around her from behind to secure her and end her thrashing.

I fired up the propulsion unit, full throttle, and let the wind of our passage overpower the sound of her gasping.

Fwooomp! I dropped her to the wooden deck. She wasn't prepared for it. Her legs offered no support and she went down hard. She lay on the hot wood, body heaving.

Andy uncrossed her legs and leaned forward. She sat in the same chair I had occupied, looking no worse for the short time she spent crouching under the deck. White blouse. Blue jeans. Gold badge fixed to her belt. Black Glock holstered behind her hip. Coiled and powerful. At that moment, I both loved and feared her.

Andy briefly searched the air where she knew I hovered, then she fixed her professional attention on the wet, trembling naked woman at her feet.

"Olivia Brogan, you are under arrest for accessory to murder in the case of Robert Thanning and Davis Bates, conspiracy to commit murder in the case of Lydia Bates, accessory to murder in the case of Graciela Montoya and James Radovan." Andy held her phone in one hand, recording. "You have the right to remain silent. Anything you say can and will be used against you in a court of law. You have a right to an attorney. If you cannot afford an attorney, one will be appointed for you. Do you understand these rights?"

I maneuvered down to the deck, close, so I could hear her. Olivia Brogan heaved and gasped. Her golden hair had gone dark and hung in wet strands on either side of her face.

"Do you understand these rights?"

Closer. I could smell the sea on her. Her breath entered and left her body in rasping bursts.

"Do you understand these rights?"

"YES!" She spit the word out. Andy leaned closer.

"And would you like to waive your right to remain silent and make a statement at this time?"

I leaned closer. My lips almost touched her ear. I whispered. "Or would you like to go for another swim?"

EPILOGUE II

63

The almost empty coffee shop carried the murmur of the baristas' voices, interrupted by the occasional hiss of the cappuccino maker or growl of a blender. I arrived early to enjoy a cup of excellent Costa Rican blend and a cinnamon scone. I took a table at the back, choosing a corner that offered a degree of privacy, yet with a slight lean in my seat, I could see the front door. The shop occupied a large portion of a former industrial building. The kind of raw brick and exposed steel that coffee drinkers seem to love.

Light jazz rose and fell in the air. The scent of fresh ground beans was intoxicating.

I waited.

At two forty-five Carla Stevens stepped through the door. I leaned back in my seat. The shop matched my cup, largely empty. Time to go.

I scanned to ensure that no one could see me in my corner.

Fwooomp! I vanished.

I worked my legs out from under the table and gave myself a gentle push toward the ceiling. Pipes and beams. My favorite interior styling. Plenty of places to grip and pull myself high across the shop. Andy and I chose mid-afternoon on purpose. A scant handful of people sat with their faces buried in laptop screens. Would-be novelists or Internet addicts; I had no idea. I couldn't imagine what could keep someone absorbed like that.

Carla Stevens wore layers of brown and burgundy, with a scarf dangling from her neck and boots up to her knees. She looked from patron to patron, searching for someone. She gave up, bought a coffee, and found a table. She chose one near the front, with a view of the street. She settled in.

I performed a slow glide across the room until I floated directly overhead.

A few minutes later, she watched a young man trot across the street and through the entrance door. He, too, bundled himself against the cold and gray that made pedestrians on the streets of the nation's capital move faster. He wore a knit cap and a puffy ski jacket with stripes down the sleeves.

Pulling off his gloves, he performed the same quick search Carla had. She watched him until their eyes met.

"Stevens?" he asked.

"Yes."

"Mike Jackson," he extended a hand. "Washington Post."

"Seriously? Michael Jackson?" she smiled. He shrugged it off.

"Yeah. My parents' idea," he said. He looked around. "They grew up in the eighties. At least I plan to stay black. Are we waiting for someone else?"

"You tell me. I was told to meet you here."

"Likewise. Lemme get a cup of something. Be right back."

I worked my way into position near the wall, then pulled myself down hand-over-hand until my feet touched the floor in the corner. As long as neither one of them stood up suddenly on the wrong side of the table, I was fine.

Jackson sat down facing Stevens. He pulled a folded sheet of paper from his pocket and held it up for Carla.

"This showed up on my desk. Out of nowhere. I mean, seriously, out of nowhere. I even checked the security cameras. Nobody went past my desk." The message on the paper was handwritten in heavy Sharpie black. The name of the shop. The time and date. Carla's name.

Carla reached in her purse. She extracted a matching note with similar instructions.

"Is this about Olivia Brogan?" Jackson asked.

"Hey, I didn't call the meeting. I thought you did."

"Nope. But since I have you here, tell me about your former boss. Did anyone at the firm see this coming? Confessing to murder?"

"Slow down, cowboy. This isn't an interview."

He looked around.

"Okay. Then it's starting to feel like we've been had. You sure you have no idea what this is about?"

I reached in my jeans pocket and closed my fingers on the item I'd been carrying. Before Carla could answer, I reached between them. I opened my hand. I felt a light electric snap as the flash drive tumbled into view, fell and clicked and danced on the tabletop.

Both stared at it. Neither moved to touch it.

Jackson quickly glanced over his shoulders. The nearest other person was a solid fifteen feet away, hunched over a laptop screen.

"If I were to guess," Carla said slowly, "I think our meeting is about whatever is on that drive."

ANDY WAITED for me around the corner in the rental car. I slid onto the right front seat beside her.

"Where to, sir?" she asked cheerfully. What we had done here lifted her spirits.

"Airport, my good woman."

She flicked the directional and pulled into traffic. "Did you already file a flight plan for Essex?"

"I filed," I said. "But not Essex. Waukesha County."

She glanced my way, questioning.

"I want to make a stop."

"Where?"

"Children's Hospital. I'll explain on the way home."

DIVISIBLE MAN: THE SEVENTH STAR
March 2, 2018 to October 14, 2018

ABOUT THE AUTHOR

HOWARD SEABORNE is the author of the DIVISIBLE MAN™ series of novels as well as a collection of short stories featuring the same cast of characters. He began writing novels in spiral notebooks at age ten. He began flying airplanes at age sixteen. He is a former flight instructor and commercial charter pilot licensed in single- and multi-engine airplanes as well as helicopters. Today he flies a twin-engine Beechcraft Baron, a single-engine Beechcraft Bonanza, and a Rotorway A-600 Talon experimental helicopter he built from a kit in his garage. He lives with his wife and writes and flies during all four seasons in Wisconsin, never far from Essex County Airport.

Visit www.HowardSeaborne.com to join the Email List
and get a FREE DOWNLOAD.

Proceed on course with the beginning of
DIVISIBLE MAN: TEN MAN CREW

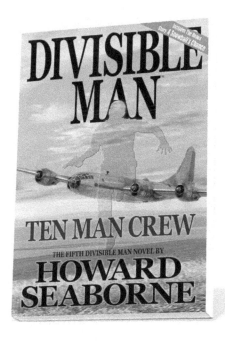

DIVISIBLE MAN: TEN MAN CREW

Dammit!

I floated in the high heat of the barn, near the roof. Pinprick shafts of sunset's last light angled through the air around me and through me. Evening crickets wound up their pickup lines outside.

I tried again.

DOWN!

Nothing.

FLOOR!

Nothing.

"Shit!" I barked in frustration.

"That doesn't sound good." Andy's voice rose from the open barn door below and behind me. I rotated in the air, using the strange core muscle that runs down my center when I vanish. For months the sensation of a controllable pivot point had been reliable and consistent.

At least that works.

"God, it's hot in here, Will. Why not fly outside? It's a beautiful evening."

She stepped out of the framed light and into the shadows of the barn loft. In short shorts, sandals and a tank top, my wife reminded me once again why I like summer best of all. Tonight, she tied her flowing auburn hair in a high ponytail, lifting it off the back of her slender neck for the sake of cooling. In each hand, she held a glistening bottle of Corona with a green lime wedge jammed in the neck.

So many reasons to love this woman.

I pushed the thumb slide on the power unit in my hand. Unseen, a six-inch carbon fiber model airplane propeller turned, blowing propwash air across my forearm, pulling me forward. I performed a spiral around one of the central barn beams and eased to a landing on the uneven wooden floor.

Fwooomp!

I reappeared in stride, mildly startling Andy. It's been a year and it still catches her by surprise. She extended the cold beer to me. Free of the cool sensation that *the other thing*—the only name I've come up with for it—wraps around me, the barn heat hit me.

"Seriously," she said, "it's fifteen degrees warmer in here."

"Yup. Old barns. You should stack hay bales in one of these sometime when it's a hundred and ten in the loft."

Andy adopted a strangely distant gaze, fixing her gold-flecked green eyes on me and not on me at the same time.

"What?"

"Oh, just picturing you, shirtless, all shiny and sweaty, heaving around fifty-pound bales. My beefcake farmhand."

"Maybe we could get that on a calendar for you." I took her musing as an invitation and stepped closer. "Want some slippery sweat on your skin? Some hay in your hair?"

"Yuk. It is way too hot in here."

"What kind of seductive farmer's daughter are you?"

"My father is a lawyer and a corporate CEO. He wouldn't know a plow from a cow unless you itemized them in an annual report. Let's get out of here."

Outside the barn, the cool evening air washed over my skin and made her point. We walked toward our rented farmhouse. The rim of the sun slipped beneath the horizon, leaving a pale blue, cloudless sky and the false promise of an endless twilight. I sent a splash of delicious chilled refreshment down my throat.

"You didn't answer."

"What?"

"Why do that in the barn? It's a beautiful evening."

"Once I'm gone the heat doesn't affect me." I shrugged. "I dunno. That's my original training space. Area Fifty-One. It feels...comfortable. It's safer, too. I'm being cautious—trying something I don't understand. You don't want me to go shooting off into space."

"I appreciate the caution." She slipped her hand in mine. "Any luck?"

"No."

She didn't press and thankfully didn't offer suggestions. *Maybe you need to focus. Maybe you've got too much on your mind. Maybe you shouldn't try at all.* The last thing I needed was Andy coaching from the sidelines. I had that going on in my head without her.

And how are you doing?

Getting nowhere faster than usual.

On several occasions while in the vanished state I propelled myself by simply *thinking* a direction or objective. The first time it took Lane Franklin and me through the window of a burning building. The second time it lifted both Andy and me to the ceiling of a motel room seconds before a now-dead Nazi shot up the bed we slept in. The third time—the longest sustained event to date—it launched me halfway across Essex County carrying Andy's nearly-drowned sister Lydia to a hospital.

For months I've tried to recreate the effect, without success.

"Maybe the effect is a by-product of adrenalin," she offered. "We don't know what happens to your physiology when you do what you do. Mix in a shot of a chemical compound that jolts the human body the way adrenalin does—I don't know—maybe it turbocharges you."

"I don't think so. I've pumped plenty of adrenalin on several occasions and nothing happened. I think it's something else."

"Like what?"

"Mental. Brain waves. Neurons firing in the right combination with those wires in my head. The difference between generated thought and a flash of pure instinct."

"Uh-huh. Speaking of those wires—"

"Yeah, yeah. Stephenson wants me to see him for an updated scan. We just did that, for chrissakes!" I sometimes wonder if the neurologist we trust with my condition is more interested in me as a specimen than as a patient.

"In February. It's been a while."

"Nothing changed in February. Nothing is changed now."

Andy answered with a skeptical expression that dismissed my baseless assumption.

Change the subject.

"Hey, it's a gorgeous night. Let's take a joyride."

She stiffened slightly. My wife does not like vanishing and flying with me. Our first experience together introduced the possibility of first dying from hypoxia, then hypothermia. That was followed closely by a near-death incident with a tall building. The bad start stained the experience. I harbored hope that a gentle scenic tour of Wisconsin farmland on a summer evening might scrub the bad memories.

"Slow and easy. Just for fun," I said. "I'll even let you drive." I held the propulsion unit out for her.

"Oh, no. Not me. And you've been drinking." She pointed at my half-finished beer.

"Lame." I flipped the bottle onto the lawn. Foamy gold spray spun from the neck.

"That's a shameful waste."

I took her bottle and repeated the gesture with excellent aim. The bottles clinked together in the grass.

"Works best if we do this," I said. I put my left arm around her and pulled her close. Catching a sparkle in her eye, I leaned into a kiss and held it. She kissed back energetically.

Fwooomp!

We vanished.

She pulled her lips from mine. "God! I told you! That's just weird!"

We began to float. She tightened her grip on me. I tapped my toes on the gravel and started a vertical vector.

"Wait! How many propeller-thingies do you have?"

"It's called a ZAP."

"No, it isn't. How many?"

"Just the one."

"No! Will, go get your vest! We need backups!" She transmitted urgency through fingers digging into my waist. Andy's fear of floating out of control like an untethered astronaut had foundation.

Choosing not to sabotage this exercise with an argument, I aimed the power unit straight up and pulled the slide into reverse. The prop hummed. We ceased ascending and slowly descended to the driveway.

Fwooomp! We reappeared. She stepped away abruptly to guarantee I wouldn't make us disappear again until we were properly equipped.

Anything to make her feel better. I turned to make the quick trip to the house when we both heard a vehicle approaching from the west on our narrow country road. A car rolled into view a quarter of a mile away. Twilight remained strong and the car ran without headlights. I stopped and watched it approach. Instead of rolling past on the whisper of its tires, the car decelerated and eased into our driveway.

"Do you think he saw us?" Andy asked quietly, as if the driver, inside a closed vehicle seventy feet away, could hear her.

"Not a chance." I strolled to the grass and picked up the two Corona bottles. Most of one had drained out, but the other still carried a healthy third of the golden liquid. I handed Andy the empty.

The car crunched to a stop on our gravel driveway. Reflections in the windshield obscured the driver. The car was a mid-sized silver Nissan sedan, looking new. With an eye trained by my police detective wife, I noted the Iowa plates.

The driver stepped out.

"Oh, shit!" I muttered out of the side of my mouth. "I know that guy!"

"Hi! Beautiful evening!" The driver eased around his door and closed it. He walked toward us casually, pitching a disarming smile our way. The smile conflicted with the shoulder holster he wore over a black polo shirt. A semi-automatic handgun hung under his left armpit.

I eased the power unit into my back pocket and slipped my right arm around Andy's waist. In my head, I closed an imaginary grip on a set of imaginary levers. Pushing those levers forward would make us vanish in less time than it would take for the man to reach for and touch his weapon. Andy tensed beside me. There wasn't time to explain, nor was there time for me to come up with a clue as to how this man had found me.

Instead of reaching for his weapon, he slipped his right hand into his trouser hip pocket and pulled out a flat black wallet.

"Detective Stewart?" he asked Andy.

"And you are?"

He flipped the wallet open. "Special Agent Lee Donaldson." He didn't need to add "FBI" because the imprint on his ID left no doubt.

"May I?" Andy reached for the wallet. He gave it to her. She examined it closely.

It's fake, I thought. *It has to be!*

"What can I do for the FBI, Special Agent Donaldson?" Andy handed the wallet back to him.

"First off, I apologize for dropping in like this. I had hoped to see you at your office, but when I called, your dispatcher said you were off duty. I just got here and thought I'd at least drive by. I saw you from the road and decided to take a chance. I hope you don't mind."

"I guess that will depend on the nature of your visit. Got here from where?"

"Pardon?"

"You said you just got here. From where?"

"Oh!" He chuckled. "Sioux City. I'm with the Sioux City field office."

Bullshit!

"And what does the Sioux City field office of the FBI want that a phone call couldn't handle—not meaning to sound rude."

"No, no. You're quite right. It was my bad to just drop in like this without calling. If you'd rather, I can make an appointment to meet with you. However, I would ask if you can make time for me tomorrow. I have to be back in my office first thing Monday morning."

"That is a shitload of driving," I commented. "All the way here from Sioux City today, then all the way back again? Must be important."

Donaldson glanced at me. He had the same military bearing, the same buzz-cut hair and the same drill instructor jawline I remembered. His eyes were a muddy green brown, but they powered a sharp gaze. He briefly studied me. I searched his expression for recognition, but he showed no sign.

There's no way this is a coincidence.

"This is my husband, Will."

I traded a handshake. As expected, he closed a tight grip, which I returned in kind.

"Pleased to meet you."

"Beer?" I lifted mine.

"Thank you, no. But I wouldn't turn down a glass of water." He turned to Andy. "That is, unless you prefer to meet with me tomorrow?"

Andy shook her head. "Nonsense. You're here. Come inside, please."

Rather than head for the back door, Andy led us past Donaldson's parked car to the front of the house and the screened porch.

"I'll get you that water," she said. "Please, make yourself comfortable." She gestured at our motley collection of wicker furniture and the old chaise lounge I like to occupy on summer evenings. Then she hurried away through the house.

Donaldson remained standing but turned to face the front yard. "This is a nice property. Quiet. Family farm?"

"Rental." I considered stopping there. Freezing him out. Then I thought about Andy's motivation for taking us around the house to the porch, rather than through the house via the kitchen. I stepped up beside him. "It's quiet, alright. Except when they're picking the corn. We're practically an island in corn fields here. You must be used to that sort of thing in Iowa. Oh, and then there's the manure spreading. Once in a while, they buy some liquid manure from a couple dairy farms that have big vats on the west side of town, and they fling some pretty ripe stuff. It reeks for a few days. Mostly at the tail end of winter." I went on for a few minutes about farming, about our landlord, and about Essex County. I was about to launch into a monologue about Essex County Air Service when Andy reappeared. She handed Donaldson a tall glass with ice and water.

"Thanks," he said. "Did I check out?"

She smiled and held up her phone. "Yes. You did."

He returned the smile. "What got your guard up?"

"I did," I said quickly. "I recognized you when you drove in. I told her the last time I saw you was at the wedding at Cinnamon Hills. You were private security for some rich guy." It was a two-part lie in that there hadn't been time to tell Andy how I knew Donaldson—and Cinnamon Hills wasn't the last time I saw this man.

The last time I saw this man, I was about to put a gun to the head of his billionaire boss, Bargo Litton.

ALSO BY HOWARD SEABORNE

DIVISIBLE MAN

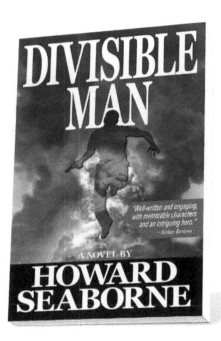

The media calls it a "miracle" when air charter pilot Will Stewart survives an aircraft in-flight breakup, but Will's miracle pales beside the stunning after-effect of the crash. Barely on his feet again, Will and his police sergeant wife Andy race to rescue an innocent child from a heinous abduction—*if Will's new ability doesn't kill him first.*

Available in print, digital and audio.

Learn more at **HowardSeaborne.com**

ALSO BY HOWARD SEABORNE

DIVISIBLE MAN: THE SIXTH PAWN

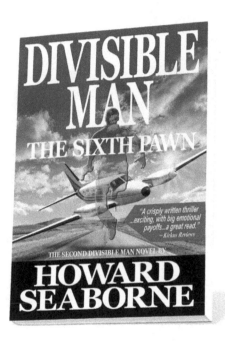

When the Essex County "Wedding of the Century" erupts in gunfire, Will and Andy Stewart confront a criminal element no one could have foreseen. Will tests the extraordinary after-effect of surviving a devastating airplane crash while Andy works a case obstructed by powerful people wielding the sinister influence of unlimited money in politics.

Available in print, digital and audio.

Learn more at **HowardSeaborne.com**

ALSO BY HOWARD SEABORNE

DIVISIBLE MAN: THE SECOND GHOST

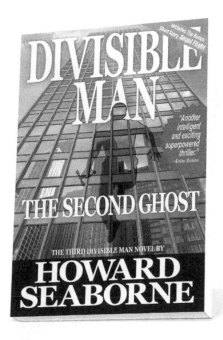

Tormented by a cyber stalker, Lane Franklin's best friend turns to suicide. Lane's frantic call to Will and Andy Stewart launches them on a desperate rescue. When it all goes bad, Will must adapt his extraordinary ability to survive the dangerous high steel and glass of Chicago as Andy and Pidge encounter the edge of disaster. **Includes the short story, "Angel Flight,"a bridge to the fourth DIVISIBLE MAN novel that follows.**

Available in print, digital and audio.

Learn more at **HowardSeaborne.com**

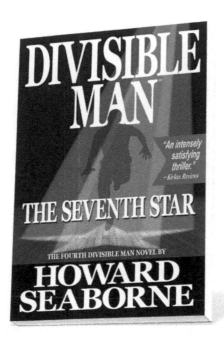

ALSO BY HOWARD SEABORNE

DIVISIBLE MAN: TEN MAN CREW

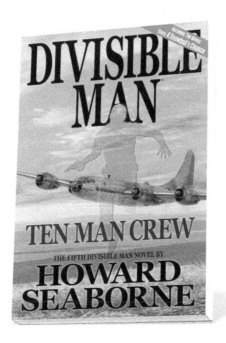

An unexpected visit from the FBI threatens Will Stewart's secret and sends Detective Andy Stewart on a collision course with her darkest impulses. A twisted road reveals how a long-buried Cold War secret has been weaponized. And Pidge shows a daring side of herself that could cost her dearly.

Available in print, digital and audio.

Learn more at **HowardSeaborne.com**

ALSO BY HOWARD SEABORNE

DIVISIBLE MAN: THE THIRD LIE

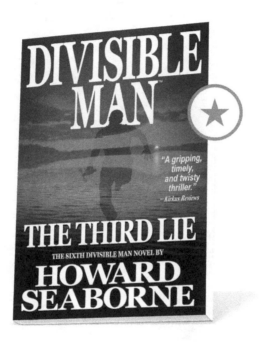

Caught up in a series of hideous crimes that generate national headlines, Will faces the critical question of whether to reveal himself or allow innocent lives to be lost. The stakes go higher than ever when Andy uncovers the real reason behind a celebrity athlete's assault on an underaged girl. And Will discovers that the limits of his ability can lead to disaster.

A Kirkus Starred Review.

A Kirkus Star is awarded to "books of exceptional merit."

Available in print, digital and audio.

Learn more at **HowardSeaborne.com**

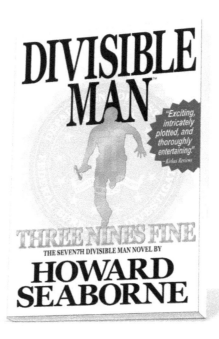

ALSO BY HOWARD SEABORNE

DIVISIBLE MAN: EIGHT BALL

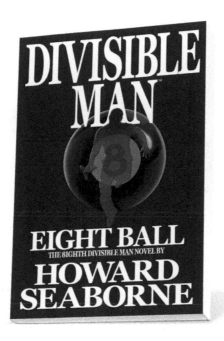

Will's encounter with a deadly sniper on a serial killing rampage sends him deeper into the FBI's hands with costly consequences for Andy. And when billionaire Spiro Lewko returns to the picture, Will and Andy's future takes a dark turn. The stakes could not be higher when the sniper's true target is revealed.

Available in print, digital and audio.

Learn more at **HowardSeaborne.com**

ALSO BY HOWARD SEABORNE

DIVISIBLE MAN:

ENGINE OUT AND OTHER SHORT FLIGHTS

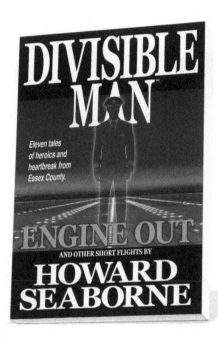

AVAILABLE: JUNE 2022

Things just have a way of happening around Will and Andy Stewart. In this collection of eleven tales from Essex County, boy meets girl, a mercy flight goes badly wrong, and Will crashes and burns when he tries dating again. Engines fail. Shots are fired. A rash of the unexpected breaks loose—from bank jobs to zombies.

Available in print, digital and audio.

Learn more at **HowardSeaborne.com**

ALSO BY HOWARD SEABORNE

DIVISIBLE MAN: NINE LIVES LOST

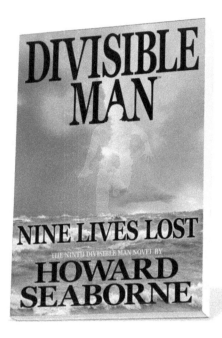

AVAILABLE: JUNE 2022

A simple request from Earl Jackson sends Will on a desperate cross-country chase ultimately looking for answers to a mystery that literally landed at Will and Andy's mailbox. At the same time, a threat to Andy's career takes a deadly turn. Before it all ends, Will confronts answers in a deep, dark place he never imagined.

Available in print, digital and audio.

Learn more at **HowardSeaborne.com**

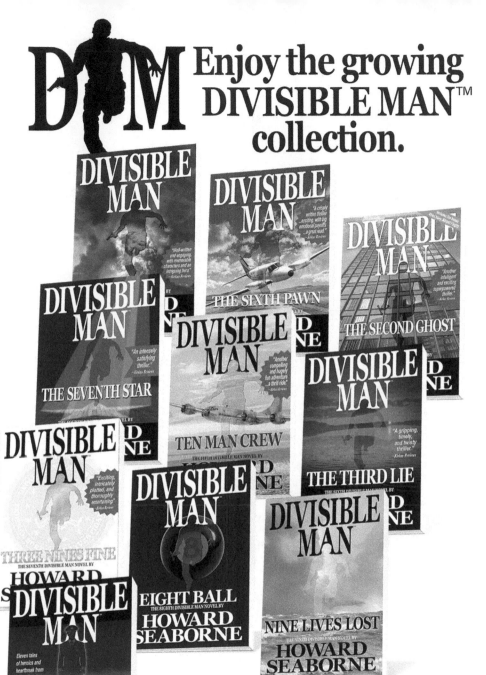

CPSIA information can be obtained
at www.ICGtesting.com
Printed in the USA
LVHW081235180922
728646LV00025B/1007/J